It's Behind You

KEITH TEMPLE

It's Behind You

KEITH TEMPLE

HandE Publishers Ltd

Published by HandE Publishers Ltd
Epping Film Studios, Brickfield Business Centre,
Thornwood High Road, Epping, Essex, CM16 6TH
www.handepublishers.co.uk

First published in the United Kingdom 2010
First Edition

ISBN 978-1-906873-28-8
A CIP catalogue record for this book is available from
The British Library

Copyright © Text Keith Temple 2009
Cover design by Ruth Mahoney
Typeset by Ruth Mahoney
Edited by Natalie-Jane Revell and Kayleigh Hart

Printed and bound in England
by CPI Bookmarque, Croydon, Surrey

For
Moraq and Henry

DRAMATIS PERSONAE

AT THE OLDE TYNE THEATRE PRODUCTION OF

'Cinderella'

Starring...

CARINA HEMSLEY   DOUGIE SPINK   SYLVIE GOGGLE
LAUREN WENTWORTH   BEN TINGLE
JUSTIN COATES   BRENDAN BERRY

DRAMATIS PERSONAE

AT THE OLDE TYNE THEATRE PRODUCTION OF

'Cinderella'

Miss CARINA HEMSLEY *Fairy Godmother*
EGOTISTICAL FORMER SOAP MATRIARCH 'CORA SMART'

Mr DOUGIE SPINK *Baron Hard-Up*
A LOUCHE SIT-COM STAR OF THE 1970'S

Miss SYLVIE GOGGLE *Wicked Step-Mother*
ALCOHOLIC CLASSICAL ACTOR

Miss LAUREN WENTWORTH *Cinderella*
NAIVE AND BEAUTIFUL, AT THE START OF HER CAREER

Mr BEN TINGLE *Prince Charming*
AUSTRALIAN MODEL TURNED ACTOR

Mr JUSTIN COATES *Ugly Step-Sister*
JOBBING PANTOMIME DAME

Mr BRENDAN BERRY *Ugly Step-Sister*
ANOTHER JOBBING PANTOMIME DAME

Mr JEZ THOMPSON
THEATRE OWNER AND DOUBLE GLAZING ENTREPRENEUR

Miss HEIDI THOMPSON
WIFE OF JEZ, SERIAL SHOPPER AND HEDONIST

Mr CAMPBELL GARIBALDI
TENSE THEATRE DIRECTOR AND ACTOR

Miss JACKIE HUMBERT

CARINA'S UNPAID PA AND PRESIDENT OF THE
CARINA HEMSLEY APPRECIATION SOCIETY

Miss IRENE

BOX OFFICE KIOSK STAFF

Mr MATTY SWAN

STAGE DOOR OPERATOR

Mr GORDON CRABTREE

AN OBSESSED 'CORA SMART' FAN

Mr PAUL MILLER

THIRD EX-HUSBAND OF CARINA HEMSLEY

AT A1 TV STUDIOS, HOME OF DAYTIME SOAP 'WINKLE BAY'

Mr RUFUS FRENKEL

HOT-SHOT YOUNG PRODUCER

Mr CARL ROGERS

LAID BACK EXECUTIVE PRODUCER

Mr MICK FLYNT

SELF-STYLED SOAP GURU AND STORY CONSULTANT

Mr JEFFREY CARTER

ACTOR WHO PLAYS REVEREND JOHNNY ARLINGTON IN 'WINKLE BAY'

Miss JULES

EFFICIENT RECEPTIONIST

THE POLICE

Mr D.I ROY NEWALL

A DOWN TO EARTH NO-NONSENSE DETECTIVE

Ms D.S. PAULINE CLIFTON

ANOTHER DOWN TO EARTH NO-NONSENSE DETECTIVE IN LOVE WITH HER BOSS

Chapter One

A tide of grimy water sloshed from a kerbside puddle onto the pavement as the black and white mini-cab slowed to a halt in front of the equally grimy 'Olde Tyne Theatre'. Inside the taxi, amidst the pattering of rain on the roof and monotonous whir of wiper motors, the driver glanced furtively at his passenger in his rear view mirror. She looked every inch the 'Glamorous Celebrity' in her dark glasses, bright red hair and fur coat. Despite the 'No Smoking' sign she sucked away at a cigarette on the end of a long black holder, her sharp cheekbones looking even more jagged every time she inhaled. He had considered asking her to put it out but lost his nerve at the last minute, remembering her headline-grabbing reputation for confrontation and public outbursts of physical violence over the years. The smoke, together with the condensation forming on his mirror, made her look vague, blurred, like a photograph taken with a filtered lens - just as she had appeared on the telly, in fact. He craned his neck around to talk to her and the illusion shattered. This was a woman who looked attractive from afar. Close up, he could see the heavy frown marks, the deeply etched misery lines around the mouth, still canyon-like underneath the layers of powder. Here was a woman who did not laugh very often, he thought. But wasn't there some rumour about radical plastic surgery a few years ago?

What was it? He gave up trying to recollect. Whatever it was, it hadn't been radical enough.

From the voluminous carpetbag at her side, another, equally ancient and cadaverous head reared up and peered myopically through bulbous teary eyes at the driver. Part trembling poodle, part budgie foetus he surmised, it sniffled and wheezed asthmatically before curling up again inside the bag when he spoke.

'We're here,' he said.

His passenger didn't reply. As far as he could discern, she seemed to be staring out at the grey stone exterior of the theatre. Embarrassed by the silence, the driver made a stumbling effort at conversation.

'Erm. So, erm, when are you going back into *winkle*?' he asked amiably.

The response, a derisory snort, made him turn around quickly and stare nervously ahead.

'When Hell freezes over.'

The voice was husky and deep. So deep it was almost masculine. She stubbed her cigarette out aggressively against the window, dropped it on the floor and peered behind her at the passing traffic.

'Drive on,' she commanded.

'Where to?'

'Around the block. Anywhere. Then back here.' She seemed tense, uncomfortable.

The cabbie shrugged nonchalantly, put the car into gear and slipped into the slow moving stream of traffic again. If the lady wanted to throw her cash around, it was fine by him. Christmas was only three weeks away: he needed the money. He smiled at her in his rear view mirror, just to put her at her ease but her features remained frozen behind the sunglasses and he was left feeling foolish. He'd had one or two famous people in the back of his taxi over the years – a loud-mouthed lass from *Big Brother*, Tony Bennett's second cousin and an ex-boxer who'd been on the receiving end of a good thumping from Michael Caine in 'Get Carter'. They'd all been quite pleasant and chatty. This woman was a Star of a different sort: a frightening all-consuming, charmless thing that sucked in light and energy and goodness and gave nothing back. A human Black Hole, mused the taxi-driver. The Black Hole lit up another cigarette and blew smoke into the front cabin. Wispy fingers of nicotine and tar curled around his throat, waking him from his disturbed thoughts. He indicated left, turned the corner, put his foot down and was back in front of the theatre in no time at all.

'Were we followed?' she asked.

'I don't think so,' replied the cabbie.

The actress nodded, relieved. A small crowd of pensioners in plastic rain hats and see-through raincoats had now gathered under the theatre portico. This seemed to please the Black Hole. The red gash of her lips settled in a grim travesty of a smile. She leaned forward towards the driver.

'How much?'

'That's ten pounds please.'

Heavily painted eyebrows shot up above the rim of her sunglasses and hovered there, like big black rearing caterpillars.

'A tenner? For a few paltry miles? You're shittin' me!'

The driver felt his testicles retract inside the safety of his pelvis. He stuttered a reply.

'That's what it says on the meter.'

She exhaled and snorted indignantly. Scrawny talons grabbed at a large leather handbag, more weapon than fashion accessory, took

3

out a five pound note and waved it at him.

'Call it a fiver and I'll throw in a signed photo.'

Weak in the presence of ego, the cabbie could only nod. The deal done, she alighted from the taxi in front of the gathered crowd. As he pulled away, he heard the loud gasps and cries of 'we love you' as an appreciative hoard took in the sight of its favourite bona fide ex-soap star. He continued to stare at her through his rear view mirror – standing there in front of her fans, arms outstretched in a voluminous fur coat. As he stared it seemed to him that the further away he drove, the larger her image seemed to loom until it filled his mirror. Unsettled, he blinked rapidly until normal vision resumed. The Black Hole receded. He turned the corner and she was gone. Later on, he would remember that moment and watching the news with his wife, he would say, 'I had a premonition about this. I did. I saw it coming.'

On the pavement outside 'The Olde Tyne Theatre', Carina Hemsley, former leading actress of soap opera *Winkle Bay*, Miss Crumpet 1977, winner of seven '*Soap Star of the Year*' awards, Patron of the Rolf Harris Donkey Sanctuary and the distinguished recipient of the Domestos '*Lifetime Achievement Award*' for services to Popular Drama, stood in God's spotlight, basking in the cold warmth of a dreary winter sun and the adoration of her fans. She grinned and paraded like a performing chimp, posed for photos, rolled her eyes good-humouredly when the crowd called her 'Cora'. She knew better than to correct them, for what was the point? Some of them were on prescription drugs: most of them had lost a serious amount of brain cells. She would always be 'Cora Smart', strong willed mother and Chief Executive of Smart Fish plc – 'The best fish gutters and kipper smokers in Northumberland.' She was Cora first and Carina second.

'Are you coming to see the show?' she asked.

A universal 'yes' went up.

A large woman advanced and put an arm around Carina's shoulder.

'When are you going back to *Winkle Bay*, Cora? We miss you.'

The woman buried her head in 'Cora's' neck. Carina, overwhelmed by the stench of wet wool and urine, struggled to overcome the urge to vomit. In an impressive display of her acting talents, she hugged the fan, stroked her head, kissed her brow, stunning the overwhelmed woman and rendering her so useless, that when she was propelled back into the crowd by a well placed shove to the spine from the soapstar's boney hand, she barely noticed.

'Ah, bless you, my love,' Carina crooned. 'God bless you. Never say never, as the saying goes. But you mustn't hold your breath, sweetheart.'

An old man elbowed his way to the front, knocking several of his less than nimble friends off-balance. He took her other hand and brushed his cheek with it.

'It's not the same without you, Cora.'

Carina pouted and air kissed him.

'No, it's not, is it?' she said, tucking her chin into her scarf to hide her unprofessional smirk.

She managed to convert the evil cackle which started in the back of her throat into a delicate cough.

'We've worked it out,' he continued. 'You're only in the Farne Island Psychiatric hospital. You could easily escape and jump on a boat back to *Winkle Bay*.'

Carina closed her eyes emphatically and shook her head. A portentous silence befell her audience. She had something important to say.

'The thing is,' she breathed, 'I'm not sure I want to go back.'

A gasp of shock went up from the crowd.

'Don't get me wrong,' she said, hurriedly. 'It's still a great show. Oh, I don't watch it all the time - I can't. I'm a busy actress but I look in on it now and again because I like to see what my good friends are up to. After five years of being away, I still miss my on-screen family. I love them. They're a part of my *soul*.'

The crowd approved.

'The twins need you,' gushed one lady. 'They're not conjoined anymore. They had an operation in Brazil. Abel Fenwick did a sponsored row around Holy Island to raise the money.'

Another woman nodded. 'And he's only got one arm.'

'He went round in circles most of time,' chipped in her friend. 'Ooh, it was upsetting.'

Carina took off her sunglasses and tapped them across the palm of her hand, waiting for the focus of attention to return to her.

'I have to say...' she said, as her audience calmed down - their memories of Abel Fenwick's heroism abating, '... from the little I've watched, things aren't what they were. And the proof of the pudding is in the viewing figures, isn't it. The viewing figures say it all. Now...' and she paused again before uttering three powerful words. '... My last episode.'

A reverent murmur echoed around the theatre entrance.

'When I had my nervous breakdown. Remember?'

'*Best Nervous Breakdown in a Soap Award, 2003*,' interjected a voice at the back.

'As well as *Best Dramatic Exit*, that same year,' piped up another voice.

Carina acknowledged another round of applause with a smile and a modest shake of her head.

'Bless your kind hearts,' she said with a quivering lip. 'Anyway, so you'll remember it well, how I tried to blow up the kipper curing shed? Do you know how many people were watching...?'

Looks of consternation were exchanged. The crowd wasn't sure. But before Carina had chance to enlighten them, a reedy, girl-boy voice called out from somewhere in the crowd, 'Three-point-seven-five-million.'

An appreciative gasp went up. Everyone turned to stare - including Carina, narked at having the lime-light stolen away. The new focus of attention, a large man in a baseball cap and green army surplus parka, younger (by about thirty years) than the other fans nearby, faded back into the shadows of the theatre entrance. He gazed down shyly at the ground, his features hidden behind the brim of his cap and a beard of several days growth.

'Yes!' Carina exclaimed, clapping her hands. 'Well done! Nearly four million.'

The sunglasses went on again and she nodded triumphantly.

'Four million people watching *me*!'

She waved her hand away modestly at the round of applause.

'Three-point-seven-five-million,' repeated the bearded man. 'That's not taking into account...'

'Yes, thank you,' interrupted Carina, irritated. She had moved on; there was another point to make. 'How many people watched the Christmas special last year when the lighthouse fell on Ezekiel Smart Junior?'

The old man with the sharp elbows turned around, wondering if the clever young lad in the anorak knew but he was nowhere to be seen. Carina took in the gormless expressions around her.

'Two mill-ion,' she said slowly, emphatically.

A weak voice piped up,

'There's too much sex in it nowadays.'

'No there's not,' said another. But they all agreed that it wasn't the same. Carina grinned, then tucking in her chin again and effecting a wide-eyed *Diana, Princess of the People* pose, said, 'Rufus Frenkel. The producer. The man who calls the shots. The Head Honcho, The Judas...!'

The very mention of the man who had ended her career so heartlessly and so quickly, made the bile rise in her throat. She swallowed, forcing back the bitterness. Her serene smile returned.

'If you don't like what he's doing with the show - write to him. Tell him. Tell him what you've said to me. *Winkle Bay* is yours. It belongs to the people.'

The applause pleased her.

Carina looked up sharply as the familiar odour of Lily of the Valley and dirty underwear wafted back. The smelly woman was at her side again.

'They should never have sacked you.'

Carina's eyebrows became inverted.

'I wasn't sacked,' she hissed through gritted teeth, 'I resigned.'

But the woman was either too stupid or too short sighted to see the pursed lips and raised eyebrows to realise that this was not a healthy subject to pursue.

'They got rid of you after you had that facelift, didn't they? That's what the paper's said. You went all bloated. And they put that photo of you, next to the one of a baboon's bum...'

Carina shook her head furiously.

'It was an allergic reaction to pineapple!'

But her explanation went unheard. They had stopped listening. The Celebrity Paradox had kicked in again. Twenty five years of fame and of meeting *her people* had taught her a thing or two about fan behaviour: it went through three distinct phases. The first, the *Thrilled Phase*, involved hysteria – the fans just couldn't quite believe they were actually talking to her and that she was real. Result? Temporary paralysis of the senses. They could barely string a sentence together.

The second stage, which consisted of excitement and inquisitiveness, was the *Adoration Phase*. Result? Gushing conversation and sycophancy. It was her favourite phase.

Carina had called the third part, *The Rude Bastard Phase* because after a while, fans forgot that they were in the presence of a real person, a mortal creature. They would revert to habit - of criticising, grumbling in front of her as they would when sitting in front of the telly at home. 'Isn't her dress awful?', 'She looks thinner on telly' etc. - Usually Carina didn't mind the comments. She was a celebrity, she was famous, she was rich. Being talked about meant you'd arrived! Or that's how she'd felt when she'd been in long-term employment.

This time the comments struck home.

'She's got a bit of a turkey neck going on.'

'... Is it a wig?'

'Somebody like her should be in panto at the 'Theatre Royal'. What's she doing in this dive?'

Carina inhaled and drew herself up to her full height. Pulling her collar around her neck, protectively, she managed a curt 'Enjoy the show', before disappearing down the side alleyway and crashing through the stage door entrance in a foul temper. Inside the building, Irene, on stage door sentry duty waved at her tentatively as she swept by, muttering something that sounded very much like 'senile old fuckers' under her breath.

Chapter Two

As Carina strode through a series of dingy backstage passageways towards Dressing Room Number One, she paid scant heed to the series of black and white prints lining the walls of 'Stars of Yesterday' which served as a reminder of the Theatre's former glory and the fickle nature of the entertainment industry. Wedged in the wall space above chipped majolica tiles and below an ancient, sprawling system of rusting pipes, a host of big names, long since departed to the 'Big Variety Theatre In The Sky,' gazed down from their dusty mahogany frames. Stan Laurel, Charlie Chaplin, The Crazy Gang, Harry Houdini, Lulu amongst them, had all performed on the small, intimate stage to packed houses in the good old Variety days. But their time was long gone and if Carina ever glanced in their direction it was only to see beyond them - to check her reflection in the glass frames. A more thoughtful artisté might have seen the collection, this far-stretching gallery which disappeared into the gloom, as a warning to present day entertainers, of the transience of fame. Of mortality. But not Carina. There were far, far more important thoughts and schemes going on in her mind - all of them revolving around herself. Besides, she refused to accept the notion of her own celebrity sell-by date... or death. 'Keep on going. No matter what,' was her motto. Or to be more specific - 'fuck 'em!'. A sentiment shared, it seemed, by the building around her.

Despite the advent of cinema, then later, television, and more ominously - the machinations of the City Planning Department, the Edwardian theatre had somehow managed to adapt to the requirements of the times. For a while, during the Sixties, the theatre, which had been closed for some years, became 'The Coliseum Bingo Hall'. Afterwards it re-invented itself as a children's cartoon club. Unfortunately, the club's opening coincided with a Saturday morning television revolution and it soon became apparent from the box office receipts that kids preferred to relax in front of the telly and goggle at real life idiots making fools of themselves on TISWAS and Swopshop, rather than sit in a draughty auditorium to watch tired old animated rabbits and cats with speech impediments doing the same.

For a brief period in the mid to late Seventies, a lurid neon sign advertised it as a venue of a rather different kind - the 'Kinky Triple X Members Only Club'. Sadly, for the owners, pornography turned out to be only slightly more of a crowd puller than Bugs Bunny and Elmer Fudd. The advent of the video age turned out to be its death knell, since members no longer had to jump on a bus, sneak down a side alley-way in dirty macs and knock furtively on the entrance door before being able to receive their nightly fix of filth: they could view it 'til they went blind in the comfort of their own living rooms. The cinema closed.

During the Eighties it reverted once more to 'The Olde Tyne Variety Theatre', under the ownership of a private consortium headed by Jez Thompson, a self confessed variety theatre nostalgia freak who ploughed the profits from his fitted kitchen and double glazing empire into financing his dream - to restore the building and re-invent it as the premier entertainment venue in the North of England. He succeeded in neither. A costly divorce combined with the bottom falling out of the double glazing world meant that money was tight. 'Restoration' turned out to be nothing more than a lick of paint here and there. More importantly, the building's dubious recent past proved difficult to shake off. No matter how much Jez tried to hail it as a monument to Variety and celebrated home to historical first time performances by stars of the silent screen, 'The Olde Tyne Variety Theatre' was forever etched in the public's collective mind as the dirty old man's porn club in the middle of Newcastle's red light area. Parading prostitutes in the alleyways outside, a line up of third rate comedians, dubious hypnotists and lack-lustre whodunit thrillers on stage, inside, didn't help his case much either.

Yet such as it was, the theatre had survived a century of change. Despite the rise of the electronic, multi-channel, game station era, it was putting a few occasional bums on seats and providing employment to a small technical and front of house work force. It was still standing. Just about.

Upstairs, in the General Manager's office, Jez Thompson was discussing the latest problems with his pantomime director, Campbell Garibaldi. The first week of the Christmas pantomime had been and gone; box office returns were poor. As far as Jez was concerned, he'd invested a considerable amount of money in getting everything right - a good cast with star names, decent sets and costumes, an experienced director. But it was money down the drain if nobody wanted to see the damned show. A few changes would have to be made in order to effect a reversal of fortune. Campbell was not going to like what he had to say so he had to be careful. These delicate artistic types with their principles and shaky egos were incapable of handling criticism. Especially this one. He was forever weeping and wailing about the place. Luckily he knew how to handle him. He had a strategy and he was about to put it into effect. Why, oh why, though, hadn't he listened to his gut feelings in the first place?

Jez had been persuaded by Heidi, his fiancée, to hire the sensitive Scottish-Italian after she read an article about him in one of the Sunday magazines. He'd directed 'Baked Alaska and Crisps' a musical two-hander about gluttony and global warming, set to the songs of McFly, which had gone down at storm at the Edinburgh Fringe. Heidi thought he was just the right person to bring something different to the next Christmas production. He could see where she was coming from. In the past, 'The Olde Tyne' had made the mistake of trying to compete with the two big Newcastle theatres. But 'The Palace' and 'The Royal' had bigger budgets, bigger names. Jez's panto productions looked cheap and amateurish by comparison. Mainly because they were. The solution, Heidi suspected, was simple. They had to provide folk with an alternative kind of pantomime. Something trendy. Something cool. Campbell Garibaldi seemed perfect. A hit with Fringe audiences and the newspapers, he was an actor and a writer too – they could commission him to cast his 'alternative' eye over Cinderella. The cult following the director enjoyed might also, they hoped, bring in a new audience. So far it hadn't. More worryingly, the old audience seemed to be staying away as well. He should have gone with his first impressions and never allowed the idiot to set foot in his theatre. Alarm bells had started to ring at their first meeting when the big whingeing baby had gone on at length about Cinderella's Wicked Step-Mother and her lesbian fixation. Furthermore, any man approaching forty who uttered 'that's a bunch of cool' at every opportunity and smoked matchstick thin roll-ups when he could afford proper ciggies needed a good kicking.

Campbell Garibaldi watched him pace around the room and found it difficult to concentrate on the problem in hand. Not because of the pacing. It was more to do with Jez's newly dyed hair, eyebrows and beard. Yesterday all his hairy bits were a dull, but quite natural looking grey. Today they were a uniform chocolate brown with a hint of ginger. Had he used hair dye or gloss paint? There was also a suspicious tightening around the eyes. He looked like Fu Manchu. No. Worse. It was as if he'd been embalmed. The things some blokes did for the sake of a younger girlfriend. Didn't they get it that most women much preferred their boyfriends to look distinguished rather than dead? How could a man get to such a great age without realising that beauty came from within? Inside! That's where it counted. Poor Heidi. Having to put up with such a Neanderthal thug. Suddenly Campbell realised Jez was looking at him, waiting for a response.

'Sorry. What?'

'I said, we have to make some changes.'

Campbell's eyes narrowed. He'd been expecting something like this.

'It's too late for that.'

Jez, sensing his Director's defences rising, continued quickly.

'Nothing major. I love what you've done... most of it. The Ugly Step-Sisters buying their outfits from Primark due to the credit crunch - great stuff. Kids get it as well. And all that searching for an organic pumpkin - spot on...'

'But?' Campbell levelled.

Jez sat down at his desk and consulted a scribble filled notebook.

'The ending. I thought we might get away with it but audiences don't like it. We can't have Cinderella going all Germaine Greer, telling Prince Charming they don't have to get married to live happily ever after.'

Campbell snorted indignantly. 'Why not? It's the truth. How many kids sitting out there come from broken homes, single families? Statistically speaking...'

Jez interrupted. '... You can't talk statistics about a fairytale. Everybody knows Cinderella marries her prince. They live happily ever after. End of story. It's a fact.'

'I just think people expect too much from marriage. If we can let kids know from an early age that it's not the be-all and end-all of everything - that there are alternatives. We'd be helping a lot of children out there. A lot of adults, as well.'

Jez shook his head, irritated. The big soft lump was going to cry - he could see his Adam's apple bobbing up and down and his voice had cracked.

'We're providing entertainment, Campbell, not a therapy service.'

He sighed, deciding to come clean.

'Look, the bottom line is, I've had complaints from The Girl Guides. They're our major block bookers and if they start boycotting us, we're buggered.'

Campbell said nothing. Jez continued.

'It's only a line change. A small detail. Hardly worth arguing over.'

The director nodded, resignedly.

'Okay. I don't like it, but okay.' He paused. 'Anything else?'

Deft fingers flicked through the notebook and stopped on one particular page.

'A word of warning to the 'Little People', ' said Jez. 'When they're sitting on the edge of the stage tossing sweets into the audience, tell them not to hurl them like bullets. They'll put someone's eye out.'

'I'll tell them,' Campbell replied and stood up.

'One more thing.'

Campbell sat down again.

'Carina.'

'What about her?' he asked tentatively.

'Make-up,' said Jez. 'She's the Fairy Godmother - not Cruella De Vil. What is it with the eyebrows?'

'I've already told her. She said they're her trademark.'

'Well, something has to be done. She's good with the geriatrics - she can do no wrong with them, but the kids are terrified of her. When it comes to the audience participation bit, she's never had a willing volunteer yet under seventy for the on-stage sing-along. The little bastards have to be dragged out of their seats, kicking and screaming.'

Campbell leaned forward, ran an idle hand along the edge of the oak desk, carefully choosing his words before he spoke.

'Can I be frank with you?'

'O'course, pal.'

'You know I didn't want Carina in this show, she was foisted on me.'

Jez closed his eyes, anticipating the tirade.

'Since arriving at this theatre she has undermined my authority at every opportunity. She criticises her colleagues on a daily basis, chipping away relentlessly at their confidence. She's troublesome. She's deeply unpleasant, she can't act to save her life...'

'... She's one of the biggest soap opera icons of the last forty years!'

'She's crap!' complained Campbell vehemently, throwing

himself back in his seat, emotionally exhausted. He reached for the little roll-up behind his right ear. Jez looked at it with distaste, and offered him a proper cigarette, which was refused.

'So what's your point?'

'It's rather unfair,' said Campbell, exhaling, 'that you seem to be blaming me for the failure of this pantomime, when it's not my fault at all. The script is good. It gets laughs. Most of the cast are tremendous.'

'I agree.'

'So you can't blame me when people don't come to see it. She was brought in on the strength of her name, her following, to give this production a higher profile. But if you're not on television, you're nobody in this business. And she hasn't been on screen for five years. She's washed up. Her career's behind her. And she knows it. So if you've got a problem with empty houses - talk to your so called 'Star' about it. The publicity rollercoaster you expected she'd bring along with her ain't happening.'

Jez smiled inwardly. So far the conversation was going exactly the way he wanted it to. It was easier than conning old dears out of fifteen grand for replacement double glazing.

'It's not that simple, Campbell,' he said.

'I think it is,' whined the director, his Adam's apple bouncing alarmingly again.

'Look at the competition we've got this year. Martine-Whatsit in 'Mother Goose' at 'The Grand'. The Chuckle Brothers are packing them in with 'Babes In The Wood' at 'The Royal'.'

Campbell puffed away nervously on his cigarette with shaking fingers, his energy spent. He rolled his eyes hopelessly at the ceiling. Jez drummed the table with his fingertips and glanced askance at him slyly.

'We have to do something,' he said slowly, 'I can see that. But what? We can't sack our leading lady. I can't afford to pay her off and hire someone else.'

'What can we do?' Campbell wondered, with more than a hint of desperation.

Jez pretended to think for a moment.

'Well, there is one thing.'

Campbell sat up, now that a glimmer of hope had appeared on the horizon. Jez opened a drawer in his desk and took out a large manilla envelope. The director stared at it blankly. It was only when Jez delved inside and withdrew the small bundle of letters that realisation dawned.

'No!' he exclaimed. 'We discussed this. You can't. You said you wouldn't.'

'Desperate times call for desperate measures, pal.'

Campbell's reply was quashed by a silencing hand. Jez picked up the phone and stabbed up a number.

'Morning Irene. Is she in yet?... Good. Trot along and ask her to come up, would you? I'd like a word... thanks.'

He replaced the receiver with a grin.

Campbell rocked back and forth in his seat. He was sweating.

'We agreed, it was down to a crank.'

'We don't know that for sure, though, do we?'

'But it'll affect her performance. It's already dreadful, as it is! Cringingly awful, in fact'. He shuddered as he thought about the previous night's show. Then something else struck him.

'God! If you tell her, she'll do a runner. We won't see her for dust.'

'Oh, I don't think so. Whatever you say about Carina, she's a pro. She'll stay. She has a contract. And she needs the money.'

'If she finds out about this, our lives won't be worth living! She'll be unbearable. More unbearable!'

'But think about the publicity.'

'Sod the publicity!'

Jez slammed a fist on the desk causing Campbell to jump in his seat. The cigarette dangling on his lips fell into his lap. He scrabbled anxiously for it, rescued it and stuck the stump back in his mouth with shaking fingers.

'If this panto closes early,' said Jez slowly, 'Carina won't be the only one who comes out of this stinking of shit. We'll all be tarred with the same turd. So think about it. Publicity is everything!'

Campbell sat there, depressed and on the verge of tears. Jez got up, went round the desk and patted him on the shoulders.

'Publicity aside, we have to do this. It's our duty. Carina has a right to know. And so do the police.'

Campbell nodded slowly, biting his nails.

'But nothing's happened so far.'

'There was another one yesterday. Much more violent in tone. With a picture.'

Jez opened the envelope on the top of the file and offered Campbell the note. A rather crude drawing in red biro, showed a woman hanging from a gibbet. 'Is that Carina?' he asked doubtfully. 'It could be Marge Simpson.'

The director flicked at it contemptuously. Jez grabbed at the sheet.

'Careful!'

'Oh, sorry. Forensics'll want it in one piece, won't they!'

'So will the Daily Mirror. They'll pay good money for photos of this lot.'

'I suppose so,' said Campbell quietly.

19

'That's better,' soothed Jez, patting his shoulders again.

'Now, keep your gob shut and let me do the talking. It'll be fine. It'll be a... a... bunch of cool! '

A few minutes later, when Carina threw open the door and paused dramatically in the doorway, fur coat and bag slung over her shoulders, hands on hips, cigarette holder balanced between fingers like a javelin, as she always did whenever she made an entrance, Campbell had regained his composure and Jez oozed charm by the bucket-load.

'Come in, my love, come in. You look wonderful today. How are you?'

Carina sashayed into the room and lowered herself gently into the chair pulled out for her by Campbell. Fluff, the trembling dog, poked its head out of the bag on her knee and looked around bewildered. Carina went into offensive mode.

'Good of you to ask. And since you have, I'll tell you. Things aren't exactly hunky-dory in Carina-world. In fact, Carina is very-pissed-off, cock.'

She spat out her demands. 'I want new digs. I don't like sharing. Especially not with that miserable lot. And no bungalow this time. I can't stand them. I'm coming down with claustrophobia just thinking about it.'

She looked down at the shuddering poodle.

'Fluff's the same. Look at her!'

Jez gazed down at the canine/chicken creature and wondered how Fluff's claustrophobic angst differed from her usual tremorous decrepitude.

'I'm sorry to hear that, Carina,' he said, diplomatically and began sifting through his trouser pockets.

'I've got something for her,' he declared, producing a small bag of Revels.

'Maybe these will help settle her.'

He tipped a few into his hand and went forward to administer them to the dog.

'No chocolate!' screeched the soap star. 'She's diabetic for God's sake.'

Jez backed away, tipping the sweets into his mouth.

'So, what are you going to do about it?' Carina pressed on, 'Because actually I should be in a hotel.'

She stabbed out a list on the fingers of one hand.

'The Chuckle Brothers! The Krankies - they've all got a suite each at the...'

Carina let the sentence die on her lips, for she had looked up and noticed for the first time, quite late into the meeting - as is the habit of most self-obsessive's who barely notice the world around them and the people in it, that something was different.

'... What the bloody hell's happened to you?' she barked. Jez began to redden.

'Me?' he said. 'Nothing.'

'You've coloured-in your beard wi'paint.'

Jez surveyed her thickly pencilled eyebrows sombrely and swallowed his retort. Antagonising his leading lady would get them nowhere.

'Carina, something's come to our attention that we think you should know about.'

Carina noticed his serious tone and sat up, all ears.

'Has that fitness instructor been tittle-tattling to the press again?' she roared. 'Because he's a liar! I never, ever paid him for sex - I don't care what he says. That five hundred quid was just a loan.'

'No!' said Campbell quickly. 'It's nothing like that.'

21

Jez pushed the file towards her and opened it, revealing the bundle of letters.

'What's that?' inquired Carina. 'Fan mail?'

Campbell and Jez exchanged a look.

'Not exactly,' said Jez. 'They're more... Well, I suppose you could call them hate mail - poison pen letters.'

'About me?'

Jez nodded. 'It's probably nothing but we think it's only fair that you should know,' he purred smarmily as Carina sifted through the dozen or so envelopes. 'But it looks like some nutter wants you dead.'

For once Carina Hemsley was speechless.

Chapter Three

Detective Inspector Roy Newall fiddled rather clumsily with a fresh pair of latex protective gloves and proceeded to study each of the eleven letters, now spread out across Jez's desk, one by one. They were all of a standard A4 size: their short unpunctuated messages made up of colourful cut-out letters from glossy magazines, glued unevenly into place. In his long but fairly undistinguished career, Newall had investigated many things - murders, suicides, kidnappings, revenge attacks, muggings, but death threats of this variety were something of a novelty for him. In fact it all seemed rather melodramatic - he'd only ever seen hate mail like this, in old films and bad TV thrillers. Could they really be genuine? Could he care? Actors! They were a weird bunch. And theatres! All that arty stuff was bollocks, wasn't it? He hated the theatre. Mind you, that Cora Thingy, the bird from *Winkle Bay*, he'd seen her on the telly once or twice. She was quite fit. His wife used to watch the show. She seemed the spirited, lively type. He remembered they'd seen her in the Quayside Lodge Restaurant a few years ago. She was pawing some bloke and playing footsy with him under the table – it was a short tablecloth and left nothing to the imagination. Newall hadn't been able to take his eyes off them all evening. His wife was disgusted by their behaviour. 'How the mother of Siamese twins and a daughter with ME could sit at a table and behave like that, I do not know,' she had exclaimed when they left. She'd even boycotted the programme. It had been on the cards for a while. She'd complained about the loose morals of the characters for some time. Whether she watched it now, he knew not. They were no longer together. Marital status? Divorced. Estranged. In events worthy of a *Best Ironic Moment In A Soap Award*, Newall's wife, Pat, tired of sharing her husband with the other love in his life - his job, had enrolled in a sign language class to keep herself occupied of an evening. Becoming proficient in finger-spelling and signing, she'd taken exams, passed them and found a worthy job signing plays for deaf audiences at 'The Grand Theatre'. In a short period of time she made new friends: her life had reason, meaning. Culturally and socially, she felt she'd found her Home. She became a more relaxed woman - almost. Two things, and two things only, aggravated her delicately balanced psyche: sex stuff, and coarse, dirty language. She hated both with equal passion. Ergo, she hated her husband who pestered her for the former and used the latter to serious excess. The theatre job protected her, pushed her problems to the background... Until that fateful day, when she was forced to confront her inner demons: she turned up for work to be told she'd been booked to sign a performance of 'The Vagina Monologues'.

For someone who spent most of her life blanking out any mention or thought of sex, the idea of having to interpret, *in public*, the crude conversations of a group of women obsessed by their downstairs departments, made her feel sick. What was wrong with monologues about cake decoration or netball, for crying out loud? The script sent Pat screaming, psychologically-speaking towards the edge of a great, dark abyss of insanity. Nauseous every time she picked up the script, she attempted to wiggle her way out of the contract, but she was stuck with it. The only other interpreter the theatre could lay its hands on at such short notice was a single, forty year old man who, after a short discussion with his mother, declined the job, admitting he felt rather uncomfortable and unfamiliar with the subject matter.

Pat considered resigning or feigning illness, or resorting to censorship, on the night. Yet something within forced her to go through with it. Perhaps she was tired at playing the frightened mouse all her life. Perhaps it was because she was a decent person who didn't like to let people down. Whatever the reason, she turned up for the interpretation and although she started the evening signing with shaking hands and with eyes closed, the more she concentrated on the words, the more she started to enjoy herself. To connect. To think. Her inhibitions left her. She realised she wasn't inhibited at all. It wasn't sex she hated. It was sex with her husband. She started to listen to the voice in her head, the voice she had been too frightened to listen to for years - the voice which had been telling her to get out of her loveless marriage and to start life afresh, because it was never too late. She went home that night, told Newall about her on-stage epiphany, packed her bags and left. Never to return.

Newall became aware that the others in the room, puzzled by his silence, were staring at him.

'What is it, Boss?' asked his colleague, D.S. Clifton. 'Have you found something?'

Newall coughed, in order to give him time to think of an excuse. Damn his bloody ex-wife. Was she destined to haunt his thoughts forever more?

'No, no. Just thinking.' He clapped his hands together lamely and straightened up, trying to maintain some semblance of

25

professionalism. 'The sheer volume of correspondence suggests to me that their author - or authors, are passionate enough.'

Clifton nodded. 'Passionate enough to carry out their threat?'

Newall scratched his nose. 'Difficult to say.'

Jez read the letters over Newall's shoulder.

'That was the first one,' he said.

Clifton, her fingers latex-protected also, pushed the envelope around the desk.

'Newcastle post mark, November 9th. Three weeks ago.' She looked at Jez and Campbell curiously.

'You've been receiving these letters for three weeks and you're only informing us now? Why?'

Jez smiled his most flirtatious smile, the dazzling white-toothed one which usually served him well, when dealing with women.

'We thought it was some crackpot. And we didn't want to worry, Miss Hemsley. She's a bit delicate at the moment. This is her first time in theatre. We wanted her to have a stress-free honeymoon period, while she got used to things, if you see what I mean.'

'Yes,' said Clifton, returning an equally dazzling smile, which suggested she understood and sympathised with his good intentions. 'Keeping her blissfully unaware about death threats would keep her stress-free.'

The smile suddenly vanished and her expression became hard.

'And then, if the threats were real and she was bumped off, there'd be no more stress at all for her - *ever*.'

Jez, his charms having let him down once, tried to win her over with his second offensive: humour.

'I can't imagine Carina getting bumped off by anyone,' he opined jovially. 'She'd do what any self-respecting gorgon would do - glare at her attacker and turn him to stone.'

26

Clifton didn't seem impressed so Jez decided not to use his third flirtation weapon - touchy-feely-ness. He was now a tiny bit afraid of her. Hair swept back, make-up free, baggy combat trousers and clumpy boots, she'd probably stamp on his balls if he attempted to stroke her arm. He decided to address any further comments and witticisms to the fatter, old cop. He was on safe ground there.

'The first letters weren't death threats, they were quite vague, really,' piped up Campbell.

Newall nodded. 'Get rid of Cora,' he read.

'Yes,' Campbell continued. 'And he keeps referring to her as 'Cora', which is another reason why we weren't too worried. 'Cora's' a fictional character. Whoever wrote this is living in a fantasy world.'

'You don't think that's worrying?!' Clifton was incredulous.

'This last one,' said Jez. It came yesterday. That's more unpleasant.' He tried to look sincere. 'That's why we've called you now.'

Newall squeezed between the desk and the wall and picked up the last letter, which read, 'The Bitch Must Die.'

'Has anybody else touched these - apart from yourselves and Miss... Erm...?'

'Hemsley?' said Clifton helpfully.

Jez and Campbell shook their heads. Newall turned to his Sergeant. 'Bag them up, then we'll pay Cora a visit.'

'Carina!' said Clifton.

Newall looked irritated. 'That's what I said.'

Clifton thought it prudent not to argue. Newall stopped in the doorway.

'Just one other thing. Has Miss Hemsley any enemies?'

Jez and Campbell exchanged another look.

'She's a darling!' Jez declared. 'I can't imagine why anyone would

27

want to hurt her.'

Clifton and Newall left the room, shutting the door behind them. Jez waited a moment, listening to their receding footsteps before reaching for the phone.

'What are you doing?' asked Campbell.

'Putting the publicity machine in motion,' grinned Jez.

Chapter Four

Downstairs in her dressing room, with only an hour to go until the matinée performance, Carina dabbed her runny nose with shaking hands as she informed Cinderella, Prince Charming and the Wicked Step-Mother of the distressing news. Gone was her haughty, chilly exterior. It had been replaced by fear and self-pity. She seemed smaller, fragile, almost, as she sat in front of her dressing table mirror, its harsh glowing electric bulbs highlighting every line and wrinkle on her weary face. Matters were made worse by the rivers of mascara which had run down her cheeks and cascaded onto the fur collar of her coat.

'I know I've done some terrible things in my time,' she managed to say between sobs, 'but I'm not a bad person. I'm not.'

'Of course you're not,' said Cinderella - eventually. She sounded genuine enough but she really hadn't meant what she'd said. She'd felt obliged to say so only because it looked as though nobody else was going to. And that didn't seem right when Carina was so obviously and genuinely upset. Nasty old person though the woman was, Lauren Wentworth refused to abandon her own moral code and sink to Carina's level. She had a strong sense of right and wrong, good and bad and while Carina tested that moral code to the max, on a daily basis, Lauren kept telling herself that she was a better person: goodness and kindness would win the day. Since meeting her on day one of rehearsals, Carina had taken a dislike to her, made life extremely difficult for her. Lauren put it down to fear and lack of confidence, or maybe it was just one of those things - you can't be liked by everyone.

Lauren was too nice and too dense to realise that Carina's hatred for her was borne out of simple envy. She was young, she was pretty, she was popular. She had the lead role...

Earlier in the year, when approached by Jez to join the cast, Carina had demanded the role of Cinderella for herself and was more than a little upset by Jez's response. He felt that audiences would find it extremely difficult, nay impossible, to suspend their disbelief if they saw her in the role of a naïve, innocent teenager on the verge of sexual awakening. Besides, Ben Tingle, the Australian model famous for his washboard stomach and a series of Pot Noodle adverts, had been booked to play Prince Charming and he was only twenty. The casting would be out of kilter if Carina played Cinderella. No, no, the role of Fairy Godmother was a much more appropriate and challenging character for an artisté of Carina Hemsley's calibre. The Star, spurred on by erotic thoughts about backstage dalliances with young Tingle, disagreed, but several persuasive calls from her agent, urging her to do the sensible thing, led to Carina reluctantly agreeing to Jez's terms. To this day though, the sight of Lauren on stage in her ragged dress, sweeping the kitchen with her broom and 'tra-la-laa-ing' all over the place, made her blood boil. To add insult to injury, the little slapper had actually copped off with Ben Tingle.

'Bless you, my love,' said Carina graciously. 'It's nice to know that you all care.'

Carina dabbed at her eyes and affected a grateful smile. Lauren smiled back, encouraged by the first pleasant thing Carina had ever said to her. Perhaps they could be friends after all.

'Group hug?' she suggested.

'If you don't mind, my sweet,' said the Wicked Step-Mother, Sylvie Goggle in her unctuous theatrical tones, 'I'd rather not be groped today. My back's gone.'

She hobbled off, back to her own dressing room. Carina, on the other hand, opened her arms wide. Lauren first, and then a more unwilling Ben, leant over her. Carina turned a cheek vaguely towards Ben, then aimed her pouting red lips with precision-like aim at his mouth. He froze in shock as her slippery tongue pushed back the barrier of his lips and flicked around his tonsils like a hot worm. A wandering scrawny hand slid over his buttocks and held them firmly, making escape impossible.

'What's this? A gang bang?' said a plummy voice from the doorway. 'Make way for Hunt.'

The threesome were joined by an older, ruddy faced man who enveloped them all with his large frame. Another pair of hands slid over his rump, pushing Carina's aside. Ben reddened, struggled free from the tangle of limbs and scurried backwards towards the door.

'What's your hurry, love?' asked Dougie Hunt, a picture of innocence.

'Lunch,' replied Ben breathlessly. He turned, bumping into Clifton and Newall on his way out and was gone.

'Catch you later,' said Dougie, calling after him. Hunt adjusted his tie and ran a hand through his thinning thatch, then winked at the woman Sergeant.

'Well, hello. Who have we got here?'

Clifton held up her I.D.

'D.S. Clifton and D.I. Newall,' she said matter-of-factly. 'Miss

Hemsley? Could we have a moment of your time?'

Carina's face took on a tragic expression. She nodded curtly and stared forlornly into the mid-distance. When Hunt and Lauren showed no sign of leaving, Newall said, 'In private, please.'

Lauren squeezed Carina's hand. 'We're around if you need us.'

Hunt paused on his way out and turned to Clifton. 'I'm in Dressing Room Number Two,' purred the old ham. 'Do drop in.' He winked at her again before draping an arm around Lauren and sauntering out.

'Is he for real?!' Clifton asked.

'No.'

Newall closed the door, pulled up a chair and sat opposite the actress. She was certainly knocking on a bit, he mused, but there was no doubt about it, she oozed sex appeal. She had presence. Carina crossed one leg over the other and Newall found himself staring at her foot. The right foot with the extremely dexterous toes he'd seen go to work on a man in a restaurant some years ago... And her smell. He couldn't place the perfume she was wearing but it was heady and wonderful.

There was an uncomfortable silence. Clifton glanced askance at her boss. He seemed to have gone into some kind of trance.

'How are you feeling?' she inquired after a pause. Newall woke from his reverie.

'Yes,' he said, rather too loudly. 'How are you?'

Carina shrugged. 'Shocked, I suppose. Stunned.' She was in soap-star mode now and rifled in her handbag for a cigarette holder and cig. Fluff's head reared up from within. Clifton couldn't help herself.

'What's that?' There was no disguising the disgust in her voice. Carina glared at her sharply as she lit up.

'This is Fluff. My best friend. My companion. We're inseparable.'

She lifted the dog out of the bag and sat her on her lap. Fluff weaved around, shaking uncontrollably on turkey-drumstick legs, and peered myopically across at the two police officers.

'That's nice,' opined Newall, rather pathetically. Carina smiled at him sweetly. Clifton stared at her boss aghast. He was blushing. What the hell was wrong with him?

'Anyway,' she said, turning the topic of conversation back to business. 'We've looked at the letters and we'll take them away with us for further analysis but judging by their contents, I would say they're probably the work of a crank.'

Newall nodded. 'Someone who gets their kicks out of writing nasty letters rather than acting on them.'

'You think?' Carina didn't seem too sure. 'What about the mounting threat of violence in them? The increasingly horrible things he says?'

Clifton was about to reply but Carina was warming to the subject now.

'I mean, the first one just says I'm a bad woman and the last one says I'm a bitch and I'm going to die.' Her voice started to tremble. 'Can you imagine how I felt when I read them - all in one go! I couldn't believe it. Jez should have told me about them when they first started arriving.'

She reached for her hankie and dabbed at her nose.

'I think they were just trying to protect you,' said Newall.

Carina blew into her hankie.

Clifton took out her notebook and a pen and opened it.

'Miss Hemsley. Do you know anyone who might have a grudge against you?'

Carina exhaled loudly and watched the cloud of smoke

thoughtfully, as it travelled across the room.

'I don't know.'

'Think for a moment.'

'There's my ex-husbands, I suppose.'

Clifton clicked her pen into action.

'Barry Peel. Garage mechanic - lives in Berwick now. Customises old Hillman Imps. Body builder. Or he was. Looks more like a sack of old conkers these days.' She paused to check her nails. 'But I doubt if it's him. He's more 'Classic Morris Minor Monthly' than 'Hello Magazine'.'

Newall stared at her. 'Sorry?' Carina stared back.

'The letters. All the cut out words in them. They came from 'Hello Magazine'.'

'Are you sure?' asked Clifton as she scribbled away.

'I should know. I've flicked through enough of them. You're looking for a celebrity magazine reader.'

Clifton paused. 'That narrows the field to a few million.'

But Carina wasn't listening. She'd returned to her list.

'Can't be my second ex.'

'Why not?' wondered Newall.

'He's dead.'

'I'm sorry.'

'I'm not. He was a bastard. Now, my last ex, Paul – he's another bastard, but living – I'd like it to be him. And he did tell me once he wanted me dead. He wasn't too happy when the gravy train left him. But it's not him either. Sadly.'

Newall nodded in agreement.

'All those letters refer to me as Cora,' she continued. 'Not Carina. They're confusing me with a character they see on TV...'

'... Or saw on TV,' interrupted Clifton. Carina stared at her down the barrel of her cigarette holder, then exhaled a heavy cloud of aromatic Gitanes smoke in her face.

'The character lives on in people's hearts and minds,' she said flatly and tickled her dog under the chin. Fluff responded by jumping off her lap onto the floor and proceeded to lurch around the room, sniffing at the carpet.

'Of course, it might be one of this lot having a joke,' she suggested, gesturing at the door. 'A sick joke,' she added.

Newall seemed intrigued. 'Why would they do that?'

'Professional jealousy. I get top billing. They don't.' She sighed. 'Oh, look. I don't know. It probably *is* some crackpot who reads crass celebrity comics and watches *Winkle Bay* and doesn't have a life.'

But Newall and Clifton weren't listening. They were watching Fluff, who had wandered into a corner and was relieving herself on the carpet. Carina, if she noticed, seemed unconcerned.

'When Cora was pregnant with Jimmy Flynn's love-child and went away to have an abortion, I got hate mail by the sack load. The worst one came from the Pope.'

'The Pope?!' marvelled Newall, with one eye still on the peeing dog.

'According to the signature. As far as I know, though, he doesn't sign off his official correspondence with 'Yours Disgustedly, The Pope'.'

Having finished emptying her bladder, Fluff staggered back to her mistress and lay down at her feet. Carina picked up the creature and kissed it on the nose. Newall and Clifton were still staring at the urine soaked carpet. Eventually, Carina said, 'So I won't say I'm not upset by this - because I am. Its been a nasty shock. Nobody goes out of their way to be hated. I might look like a hard-nosed cow but underneath it all,' and here she paused, 'I'm only human.'

She clasped the dog to her bosom and kissed it again. Clifton snapped shut her notebook and clicked her retracting biro. Roy Newall stood up and offered her a hand in farewell.

'Well, thank you for your time, Miss Hemsley.'

'Carina,' she replied, shaking the hand. Newall beamed at her. Clifton searched through her pockets and brought out a business card.

'If you need to contact us, or if you think of anything that might help our enquiry... Please give us a call.'

'Anytime,' added Newall.

'Thank you,' replied Carina, getting up. 'Actually, there is one more thing.'

Newall paused on the threshold. 'Yes?'

Carina deliberated a moment before replying.

'You probably think I'm imagining it,' she said hesitantly. 'But before I found out about all this, and for some time, really, well, I've had a sneaking suspicion I'm being followed.'

Newall walked back into the room.

'Have you noticed anyone?'

'No. It's just a feeling. Had it ever since I started this production.'

Clifton didn't seem too impressed.

'If you do see someone, call us straight away,' she said matter-of-factly.

'I will.'

Newall looked back at her as he closed the door. She seemed quite small and defenceless, in sharp contrast to the personality, the celebrity he'd seen in newspapers and television over the years. She smiled wanly at him and waved. He waved back self-consciously.

Clifton, who had paused in the corridor to study a photo of Houdini on the wall, set off after him.

'I think she likes you, boss.'

Newall shook his head and grimaced. 'Behave.'

'Sorry. But I think she does.'

'I wonder if she really is being followed,' he mused, ignoring her.

Clifton was cynical.

'Maybe we should talk to the Pope. See if he's got an alibi for his whereabouts the past few weeks.' When he didn't laugh, she chided him. 'Oh, come on, Boss, where's your sense of humour?'

Newall strode off into the gloom.

'I hate theatres,' he said when she caught up with him.

'Why?' she asked, intrigued.

'Bad memories.'

'Don't tell me - you were found in a reed basket outside the stage door of 'The Palladium' as a baby!'

'Something like that,' he replied, thinking of abandonment and divorce. He threw open the heavy exit door and headed out into the cold, wet December afternoon.

Chapter Five

'Gordon! Gordon!'

The old woman's muffled cries for attention echoed up the narrow staircase and floated around the small bedroom where thick, grubby fingers, holding a pair of tweezers were sticking down the last two cut-out letters on a white sheet of paper with a dab of glue. Satisfied with the result, Gordon picked up the sheet and blew gently on it. Tiny snippets of paper and discarded cuttings fell in a shower of confetti, landing on a rusty, ancient biscuit tin perched on top of old issues of celebrity magazines scattered on the floor. Gordon brushed the lid of the biscuit tin clean with a gentle, caressing movement, then he folded the letter neatly, slipped it inside an envelope, and sealed it by dragging a small sponge across the gummed border. Such was his concentration that he failed to hear his mother calling until he'd made sure the envelope was sealed securely.

'Gordon!'

This time the cry reached his consciousness. Gordon leaped to his feet, slipping on one of the opened magazine's glossy pages as he bolted for the door. He kicked it out of the way, ran down stairs and entered the darkened living room, breathing heavily with the exertion of taking the steps two at a time.

'What's the matter, Mam?' he gasped, checking her over for signs of damage. But nothing seemed to be amiss. She sat there, in the shadows, with one gnarled, arthritis-deformed claw of a hand pointing at the flickering television screen.

'Do you need to go pee-pees?'

'Look!' she tried to say, still pointing. Gordon froze. On the early evening regional news, a reporter was interviewing Carina in her dressing room. The actress, fresh from a successful matinée show, was giving another performance, this time for the smaller screen.

'... I owe it to my fans to continue,' she was saying. 'I'm not going to be put off by some crank. A coward.' She leant closer to the camera. 'Can I say something, my darling?' she asked the reporter. 'This is for the lunatic out there, wherever he... Or *she* is.' The dark eyebrows descended and hooded her eyelids as she peered down the camera lens. 'Get some help, you sicko, 'cos you aint going to stop me. The show goes on!' In the back of shot, members of the cast could be seen clapping and cheering.

Gordon's mother tried to clap too, but the effects of her debilitating stroke made it difficult. Gordon took out a handkerchief and wiped a trickle from the corner of her twisted mouth.

'What did the doctor tell you about not getting over-excited?' he said, without taking his eyes off the screen. The old lady's rebellious laugh turned into a rasping cough.

'Cora!' she managed to say between gaps in her coughing fit. Her words tumbled out, jumbled and indistinct. 'Co-ra!' she slurred. 'Terrible thing! To Cora!'

At least that's what Gordon interpreted the noise as. He wanted to say so much to his mother, to explain but had to bite his tongue. He knew she wouldn't understand. Some time soon he would be able to reveal everything. But not yet. Instead, he tapped the gnarled hand which clutched the TV remote with a grip of iron, then knelt down and kissed it.

'I know. It *is* a terrible thing,' he pronounced, with as much solemnity as he could muster.

He smiled to himself, knowing she couldn't see his expression in the darkness. On TV, the recorded report had ended and the news anchorwoman was telling everyone about a fundraising event Carina would be attending at the weekend and wasn't she a 'trouper'? Gordon's mother lost interest. Her heroine had appeared on the screen for a moment, shone briefly, then vanished, just as she'd done five years ago.

'I mish her,' she whispered plaintively. 'She should neva haff left.'

'I know.' Gordon kissed the hand again. Then he couldn't help himself. He wanted to cheer her up. 'I saw her today.'

Gordon's mother spun around. 'Where?' she slurred.

'Outside 'The Olde Tyne Theatre' with a bunch of fans.'

The old lady gasped. 'I spoke to her,' he bragged.

'What you shay t'Cor?'

'Three-point-seven-five-million.' His bulky frame became animated as he described the crowd outside the theatre and how he'd corrected Cora Smart in front of all her fans.

'She said four million had seen her last episode which isn't actually correct. It was three-point-seven-five-million. That was going on the first viewing, people who watched it on the night and didn't take into account the people who'd taped it - and then when you added those and the omnibus figures, the final result was more like four and a half million, which is fantastic for a daytime show!'

But his mother was no longer listening. Her concentration,

weakened by heavy prescription drugs and damaged synapses, was sporadic and fleeting. Gordon stared at her, trying to peer past the reflected image of the TV screen in her spectacle lenses, to see if she'd fallen asleep. He hoped she had. He'd already said too much to her. But no, the eyes weren't fully closed. He dabbed at the rivulet of saliva in the corner of her mouth again and said, as if talking to a toddler, 'Are you sure you don't want to go pee-pees?'

She reacted like a child by shaking her head fervently, petulantly. Gordon, on hands and knees, felt his way across the floor and reached for an electric plug.

'Shall I put the Christmas tree lights on? Shall I?' His voice became increasingly shrill as he repeated himself in the hope of getting some response.

'The Christmas tree lights?' He waved the plug at her. 'Shall I put them on? I will. Shall I?' When no reply was forthcoming, he rammed the plug into the socket.

In the bay window, tiny coloured stars on a plastic tree, and larger, brighter bulbs around the window, lit up the place like Santa's Grotto, throwing intermittent splodges of bright light across Gordon's mother as she sat in her chair in the centre of the room. She was a big woman, bloated from drugs and bad diet, dressed in clothes - skirt and silky blouse - which seemed too small, too short and too young for her. Rolls of puckered, wrinkled fat hung down from her legs below the skirt like molten mishapen wax and rippled every time she coughed or moved. The silk of her blouse was tight, shiny and smooth over her distended belly. However, nothing that lay below the neckline could prepare for the shock of what lay above it. The sheer mass of her body was quite overshadowed by her face. It was porcelain white, powdered and buffed, with garishly rouged cheeks. Heavily pencilled eyebrows, unmoving on her forehead, gave her a permanently startled look and there was something obscene about the bright scarlet lips, imprisoned between thick jowled cheeks. The lop-sided red wig on her head made her ancient features even more of a travesty. She had been turned into a grotesque imitation of her favourite soap actress: turned into an older, over-inflated, mentally-challenged version of Cora Smart. Only this was an extreme make-over too far: a parody bordering on the horrific. It was the stuff of nightmares.

Gordon, the architect of his mother's cosmetic re-enhancement, grinned winningly down at her as the kaleidoscope of lights flashed on and off and on again, around her.

'Is this a perfect tree, or what! Isn't this all lovely? Don't you think it's beautiful? It's like Heaven. It is, isn't it! Just like *Heaven*!'

The old lady nodded. Her doting son picked up a blanket off the settee and wrapped it around her legs.

'I'm just nipping out for a minute - to the post box,' he said, tenderly. 'I won't be long. And when I come back, I'll take you to the toilet. We'll have some tea. Then we'll settle down to watch *Winkle Bay*. All right?'

The over-made-up face broke into a gruesome smile.

Chapter Six

Carina lay in bed, physically exhausted after Saturday's two matinées and an evening show and the cumulative effect of having to pitch her performance at an audience of children and idiots. She took some consolation in the fact that at least the show was finally pulling in the punters. The empty gaps in the stalls were fewer and less embarrassing than they had been at the start of the run. She put the swelling ranks of the audience down to her unpleasant plight, now that it had been splashed across the newspapers. Most of the theatre-goers hoped they might be party to a gruesome assassination attempt on Carina's life by the shadowy author of the death threat letters. So far they must have left disappointed. Apart from the odd balloon bursting in the auditorium and one of the wheels falling off Cinderella's pumpkin coach, each performance had passed uneventfully. Carina was alive and well.

To her own surprise, she'd rather enjoyed the last few days. Colleagues, even the ones who despised her - which was ninety-nine-percent of the cast, had tried their best to console and cajole her in her hours of need. Management had taken to sending down bottles of champagne after each performance and even though she felt the majority of after-show punters clamouring for her at the stage door were waiting for her to drop dead from a drive by shooting/arsenic poisoning/surprise mugging, she was enjoying the attention. It was nice to feel wanted again. As she stared at the chink in the curtains where daylight sought to invade the room, mulling over events of the past few days in her mind, a warm feeling suffused her body.

For the first time in nearly five years, she'd experienced something of her former life, with journalists and photographers ringing and offers of satellite link interviews on breakfast television coming in. Of course, it wasn't anything like the scale she'd been used to in the past. When she'd had the face lift and was at odds with *Winkle Bay* executives, the paparazzi were everywhere. Then there was the furore around Paul, her third ex, and his sordid kiss and tell revelations - accusing her of being a violent, husband-beating alcoholic. On the back of those, Carina did the rounds of the chat-shows for weeks, expressing her regret time and time again and vowing, after a successful stay at 'The Priory', that she'd never lift her fists in anger again. And she'd been true to her word. Post divorce from Paul, whenever she felt the urge to throttle someone, she took a deep breath, then made a quick phone call to an accommodating thug she knew who charged very reasonable rates for short, swift acts of grievous bodily harm and got on with her life, happy in the knowledge that those who offended her were paid back big time. Of course, this wasn't an exact re-enactment of her heady golden days. No. The press interest she'd engendered this time around was relatively low key. Tabloid front page news she wasn't. A quarter page here, a column inch there, with an accompanying photo the size of a stamp. The telly stuff had mostly been regional. Still, she'd given two interviews to Sunday tabloids and posed for photos, which was better than nothing. Things could only get better. She was back! Or nearly back. Heading for the top again. All the way.

A gentle tap at the door made her sit up and check her appearance in the dressing table mirror opposite. Without her trademark red wig and war paint, the piggy-eyed woman who stared back at her bore no resemblance to the glamorous soap world vamp.

'Hang on,' she barked gruffly, quickly applying lipstick with one hand and reaching for her wig with the other. Then, realising her trusty sunglasses weren't on the bedside table, she groped around herself on the duvet.

'Shift!' she hissed at Fluff, who was sleeping soundly at the bottom of the bed. Sluggish and dazed, the creature was too slow to move. A milli-second later, Fluff sailed through the air - eyes a-boggling, after a well placed under-duvet kick from her owner. She landed on the floor with a whimper and scurried into a corner of the room where she trembled and shook inconsolably. Carina picked up her sunglasses and pushed them onto her face. She made a mental note to herself to tackle Jez Thompson again about a hotel suite of her own. There was just no damned privacy in this squalid dump.

'Come in.'

Dougie Hunt's head appeared round the door.

'Everything all right, darling?' he asked. 'Did you sleep well?' He rolled out his most concerned, sympathetic expression and let his eyes wander casually over to the dressing table mirror in order to make sure the look was as good as he felt it was. Yes. Magnificent. His face really had taken on an expression of genuine solicitude, when all he wanted to do was laugh hysterically at the sight of the silly old witch wearing sunglasses in bed. God he was good. If only his ears were a bit more symmetrical though, he thought as he glanced again fleetingly at his reflection. He sighed. The line between leading man and geeky character actor was a fine one.

Never mind.

'Mmm?' he muttered, aware that Carina had spoken.

'I said, I haven't slept a wink.'

He tipped a nod at the sunglasses.

'Glaucoma?' he queried.

Carina frowned at him.

'I had a nightmare. Kept thinking there was a man at my bedroom window.' She shuddered, then frowned at him again as the ghost of a smirk flickered over his face.

'Nightmare darling? Or wishful thinking?'

'Did you want something?' she enquired coldly.

Dougie nodded, pulled his unfeasibly short dressing gown around his corpulence and said, 'There's someone to see you.'

Carina sat up.

'Press?'

'Alas my love, no. A timid little mouse. Goes by the name of Jackie.'

Shit! Bollocks! Bloody woman. Carina sank back against the pillows.

'Tell her I'll be out in a minute.'

Dougie strode into the living room where the timid mouse was sitting in an armchair, attaché case on her lap, twisting a strand of mousey hair around a finger. Jackie let go of the stray lock and hugged her attaché case to her chest, either as a comforter or a shield against Dougie. Dougie grinned back at her.

'Her Divine-ness is just making herself presentable,' he said. 'She'll be about an hour.'

The sarcasm was lost on her. Jackie merely nodded politely and looked around the room, unnerved by Dougie's intense stare.

'It's awful, isn't it?' she said eventually.

46

'Isn't what awful?'

'This poison pen business. Poor Carina, she doesn't deserve it. All the things she does for charity as well. It's just not fair.'

Dougie shook his head sympathetically and decided to have some sport. He circled her like a cat closing in for the kill and sat down in the chair opposite.

'So what's your connection with Carina, my darling?' he asked. 'Are you a friend?'

'No, no. Not exactly. Well...'

'Lover?'

'What?! No! Friend! Yes! We're friends. I've known her for years... She's taken me into her confidence on many an occasion.'

'Really?'

'I run 'The Carina Hemsley Appreciation Society',' she stated portentously. 'I'm the President. I produce a newsletter four times a year and...'

The rest of the sentence stuck in her throat as her jaw dropped open. Her face reddened. She'd noticed something out of the corner of her eye. Dougie had crossed one leg over his knee, revealing the fact that he wasn't wearing anything under his dressing gown.

He grinned at her again, apparently oblivious. 'Go on, my love.'

Jackie's eyes whirled around in their sockets, taking in the ceiling, the tatty Monet prints on the walls, the view outside the window. Anything but the little gnarled stump and accompanying fuzzy bag of conkers poking out of Dougie's tartan dressing gown.

'Erm... You've... er... you've... four times a year,' she managed to say. 'And a signed Christmas card.'

'That's nice. Is your little club popular?'

Jackie fixed her eyes on a framed print of *Tyne Bridge in Winter* on the wall behind Dougie's head and concentrating hard, said, 'Yes. It is.'

Dougie nodded.

'I bet you're always on the look out for new members, though.'

'Yes,' Jackie replied, turning a funny puce colour.

Chuckling to himself Dougie stood up, pulling his robe around himself tightly. Carina, also robed up and with her head in a turban and her eyes screened by her Ray-bans breezed in. Jackie leaped out of her chair and bounded over.

'Oh, it's lovely to see you. You look well,' she gushed. 'Really well. Considering. I've been so worried about you. Desperately worried. Yes indeed-y.'

She made a half-hearted attempt to lean over and kiss 'The Star' but she saw the caterpillar eyebrows descend, drawing down a frown and thought better of it. Carina looked at her strangely, taking in the flushed face and twitching limbs cowering behind the attaché case.

'Have you been drinking?' she asked suspiciously.

'No!' Jackie squeaked. 'I haven't. I'm just a bit hot, that's all.' Behind her, Dougie mimed tipping an imaginary glass to his lips and nodded fervently at Carina, before slipping out of the room with a chuckle.

'Right, then!' said Carina, 'Spill!'

She sat down, loading a cigarette into the holder. Jackie too, sank back into the armchair and rubbed her brow, still unable to quite believe what she'd just seen. Aware that Carina was studying her beadily, she laid her attaché case flat on her knee and clasped her hands together over it.

'Actually, Carina, there isn't much to spill.'

The large black caterpillars gathered together above the shades

48

and reared, poised for attack.

'What do you mean?'

Jackie swallowed. 'There's only one piece in the Sunday's,' she said, opening up the attaché case and taking out a selection of newspapers. 'And it's not really about you. It's more about *Winkle Bay* and the falling viewing figures.'

Carina snatched the paper and studied the small article ringed with red pen.

'It's a nice photo of you though,' Jackie opined. 'And the caption's nice. "Cora Smart – a face from the good old days".'

Carina threw the paper at her. 'I don't want to be remembered as someone from the good old days! Christ, it sounds like I'm an old bloody relic! I want to be remembered for today! Tomorrow! Not bloody yesterday!'

Jackie cowered in her chair, bit her thumbnail and concentrated hard on preventing her bottom lip from trembling. It wasn't nice when your idol and heroine hurled abuse at you, no matter how frequently it happened. Usually she coped with it by telling herself that actors were temperamental, delicate – it's what separated them from the masses. Creative types were passionate. Delicate. It's what fuelled their art. She'd read that in Chat Magazine. But today Jackie was feeling delicate and vulnerable herself. It was eight months to the day since... since... Change the subject, she thought as her heart felt suddenly heavy and the salt in her tear ducts started to sting.

Sitting opposite, Carina saw the watery eyes, the mouth puckering into a dog's arse in spasm and felt her fury rising. Any other human being might have felt pity. But not Carina. Weakness only inspired anger. She pressed on, refusing to allow for human frailty.

'You did ring The Mail and tell them about attendances being up by seventy per cent, thanks to me?'

'Oh yes!'

'And what did they say?'

'*That's nice.*'

Carina sprang from her chair, livid, and started pacing the floor.

'And what about the Sunday Mirror? You speak to them?'

Jackie's head bobbed up and down as she fought off emotional collapse.

'I told them all about how brave you were being, insisting the show went on as usual and how you were dying inside, sort of thing.'

'And?'

Silence.

'Well?'

Jackie sighed. 'They weren't interested. They just wanted to know if you were... canoodling with anyone in the cast.'

'*Canoodling?!* Is that what they said?'

'No. They used the 'shh' word.'

Carina stared at her contemptuously.

'How old are you, woman?' she spat. 'Eight? Shagging! Just say it. Shagging! Christ, my fan club's being run by Mother-Fucking-Teresa!'

Jackie, pulled the attaché case from her knee, placed it protectively across her chest and began to rock back and forth on the chair. Carina tutted, for now Fluff was whimpering at her heels. What did she do to deserve being surrounded by such needy, neurotic creatures?

'Is there anything else I should know?' she ventured, coldly.

'One or two things,' Jackie said, in a small whiney voice.

'Rufus Frenkel at *Winkle Bay*.'

Carina spun around. 'What about him?'

'He rang me yesterday.'

Carina could barely contain her excitement. 'I knew it. I knew he would. What did he want?'

Jackie swallowed. 'He wants you to stop asking the fans to write in asking for the return of Cora. He says it's never going to happen. Ever.'

Carina tapped the end of her cigarette holder against her front teeth as she struggled to keep her temper in check.

'Oh really?'

'Mmm,' said Jackie. 'He thinks you should at least attempt a show of dignity and self-respect.'

Carina inhaled deeply, blew out a stream of smoke and advanced on Jackie. She stopped in front of her, hands on hips, head tossed back defiantly.

'I hope you told him where to get off,' she said malevolently.

Jackie shrugged uncomfortably and mumbled something incoherently.

'You didn't say anything, did you!' snapped Carina. 'You just let the little weasel walk all over my character and you took it like the big wet bloody lettuce that you are.'

Jackie reached for the handkerchief up her sleeve. The tears were gushing now and she was unable to stem the tide.

'I couldn't think. He was so horrible...' she managed to stammer.

'Who made that programme what it is today? Me. Who pulled in the punters? Me. That's what you should have told him. You're the President of my fan club, woman!'

She hunched her shoulders and putting on a little-girl voice, mimicked Jackie. '*He was sooo horrible!* Pathetic!'

'Leave me alone!'

The anguished outburst, so out of character, made the actress's head jerk back in shock. Jackie had found her voice at last.

'I'm not your secretary!'

'What?' asked Carina, unable to believe her ears.

Jackie, a mass of raw nerves and emotion, pressed on. 'You don't pay me! I get no thanks from you for what I do. You don't seem to appreciate all the hard work I put in!'

'All right, keep your hair on!' muttered Carina petulantly.

'I'm just an ordinary housewife who's trying her best!'

'I know, love. I know!' said Carina, quickly changing tack. She realised she'd gone too far. It didn't do to antagonise the unpaid help. 'And don't say you're just a housewife,' she added. 'You're marvellous.'

The sudden shift to kindness and concern only made the tears flow faster.

'I'm not,' she wailed. 'You're sick of me...'

'What made you think that?' protested Carina.

But Jackie wasn't listening, she was on a roll.

'... The kids are sick of me...'

'No!'

'... Alan's definitely sick of me...'

Carina was about to protest again but thought better of it.

'Is this what it's all about, my love? Alan?'

Jackie nodded slowly. 'It's eight months to the day since he vanished.'

'Ahhh!' Carina exclaimed. 'I didn't realise. Poor lamb.' She perched on the arm of the chair and stroked Jackie's hair.

'Why hasn't he been in touch?' Jackie wept. 'Why did he just walk out like that? You don't know what it's like, the not knowing, Carina.'

'It's been awful for you.'

'I keep thinking I see him. In the street. In a car. On a bus.' She blew her nose. 'But it's never him. I think something's happened to him, Carina. Something terrible.'

'No!'

Jackie shook her head. 'Eight months. And in all that time he hasn't touched his bank account, his savings... He wouldn't walk out like that. Not without good reason. He wouldn't. Would he?'

'He was a bit of a bastard,' said Carina, trying to sound helpful. 'And he *was* shag... canoodling with that cheap slut from Blockbusters last year.'

Jackie blew into her hankie again. 'We were over that. We'd moved on. He loves his kids.'

'What do the police say?'

'They just keep telling me there's nothing to report.'

Carina took Jackie's hands and pulled her up out of the chair. 'Come here,' she said, hugging her tight.

'He'll turn up when he wants to.'

'Will he?' asked Jackie plaintively.

'I'm sure.'

Jackie nodded again, trying to be brave. She buried her head against Carina's breast. Carina grimaced and patted her on the shoulder.

'If I seem to be taking you for granted,' she purred, 'It's only because I'm trying to take your mind off your problems. That's all. Work, work, work! Best thing for a troubled lass.'

Jackie smiled. 'Thank you.'

'That's better.' Carina air-kissed her. 'Now, how does a big old fashioned Sunday dinner sound to you? Roast beef, Yorkshire pudding, veg, trifle... a bottle or two of nice wine?'

Jackie grinned, flattered, and wiped her tear streaked cheeks. 'I'd like that.'

'I'm going to cook it myself. I'll invite Dougie and some of the cast along, make it a cosy little gathering. Just my way of saying thank you to everybody for being so kind over the past few days.'

'And that includes you,' she added magnanimously.

Jackie suddenly felt teary-eyed again. This woman was so misunderstood. Underneath the hard exterior lurked a heart of gold. She was a genuine person, despite being a living legend. And Jackie felt privileged to be included in her inner retinue.

'Won't you be a bit pushed?' she enquired. 'You're guest of honour at the fund-raiser tonight.'

'Oh, yes!' said Carina, trying to sound as if she'd forgotten. 'What am I going to do?'

She looked at Jackie, wide eyed. And waited.

'Maybe I could help...' Jackie started to say after a pause. Before she'd had chance to finish the sentence Carina was calling her an 'angel' and a 'love'. Digging around in her dressing gown pocket she produced a piece of paper and thrust it into Jackie's hand.

'Here's the shopping list.'

Jackie stared at her bemused.

'Well, I can't go down the supermarket sweetheart,' continued Carina. 'I'll be mobbed.'

'Yes. Of course.'

Behind them, Fluff started scratching frantically at the lower panes of glass in the french windows overlooking the garden. She looked back at her owner with pleading eyes but was ignored.

'Don't take too long, eh? 'Cos you'll have to get back and put the dinner on. We'll want to eat at seven, if the charity do starts at half eight.'

Jackie leapt up.

'Of course.'

As she reached the door, Carina dug her hands inside her pocket again and called out, 'Hang on, flower.' She pulled out Fluff's dog lead. 'Take the dog with you. She needs to go pee-pees.'

Chapter Seven

A thick fog, cold and dank, rolled off the sea front at Whitley Bay, making the avenue of dilapidated amusement arcades look even more depressing. Even in summer, when the crowds came, an air of sadness hung over the place but the present clouds of mist made the place look even more abandoned. Vague silhouettes of occasional joggers could be glimpsed trudging along the promenade until they too vanished, ghost-like into the mists. Pauline Clifton, warm and comfortable in the passenger seat of her boss's car, shivered as the fog swirled in the road ahead.

'How depressing,' she muttered, sinking lower into her seat.

'Shush!' Newall, concentrating on his driving, frowned. The weather had done nothing to lift his spirits either. A late night spent drinking alone in front of the television made concentration very difficult.

'I set fire to the settee last night,' he said eventually.

'Why?' asked Clifton, startled.

'There wasn't anything decent on the telly.' He looked at her askance. 'I fell asleep with a fag in my hand.'

'Oh, Boss!'

'I know, I know. But it could have been a lot worse. I was fine. And there's only a little hole in the arm of the settee. I covered it with a coaster. Might have to touch up the ceiling though.'

'You know Boss, if you fancy a night out, all you have to do is ring me. I hardly go out, myself.'

'What about your fella? The deep-sea diver. Wouldn't he mind?'

Clifton shrugged. 'He really wouldn't. We broke up.'

'Oh. Bad luck.'

There was no more time to pursue social conversation. The fog lamps had picked out a large sign at the bend in the road bearing the legend 'Four Seasons Caravan Park.' Newall slowed and started indicating.

'Four Seasons,' scoffed Clifton. 'That's a joke. We only get one season here. Permanent winter.'

The car turned into the caravan park and stopped. The private road ahead disappeared after only a few feet. They were surrounded by a wall of white impenetrable mist.

'We'll never find it, Boss. It's bad enough when you can see. The place is a maze of trailers.'

'What number are we looking for?' Newall asked, ignoring her comment.

'One hundred and eleven.'

Newall pulled on his leather gloves, opened the door and climbed out.

'Let's go.'

Clifton sighed and was about to complain again but Newall's outline began to fade as he strode into the fog, so she dashed after him to avoid losing him. They edged their way gingerly along the road, straying onto muddy grass verges occasionally to check the signposts at each intersection.

'Twelve to twenty,' Newall said, tapping one of the signs. 'We're getting warmer.'

'Speak for yourself,' said Clifton, adjusting her scarf and stumbled against a stone marker at the road side. 'You don't really think the second ex has anything to do with those letters?'

'I don't know,' came the honest reply. 'I've seen the cuttings and he did seem bitter when they divorced.'

'Seems like he had a lucky escape to me,' opined Clifton. 'She's a complete monster.'

'Oh, I don't know about that. I can see what blokes see in her. There's something about her.'

'God! You fancy her!' Clifton couldn't help her outburst.

'Rubbish!' exclaimed Newall. 'I'm being objective.'

'If you're being objective Boss, then so am I. I can see why a lot of people might hate her guts. She's selfish, demanding and manipulative.'

Newall didn't dispute her observations. Emboldened by this, Clifton pressed on.

'It wouldn't surprise me if she sent the letters herself. But then again, I don't think she's that good an actress.'

Her cackle ceased abruptly when she realised Newall wasn't laughing along with her.

'I think we're looking for a disgruntled fan,' she said quickly. 'Maybe she didn't reply to a letter, or forgot to send an autographed photo.'

'Possibly,' muttered Newall.

Clifton thought it wise to say nothing more. She knew Newall well and respected him. She also knew of the politics at play here. If the local media hadn't been clamouring for answers along with the odd tabloid reporter ringing up to harang his superiors about 'Poor Cora', the time spent on this investigation would have been negligible. They had to be seen to be doing something.

They took a right turn and strode on in silence until a tall object loomed in the near distance. 'Oh, I don't believe it! We're back at the beginning!' shrieked Clifton. The sign post in front of them read 'Trailers 12 - 20'. She stomped her feet petulantly. Her toes were freezing.

Paul Miller was awakened rather rudely from a deep, deep sleep by an officious-sounding knocking on his trailer door. Who the hell was this? Disturbing his peace on a Sunday morning. He looked at the clock. Afternoon, then. Even so. It still wasn't on. He buried his head in his pillow and hoped the person or persons would go away. But the knocking continued. Miller sighed.

'I'm coming!' he croaked and threw back the duvet exposing a bare torso of a deep orange colour which seemed strangely luminous in the half-light. Pulling on jeans and a t-shirt he lurched over to the door, threw it open and squinted at the two figures staring up at him. The middle aged man, balding and overweight was formally dressed in a black suit and overcoat. The woman, younger and prettier, was also in a suit. Quite expensive by the cut of it. Armani? They both wore the same smug expression.

'If you're with the Mormons,' he said contemptuously, 'I'm not interested.'

The couple exchanged puzzled looks and flashed their warrant cards at him.

'Oh!' he exclaimed.

'Mr Miller? Could we have a word?' Newall recognised the fake tan and bleached hair from a night in the Quayside Lodge restaurant several years ago. He was younger then, fresher-faced. There were bags under the eyes now and the golden wavy hair was straw-like this close-up, more obviously dyed. Miller stood back to admit the officers.

'It's about the third degree burns, isn't it.' The officers said nothing, let him continue. 'Well, it's not my fault,' he said. 'I only rent out the sun beds and if some ginger-minger's stupid enough to lie under one for an hour, that's got nothing to do with me. I told her...'

'Mr Miller!' Clifton cut in, 'We'd like to talk to you about your ex-wife.'

Miller closed the door sharply.

'She's not dead?' he asked hopefully.

'No,' said Clifton.

Miller sighed, disappointed.

'Would you like her to be?'

'Too right.' Remembering who he was talking to a little too late, he added quickly, 'I mean, no. No.' But unable to help himself he added, 'Maybe maimed a bit. In a car crash. Has she been involved in a car crash?'

The detectives shook their heads.

'Mr Miller,' began Clifton. 'Your ex-wife has received a number of letters recently from an anonymous source, threatening her life.'

Miller stared at them blankly.

'Have you got anything to say to that? '

He nodded. 'Good on them,' he said, and laughed.

Clifton, chilled to the bone and worried about the lack of feeling in her feet, snapped at him.

'We're treating this very seriously, Mr Miller. So I suggest you do likewise.'

Miller's smile disappeared. 'You don't think it was me?' he asked incredulously.

'You tell us,' Clifton said.

'Of course it wasn't. Why would I? I haven't seen her in six years.

I don't want anything to do with her.'

'Your divorce was rather acrimonious.'

'Only because of Fluff. I didn't want her money or her things. Just the dog.' A note of hysteria crept into his voice. 'She was mine. I bought her. I was the one she went to when she needed love and affection.'

He picked up a framed photo of Fluff, taken in happier times, when she had a healthy coat of fur and touched the image fondly.

'She knew I loved that dog. That's why she wouldn't let me have her.'

He gazed at the photo, lost in thought.

'How is she?' he asked, after a moment, when he had calmed down.

'She's holding up well,' opined Newall. 'Going on stage every night. Refusing to give in.'

'Not her!' snapped Miller impatiently. 'Fluff!'

'As well as can be expected,' said Clifton.

Newall flicked through his notes. 'You used to be Carina's hairdresser? That's how you got together?'

'That's right. Almost right. I don't remember how we actually *got together*,' said Miller. 'I woke up in her bed one morning after a night out. And that was it. She said we were going to get married. I swear she must have drugged me. I couldn't remember a thing.'

'It must have been quite hard for you when she sacked you and divorced you at the same time?'

Miller didn't deny it. 'For a while it was. When all you're remembered for is being Mr Carina Hemsley. But I moved on. Gave up the hairdressing. Had to.'

He held up two shaking hands. 'Nerves. She did that. With all her unnatural demands.'

61

Newall looked up, interested. 'Such as?'

'She just wanted sex all the time. There was no love. No feeling. I was just an object to her. She's like a vampire. Sucks you dry then spits you out.' He shivered and stood up. 'But I'm over that now. The sun bed business is doing okay. I'm expanding into spray tan. Going mobile. *Tan In A Van*. I'm a success in my own right now. And I've done it without her help.'

Clifton took in the chipped mugs on the counter, the threadbare carpet and tatty furniture, all wrapped up in the aroma of damp and suspected that Miller's idea of success differed from her own.

'Do you keep up with her progress?' wondered Newall. 'In the celebrity mags? That sort of thing?'

Miller laughed ruefully. 'Wouldn't touch them with a ten foot barge pole. I know she's not in *Winkle Bay* anymore. And she must hate that. So I'm pleased. But celebrity life? Don't miss it. It stinks.'

'Well, thank you for your time, Mr Miller,' said Newall politely, and opened the door. Salty sea air seeped in, mixing with the smell of damp. Clifton got up to follow. Warm vapour escaped from her mouth as she stepped out into the cold.

'It's very cosy here,' she lied. Miller nodded and leant against the doorway.

'Can you think of anyone who might have it in for Miss Hemsley?' Clifton added.

Miller started to laugh a high pitched nasally laugh that grated on the senses like nails down a blackboard. His sides shook and he wrapped his arms around his ribs as if he was in pain.

'I feel sorry for you lot,' he managed to say, wiping tears of mirth from his face with the sleeve of his t-shirt.

Clifton stared at him, not understanding. 'Why's that?'

'You don't have the manpower or the time to investigate every single person who holds a grudge against Carina. She's the most hated woman I've ever met. She is!'

Newall and Clifton walked away slowly, retracing their route to the car. When Clifton looked back, Miller and his caravan had disappeared into the white mist. Only his laughter remained, echoing around the camp site until it was drowned out by the lonely cry of gulls somewhere high above them.

Chapter Eight

Ben Tingle jumped out of the taxi and opened up the umbrella to protect his girlfriend from the pouring rain. She slid out of the cab demurely and they both stared over at the bungalow, Lauren with anticipation, Ben with a sinking heart. When the call came from Carina inviting them to an early evening Sunday dinner before going on to the fund raising benefit, he had wanted to refuse. It was bad enough spending time with her in a professional capacity never mind having to endure some extra-curricular hours with the groping old dragon. Ever since day one of rehearsals she'd grabbed him and poked him relentlessly, making it quite clear what she was after. The thought made him ill - his own grandmother was younger than Carina Hemsley. He was sure he had good grounds for a sexual harrassment in the workplace suit but his agent had made him aware that it wouldn't serve his macho persona very well if the press ever got their hands on it. So he was forced to tolerate Carina getting her hands on *him* once in a while. He didn't know what was worse - Carina trying to stick her tongue down his throat when she got the chance or the tugging at his crotch in the wings every night before the ballroom scene. Actually he did know what was worse. It was neither of those things - which were bad enough. It was Dougie Hunt trying to do the same. The situation was becoming intolerable. He'd tried to put Carina off by telling her he was with Lauren but she only laughed and said 'Lauren *Who*?'. With Dougie, he'd socked him on the mouth the last time he followed him into the loo but the very next day in the finalé, he'd assaulted him behind the pumpkin carriage. Short of running onto the stage shouting 'Baron Hard-Up's a shirtlifter,' there was little he could do but fend him off until his cue. Anyway, who would have believed him? To the world, Dougie had a reputation as a ladies man. He remembered him from those old sitcoms from the Seventies - swanning around in a cravat and a smoking jacket smooth-talking women into the bedroom with his ridiculous 'Well, aren't you a *peach*?!' catch-phrase. Even as a kid he thought the guy seemed unreal. As an adult, years later, finding himself on the end of the very same chat-up line was sickening. Explaining his problem to Lauren hadn't worked at all. She didn't seem to understand. The trouble was, she was too nice and trusting and believed everybody in the world was sweet and kind. What's more, there were never any witnesses around when the attacks happened. Carina and Dougie were obviously old hands at this game. He felt isolated and alone.

Lauren admired her boyfriend, standing in the orange glow of a street light in his tux and dickie-bow, looking rather forlorn. 'You look gorgeous,' she said.

'You're not so bad yourself,' he muttered, a little distracted. She did indeed look stunning. He just wanted to be alone with her. Away from this dump. Away from these weirdo people. Apart from meeting Lauren, he wished he'd stayed in Sydney and never agreed to a career in acting. Modelling was so much easier. There was none of this walking and talking business. You just turned up for the shoot, flexed your muscles and posed. Then went home a few thousand dollars better off.

Lauren grabbed his hand and squeezed it. 'It'll be okay.'

'Don't leave me alone, yeah?'

'Looking like that? No chance.'

They waved the taxi away and walked down the holly-lined driveway and up the disabled ramp to the front door.

'What's with the ramp?' Ben asked. 'It's like an old lady's house.'

'It's one of Jez's properties,' Lauren replied. 'Dougie says it's got a sit down bath and hand rails all around the place.'

'Carina should feel at home, then.' He caught Lauren's frown. 'Okay, I'll be nice. But only because someone's trying to kill her,' he added.

Before Lauren rang the doorbell, she turned to Ben, suddenly anxious.

'Do you think I should tell her?'

'Yeah! Of course! Tell everybody! I would!' came the reply.

Lauren wasn't so sure. 'Maybe I'll see how it goes. I mean it's only an audition. Nothing definite.'

'You'll get the part,' Ben assured her. He kissed her as she pressed her finger on the doorbell. They were still entwined when the door opened, light spilling over them from the hallway.

'Aren't you two sweet?' Dougie grinned at them. 'I could eat you both.' They quickly separated. He beckoned them in with a cocky tip of the head. Ben skirted around him suspiciously. 'Look who's here every one. It's Cinderella and her Prince Charming,' said Dougie as he led them into the candle lit dining room. The group sitting around the table glanced over: Campbell, a permanent picture of apprehension, Jez and Heidi (she, in stark contrast to her husband's black/ginger hair and beard, a slave to bleach and depilation), and Brendan and Justin, the Ugly-Sisters, who, off duty and in men's clothing, resembled ugly brothers.

'No Sylvie?' asked Lauren.

Brendan shook his head. 'Poor thing's a bit tired. She's...'

'... Pissed again,' interrupted Dougie. He pulled out a chair for Lauren. 'You sit there, my darling,' he commanded gallantly, then guided a reticent Ben further around the table. 'And you, handsome, can sit here, next to me.'

Realising he was trapped, Ben slid into his seat and fumbled nervously with his napkin.

'This is lovely,' cried Lauren, gazing around at the flickering candles and the tealights on the old oak sideboard which someone had placed rather artistically amongst some freshly picked branches of holly. The dark shadows they threw on the walls took the curse off the spiral patterned Seventies wallpaper and made the place look warm, even if the atmosphere remained a little frosty.

'Isn't it,' said Justin without much enthusiasm.

'It's all so gorgeous,' she gushed. 'And so Christmassy. And we're all together. Like a family.'

Campbell looked up from rolling a cigarette in his lap. 'Christmas has got nothing to do with 'family' these days. It's about big corporations making big money. It's obscene! And the damage to the environment caused by all that wrapping paper...'

'Can't you just enjoy yourself for once?' snapped Jez. 'Christ! What a kill joy.'

Campbell's hands started to shake and bits of tobacco fell out of the unsealed cigarette paper.

'He's right though. It's all a big con,' said Heidi, smiling supportively at the director. Unseen by her husband, she took the cigarette from Campbell's shaking fingers, moistened the gum with her tongue, rolled it expertly and handed it back.

'Where is she?' asked Lauren.

'In the kitchen,' replied Brendan, 'checking on her cauldron.'

'Don't be horrible,' protested Heidi. 'I think it's really nice of her to go to all this trouble. Isn't it, honey?' She struck a match and lit Campbell's roll-up.

Jez grunted. He had no idea why they were all there. From what he'd gathered, kind and selfless acts *and* Carina Hemsley did not go together. There was always an ulterior motive with that sort of person. He should know. He was that sort of person too. Or was he being too hard on her? The charity fundraiser event had been organised some time ago. Perhaps he was wrong in assuming that Carina was taking advantage of the death threats to gain sympathy and attention. But what the hell?! As long as she was pulling in the punters - and she was - he would indulge her as much as she liked.

'Budge up, cock.'

Jez tried to pull his chair nearer the table in order to let Carina pass. Dressed in a shimmering gown which twinkled in the candlelight, she really did look like a relic from Hollywood's golden era: cigarette holder dangling at an angle from her mouth, 'hair' and make-up perfect, she stood in the doorway holding a tray of cocktails, striking a pose.

'Margarita's everybody?' She shmoozed her way around the room - 'Thanks for coming, my darling,' and 'So lovely to see you,' handing out drinks as she went. Stopping beside Lauren, she ran a finger over the young girl's shoulder.

'What a gorgeous dress, flower,' she cooed. 'You look beautiful.'

Lauren grinned, flattered by the attention. 'Thank you Carina. So do you.'

Carina blew her a kiss and passed on. When she reached Ben and held out the tray for him to pick up his drink she grinned at him wickedly and raised the tray high above her head, forcing him to stand and reach up for it.

'She's such a tease,' said Dougie. Ben sat down promptly.

'I'll make do with water,' he said.

Carina lowered the tray within reaching distance.

'Big girl's blouse,' she said, with more than a hint of ice in her voice and set the cocktail down in front of him, then yelled, 'Jackie!'

Jackie appeared in the doorway wearing an apron over her clothes. She smiled at the guests and brushed a stray lock of hair from her face with a bandaged hand. As she did so, Ben and Lauren gawped impolitely at her face. There were several rather livid scratch marks down one cheek and across her forehead which were starting to swell around the edges.

'What happened to her?' asked Lauren.

'She fell in the holly bush,' replied Brendan, trying not to laugh. He pointed to the Christmas decoration on the sideboard.

'Trying to make a festive display for Boss-In-Boots.'

'Dinner in five minutes,' barked Carina without looking at her injured 'assistant'. She had picked up her own Margarita and was about to move into the seat on the other side of Ben. The Aussie beefcake sat rigid in his chair, with the haunted look of a condemned man.

'Yes Carina. Everything's ready,' gushed a harassed Jackie. 'Just about to mash the potatoes.' She scurried out.

Carina tapped her glass with a spoon and cleared her throat. A hush fell upon the room.

'I'd like to say a few words,' she began.

Brendan turned to Justin and whispered, 'We'll be here for a week.'

'You know what I've been going through recently. I've been living a nightmare, never sure who or what might be lurking around the corner.' Carina's voice cracked. She took a few seconds to compose herself. 'But I have to say, you've all helped me enormously. You're true friends.' She reached over and grabbed Ben's hand in a vice-like grip. 'True friends,' she repeated. Ben, unable to free his digits from the iron claw, picked up his Margarita with his other hand and gulped it down in one. Dougie, never one to pass up the opportunity to hog the lime-light, stood up with his glass.

'I'd like to say something too,' he declared. 'A toast. To Carina's bravery and sublime professionalism.'

The others held up their glasses and turned to Carina.

'Bless you my darlings,' she said, visibly moved. 'When we started rehearsing, I never dreamt...'

She was interrupted unceremoniously by the arrival of Jackie, who staggered in with a tureen of steaming vegetables in each hand and two more balanced precariously on her arms.

'Dinner's ready!'

Carina glared at her. 'Do you mind? I'm talking,' she snapped.

'Sorry. Sorry!' Jackie gasped and hovered behind her, transferring her weight from one foot to the other as she tried to balance the plates.

'Where was I?' She glared murderously at Jackie. 'Oh yes. In the beginning I thought this was going to be like any other gig. Get in, do your stuff, get out again. But you've made this so, so special for me...'

'I'm sorry!' shrieked Jackie, dancing around on the spot. 'The plates are hot!'

'Oh, put the bastards down, then,' Carina snarled. She glowered at the poor woman. Ben used the diversion to reclaim his imprisoned

70

hand. He snatched it out of Carina's grasp and sat back in his chair, relieved.

'It's roast beef, yorkshire pudding, carrots, peas, mashed potatoes,' said Jackie, plonking plates in front of the guests.

'Thank you. It looks lovely,' said Heidi. The chef smiled at her gratefully and hurried out to the kitchen. Campbell stared down at the plate set in front of him and tried to shut out the crap he was being forced to listen to. Heidi, noticing, rubbed his shoulder affectionately. 'Are you okay, Campbell?' she inquired. He nodded politely, moved by her concern. This woman was amazing. She was a beacon of goodness. What she saw in the old heathen she lived with was a mystery to him.

'Hope nobody's a vegetarian,' cackled Carina.

'Actually, I am,' said Campbell. Carina turned to him contemptuously.

'Figures,' she said, draining her glass.

'Oh, well,' she sniffed, 'Enjoy your carrots and peas.' Campbell pushed the vegetables around with his fork, forlornly.

Carina winked at Ben. 'I could never give up meat.'

Dougie concurred.

Jackie brought in the rest of the meals and made sure everyone had what they needed. It was only when she returned with her own dinner that she realised there was nowhere for her to sit. She hovered over the dinner guests, a piteous figure, nervous and feeling excruciatingly self-conscious. A gentleman at heart, Brendan offered to give up his place but Carina was having none of it.

'What's wrong with the kitchen?' she bellowed.

Jackie slunk out, red faced, plate in hand and sat alone in front of the gas cooker where, no matter how hard she tried, she was unable to quash the rebellious voice inside her head, telling her life might have been much easier if she'd stayed with 'The Olivia Newton-John Fan Club' all those years ago and never transferred her allegiance to *Winkle Bay*.

'She's a good person, really,' she said out loud.

Sighing, she picked up a knife and fork and stabbed at her food but after spending hours preparing the meal she found she wasn't hungry. As a distraction, she tried to think about her husband: tried to imagine all the possible scenarios which might account for his prolonged absence. Like amnesia. Resulting from a car crash. He could be lying in a hospital somewhere... in a coma...

Jackie brought herself out of her reverie with a jolt. Something strange was happening to her daydreams, she noted, with a pang of guilt. This was the second time it had happened, in as many days. Whenever she'd thought of Hubby-Dearest recently, she hadn't quite been able see his face clearly in her mind's eye. The familiar features she'd woken up to every morning for the last fifteen years somehow didn't seem so memorable. And he'd only been gone a few months. Jackie couldn't understand it. Was she so shallow it was a case of 'out of sight, out of mind?' No! Surely not. It was the stress talking. She loved Alan very much. And if she couldn't see him clearly, perhaps it was due to the drugs she was taking for her depression. Didn't they block things? Nerve endings? Affect the memory? Or was this the start of something more serious? Something mental. The more she thought, the more she felt herself beginning to unravel again and this was something else she had to reproach herself for. She had to keep herself together for the kids. For Carina. They all needed her. Jackie focussed on the thickest piece of beef on her plate, drew the blade of her knife slowly, forward and back, forward and back, in the same groove, carving an incision with the edge of the blade, until it separated, then fell off the larger tranch of beef. Her breathing and nerves steadying, she popped the meat into her mouth and chewed. It was delicious. Not too brown, not too pink, just perfect. But of course it was. She was a good cook. The best. Alan had told her so. On several occasions. He loved her cooking. She tried to sidetrack her thoughts, move away from her pre-occupations. Were Carina's guests enjoying the meal? Was Carina? She supposed they must be. It sounded very quiet in there. All she could hear was the metallic grating and clashing of cutlery on china and the low murmur of voices.

Alan's favourite Sunday dinner was roast chicken. With homemade pork and sage stuffing. Oh, no! She was back to that again. Alan. And Alan's love of food. Her food. Her cooking. Dark thoughts leaked into her mind, staining her daydreams, unsettling her stomach with their poison. There was no escaping the notion: something terrible had happened to Alan. She had no proof to back it up, no theory of possibilities, only the nagging knowledge that even a fling with Hannah from Blockbusters - with everything that entailed - long legs, a great figure, free dvd's: none of those temptations were enough to keep him away from Jackie's home-made apple crumble and the kids for longer than a month. No, she feared the worst.

Jackie guided a few peas onto her fork with her knife and quickly shovelled them into her mouth before emotion rendered her lips rubbery and useless. Such was her distraction, she failed to see the shadowy figure watching her through the kitchen window.

Uncomfortably warm from the effective electric fire and from the number of bodies squashed around the small table, Carina tipped half a glass of Rioja down her dry throat and held it up for Dougie to refill. Unlike her glass, the plate of food in front of her remained untouched. Waving bye-bye to the enjoyment of eating was one of the pitfalls of Celebrity. The camera put an extra ten pounds on a person, though in Carina's view it was more like ten stones. She glanced at Lauren, enviously, who was tucking in to her dinner without a thought for her calorie intake. Lauren looked up, saw her staring and smiled winningly.

'The food is delicious, Carina. Absolutely yummy,' she said. Carina swallowed her wine and managed a half-hearted sickly grin in return. The others agreed.

'I'm so glad.'

She reached down and picked up a startled Fluff off the floor, but not before taking another glug of Rioja to numb the hunger pangs. Fluff's eyes bulged alarmingly as Carina's heavy handed strokes pulled the fur back from her quivering head.

Lauren dabbed at her lips with her napkin and cleared her throat.

'Actually, Carina, I've got some news.' All eyes turned to her. All eyes except Dougie, who was focussing intently on Ben.

'Don't tell me you've got her up the duff?' he snorted.

'What are you talking about, you weirdo?' snapped Ben angrily. 'Jeez!'

'No, it's nothing like that. God, no,' said Lauren, blushing. 'I've got an audition for *Winkle Bay*!' She ended the declaration with an excited little squeak.

Brendan and Justin clapped and cheered. Carina remained stoney faced.

'As what?' she inquired, with a dangerous quaver in her voice. 'What part is this?'

'Daisy Smart.' Lauren hugged herself tightly, such was her excitement. 'Your grand-daughter.'

'That's fantastic!' Carina bellowed. Her voice came out louder than planned. She seemed as shocked as everyone else by the decibels. Fluff jumped off her lap. 'Really fantastic,' she repeated, at a level more acceptable to the human ear.

'I think this calls for a celebration,' said Jez.

'Oh, no. It's only an audition,' Lauren said modestly. 'I might not get the part.'

'You'll get it,' Ben opined with all the misplaced optimism of youth.

'Of course you will, lovey,' said Carina, with all the insincerity of bitter age. Her eyes took on a glazed look as she loaded a cigarette into her holder.

'I think it's a big mistake.'

The others turned to Campbell, who had placed his knife and fork on his plate and looked like he was about to launch into one of his puffed up lectures.

'Oh here we go,' muttered Jez.

'You're a terrific actress, Lauren,' he said. 'Superb. And I love you immensely. So don't take this the wrong way when I tell you that it will be the end of you as an actress of quality. You'll develop bad habits, your ego will take over and you'll lose your integrity. Stay away from the soaps.'

Before Carina had chance to stub out her cigarette on his nose, a piercing scream from the kitchen saved his life. Jackie rushed in, and fell to the floor, a quivering wreck.

'Looks like pudding's off,' Dougie said.

Carina poked at her with her foot. 'Get up!' she hissed. 'Get up you silly bitch!'

'Call the police!' Jackie managed to gasp. 'There's a man outside.'

'Really?' said, Dougie, perking up.

Brendan bent over her and helped her up.

'Ignore her,' instructed Carina. 'She's hallucinating again.'

'I'm not!' Jackie weeped.

'Ever since her husband buggered off, she's imagined seeing him in all sorts of stupid places,' Carina explained.

'NO!' wailed Jackie. 'It wasn't Alan. It was a stranger.'

'Good looking?' wondered Dougie.

'I don't know,' sobbed Jackie. 'All I could see were his terrible eyes. Burning through the glass.'

Ben leaped up and raced through to the kitchen.

'Nobody there now,' he called back.

'See?' said Carina unsympathetically.

'Maybe we should look outside,' ventured Lauren. The men exchanged nervous glances but made no attempt to move.

'Call the police,' Campbell squeaked.

Carina tutted, drew herself up bravely and teetered over to the window. Drawing the curtain aside she gasped and staggered back. They all turned to stare at the sheet of paper taped to the outside of the window. 'The bitch will die' read the message in the now familiar patchwork of cut out letters. Her guests gathered around her with words of support.

'I told you there was somebody there,' said Jackie.

Carina reached for the nearest glass of wine and knocked it back thirstily.

'I'm telling you this for nothing, mush,' Carina said, turning to Jez, 'I'm not staying another night in this place. You can put me up in a bleedin' hotel.'

Jez thought it wise to give in to the Star's demand. He felt rather shaken, himself. Ben returned to the dining room and took in the multi-coloured message.

'I don't understand,' he said. 'Why would anyone want to frighten an old lady?'

A dreadful silence descended. Even Jackie momentarily forgot her panic attack.

'Of course you don't understand,' Carina managed to say. 'How could you, my love? That would require a brain.'

She'd gone right off handsome beef-cakes.

Chapter Nine

The room was really no more than a cupboard but the boxes of crisps and nuts had all been stacked to one side and a small battered dressing table now took pride of place against one wall. Carina sat before it, fixing her make-up. If she was nervous, she disguised her feelings well. Fluff, on the other hand, sitting in her basket on the floor, shook and trembled every time a distant cheer went up from the bingo crowd in the entertainment room beyond. Carina smiled at her reflection, took a big mouthful from the large glass of brandy at her side and turned to acknowledge the officious sounding knock at the door.

'Come in.'

D.I. Newall entered.

'Only me, Miss Hemsley,' he said, slightly intimidated by the shimmering vision before him.

'Hello, my guardian angel,' she purred. 'And it's Carina. Call me Carina.'

Newall pushed a box of pork scratchings aside and drew up a chair.

'Are you sure you want to do this?' he asked. 'You don't have to, you know. I'm sure your audience would understand.'

Carina reached over, picked up a Barbie doll, boxed up and

dressed with a single satin ribbon and brandished it at him.

'I've promised a dying little girl a trip to Lourdes,' she said. 'We're going to raise the money tonight and send her on her way. I'm not going to let her down.'

Newall patted her hand. 'Well, I'm here. And I've got a couple of men outside. You'll be safe as houses.'

'Bless you.' She replaced the doll on the dressing table and took another swig of brandy.

'All part of the job.'

Newall's chair creaked alarmingly as he sat back. He twiddled his thumbs nervously, aware that she seemed to be drinking rather heavily. Eventually he stood up again and said, 'I bet it's a long time since you were in a working men's club.'

'I'll say!' Carina put down her glass heavily, reached for her lipstick and started to apply it with an unsteady hand. Newall couldn't help himself.

'You look great.'

She batted heavily mascara'd eyelashes at him, taking in his abashed expression.

'You're not so bad yourself.' She tried and failed to stifle a hiccup. 'I'm a bit pissed,' she admitted. 'Who wouldn't be after what I've had to go through?' Newall nodded. 'But don't worry,' she added, 'I'm a pro... Once I get out there, on that stage,' she waved an arm around expansively, 'nothing matters.'

'Whoever it is, doing this,' said Newall. 'We'll get him.'

Carina's eyelids fluttered and she moved closer to the policeman, slipping into his personal body space with ease, a trick she'd honed to perfection over the years. She noticed that Newall didn't shirk or flinch. He gazed into the dark eyes, absorbed the heady smell of her perfume which mingled sensuously with the hot brandy fumes and aroma of stale tobacco. He liked it all.

The moment was broken by further knocking at the door. Clifton entered.

'Anything?' asked Newall, trying to sound nonchalant. He walked backwards into a box of Quavers. Clifton, ignoring his uncharacteristic clumsiness shook her head.

'Nothing at the house at all. Ground's wet but the path's concrete so there's nothing. No footprints, fingerprints.'

Newall sighed.

'What about Jackie's description?' Carina asked.

Clifton grimaced. *'A pair of devilish eyes*, not much use I'm afraid.'

The door opened partially and Jackie poked her head in. Newall surveyed her scratched face and swollen features.

'What happened to you?' he gasped. 'You look like you've been mauled by a tiger.'

'Idiot fell in a holly bush. Don't ask,' said Carina, her sweetness vanishing.

'Did you get my champagne?' she snapped.

Jackie shook her head anxiously. 'They've only got Asti Spumante,' she said apologetically. Carina's mouth took a downward turn. 'I'm doing this for free,' she explained to Newall. 'And all I asked for was one little bottle of Bollinger to settle my vocal cords.' She stabbed a finger at Jackie. 'Can't you get anything right?'

Jackie ignored her outburst.

'Shall I say no to the Asti Spumante?' she queried.

'Forget it!'

Jackie played with her wedding ring but made no attempt to leave.

'Well?'

'Someone to see you, Carina.' She tried to smile but received a short stab of pain from one of her cuts which was now swollen and septic.

'Show 'em in, then,' sighed 'The Star'. She slurped back the rest of her brandy and grimaced.

'I don't think there's enough room,' Jackie whispered and mouthed '*wheelchair*.'

'Is it Little Sandy?'

'Erm... yes.'

'Hello, flower, I'm coming,' trilled Carina. She rose from her seat with a slight wobble, steadied herself and said to the police officers, 'Excuse me. My public awaits.'

Spreading out her arms, ready to embrace the 'Poor Unfortunate' known as Little Sandy, she ventured into the corridor and faltered at the sight before her. 'Little Sandy' wasn't so *little* at all. Like the rest of her furtive looking, chain-smoking family, she was decorated from head to foot in blurred, indistinct tattoos, the work of an amateur artist with unsteady hands. And eyes. Carina estimated her age to be around the twenty mark, although it was difficult to judge with the lower half of her face concealed under an oxygen mask. A long plastic tube snaked from the mask and connected to an oxygen cylinder behind the chair.

'Christ!' she blurted out, before adding hastily, 'Lovely to meet you at last, sweetheart.'

Sandy, who seemed vexed about something, remained mute.

'I had a doll for you, my darling,' Carina said, with the briefest flicker of hatred aimed in Jackie's direction, 'But I don't think you'll be wanting it, will you?'

Sandy lifted up her mask. 'No.' There was no disguising her

moodiness, her dissatisfaction. Carina, perplexed, paused for a moment, thrown by the waves of disapproval coming from the girl. It wasn't supposed to be like this. She was supposed to be grateful. And cute.

'Tell you what, Sandy treasure, I bet I know what you *would* like. Do you want to see my ickle Fluff?'

Sandy pursed her lips, pulled down her mask and looked away again.

'I'll take that as a yes, then,' said Carina who was beginning to lose her patience. She teetered back into her dressing room/bar snacks storeroom.

'Big mistake! Big mistake!' she hissed at Newall. 'It's a disaster! Bloody Jackie's cocked up big style!'

Newall and Clifton exchanged worried glances.

'She's not a little kid,' Carina explained. 'She's a big fat mess.'

She paced around the room, fuming, muttering under her breath. Then, scooping the unwilling Fluff up in her arms she lurched out into the corridor again, a vision of sweetness and charity. Sandy, who had been frowning up at the ceiling for no apparent reason, reacted badly to the appearance of Fluff. She reared back in her wheelchair, made whimpering animal sounds and threw her hands up in front of her face. Fluff reacted in a similar fashion.

'What's up with her?' Carina enquired.

'She hates dogs,' said Sandy's mother, with the kind of whistling lisp that came from an absence of front teeth. 'Hates the bastards.'

'She's scared o'them,' chimed in one of the sisters, who, on opening her mouth, also appeared to be as equally diminished in the orthodontic department.

'Rottweiler mounted her in the park once.'

'How traumatic,' said Carina, in such a way that it was impossible to work out if she was thinking about the dog or Sandy. But her comment went unheard thanks largely to Sandy's increasingly anguished squeals. Sandy's father shook her chair and shouted, 'Pull yourself together, man', without removing the cigarette from his mouth.

'Excuse us.' Carina nodded sharply at Jackie and indicated the door. Jackie followed meekly.

'Would you give us a couple of minutes, my loves?' she asked of the police officers. 'Girl talk.'

Newall and Clifton got up politely and left. Carina waited until the door had closed before laying into Jackie.

'Little Sandy?' she screeched. '*Little* Sandy? She's got to be twenty five stone.'

'I'm sorry,' stammered Jackie. 'I only spoke to them on the phone. They sent a photo... it must have been taken years ago.'

'You stupid... how's it going to look in the Press, eh? She was supposed to be cute - with plaits. And specs! The miserable hacks out there, they want tragedy and pathos. They don't want photos of me and some big minger-of-a-lass in a wheelchair! And another thing...'

She stopped to breathe the air - the brandy was making her queasy.

'When you're on the look out for photogenic people, choosing a family with only four teeth between them isn't such a good idea, lovey. It's really not.'

'Please don't shout at me, Carina,' begged Jackie, whose own teeth were starting to jangle ominously. 'My face is swelling up and it hurts.' Her head was indeed beginning to take on the appearance of a red football.

'And I'm faced with a PR stunt that's gone tits up thanks to you,' retorted Carina. She fumbled for her cigarettes and plucked at one with trembling fingers.

'Never mind,' she said quietly. 'Never mind. It'll be fine. It'll have to be.'

She tossed Fluff aside, checked her wig in the mirror, breathed deeply and heavily for a few seconds until she'd managed to compose herself again. Then she threw open the door and beamed at the small crowd in the corridor. Sandy's family surged forward again, pushing past her wheelchair to talk to Carina. They were big fans. Had always wanted to meet her. *Winkle Bay* wasn't the same now that she'd gone. They'd already been to see her in Cinderella. Twice. It was the usual punter stuff. Carina made all the right noises, gave all the appropriate expressions. Despite Sandy being the wrong kind of dying child, she would make the best of things. Newall watched her, mesmerized. Sandy, forgotten in their excitement, slapped her hand impatiently against the arm of her chair.

'Fag!' she yelled.

'Shush,' said one of the sisters, who was sifting through her fake Burberry handbag for some paper and a pen. Carina raised her hands high above her head, for silence. Newall and Clifton appeared behind her in the corridor and watched.

'I'll sign all the autographs you want after the show but right now, I'm going to get up on that stage and we're going to give those good people out there a night they'll never forget.'

She hitched up her gown and knelt beside Sandy. 'And we're going to send you, young lady, on a lovely trip to Lourdes.'

Sandy lifted her mask. 'Disney World,' she wheezed emphatically.

'Sorry?'

'Disney World!'

Sandy's mother cuffed her over the head. 'You're going to

Lourdes!'

Sandy glowered at her defiantly. 'Disney World!'

'Here,' muttered her father, 'have a fag and shut up.'

'Doesn't she want to go to Lourdes?' asked Carina.

'Oh yeah,' said the mother. 'Yeah, she does.'

'I don't.'

'Well, she did,' admitted the sister. 'Until she found out we're all going to Disney World.'

Carina blinked. 'I'm sorry?'

Little Sandy's sister stared nervously at her pen.

'You're all going to Florida?'

The others nodded. Newall and Clifton, both wanting to laugh, avoided looking at each other.

'Why can't you take Sandy?'

'Cos it'll be no fun, will it?' said the sister huffily, 'Pushing her around in that heat? She weighs a ton.'

'I want to go on the rides,' pleaded Sandy.

'There's rides at Lourdes,' muttered Sandy's Mam. 'A big bloody bus ride.'

Struggling to keep her temper in check, Carina linked arms with Sandy's Dad and pulled him to one side.

'One question, my love,' she said in a calm steely manner, 'Just how sick is she?'

The family patriarch bit his lower lip and frowned. With no answer forthcoming she pressed on.

'Sick as in *I'm-dying-and-I've-got-three-months-to-live*? Or sick as in *Ooh-er, I've-got-a-bit-of-indigestion*?' she suggested helpfully.

Sandy's Dad puffed out his cheeks and exhaled deeply. The answer seemed to perplex him. Carina, irritated, increased the pressure on his arm.

'Look, love,' she hissed. 'I haven't asked you for a definition of quantum physics. I just want to know what's wrong with her?'

'Asthma,' he whispered.

Carina let go of his arm in surprise.

'*Asthma*?!' she repeated, with barely concealed disappointment. 'So she's not dying?'

Sandy's father seemed to be in two minds. 'No,' he said. Then, 'Yes!'

Carina drummed her fingers impatiently against the wall. 'Help me out a bit, here, my darling?' she threw him an alarming smile.

'Stan,' he volunteered.

'Stan. I'm a bit confused. Is she or is she not, about to pop her clogs?'

'She could go at any time, Cora,' he assured her. 'She's morbidly obese. Living on a knife edge. Her legs have packed up already.'

Stan lowered his voice to a whisper. 'Boyfriend trouble. Four years ago. They were childhood sweethearts. Together forever an' all that bollocks.' He sucked greedily on his cigarette and exhaled through hollow cheeks. 'They were planning to live together and everything when he only buggered off with her best mate, the bastard. Heart broken she was. Shut herself away in her room, ate and smoked herself silly. Terrible.' He shook his head sadly. 'She's still pining for 'im. It's like something out of Romeo and Juliet.'

Carina's eyebrows arched. 'Is it?' she asked dubiously. 'I don't remember the part where Juliet pigged out on chips and Benson and Hedges and ballooned up like a Zepellin. Maybe I just haven't read it properly.'

Stan shrugged nonchalantly. A mistake. The gesture only served to inflame Carina's outrage.

'Let me get this straight,' she said slowly. 'I'm giving up my precious night off, risking my personal safety, to raise cash to send some greedy, lazy-arsed chav with a cough to France, while the rest of her family nick off to Florida?'

'France?!' Stan looked genuinely surprised. 'Our Sandy's going to France? Why?'

Carina stared at him incredulously.

'Is Lourdes in France? I thought it was in Cornwall.' He turned to Sandy, excited.

'Hey! You're going to France.'

Sandy sat up in her chair. 'Do they have McDonald's?'

Luckily for Sandy, before Carina could reply, Dougie hurried over from the entertainment room. 'Petal? You're on in five.' Carina didn't appear to be listening. 'Are you all right, sweetie?'

'Fine,' fumed Carina. 'How's the audience?'

'They'll love you,' said Dougie. 'They're all smashed.'

He waved at Sandy's family. 'Hello, you lovely, toothless people,' and with a flourish, he was gone.

'Is he a gay?' asked Stan, suspiciously.

Ignoring the question, Carina put an arm around his shoulder.

'Keep your gob shut about greedy guts, Florida, and 'Romeo and Juliet', or that crowd out there might just lynch you,' she spat. 'And me.' She fixed him with one of her glares.

'Right! I need a couple o'minutes to compose myself before I go out there, because right at this moment, cocker, I'm seriously tempted to walk! Okay?'

'No problem,' Stan turned to his gang. 'Come on. Give Cora a bit of space.'

'Disney World!' muttered Sandy.

'Shut your face!' snapped Carina. 'Gag her if you have to,' she commanded.

Stan grinned obligingly. Thick skinned, he winked at her. 'See you later, Cora.'

Carina curled her lip at him. Newall, Clifton and Jackie watched them go.

'Charming bunch,' said Newall.

Clifton nodded. 'We should arrest the lot of them for their flagrant disregard of the British Smoking Laws.'

'I think,' said Jackie, 'if you don't mind, I'll be getting along home now, Carina. I don't feel so well.'

But Carina was having none of it. 'Oh, no you don't,' she said. 'You got me into this shit in the first place, you're staying.'

She turned to go back into her dressing room. Newall placed his hand on the door before Carina could shut it.

'I'll be outside until you're ready.'

Carina blew him a kiss and closed the door firmly. Bending over she picked up Fluff who was cowering behind a box of crisps, staggered but rallied herself and held the creature up in her arms. Then she gathered the dog up and kissed the top of its head.

'Are we going to be a good girl for Mamma?' she cooed. Fluff regarded her askance as she reached into her handbag and removed her trusty hip flask.

Chapter Ten

In the Entertainment room, bingo was over. Disgruntled losers were clearing away their pens, commiserating with their mates, complaining about what a fix the whole thing was. Week in, week out, the conversation was the same - who won, how much and what a fix it all is, isn't it?! This week things were slightly different. There was a buzz in the room. A hint of anticipation and excitement. Cora Smart was somewhere in the building. *The* Cora Smart. Cora from *Winkle Bay* who, amongst other things, had saved a sinking shipful of illegal immigrants single handedly, breast fed a baby seal, built a lighthouse despite having only one kidney, campaigned tirelessly for Independence for Northumberland... and now she was going to sing for them live on stage. All in aid of some sick girl's dying wish to go to Lourdes. The place was filling up nicely so it looked like the poor kid would get her wish. Some of the arrivals, filing over to their tables were thrilled to see the likes of Dougie What's-his-face, that old comedy actor, selling raffle tickets in the name of charity. Yes, it looked as though it was going to be a great night.

Dougie ripped out a ticket from his raffle book and handed it to the well built lad sporting a black baseball cap and a 'Soap Queen Cora' t-shirt stretched over his protruding stomach.

'Have you come to see Carina?' he inquired.

'Not really,' came the dismissive reply. Dougie tried to peer under the baseball cap but the wearer insisted on looking down, avoiding any eye contact. Pudgy fingers snatched at the pink raffle ticket, then dropped it as Jackie made her way over. With a vague condescending smile for the shy ticket buyer scrapping around on the floor for his ticket, she nudged past him and whispered, 'She's ready' in Dougie's ear. Dougie was about to whisper something filthy back but a cry of 'Dougie, we love you' from a nearby table of pensioners diverted his attention. He danced off to bask in their adoration. Jackie sighed, visibly relieved and with another patronising smile for the 'Soap Queen Cora' man, made her way over to the front of the stage to join Carina's panto colleagues.

Gordon pocketed his ticket and scratched his head, damp from sweat, under his baseball cap. The stupid woman hadn't even recognised him. She'd stood next to him and actually smiled at him and still hadn't cracked on. A lucky escape. Scratch-face had taken him by surprise back at the house earlier on. Peeping through the tiniest of chinks in the dining room curtains, he'd observed Cora's guests tucking into their dinner and assumed they were all together. When the small woman with the cut face and bandaged hands in the kitchen looked up and screamed, he'd frozen to the spot in shock. He'd recovered, though and managed to make his legs work. Despite the chaffing, he'd succeeded in running for a minute or so without collapsing - something of a record for him.

Gordon pulled down his cap again, then followed a crowd of people heading for the bar at the back of the room, all of them anxious to get their drinks in before the entertainment started properly. He ordered a Malibu and Coke and returned to his seat, two tables away from Jackie and the panto people - near enough to overhear their conversation, but far enough away not to be noticed.

He started to relax. Things were progressing nicely. Gordon sipped his drink, enjoying the chilled sweetness as it slid down his throat. This was a bit of a treat for him. He rarely went out on an evening. And when he did, he had to take his mother along. He couldn't leave her alone in the house, it wasn't fair. Still, she would have to get used to sitting in by herself before long. Life was about to change, forever - for both of them. He had plans. He intended to experience new things. And soon he would have the means to do so. He wasn't going to be lonely anymore.

Gordon watched with interest as a bulldog faced man and a younger woman joined the celebrity table. The girl was pretty and might have been beautiful if she didn't frown so much. He guessed they were police officers. He'd been told they might be making an appearance. Not that it bothered him. His run-in with the nervous little woman proved he was safe. A booming voice from the PA system interrupted his thoughts.

'Ladies and gentlemen, boys and girls, please give a big hand for the star of tonight's entertainment, Miss *Winkle Bay* herself, Miss Carina Hemsley!'

Carina, a shimmering vision in silver, teetered on stage and strutted into the spotlight to tumultuous applause. She raised her hands in the air in a mock humble gesture.

'Hello, you gorgeous people. It's lovely to be here,' she schmoozed. And her audience responded with yells and whistles. 'Ooh, aren't you a noisy bunch? Down boys! Woof!' The clamouring continued. Carina was enjoying every minute of it. 'Thank you!' she yelled. 'But hey! Hey! Let's take a moment to remember why we *are* here.'

A hush descended.

'There's a brave young lass in the audience tonight. Where is she? Where's... what's she called? Sandy?'

Sandy's family, sitting a few tables away from Gordon, waved up at the stage.

'Bless!' said Carina. 'She's a right mess, ladies and gentlemen, but we're going to give her a night she'll never forget. So folks, I want you to dig deep into your wallets and buy as many raffle tickets as you possibly can 'cos that tragic little lamb wants to go to Lourdes!'

'Disney World!' Sandy tried to yell before succumbing to a savage wrist slap from her mother. She sank back in her chair huffily and gasped into her oxygen mask as Carina launched into a rousing rendition of 'Downtown'.

With all eyes focussed on the stage, Gordon managed to slip out of the room unseen. He would have liked to have stayed for the entire performance but there were things he had to do. And besides, before long he would have Cora all to himself...

Pauline Clifton, her ears taking a battering from her close proximity to the PA system shifted her weight from one buttock to the other, trying to make herself comfortable. She leant closer to her superior officer.

'Petula Clark would turn in her grave,' she whispered.

'She's not dead,' replied Newall without taking his eyes off Carina.

'If she heard this she'd wish she was,' muttered Clifton and grimaced as Carina hit another bum note. The strange thing was, the audience didn't seem to mind, or care. They were cheering her on, clapping along. Perhaps they'd all been hypnotised by the sheer force of Carina's personality. She exuded confidence. She behaved as if she was the most amazing thing they'd ever seen. All this she did despite having the musical ability of a talent show reject. Wasn't that part of the secret of success, pondered Clifton? Self-belief and sheer bravado? If you believed totally and whole-heartedly in yourself, then surely it followed that others would believe in you too. Newall, judging from the way he tapped his foot, had fallen under her spell. Likewise, the old couple nearby who held up and waved their ignited Zippos in the air as Carina revved up a notch for the song's finalé. Two large bodies swaying from side to side, to no recognisable rhythm, they kept colliding with one another, unable to synchronise their movements, causing a variety of bottles and glasses within a ten foot radius to vibrate and tinkle alarmingly from the shockwaves. Desperate to drown out Carina's melody-murdering vocals, Clifton focussed on the ancient pair and wondered which of them would be the first to go up in flames. She opted for the woman. Nylon shell suit, hair lacquered to buggery and a badly co-ordinated husband with a flaming lighter: she was a fire hazard waiting to happen. Didn't anybody in this God forsaken hole know that smoking in public was illegal?

'Thank you! Bless you!' Carina was blowing kisses at 'her people'. They lapped it up.

'I'll say this for her,' said Newall, 'she's got style.'

Clifton didn't trust herself to reply.

On stage, Carina patted her face demurely with a white silk handkerchief and clicked her fingers in Jackie's direction at the foot of the stage. Jackie leaped up with a glass of wine and handed it up to her.

'Ooh, it's thirsty work entertaining you lot,' Carina cackled into her microphone. She drank greedily, emptying the glass in one go. Jackie caught it cannily as it was tossed back to her and scurried away into the darkness beyond the footlights, for a refill.

'Are you all watching *Winkle Bay*?' Carina's voice boomed around the auditorium. An enthusiastic reply came back. 'Isn't it shite!' she cried. 'Ooh, I've said too much.' She cackled into the microphone, deafening her audience. For the first time that evening, Ben, sitting at his front row table, laughed. Lauren nudged him.

On stage, Carina performed a drunken little jig and launched into a rousing medley of Christmas carols. Thankfully the audience joined in and as a result, failed to notice the bum notes, or the bits where she forgot the words. At the end of the medley, Carina had them eating out of the palm of her hand. She was glistening with perspiration, a gleaming beacon under the spotlight. She'd really thrown her all into it. Even Clifton had been impressed, if not by her talent, but by her energy. Jackie rushed up to the stage with a slug of chardonnay for the gasping singer. Once again, she knocked it back in one and sent the empty glass sailing through the air for the luckless Jackie to catch. This time she wasn't quick enough. It caught the Zippo waving woman in the side of the head and shattered. The woman put down her lighter and looked around, dazed. Her husband, on the other hand, lost in his own little world, continued waving his own lighter in the air, oblivious to the fact that the music had finished and his wife had been glassed by a soap star.

An hour later, her singer's thirst quenched by several glasses of dry white wine and giddy from the love of the crowd, Carina brought her performance to an end. It was just as well. Her vocal cords had given up long ago: talking was going to be difficult for her. So was walking. She stood in the spotlight, exhausted, trying to blow kisses at the crowd but her hand just wouldn't connect with her mouth.

'I love you! I love you all!' she yelled at the whooping, chanting crowd and burst into tears. Jackie and her panto colleagues dashed to her rescue - everyone except Ben, that is. Relieved to be free from Dougie's clutches at last, he sat back with his pint, ignoring the beckoning gestures from his girlfriend.

Carina grasped Jackie in a vice like grip and wept in her face. Salty tears dripped into her septic gouges but Jackie ignored the pain and savoured the moment. This was the real Carina. The one worth waiting for. Jackie felt the lump in her throat and knew she was going to cry too. To be acknowledged, so publicly by her heroine. It was almost more than she could bear. She could see quite plainly beyond the footlights some familiar faces from the 'Carina Hemsley Appreciation Society', clapping and cheering. She hoped they had cameras with them. This was going to make the front page of the next CHAS newsletter. Without a doubt. A sweaty hand on her thigh put all thoughts of fandom out of her mind. It was Dougie. Jackie reared back to avoid his damp paws. Finding the inner strength at last to tell him what she really thought of him, she turned around to find him with his arms around Carina. She decided at that moment that she hated him but at the same time she couldn't help but marvel at his dexterity. Not only had he managed to get a grip on Carina, he'd somehow wrestled the microphone from her at the same time. He twirled it with a flourish. Carina searched her empty hands, momentarily bewildered. Then suspicion clouded her face and peered at him through heavy eyelids.

'Are you trying to hog my lime-light?' she slurred.

She tried to poke a finger at him but she was seeing double. She plumped for the wrong Dougie and missed. Dougie waved a dismissive hand at her and threw a cheesy grin at the audience.

'Ladies and gentlemen, isn't she fantastic? Let's hear it for - The One. The Only. Carina Hemsley.'

Newall and Clifton joined in the applause: one of them more

enthusiastically than the other.

The Club Secretary, a little scrawny man in a garish Hawaiian shirt joined them on stage and took the microphone.

'Before you's all go home,' he wheezed, 'I just want to let you know, we've totted up the cash from ticket sales and the raffle and we've made seven hundred and forty five quid.'

The audience cheered.

'Sandy, pet. You're off to Lourdes.'

Sandy sucked unhappily on her cigarette, refusing to look at anybody.

'I don't know what your problem is,' complained her sister. 'You've always hated Mickey Mouse.'

Sandy flung down her cigarette.

'I've always hated Jesus as well,' she rasped.

'Can we get her up on the stage?' asked the Entertainment Secretary, beckoning to Sandy's family.

'Not unless you've got a rope and pulley,' said Carina. Sandy found herself being wheeled unwillingly to the staircase at the side of the stage. Newall stood up anxiously as two men edged past them and hurried onto the stage.

'It's okay, Boss,' said Clifton. 'They're Press.'

Carina, who could spot a journalist at fifty paces, staggered over to Jackie.

'Tell you what, flower,' she said. 'Go and fetch Fluff.'

Jackie wavered. 'Are you sure? Won't all the noise scare her?'

'She's always bloody scared.'

Carina, becoming bolshy, staggered ominously. Waving a rather un-coordinated hand around in the air, she said, 'Look, we've got to find something cute for the photo... photo... tographer to whatsit... focus on. That's why they've come, isn't it. We can put Fluff on the heffelump's knee and they'll go away happy. All righty?'

It seemed to make sense. Anxious to make amends, Jackie scurried off. Carina turned to watch Sandy's family struggling and straining to climb the last few steps with the wheelchair and its occupant. Jez and Campbell went to their rescue.

'Hurry up big lass,' she called. Increasingly unsteady on her feet, she went over on one ankle. The Entertainment Manager came to her rescue. He put an arm around her. She looked at him blearily as if only seeing him for the first time.

'This stage is a death trap,' Carina said. 'Bloody-Hell-Fire!!'

The piercing scream caused her to jump and go over on the other heel. It ceased as quickly as it had started only to be replaced by loud gasps and hysterical sobbing. Newall and Clifton heard it in the auditorium above the din of the crowd. They leaped out of their seats and raced up the stairs.

'Over here somewhere!' said Newall hurrying towards the wings. They almost collided with Jackie as she tore on stage from the wings. She was shaking uncontrollably and holding a hand over her mouth. Tears poured down her cheeks. Her stinging cuts were forgotten. She stood there, shivering, pale as a ghost. The others stared at her, stupefied.

'What's the matter?' Newall demanded.

Jackie tried to speak but no words would come. Clifton went over and put a sympathetic arm around her shoulder.

'Jackie? What's wrong?'

'It's nowt,' muttered Carina unsympathetically. 'Poor daft bugger keeps seeing her husband,' she said to nobody in particular. But Jackie was shaking her head.

'Note on the door,' she stammered. Grasping Clifton's hand she pulled her towards the backstage corridor. Newall followed them out, pointing at Carina as he went.

'Stay there,' he commanded.

Jackie and Clifton stood in front of the closed door to Carina's 'dressing room' staring at the note someone had tacked up. It was the usual variety and read 'ONE BITCH DOWN ONE TO GO'. Clifton frowned. She didn't understand. Granted the note and sentiment were unsettling but Jackie's discomposure, her hysteria were out of proportion. Surely?

Newall arrived.

'More of the usual,' said his junior and put a hand on the doorknob.

'Don't!' Jackie grabbed her arm.

'What is it?'

Jackie shook her head. She didn't want to say. What little colour was left in her face drained away completely as Newall pushed in front of them and opened the door.

'Bloody hell!' he said. The police officers stared in horror. Jackie convulsed and retched.

'What have you found, then? Eh?' Carina's voice boomed down the corridor as she lurched towards them. 'Ten to one it's not her husband. I mean,' she slurred, 'what would Alan be doing in a crisps cupboard? Are you mad?'

'Stay back!' ordered Clifton. Newall tried to close the door: too late. Carina caught a glimpse of something swinging slowly in the air in the darkened room: saw the turkey drumstick-like legs dangling lifelessly, the pink tongue, the bulging eyes, even more bulging in death. Fluff had been strangled with her own lead and suspended from the light bulb flex. Shiny shards of coloured light, twinkling from her diamanté collar, flashed around the walls as the dog, part pendulum, part disco ball, revolved slowly on the end of

her leash. Carina's mouth fell open but no words would come out.
Newall caught her before she hit the floor.

Chapter Eleven

'But why would anyone want to murder a dog?'

It was a question for which Jackie could find no answer. The shock of finding a strangled poodle hanging from a light flex had left her badly shaken. Even now, some twelve hours or so after the event, strolling down the lane to her local newsagent's shop, she could feel the nausea rising in her throat as she remembered Fluff's vacant, cod-fish, terrible eyes, bulging and staring in death. A bit like they'd been in life, really, thought Jackie. Only deader. She'd stood there, in the doorway to Carina's dressing room, mesmerized, rooted to the spot, unable to scream at first, fully expecting those glassy eyes to pop out of their sockets at any moment. But of course, they hadn't and very quickly, regaining the use of vocal chords and limbs she'd slammed the door shut and fled, screaming onto the stage.

In hindsight she regretted her hysterical outburst - for Carina's sake she should have held herself together. In absence of any real family in Carina's life, Fluff was her world: she doted on the creature, took her everywhere. Small wonder she fainted. Jackie shivered, the memories of Carina's howls of pain, her grief laid so bare so publicly - for the Press contingent at the charity bash very quickly managed to get in on the act - would take a long time to forget. All she wanted to do was wrap her idol in her arms and console her. But the nice policeman seemed to have control of the situation, whisking Carina away from the glare of flashing cameras and shrieking journalists before they could upset her any further. *'How do you feel now your dog's dead?!'*

'Pigs!' Jackie said out loud. 'Heartless pigs!' Using tragedy and despair to sell newspapers. Couldn't they see that behind the quips and big smiles Carina was a devastated wreck? It almost broke her heart to think what that brave woman endured for the sake of her craft and her celebrity status. Sometimes she despaired of Mankind. The hatred, the wars, muggings, bullying, the evil things people inflicted on each other - it was all becoming too much to bear. Every day in the Daily Mail - her newspaper of choice, reports of the world going to Hell in a hand cart had become the norm. If the threat of Armageddon and world domination by Tesco's wasn't enough to contend with, they now faced the equally disturbing thought of a dog murderer at large and in their midst. Worse still, she was sure she'd seen the man. Or at least a part of him: his eyes and evil smile. Surely it was no coincidence that a stranger appears at Carina's kitchen window one minute, and the next a four legged creature is killed in a most heinous fashion. Jackie stopped in her tracks, remembering suddenly the crooked grin which had become more crooked the wider the lips stretched, revealing dirty, grey, gappy teeth. Had she mentioned this detail to the police? She couldn't recall. Damn her memory. If only Alan was here. She would have told him everything and he would have reminded her, counseled her on what to do next, what to say to the authorities. This was an aspect of Alan she missed, aside from the physical closeness: everything in the world that was a mystery to Jackie always became clearer when she talked to Alan about it. He was intelligent, and patient and caring. He looked after her. *Had* looked after her. Before he'd vanished. She rifled through her pockets and retrieved her mobile phone, checking for a sign of life, a message from her husband. It had become a habit - searching for a text or a voicemail, some presage of Alan's return. Inbox empty. Again.

She considered her children. Evie and Christian. They thought their father was dead. Evie claimed she'd had a dream where she'd seen Alan in a ghostly shroud beckoning to her from the entrance to a dark tunnel. This was emphatic proof that her father had 'passed over'. Jackie put the dream and the jargon down to watching too many Derek Acorah shows back to back and the desire to be centre of attention in the school playground after a recent downturn in popularity. Something to do with not having the right kind of bag. Death and pity - girls just loved to revel in the emotional turmoil of it all. Her son's reasons for preferring death to disappearance were even easier to fathom. Christian had had his eye on Alan's Philishave for some time and used Alan's 'death' as a neat excuse to nab it for himself and sell it on ebay. Along with a silver money clip, his Longines watch, Mulberry wallet and a Penhaligon's money tray. Christian, Jackie reflected, was turning out to be most inappropriately named. Eight year old boys were so sophisticated these days. They knew their brands.

Then there was her mother. Alice hoped her son-in-law was dead - they'd never seen eye to eye, especially after the affair. Alan's parents, on the other hand thought their son had committed suicide and blamed Jackie for sending him 'over the edge'. They'd even called her 'mental' during one vitriolic outburst, citing the nervous breakdown a few years ago and her subsequent obsession with cleanliness and soap operas as the cause of Alan's woe and misery. Which was nonsense of course. She'd never had a nervous breakdown in her life. Gone away for a rest after trying to strangle a man dressed up as the Honey Monster during a Sugar Puffs promotion in Asda a few years ago, yes. Breakdown, no. Jackie had not lost control: she'd known what she was doing all the time. She was trying to protect her children from Evil.

Alan's best friend Johnny was also convinced her hubbie had shuffled off this mortal coil - all because of a pair of pants. He'd left his Hugo Boss trousers at the dry cleaners before he'd disappeared - his favourite strides, according to Johnny - no way would he have allowed them to lie uncollected if he'd just done a bunk. He'd have picked them up first, then vanished. Alan always liked to look good, Johnny had said in his usual damning, criticizing manner. Jackie resented the implication that her husband was materialistic and a bit of a narcissist. Yes, he used moisturisers and spent a lot of time admiring himself in mirrors and in shop windows but that was because he was a perfectionist. He liked to look good for her! Johnny had always been jealous of his better looking friend, no matter how hard Alan had tried to help him in the past - dragging him to the gym in an attempt to get his weight under control, taking him abroad every year to give the poor guy a holiday. And how had Johnny repaid his friends selfless gestures when recounting them to the Police? By slurring his character and reputation, claiming his Good Samaritan efforts were just an excuse to get away from his wife and score with women! Not only that, he'd even told her he'd confessed to the police that he thought *she*, Jackie, might have something to do with Alan's 'murder'. Because of all the 'affairs'. It was all down to jealousy. Ludicrous! There was only one jealous creature around Alan and it certainly wasn't her. It would be a long time before she'd welcome that man back in her house again. Knocking on her door late at night in a drunken state asking where she'd buried Alan, indeed!

'He is not dead!'

Mr Dillan the newsagent looked up from the till. The three people in front of her in the queue, also turned around to stare. Jackie cleared her throat, pretended to cough and stared down at her feet until it was her turn to be served. She was sure Carina would be too traumatized to pore over the morning newspapers, to read the column inches relating to Fluff's death but one could never really tell with Carina. She was such a pro. Dedicated to her scrap book. And people dealt with their grief and pain in different ways. Some wallowed in it, others, like herself, got on with their lives, as if nothing had happened. An occasional twitching of the eye, spasmodic collapse of the muscles controlling the mouth and hiccups were the only outward sign of the swirling emotional maelstrom raging around within. Yes, she and Carina were very similar. They suffered and endured in silence.

Jackie prepared to muster her most sorrowful expression. She anticipated a melodramatic response from Mr Dillon who knew her connection to Carina and must have seen the reports of last nights events, if not in the broadsheets, certainly in the tabloids. Fluff's murder must feature somewhere near the front pages. She strained to see the piles of papers on the counter but she wasn't wearing her glasses. Everything more than three feet away was a blur. The man in front of her pocketed his cigarettes and moved away.

'Ah, there you are,' said Mr Dillon, shaking his head sadly as Jackie moved forward. 'What a terrible to-do.'

Jackie nodded, 'I know.'

'Who would have suspected?'

Jackie sighed and tried to look tragic.

'Who could have known', continued Mr Dillon, 'that he was

such a dirty dirty old dog?'

Jackie, puzzled by his words, momentarily forgot about her tragic expression.

'Sorry?'

'Did you know?' Did you all know he was a dirty disgusting dog?'

'Oh no, Mr Dillon,' Jackie replied, 'He wasn't a *he*. Fluff was a *she*.'

'Fluff?' repeated Mr Dillon, he looked her up and down rapidly, wondering if she'd been drinking. He'd had his suspicions before. Sometimes when she picked up her papers of a morning she'd twitched and reeled in a very queer manner.

'You're just trying to protect him, aren't you. That's what you're doing. Nice lady, you don't have to.'

Jackie frowned. This was not the reaction she'd been expecting. Sympathy, horror, outrage, perhaps. Although she could certainly discern outrage in Mr Dillon's voice. But amidst the outrage she could also detect contempt. Strange.

'It's all here. All the filthy details.'

What was the man talking about? Jackie fumbled in her handbag for her glasses. She slipped them on with shaking hands, gazed down curiously at the familiar face on the front pages of all the tabloids and gasped.

Chapter Twelve

A baying crowd of press hacks had gathered outside Carina's bungalow as Jackie pulled up in her car. For a moment she contemplated putting her foot down and driving away, never to return, for the thought of having to squeeze past this howling mob filled her with dread, made her skin crawl. She knew her personal body space was about to be invaded several times over: she could look forward to having questions screamed rudely in her ear from all angles. She'd seen it happen to Marilyn Monroe, Princess Diana, Take That and now bizarrely it was her turn. Perhaps if she drove away, just a mile or two, she could stop at a layby and ring Carina on her mobile. But no, that was the cowardly way out. Carina needed her right now. She wasn't going to let her down. And perhaps she could use the experience to her advantage.

Jackie checked her make-up in the rear view mirror, touched the tender scratch marks from yesterday's accident in the holly bush. They were still there, obviously, but not so inflamed and infected. Yes, she thought, she would do. There were photographers present. Her image could end up in the newspapers. And if Alan, wherever he was - in a clinic, perhaps, somewhere, recovering from amnesia, picked up a paper over the next few days and saw her face staring up at him - well, it might prove to be the vital jog his memory needed.

One glimpse of her and Alan could be home for Christmas. Jackie flicked back a piece of stray hair with a toss of her head, grabbed her briefcase, leapt out of the car and charged into the throng of violent, joshing bodies.

The journalists separated, parting like the Red Sea after the command from Moses. A clear path appeared for her along the pavement to the garden gate where a police officer stood, tall and imposing. The press hacks weren't interested in her. At all. She sidled up to the policeman who waved her through. As she reached the front door one of the reporters shouted something but his words were lost to her on the December winds. Her reedy reply of 'No comment' also vanished into the chill morning air.

The door opened and Carina's turbaned head poked out. She wore the obligatory celebrity sunglasses but neither celebrity fashion accoutrement could mask the fact that she looked pale and frail. The flashes from what seemed like a million cameras clicked and exploded over the garden hedge together with the buzz from a thousand questions all asked at once. Carina waved graciously with one scrawny hand. The other lassoed itself around Jackie's shoulders, pulling her inside. The door slammed shut.

Carina leant against the wall, gasping for air as if the whole exercise had been too much for her. Jackie could still hear noise from the rabble outside but it was distant now thanks to Jez Thompson's double glazing efforts.

'Are you all right Carina?' Jackie asked. 'You still look terrible.'

'I can always rely on you for words of support and encouragement,' replied Carina sarcastically.

'Sorry, it came out all wrong. I meant you weren't wearing any make-up so you look...'

'Yes, all right. Never mind. Come with me.'

She guided Jackie through the dingy hallway to her bedroom, sat down on the bed and gazed wistfully into the middle distance. Jackie struggled to think of something appropriate to say but gave up. She perched gingerly on the end of the bed.

'I can't stay here any longer,' Carina said eventually. 'Too many memories.'

Jackie nodded.

'Everywhere I look, I see my lickle-ickle Fluff.'

'I know,' Jackie managed to say, hoping she sounded suitably sympathetic. Secretly she wondered why Carina had started to speak in baby words. It was all a bit unsettling. Grief, perhaps. And shock.

'And I'll have to buy a new handbag. Everytime I pick it up I expect to see my ickle darling looking up at me.'

Jackie reached over the bed and squeezed Carina's hand and was rewarded with a brave smile.

'I'm so tired, Jackie.'

Still wearing her sunglasses, she lay back on the bed, resting her head against plump pillows. Jackie jumped into action, becoming mother hen. She pulled back the duvet and repositioned it over Carina, tucking it under her chin.

'Then you must stay in bed until you feel better. Get some sleep.'

'I can't,' said Carina, though Jackie noticed she hadn't resisted her efforts to make her comfortable. 'I've a matinée in case you'd forgotten.'

'Ah, about that...' Jackie wondered how she was going to break the news.

'Maybe I *could* get some sleep if the press'd just leave me alone...'

'Carina?'

'Luckily that lovely Inspector placed a guard duty at my door. What a nice man. Isn't he, darling?'

'Yes, but...'

'I could fall for a hunk like that. You know he put me to bed last night? Sat in the lounge until the sleeping pill took effect. I didn't want to be alone in the house. God knows where Dougie got to...'

'Well...' Jackie knew the answer to that one.

'I know I shouldn't ask but I can't help wondering. No. No... perhaps not,' Carina hesitated, 'Is there anything in the papers?'

It was Jackie's turn to hesitate.

'There was a piece... in The Mail.'

Carina's furry caterpillar eyebrows took off in unison.

'The Mail? One piece? Is that all?'

Jackie nodded.

'Then what are the paparazzi camped outside for?' asked Carina.

'The thing is...'

'Tell me 'cos I don't understand. They've been out there since the crack of sparrows. I'm a prisoner in my own home.'

'The thing is Carina. They're not here to see *you*.'

Carina laughed an empty harsh laugh.

'Don't be silly girl. Who else would they be here to see?'

They could hear the roar outside, the unmistakable sound of the press pack smelling blood that no amount of double glazing could mask. A moment later the front door slammed shut. Carina leapt out of bed and hurried along to the lounge just in time to see a dishevelled looking Dougie making for his room.

'Dougie?' she called.

'Not now, lovey!' He tried to sound nonchalant but there was a definite tremor in his voice as he spoke. 'I need a bath.'

'But where've you been?'

She heard a muffled word which sounded very much like 'hotel' as Dougie's door closed.

Carina returned to her own room where Jackie was laying out the morning tabloid newspapers on the bed. Carina stared at the headlines and read them out loud.

'Dirty Dougie!'

'Baron Hard-On!'

'Has-been sitcom Star in Gay Outdoor Sex Shocker!'

She lowered herself onto the bed as if it was all too much for her. Jackie sidled over to her.

'Apparently he was caught by the police, doing naughties with two men in Jesmond Dene last night.'

'The dirty, dirty bastard!' said Carina.

'I know,' agreed Jackie.

Carina turned an odd purple colour, a colour which frightened Jackie. She'd never witnessed a human go purple before. She was breathing heavily too. Oh, God, she thought, Carina's having a heart attack. Or a stroke. What should she do? She was contemplating screaming for help when Carina came to.

'What a sorry state of affairs, eh, Jackie my love?' she said, shaking her head sadly.

'What kind of a world are we living in when the tale of a fat old queen's gang-bang in a park is more important than the strangling of an innocent poodle!'

'And not just any poodle,' added Jackie with brevity. 'A celebrity poodle.'

Carina's pained eyes closed briefly, with a small flutter. Then they snapped open.

'I honestly despair,' she said, staring through the window at the trees blowing in the wind in the garden.

'There's talk in one of the papers of the pantomime closing.'

Carina seemed transfixed by the view outside. She was unmoving. Still in shock, Jackie suspected. She was not her usual ebullient self. There was a spark missing. No wonder, the woman must be exhausted. As if to contradict her, Carina turned away from the window and Jackie saw that the dark hairy caterpillars were lowered over bright steely eyes.

'After everything I've been through lately? It'll close over my dead body,' she said defiantly.

Suddenly finding the energy she needed, Carina jumped up off the bed. Reaching in the pocket of her dressing gown she took up her trusty cigarette holder, rammed a cigarette home into the filter and lit it.

'Get onto that useless ex-husband of mine,' she said. And for clarification added, 'The last one. Paul. You've got the number, haven't you? Tell him about Fluff. It'll sound better coming from you. I'm warning you now though, he'll weep and wail like a girl down the phone. If he does, hang up.'

Jackie pulled out her mobile.

'And when you've done that, call Jez Thompson and that useless director. I want a meeting at the theatre. A.S.A.P.!'

Launching a swirling cloud of smoke into the air with two drags of her cigarette, Carina swept out of the room. Jackie heard her stentorious voice booming along the corridor: 'Dougie? Dougie!'

Dougie, lying on his bed fully clothed, pulled himself up on one elbow.

'Go away,' he called out melodramatically, 'I want to be alone.'

'It's a shame you didn't think to say that last night, sweetie,' came

111

the muffled reply.

Dougie knew Carina was right up to a point, but did she have to say it? He'd only been trying to have a good time. Nobody got hurt. It was consenting adults looking for excitement, that's all. Oh, it was so unfair. Anger and self-pity fought a confused battle within him. Neither won but the tears of self-pity which started to roll down Dougie's cheeks were a release of some sort. The pressure lifted. The pain in his head and throat abated somewhat.

'It's all very well to say that in hindsight,' he called out defiantly, 'but they were very nice young men. We were only chatting about how picturesque the waterfall looked and then one thing led to another...'

Carina threw the door open and marched in.

'I'm not interested in the gory details...' she started to say but Dougie was on an indignant roll.

'That arresting officer! What a vile thing. Do you know he had the cheek to call us *degenerates*? He! He who hid in the bushes for ten minutes before eventually making himself known to us. Arrested by a Peeping Tom Copper, I was! I said, "You're in no position to feel morally superior over us, Miss Plod."'

He sat up with some difficulty. A night in the cells had eaten into his reserves of strength.

'Do you think my career's over?' he asked.

Carina shrugged.

'I mean everybody knows I'm an old faggot now.'

'They've always known, darling!'

'No,' he interjected, 'There was speculation - a whiff of camp but now they *really* know. I won't be asked to play a romantic lead again.'

Carina snorted.

112

'When was the last time you played the romantic lead? 1962?'

She inhaled on her cigarette thoughtfully before producing a handkerchief and handing it to Dougie.

'You should know there's talk of the pantomime closing,' she said.

Dougie whimpered.

'It won't come to that though. You're going to go out on stage tonight as if nothing's happened.'

'I don't think I can, darling.'

'You can. And you will! Because what are we without the bright lights and the adoring fans? Ordinary!'

Dougie looked at her in wonder. Wonder tinged with puzzlement.

'Why are you being like this? I don't understand.'

'We're a team,' Carina said. 'An ensemble. A troupe. All for one and one for all. We stick together no matter what.'

Dougie, shocked by this unexpected display of solidarity, found himself unable to speak. Had he been dreaming? Was he dreaming still? This wasn't right. It was beyond expectation. His worst fear was that Carina would insist on his removal from the pantomime. He'd thought about it all night long in the police cell. He knew what she was like - even before they'd appeared together on stage he'd heard of her selfish reputation, it was legendary. Leaked stories in the Press during her *Winkle Bay* days, of tantrums and machiavellian manoeuvres to oust the younger, better looking competition: demands for champagne chilled at specific temperatures in her dressing room. Her evil-doing and appalling behaviour had provided actors in green rooms and theatres up and down the country with a supply of astonishing and embarrassing anecdotes for years. Yet here she was, being nice to him. Being human. It was all too much for him.

'I thought you were a dried up old witch,' he sobbed. 'But you're not, are you. Deep down inside, you're a really lovely woman.'

Carina smiled.

'Let that be our little secret. If you tell anyone, I'll have to kill you.'

Dougie blew hard into the perfume-laced hankie. Suddenly he felt light headed with relief. Somehow things didn't seem so bad. Maybe he could save his career after all. With this strong, strident, good woman on his side, he could achieve anything.

'Dry your eyes and get your coat,' ordered Carina.

Dougie blew his nose one last time. 'I can't possibly go outside - the press are going to crucify me.'

'Rubbish,' snorted Carina. 'Just do what George Michael did.'

Dougie thought long and hard. He didn't have the necessary talent to write a chart topping hit about outdoor sex. A play though, that was within his grasp. He would write a play about an orgy by a waterfall... or maybe not. It seemed too much like hard work.

Carina's voice broke into his reverie. 'Smile and say so what!'

'Hmm?' he murmured. 'Oh. Yes. Shrug it all off. Easier said than done.'

Carina grabbed his hand and tried to pull him off the bed.

'Where are we going, Carina, my love?' he inquired.

'We've got an appointment,' she replied mysteriously. 'At the theatre.'

Dougie stared at the scarlet, nail-varnished talons gripping his own pudgy digits. He pulled the hand closer and raised it to his lips.

'You know?' he said tearfully. 'That's what it's all about. The nooky doesn't matter really. I just want to hold someone's hand.

Silly isn't it. But I don't think there's anything more romantic or sexier, than entwined fingers. It says so much about belonging and being wanted.'

He looked up at Carina and noted the bored expression.

'Sorry,' he sighed. 'I think I must be hungover.'

Chapter Thirteen

Pauline Clifton yawned and stretched as she got up from her sofa. Her neck screamed in pain as she did so and her shoulders went into spasm. Once again she'd fallen asleep downstairs: once again she'd slept in a stupid position, probably with her mouth open. Dribbling. She sighed. On reflection it didn't matter where she fell asleep or what she looked like when she was in the land of nod. Who would notice? There was nobody waiting for her in her bed. Probably just as well, she thought. She'd been single for twenty three weeks now. The number '23' flashed in front of her like a neon road sign. She shook her head with difficulty and the image flickered and disappeared. Too many months. And things weren't going to change in the near future if she didn't do anything to change the situation. Some chance of that. A combination of work and not knowing if the man she fancied, fancied her back, made everything so difficult. The fact that she'd lied to Newall about having a boyfriend recently only made her feel worse. What on earth possessed her to invent fictional Pete? A *diver*? Why couldn't she just come out and *ask* Roy Newall for a date? Why complicate things with a pretend boyfriend? What the Hell was wrong with her? It wasn't like she was repulsive or unattractive. Or even nervous around men. Just *this* man. She wanted the unattainable. No, not the 'unattainable', that was the wrong word. 'Inappropriate!' That was it. The man she wanted - well, it would be inappropriate to pursue him. There was too much baggage. She could see it all ending in tears. Her tears. But was that such a bad thing? Better for a relationship to end in tears than to never begin in the first place, surely. Or perhaps not. She cast her mind back over her last *real* relationship of one year standing which had started off so promisingly, taking her to physical heights of rapture and excitement, only to come crashing down to earth in a blaze of acrimony and blame six months later with much weeping and wailing on her part. Paddy the jockey had been a big mistake. What was it with little men? Their egos were impossible. And the lies. He cheated on her, deceived her, stole from her and when she found out and confronted him (shamefully late in the day, a fact which made her seriously question her sleuthing skills), he ditched her, claiming she'd never shown an interest in his career, made his weight yo-yo out of control by plying him with too much beer and pasta, and refused to iron his jodhpurs. She wished to God she'd never met him. Had there been any advantages? Had she learned anything from her time with Paddy? Perhaps one thing. Begrudgingly and rather superficially, she thought back, remembering a night when Paddy and a couple of jockey friends had arrived for dinner and drinks. Looking around her living room, she observed with some satisfaction to herself that a minimalist room full of jockeys, still looked like a minimalist room. They don't clutter up the place the way bigger people do. She considered again. Two things: never date a man you can fit in your handbag, he'll only steal your purse. At least she could laugh about it now.

Bumping into the pile of dvd's at her feet, she cursed and staggered upstairs to the bathroom, where she turned on the shower and revived her spirits and aching bones under its hot, stinging jets.

Twenty five minutes later, she sailed into the office, slung her jacket over her chair and made her way to the canteen where Newall was tucking into a fried breakfast.

'That stuff will kill you, Boss,' she said.

'I know.' The knowledge of this didn't seem to put him off though. 'You hear about that actor fella in Jesmond Dene?'

Pauline laughed. 'Heard it on the radio coming into work. Hardly surprising.'

'Is it?' Newall sounded surprised. 'I thought he was trying to chat you up.'

'That sort'll chat up anything with a pulse.'

Newall returned to more pressing matters - the Fluff murder.

'Anything on that letter taped to the dressing room door?' he asked.

Clifton threw the report she'd picked up on her way in.

'Same kind of words taken from celeb mags. Hundreds of fingerprints on the door though. Only one of them threw up a match.'

'Oh?'

'Stanley Parker.'

The name meant nothing to Newall.

'Father of 'Little Sandy'?'

Newall looked interested.

'Don't get too excited,' said Clifton. 'He's got form yes, but it's drug dealing and petty theft. Ten years ago. And as far as I remember he was in the entertainment room with his family most of the time. Could've sneaked out I suppose.'

Newall nodded and let his knife and fork clatter down on an

empty plate. He yawned.

'Late night?' inquired Pauline.

'You could say that.'

Was it her imagination or was Clifton's boss blushing. He was! A pang of jealousy stabbed at her heart.

'How long did you stay with Carina?' she asked suspiciously.

"Til she fell asleep,' came the reply. 'Then I went home.' Newall had tried to sound nonchalant but he'd failed miserably and Clifton was not fooled. She detected the slight quiver in his voice. That oft heard quiver in a man's voice suggestive of a lie. An image of her jockey friend swam into view. It was quickly squashed.

'What time was that?'

'About three... ish.'

'Three-ish in the morning?'

Newall regarded her with a frown. Clifton looked away.

'I'll trawl through those tapes again,' she said, getting up.

Two hours later Newall, at the wheel of his car sped along the Great North Road, out of the City. The grey skies of early morning had given way to a brighter creaminess and the clouds on the horizon looked ominous.

'I think it's going to snow again,' said Clifton, beside him in the passenger seat.

Newall didn't answer. His earlier encounter with his younger associate had left him unsettled. He'd detected a note of disapproval in her voice when he'd talked about Carina in the canteen. Had she picked up on something? They'd worked together for quite a while now and they each knew the other's way of thinking, their foibles and feelings quite well. Up to a point. Newall never asked about Clifton's love-life and vice-versa. Their personal lives were taboo. Why, he didn't know. It was just the way things had worked out, and neither strayed beyond those boundaries. But this morning it was as if she'd read his mind. He could see she knew something was different. He'd behaved out of character, given himself away. Newall, like Clifton, was well aware that to take a woman home after a traumatic experience and sit by her bedside for several hours was above and beyond the call of duty. He'd never done it before. With nearly thirty years of police work behind him, he'd consoled - professionally-speaking of course, a fair amount of women who'd witnessed violent and terrible things but never once had he sat at their bedside until they fell asleep. Somehow he hadn't been able to help himself. There was something about this woman, Carina Hemsley, that appealed to his protective instincts. And, if he was honest with himself, she also appealed to his more basic instincts. Had she not been drunk and traumatised, who knows what might have happened?

'I think this is it,' he said eventually, pulling up outside a particularly unkempt terraced house. There was an old Volkswagen camper van rusting away on the driveway and an ancient rusting cooker beside the front door. They made their way up the front path, avoiding obstacles along the way: an oil drum, a tired wheelbarrow and the chassis of a Silver Cross pram.

A flurry of white flakes started to fall from the sky as Clifton's finger made contact with the door bell. The words on the tip of her tongue turned into a silent scream as a sharp surge of electricity flowed through her body. Newall pulled her finger off the bell, breaking the circuit. She stammered a thank you.

'Are you okay?'

Clifton nodded. 'I'll live. I think,' she said, patting down her hair which was suddenly alive with static.

'Bloody dangerous,' grumbled Newall.

He knocked loudly on the door but it was some time before it creaked open a crack. A suspicious pair of eyes partially obscured by an oxygen mask peered through at the officers.

'Hello Sandy,' Clifton said brightly. 'Is your Dad in?'

Silence.

'Sandy, we'd like to see your father. Please?' Clifton reiterated.

Sandy fumbled behind the door and eventually a large hand holding a matchbox snaked out towards them.

'Here!'

Clifton and Newall exchanged a bemused look. Pauline took the matchbox and opened it. They both gazed down at the contents - a fine dark grey pile of ash.

'What's this?' asked Newall, beginning to lose his patience.

'My Dad.'

The penny dropped for Clifton.

'Stan's your Step-Dad?' The girl nodded.

Clifton stared at her with concern. 'You keep your Dad's ashes in a matchbox?'

'Can't have been a tall man,' Newall observed.

Sandy, with great difficulty, opened the door wider. She turned her wheelchair around to face them and gasped in air from her oxygen mask before saying, 'We had to share him out... between my brothers and sisters... and Nanna and Grandad.'

'Who is it?' a voice barked loudly from somewhere within.

'Police. To see Dad. I've told them he's dead.'

'Actually, Sandy, it's our mistake and I'm very sorry,' said Clifton. 'It's Stan we'd like to see.'

Sandy waved them in. A wave of stale beer and tobacco greeted them as they entered the lounge. Stan, bare chested and puffing away on a roll-up cigarette sat up in his armchair, a look of alarm on his face.

'Who are you?' he scowled.

Newall and Clifton produced their warrant cards.

'D.I. Newall and this is D.S. Clifton. We met last night at the charity do,' Newall reminded him.

'Oh, aye,' said Stan warily. 'Terrible, wasn't it. Poor Cora.'

He tutted and grimaced, exposing rotten yellow teeth. Clifton studied his tattoo covered torso and tried to work out what they were supposed to be. She could make out bare breasts on several figures up and down his arms, knives and swirling patterns on his chest but they had lost all sharpness. The result was a blotchy, green mess of faded ink that only succeeded in making him look grubby.

Sandy propelled herself further into the room. 'Don't want to go to Lourdes,' she winghed.

'Shut it!' hissed Stan.

'Mr Parker,' started Clifton, 'we'd like to ask you about your movements during the concert.'

Stan looked at them blankly. 'What do you mean?' he asked defensively. 'You know where I was. I was in the entertainment room.'

'All the time?'

'Aye. I went to the bog.'

Little Sandy said, 'You were away a long time.'

'A man can have a crap if he wants, can't he? Jesus! It's not against the Law!' Stan scowled at his Step-Daughter. Then threw the officers a sneer. 'You want to pin that dead dog business on me! I didn't touch it! Why would I?'

'We're only asking, Mr Parker,' Newall said reasonably. 'Your finger prints were on the dressing room door and you were prosecuted by the RSPCA...'

Stan leaped out of his chair indignantly, splodgy tattooed beer belly wobbling in all directions like a sagging balloon.

'Our Goldie ate that rabbit by accident. It shouldn't have been in our garden in the first place. Anyway, I wasn't even there when it happened. I told the court, I love pets. And of course my fingerprints were on the door. I probably touched it when we went to see Cora before the show. The whole family's prints'll be on the bloody door.'

He sat down, exhausted by his tirade.

Newall pressed on. 'So you're saying you went to the toilet and returned to your seat. You didn't go anywhere else?'

'No!'

'Boss?'

Newall spun around, noting the urgency in Clifton's voice. He looked to where she was pointing. On a coffee table next to the television lay a pile of celebrity magazines. Some of them were open and intact, others had pages ripped out of them and there were holes in the paper where pieces of text and photos had been excised.

Newall turned back to Stan. 'You want to explain all this?'

'Bloody Hell!' Stan exploded. 'When did it become illegal to read Hello Magazine?'

Chapter Fourteen

The meeting was not going well but it was as Jez expected. Carina's early morning call demanding 'a little chat' had put him on red alert. And later, as the Star entered his office, brusque and perfumed, with Dougie Hunt on her arm, he knew he was in for a hard time. He'd asked Campbell Garibaldi to sit in with him - even if he was a spineless creature and quite useless: he sat on a chair at the side of his desk, quivering like a nervous lap dog. A bit like Fluff, actually, he mused. He wondered why he hadn't thought of that before. Fluff and Garibaldi - separated at birth. He was contemptuous of the idiot but at the same time felt quite comforted by his presence. Afterall, wasn't that the whole point of lapdogs?

So far Jez had been a model of concern and sympathy to both actors: expressing regret over Fluff's untimely demise, offering words of understanding to Dougie. Not that he really understood anything about the big idiot. Fancy behaving like a dog on heat in a public park, especially in winter, the silly sod. What was he thinking of? At some point he would have to ask Carina to leave the room in order to sack him. He wasn't looking forward to it but it was an inevitability. After the events of the previous evening, Dougie could hardly expect to remain in a family panto. He'd already received several emails and phone calls from church organisations, unhappy with his devilish presence. He couldn't help but marvel at the man's front though. He didn't seem remorseful at all. From where he was sitting it looked like butter wouldn't melt in his mouth.

Jez had already acquiesced to Carina's demands for a fancy suite at the Valmont. And for a car with a personal driver: quality champagne and a plasma TV in her dressing room. She was bringing the punters in, in droves, it was the least he could do. From a security point of view she was probably safer in the hotel, which might put an end to the death threat correspondence. There would be no Peeping Tom's peering through her windows eight floors up in The Valmont either.

So it was Happy Luvvies all round at first, until Carina's subsequent demand for a total re-write of the panto had caused Campbell to convulse with indignation. Jez glanced sideways at him. He was gulping in air, like a trout yanked out of a river.

'Be realistic Carina,' Jez said, trying to be reasonable. 'How can we re-write? We've a matinée in just over four hours time.'

'Simple,' replied Carina. 'Cancel it.'

There was a stunned silence.

'It won't take long. I'm not asking for a total re-write. All we have to do is get rid of the dwarves...'

'No!' spluttered Campbell.

'Why?' inquired Jez.

'Because they're unprofessional, they're always drunk and the Cinderella story never had dwarves anyway. Ugly Step-Sisters, wicked Step-Mother, Baron Hard-Up, yes. Little fellas, no.'

'But it's a pantomime tradition.' Campbell was shaking all over now but he'd plucked up the strength to protest.

'I don't care. They keep staring at my tits. Get rid of 'em.'

'Well, I suppose...' Jez started to say, aware that it was only a matter of time before they put a child's eye out with their aggressive sweetie throwing.

'Sorted!' Carina slapped her thigh triumphantly.

'Anything else?'

'Yes, my love.' Carina smiled sweetly, exposing perfect white teeth behind scarlet lips which reminded Jez of a great white shark going in for the kill. She clasped a talon around one of Dougie's pudgy hands.

'Now that Dougie's double life as a rampant cock-jockey's been exposed - you don't mind me saying that do you my darling?' Dougie shook his head. She patted his hand and continued. 'The best thing we can do is acknowledge it and move on.'

Jez shifted uncomfortably in his leather chair, unsure as to where this was going.

'We want to save his career. And the best way to do it, is to embrace his naughtiness and say to the world, "Okay, I've been caught with my trousers down, so what? I'm here I'm queer. Lets all have a laugh about it!"'

Campbell looked at Jez, uncertainly, then turned to Carina.

'I don't understand what you're saying,' he stammered.

'Then I'll make it simple for you, Campbell my darling!' said Carina, letting go of Dougie's sweaty hand. 'I want you to re-write Baron Hard-Up as a big old pansy thing, lots of innuendo, lots of campery. The audience will love it.'

Dougie looked worried suddenly. 'Will they?'

'Yes! They'll see your performance for what it is - you sticking two fingers up at the tabloids.'

'But the audience will expect the Baron to go off with the Good Fairy at the end,' Campbell argued. 'How can they believe that if the Baron is so obviously... not interested in her?'

'It's pantomine dear, not Ibsen,' replied Carina coldly. 'They've already accepted two ugly hairy blokes passing themselves off as sisters. A pumpkin and a few mice turning into a coach and horses? Nobody bats an eyelid. If they believe all that they'll believe anything.'

Jez cleared his throat. 'There's a problem Carina...' he started to say, choosing his next words carefully. 'I was going to have this discussion with Dougie a little later but since you've raised the subject, I really don't think we can continue with him in the role.'

'You can.' There was no mistaking the steely edge in her voice.

'I'm not so sure.'

'If you sack Dougie,' said Carina folding her arms over her chest and swinging one leg over another, 'I'll walk.'

Dougie sat up.

'Carina, please, no!'

'We're all in this together Dougie. We're a company. All for one and one for all.'

'Well, we'll have to check your contract,' Jez said.

'I don't care what it says in my contract. You sack Dougie here and I'm off.'

Jez sat back in his seat. For the first time since buying the theatre he wondered if he'd done the right thing. Rarely was he forced to put up with this kind of hassle in the world of double glazing. Once in a while, he had to fend off a phone call from a dissatisfied customer whose windows had fallen out, but that was manageable. Bearable. He didn't have some mad coot with an ego the size of an Eddie Stobart truck bearing down on him across a desk. He sighed. He knew she had him in a corner.

'All right,' he said, defeated.

'Jez!' Campbell protested.

Carina's smile returned. She reached inside her bag and took out her *healthy* menthols and lit a victory cigarette.

'I knew you'd see sense, my darling,' she said, winking at Jez. 'Just to reiterate, so we're all quite sure what it is we're doing. You'll cancel today's matinée?' Jez nodded. 'Which gives time for little Campbell here to sharpen his pencils and put his creative head on. You'll have something for us by, ooh, say, two thirty?'

Campbell, about to protest, saw the look in her eye and thought better of it.

'Good. We're a smart bunch of pro's, - it won't take us long to get the hang of new material. Ben might struggle a bit. Can he read, do we know?'

'I can always help him,' offered Dougie.

'But what will we tell the people with matinée tickets?' asked Jez.

'Tell them 'personal reasons' have forced cancellation. My God, Jez, I've lost my favourite friend in all the world and Dougie's buggery business has knocked him for six! *My People* will understand.'

She wiped a tear from the corner of her eye and looked away. How she hates exposing her emotions in public, thought Dougie.

'Yes, yes!' said Jez apologetically. 'But speaking with my business head on, we're going to lose money today.'

'Not if you extend the run,' Dougie said, sounding rather pleased with himself. Good ideas and common sense weren't his forte usually.

'Brilliant,' Carina clapped her hands. 'Dougie you are a darling.'

Jez drummed his fingers on the desk, thinking over the implications.

'Let me look into it. I'll get back to you.'

Carina turned her most winning smile on him. 'We'll leave it in your capable hands, then.'

She rose to her feet, took a drag on her cigarette and blew a cloud of smoke in Campbell's direction. He looked up at her startled.

'Chop-chop, kidda!' she said. 'You've got work to do.'

Campbell's bottom lip started to quiver. Trying to muster as much dignity as he could, he stood up and walked to the door.

'And none of your politically correct shit, either,' Carina added. Campbell's back stiffened. 'It's got to be gags, gags, gags!'

Campbell, desperate to distance himself from the dragon lady, scurried off.

With a wave of the hand and a 'Ciao babe', Carina followed him out, a docile and happy Dougie in tow. Jez relaxed visibly. The meeting could have been a lot worse. He'd fully expected Carina to make a demand for more money. Not that he could blame her. The box office receipts so far were better than he could have hoped for and if he extended the run he'd be raking in a fortune. So a slight re-write, the cancellation of one matinée and having to tolerate dirty Dougie for a few more weeks didn't seem so bad.

He wandered off into a little daydream where he and Heidi were sitting on piles and piles of money. They were laughing at the tiny figure of Carina far below them, who clambered on the hill of money but kept slipping back to the ground, shrieking and crying. Then Campbell appeared beside Heidi and the dream ended. As he stretched and became more conscious of the real world around him, Jez caught sight of his reflection in the glass door of the bookcase and all thoughts of extended runs, panto re-writes and mountains of cash were forgotten. He peered closely at his image in the glass, appalled. Perhaps it was a trick of the light. He flicked on his angle poise and peered again. No. It wasn't. The black dye in his hair and beard had definitely changed colour. Amidst the 'jet' tones he could detect an unattractive green hue. It looked awful. What was happening? Neither the box nor the instructions mentioned any side effects or problems. Not that he could recall. He'd been in too much of a hurry to read them. 'Forever Young' the product was called, not 'Forever Green'. Here's hoping it was a temporary thing. A chemical imbalance that would rectify itself. 'May fade over weeks' he recalled noting. Nothing about change of colour. Suddenly he found himself wishing to God he'd never resorted to using cosmetic products - the hair dye, the moisturisers, the fake tan. The yoga! Heidi was twenty three years his junior. And gorgeous. He'd always known that. They were both well aware of and fine about the age difference. They laughed about it often, in a relaxed, easy sort of way. Had she ever complained about his lack of youth? Or beauty? No. She'd always professed to loving him for who he was and what he was: a grey haired, potent and powerful man of fifty eight. So what had led him down this insecure path of late? Never a great fan of analysis and introspection, the outcome, after a moment's contemplation was that he 'couldn't really say'. If something was troubling him on a deeper level, it was wedged down, far too deeply to retrieve. He tidied his hair in the reflection and as he continued to look, the green-ish tint wasn't nearly so noticeable anymore. Perhaps it *had* been a trick of the light. Yes, that's what it must have been.

Pleased with the way he'd handled Carina and feeling suddenly more like his old-self - confident and brash, he reached for the phone to ring Heidi and tell her all about the meeting. Before he could stab at the number, the door blew open and Carina stood in the doorway, hands on hips.

'I forgot to mention, darling,' she said. 'You and I should have a little chat about money? Clue? I'd like some more.'

Jez sighed. He should have known it was too good to be true. The woman only had three major scenes in the pantomime and was paid a fortune for spending most of the performance twiddling her thumbs in her dressing room. Yet she still wasn't satisfied.

'And by the way,' she added, 'what's with the green hair?'

Chapter Fifteen

An unhappy band of 'Little People', loaded down with rucksacks and hand luggage passed Newall and Clifton at the stage door entrance later that afternoon. The detectives stopped to watch them as they exited the building, pulling collars and scarves up to protect them from thick snow flakes now falling in the alleyway.

'Hi-ho,' Newall said with a grin.

One of the dwarves, Big Olly, turned around sharply.

'What did you say, mate?'

Newall stopped smiling.

'Nothing,' he said. 'On a break?'

'You could say that,' Big Ollie replied. 'A long break. We've been sacked.'

'Why?' asked Clifton.

'Ask Carina.'

Clifton glanced at her watch. 'Sacked before the matinée?'

'It was cancelled, along with our employment,' Olly said, adjusting the straps on his rucksack, adding, 'I hope whoever's after her hurries up and finishes her off.'

Suddenly remembering who he was speaking to, he scooted after his mates, leaving little footsteps in the falling snow. The gang trudged onwards, turned the corner at the end of the alley and disappeared into the crowd of Christmas shoppers.

'That wasn't a very nice thing to say,' Newall observed.

'Ah well, that's showbusiness. A profession of dogs and thieves,' commented Clifton.

'How would you know?'

Clifton looked at him in amazement. She'd lost track of the number of vile characters who'd crossed her path inside the theatre. Hadn't he noticed?

'Experience,' she said incredulously and left it at that. She pulled the heavy stage door open and indicated respectfully for her boss to enter before her. Newall took up the offer, stepping into the half-light as the door clanged shut behind them. Distant voices, loud and echoing reached them from the stage area. They followed the noise and found themselves in the wings where rehearsals were underway for the revised script. Dougie and Ben as Baron Hard-Up and Prince Charming were engaging in a new piece of slapstick, running around Cinderella's kitchen set with gusto.

'You're supposed to let me catch you!' Dougie was saying, or trying to - he was terribly out of breath.

'Yes!' came the reply from the stalls. Campbell stood up and made his way to the front of the auditorium. 'Ben, you have to slow down for Dougie.'

'I don't want him to catch me. He keeps touching me up,' replied Ben plaintively.

Campbell felt sorry for the poor lad but his hands were tied. It was in his contract - if Jez demanded changes, he had to have them. So he swallowed his pride and re-wrote the script - in record time and with all the required camp-ery and innuendo. Not that anyone had thanked him for his contribution. Carina hadn't even looked at the changes. And Jez didn't seem interested. Philistine. Once again his thoughts turned fleetingly to the lovely Heidi, trapped in a loveless marriage. All that style and grace, it was wasted on Jez.

'Tell him!' commanded Carina, joining Campbell at the foot of the stage. 'It's in the script!'

'I don't care!' came Ben's outraged reply.

Lauren came forward with soothing words for her boyfriend.

'Ben, you just have to do it. You really do,' she said sweetly.

He looked at her, with pleading eyes. 'But it's all wrong.'

'What, babe?' she asked.

'If a Baron tried to come on to a Prince, he'd have him *executed*. He would!'

'Maybe in Quentin Tarantino's version of 'Cinderella', honey-pie ,' protested Dougie. 'But not in this one. Now relax and enjoy yourself.'

Campbell clapped his hands loudly. 'Once again, please, from the top.'

Dougie poked a finger hard into Ben's chest.

'And this time, slow down!' he hissed.

The two police officers, about to make themselves known, heard quick footsteps behind them in the wings. Jez, in something of a flap bounded over to them. He saw Clifton's eyes focussing on his head.

'Trick of the light,' he said quickly, patting the pockets of his jacket in search of something. Producing a folded sheet of paper.

'This has just come in. Post was late today.'

Newall and Clifton stared at the now familiar mish-mash of letters and words, glued to the white note paper.

Newall read out loud, 'Cora I'm going to make you suffer agane and agane.'

'Atrocious spelling,' said Clifton, feeling a rant about the current

134

state of the education system coming on. 'It's shameful.'

Jez produced the envelope. 'Newcastle post mark. I knew what it was as soon as I saw it. I recognised the handwriting.' It was the same childish scrawl in large capitals. 'Disguised probably,' he added.

'He can disguise it as much as he likes, we'll still find him out,' said Newall.

Jez quizzed them. 'Any joy yet?'

'We're working on it,' replied Clifton, giving nothing away. The truth was, they had little, if anything to go on. The cut out pages from celebrity magazines scattered around 'Little Sandy's' living room were actually the handiwork of Sandy herself. An obsessive *Westlife* fan, she spent most of her days poring over the magazines, cutting out photos of her idols and sticking them in a scrap book.

They were joined in the wings by Heidi Thompson who crept up behind her husband and draped her arms around his shoulders.

'Hello, cuddles,' she said, causing Clifton's stomach to churn. Grasping a fistful of hair at the back of his head and tugging it with some force, she twisted Jez around. They embraced and kissed. The kiss, a lingering, noisy one, went on for some time. Clifton tried not to laugh at Newall's expression. It had disgust written all over it.

'Don't mind us,' he said.

Jez withdrew from the clinch, pecked his wife on the forehead and grabbed her by the waist.

'This is a surprise. I didn't know you were coming in.'

Heidi held up a carrier bag.

'I've brought some herbal tea in for Campbell. He called earlier to tell me what an awful time he's having. Re-writing and re-writing.'

135

'That's his job!' Jez complained.

'I know.' Heidi tucked his chin playfully. 'But you know how sensitive he is. The camomile will calm him down.'

'I could do with some camomile myself, darlin',' replied Jez. 'You've no idea what kind of a morning I've had.'

Heidi folded her arms around his sizeable girth and kissed the nape of his neck.

'I know what my cuddles needs...' she whispered, then retracting her arms, she led him away by the hand, laughing.

Newall watched their departure. 'How bloody gruesome was that?!' he exclaimed. 'What is it with these older blokes and younger women - it's embarrassing.'

'It's got nothing to do with their ages,' protested Clifton quickly, hoping that by standing in the shadows her boss wouldn't be able to see that she was blushing. 'Older guy, younger woman - not a problem usually. It's about appropriate behaviour.'

Newall shrugged.

'Maybe.'

'Definitely!'

She wanted to say more. She so desperately wanted to say such a lot more to him but she didn't dare: now that she knew his view on older men-younger women relationships, it was pointless.

'Come on,' she heard him say.

They emerged from the wings and walked onto the stage, shielding their eyes from the bright glare of the footlights. All eyes turned to them.

'Afternoon,' Newall said, rather self-consciously.

'Well, if it isn't my White Knight,' Carina's rich tones bounced around the auditorium. Newall moved cautiously to the edge of the stage to get a better view of her. She was sitting in the stalls next to a stoney-faced Campbell. 'Come down,' she instructed, indicating the narrow flight of stairs at the side of the stage leading down into the auditorium.

Clifton followed behind her boss, staring out into the vast cathedral sized expanse in front of her. She was impressed. As a girl she had attended Christmas pantomimes with her family, and always been astonished by the magic of the theatre, been in awe of the giant proportions, the grandeur of the architecture. She'd assumed this had more to do with innocence, the gullibility of childhood. Places and things which had impressed her as a kid, often when she'd returned to them with an adult's eye had left her feeling disappointed, saddened. But this? This was different. Poised on the edge of the proscenium arch, gazing out into the huge space in front of her, she was moved by the sheer scale of it all - just as she had been when she was so young. Row upon row of plush red seats stretched on and on into the distant shadows. The boxes on either side of her, high up and imposing with their gilded stucco angels and foliage in relief looked beautiful, in spite of the obvious wear and tear that the years and lack of maintenance had imposed on them. The huge chandelier dominating the ceiling above, glass jewels now dusty and muted still glittered and sparkled in the light. Below her, in the orchestra pit, drums and keyboards and other, more mysterious instruments, disguised by protective coverings and casings, waited patiently to be brought to life. It was all as she remembered: thrilling, exciting.

A begrudging respect for the acting profession began to take hold. She understood why these strange people were the way they were. The physical gap between stage and audience was great and it required huge character and ego to be able to punch through the void, to convey emotions, to connect with all those bums on seats and make them forget their petty, mundane lives for a couple of hours. In return an actor became the focus of attention for a thousand pairs of eyes. What a buzz. No wonder the Carina Hemsley's of this world all became larger than life caricatures eventually. She and other celebrities like her needed to be the centre of attention off stage as well as on. It was like a drug to them. Returning home at night after a performance must be akin to going cold turkey. No wonder Dougie Hunt sought danger and excitement off stage. Real life must be so tedious.

Clifton clattered down the stairs after Newall. Carina was in the process of tilting her head to one side in anticipation of a peck on the cheek from him. Clifton was relieved when Newall merely proffered a hand to shake instead. Carina accepted the hand and beckoned him to sit down.

'Budge up, petal,' she said to Campbell, sitting next to her in the aisle and indicated for Clifton to take his seat. Campbell leaped up.

'I'll work on stage,' he stammered.

'I'll be up in a minute, sweetheart,' replied Carina. Campbell sloped off and she patted the velvet seats either side of her. Clifton and Newall sat. Fixing Clifton with a sweet smile, she said, 'Make-up.'

'Sorry?' asked Clifton, thrown.

'I'm curious. Is it police policy for women officers not to wear make-up?

'No,' she replied.

'Think about using some dear. It might help.'

Clifton wasn't sure how to respond so she said nothing. Already her new-found respect for actors had peaked and waned.

'How are you?' asked Newall.

Carina sat back in her seat and looked over at her large handbag on the floor beside her.

'Bearing up,' she said bravely. 'Taking one day at a time. I keep expecting to see Fluff's ickle head poking out of my bag but there's nothing there,' she sighed tragically. 'Just a packet of mints and the Daily Mail.'

Newall nodded sympathetically.

She went on. 'Have you found the bastard yet?'

'It's early days,' replied the detective. 'But we wanted you to know that we won't stop until we find the person who did this.'

'I know, Roy,' said Carina softly.

Clifton couldn't believe her ears. Roy? Roy! What the hell was going on? She looked over at Newall, who was blushing. Again! *Roy* avoided her gaze.

'I'm afraid there's been another letter,' he muttered. Carina admitted she was past caring. Newall, about to say something, thought better of it. Instead he fidgeted in his seat and watched Dougie and Ben running around on stage.

'What's with the rehearsals?' asked Clifton. She felt she had to say something. The heavy silence was getting to her.

Carina sucked in her cheeks. 'You heard about Dougie's little nocturnal adventure?'

Clifton nodded. 'The whole country has.'

'Exactly!' Carina slapped the back of the chair in front. 'We've decided to make a feature out of it. We're camping up his character, putting more of the real Dougie into Baron Hard-Up. He doesn't want what's happened to be swept under the carpet like it's something to be ashamed of.'

'Will the public accept it?'

'Course they will! Joe Public loves an underdog,' Carina chuckled.

'I should know.'

'Murderer!'

The actors on stage stopped in their tracks.

'You bloody murderer!'

The accusation echoed around the empty space. All eyes turned to the back of the auditorium where the emergency doors had burst open with a resounding crash. A man, obviously overwrought, was running towards the front of the theatre. Newall leaped up. The other members of the cast clattered off the stage to assist.

'You killed her! You did it.'

It took a moment for Newall to recognise Carina's orange ex-husband.

'Calm down, Sir,' he started to say, moving into the aisle to fend him off. Paul Miller was in no mood to listen though. His bleached hair stood up on end like a wild haystack and tears streamed down his face. In his hysterical desire to reach Carina he tried to push the policeman aside but Newall was taller and stronger than the slightly built sun-bed purveyor.

'Why did you do it? Why?' he sobbed as Newall secured him in an arm lock. Carina had grabbed her handbag as a shield and pushed herself as far back in her seat as was humanly possible. She levered herself forward assisted by Dougie.

'What's he talking about?' she managed to stammer.

'Fluff!' The act of speaking her name resulted in a further flood of tears from Paul.

'Darling, who is this man?' inquired Dougie.

'My ex,' spat Carina, slowly recovering her poise.

'Mmmm!' said Dougie, approvingly. 'Quite sexy in a tangerine-Worzel-Gummidgey sort of way.'

'You're a murderer Carina. You know you are!' sobbed *The Ex*.

'He doesn't think much of you, though, does he darling?' said Dougie.

'I loved that dog. You know I did,' Carina insisted.

'You killed her!'

'That's enough,' said Newall, shaking Miller by the arm. 'Enough!'

'She might not have strung the little darlin' up but if she'd let her stay with me, Fluff'd still be here.' He twisted around hoping to get nearer to Carina, failed to break free from Newall's grip and sank to the floor in a heap, exhausted.

'You know I'm right,' he weeped. 'She'd still be alive if I'd been given custody.'

Carina slumped back in her seat again and wailed loudly. Lauren rushed to her side and hugged her close.

'Get him out of here, Roy,' she cried. 'Please! Get rid of him.'

Newall pulled Miller to his feet. 'Come on, you,' he said gruffly, yanking on his arm.

Clifton grabbed his other arm.

'I'll give you a hand... *Roy*,' she said, unable to help herself.

They dragged him up the long aisle to the front exit. Carina put her hands over her ears to block out the hysterical shrieks and the repeated accusations of 'murderer' as they resounded around the cavernous auditorium.

Dougie pushed Lauren aside, sat down next to Carina, took her hands gently in his, moved them onto to her lap and whispered in her ear, 'He's gone.'

Carina nodded.

'What an awful man,' he said, commiserating. 'Beautiful but bonkers.'

'Story of my life,' Carina replied.

He produced a handkerchief from his back pocket. Carina took it and dabbed around her mascara.

'Don't worry darling,' said Dougie. 'From now on, things can only get better for the both of us.'

'Can they?'

He nodded the vehement, confident nod of a man in possession of psychic knowledge.

Dougie, unfortunately, was no clairvoyant.

Chapter Sixteen

That night, the audience turned on Baron Hard-Up. His camped up bufoonery was hissed at throughout the first act, so much so that by the time the safety curtain descended at the Act One interval the auditorium echoed to what sounded like the angry displeasure of a million snakes. Dougie, by no means immune to the tide of disapproval, took Carina aside.

'I don't think they like me,' he said simply.

'Don't be silly, cock,' replied Carina.

'But they're hissing at me.'

'It's a panto darling, audiences love to hiss.'

'Yes! At the baddies. The Ugly Sisters. The Wicked Step-Mother. But they haven't had a look-in tonight.'

Carina gathered as much as she could of his large frame in her arms.

'Give them time to get used to you,' she cooed. 'They'll start relaxing and when they do that they'll see how funny you are.'

Her confidence was comforting and sounded utterly convincing. It was infectious. Dougie felt marginally better. Until the curtain went up on Act Two and he launched into his routine of comic asides interspersed with smutty references to his nocturnal adventure of the previous evening. The hissing was replaced by loud boo-ing, shouts of 'Get off' and aggressive cat-calls. Dougie realised Carina's hasty scheme to redeem him with the public, well intentioned though it may have been, had gone awfully wrong. He tried to tone down his performance, ditching the silly voice, epicene mannerisms, replacing them with a masculine baritone and manly swagger: all to no avail. The damage had been done. Strolling sedately on stage to take his bow at curtain call his appearance was greeted with a universal heckling, the likes of which hadn't been heard in the auditorium since that night in 1975 when the film projector broke down midway through a screening of 'Deep Throat' and a frustrated audience of dirty mac'd film-goers had registered their dismay en masse.

Dougie remained stoic in the face of mass rejection and received many supportive slaps on the back from his fellow troupers as the curtain descended on the house for the last time that night. He shrugged off the criticism with a snort and an airy wave. Later, in the privacy of his dressing room he went to pieces.

Watching the show from his seat in the Upper Circle, Roy Newall couldn't help but feel sorry for the actor. Wasn't it hypocritical of theatre-goers to take such a moralistic stand against Dougie's al fresco interests, when they were all paying good money to see a show which glorified and made light of domestic abuse? Cinderella's situation with her family - the drudgery, the ragged clothes, the mental cruelty - it all warranted closer investigation by Social Services. Yet the audience was quite happy to turn a blind eye to the deeper, more disturbing themes surrounding the poor girl's circumstances. Newall flicked popcorn off his beer belly. The two and a half hours of sporadic entertainment had left him with a numb bum and a longing for a pint. Yet in spite of the physical discomfort he'd endured, he'd actually learned something and it was this: Carina Hemsley was extremely watchable. Not the best actress, or singer in the world by any stretch of the imagination but she possessed charisma. And vitality. In spades. On stage her presence shone, so much so that Newall found himself unable to take his eyes off her and when she was off, he counted the moments until she returned. Curiosity, together with a complimentary ticket from The Star herself had led him to this solo outing and while the screaming kids with the melting chocolates, spilled drinks and moaning parents he was squeezed in amongst weren't his ideal choice of companions for a great night on the town, he found himself cheering and joining in with the other theatre-goers with gusto. He hadn't had this much fun in years. It occurred to him, as the safety curtain fell that he really needed to get out more.

Filing out of the auditorium with the other members of the audience, Newall took a left turn, going against the flow of the departing throng and made his way to the backstage area where he waited patiently in the dank corridor near the stage door entrance. Carina, still in costume, was already signing autographs for appreciative fans in the doorway. A select few had been allowed inside the building but the other dedicated worshippers were left to stamp their feet in their cold and battle with the icy wind which blew down the alleyway from the river. A wizened old man Matty, guardian of the stage door, held the more enthusiastic fans (or the ones anxious for some warmth) at bay with a sinewy arm firmly placed across the door jamb. Further down the corridor he saw Lauren, luminous in Cinderella's wedding dress, consoling Dougie. Tears rolled down his ghostly white Regency Dandy make-up, exposing thin track marks of pink flesh in their wake. Powdered wig askew and his cherry red lipstick all smudged, he looked a sorry mess. Lauren patted him on the arm and led him inside his dressing room. Ben Tingle, loitering at a safe distance behind his girlfriend looked rather tense, hesitated a moment, before turning on his heels and withdrawing to the safety of his own dressing room.

Carina caught Newall's eye, grinned at him and waved expansively. He waved back rather sheepishly, then wandered over, feeling slightly apprehensive. He was off duty now, without any real cause to be there. Free from the mantle of police inspector he reverted to the shy, rather gauche individual he was in private. Nevertheless, the professional skills honed over thirty years of policing were never far away and he observed the crowd surrounding Carina with interest. He'd already explained to Carina that her safety was compromised every time she met with crowds of people she didn't know. It wouldn't be too difficult for anyone with a grudge against her to get near enough to inflict serious harm. Carina had rejected his concerns outright. 'Meeting Her People' she explained was all part of the job. The fans expected it and she wasn't going to let them down because of some lunatic. While her attitude irritated him, he couldn't help but admire the woman for her sheer determination and disregard for her own safety. The fans who looked up at her so adoringly hardly resembled a cut throat gang of psychopaths. Yet wasn't that the problem with psychopaths? If blood thirsty murderers actually looked like blood thirsty murderers, his job would be so much easier. This particular bunch of suspects consisted of a group of pensioners on a mini-bus outing and a few children eager to have their programmes autographed. Carina was mid-way through her favourite topic as he reached her.

'The best thing you can do is write in,' she was saying. 'Write to Rufus Frenkel, producer of *Winkle Bay* and tell him how you miss me. Tell him you want me back.'

'Oh, we do!' exclaimed one of the pensioners. 'I've got emphysema and not much to look forward to in life and the telly just isn't the same without you on it.'

'That's so sweet of you to say, my love,' said Carina, with feeling. 'Don't forget. That's Rufus. Frenkel. And he's about twelve years old, so don't go using any big words.'

She opened her arms in a grand style as Newall arrived and greeted him like an old friend. Or lover. And kissed him on both cheeks. Newall blushed to the roots of his grey hair.

'Here he is, ladies and gentleman. My wonderful protector, my Superman and an all round lovely guy.'

Such was the dramatic introduction that some of the fans resorted to applause.

'Is he your boyfriend?' asked a young girl inquisitively. Newall went red again.

'That would be telling,' said Carina coyly.

'He's a chubby lad,' opined one of the mini-bus crowd, an old crone with a thick moustache.

Newall glared at her.

Running footsteps echoed around the narrow alleyway and Newall, all alert, jogged past Carina, anticipating trouble. A flash from a camera blinded him momentarily.

'Come on boys,' Carina said to the gathering journalists. 'Give me a break. I'm talking to my people.'

'Where's Dougie?' asked one of them.

'How does he feel now his career's over?' inquired another.

Carina's lip curled nastily and she was about to lose her cool but somehow she managed to keep her temper under control. The curling lip turned into a wide, charming smile. She turned to 'Her People'.

'Have a lovely Christmas, my darlings,' Carina added. 'I must dash. It's past my bedtime.'

She blew a kiss at the crowd, slipped an arm through Newall's and withdrew to the relative warmth of the theatre. Scrawny old Matty warned the crowd to stand back and the door slammed with a metal clang that echoed down the corridor.

'Bastards,' she said. 'Why can't they leave the poor bugger alone?'

Newall wanted to say that they were just doing their job but he felt this wasn't the answer Carina was looking for so he just shrugged and took in the well manicured hand resting on his arm. The long, scarlet, polished nails had unnerved him on previous occasions but this time they aroused him. Every slight increase in pressure from the long thin fingers, every brush of her dress against his leg as they walked, sent the blood rushing to his groin. In a moment the discomfort was painful. It was like trying to contain a cucumber in a crisp packet. Difficult. And something would eventually snap. Newall made a mental note to buy new underpants. He should have invested in some when he started piling on the pounds over a year ago. Now he was paying for his laziness in a most uncomfortable way. In the hope that things might return to normal he tried to think about something abstract: his lottery numbers, the whiskers on the rude old woman.

'I don't think you're fat,' Carina said. 'I think you're just right.'

The pain returned making walking suddenly difficult for Newall. He stopped in the middle of the corridor and pretended to scrutinize one of the black and white portraits lining the wall.

'Laurel and Hardy,' he said weakly. 'I love them.'

'Me too.'

The door to Dougie's dressing room opened and Lauren looked out.

'How is he my sweet?' Carina inquired.

'Upset.'

'Oh, the little love.'

Carina marched into the dressing room with Lauren, leaving Newall to a) scrutinize the photograph of his comedy favourites, and, at the same time, b) discreetly re-arrange himself. When he eventually followed the others into the dressing room Carina and Lauren were hugging the seated Dougie, kissing the top of his head, stroking his arms. Dougie seemed impervious to the affection. He gazed into the middle distance, frowning.

'I think I'm finished,' he said.

'Rubbish. It's a glitch. A blip,' Carina argued. 'You'll see. In a few weeks, it'll all be forgotten.'

'She's right,' agreed Lauren, adopting Carina's positive stand. 'Look at Michael Barrymore.'

Carina and Dougie turned to look at her.

'What?' said Carina, contemptuously.

'Michael Barrymore,' Lauren repeated, a little less sure of herself. 'His career took a bit of a nosedive, didn't it. For a while.'

'*For a while!*' Carina's incredulity was obvious.

'Oh God!' wailed Dougie.

Lauren hugged him again and tried to salvage the situation.

'Maybe I shouldn't have mentioned Michael Barrymore, Dougie. You're not a bit like him. Not really.'

Dougie patted her hand gratefully.

'Oh, I don't know,' he said. 'I've had so many offers to appear on reality TV shows since the shit hit the fan.'

'Have you?!' Newall detected an edge to Carina's voice. 'That's nice,' she added.

'So I could sell my soul, I suppose and make an arse of myself for a while. Earn a few quid.'

'Which shows?'

'All sorts.'

'They just rang you, all these TV producers?'

'Yes.'

Carina's caterpillar eyebrows gyrated madly across her forehead. She was quiet for a moment. When the caterpillars settled down, she said, 'I'm sorry, Dougie. I think this is all my fault.' Dougie tried to interject, to disagree, but Carina was having none of it. 'Yes, my love, it is. If I hadn't insisted on all those re-writes, the public might not be baying for your blood.'

'No, no!' Dougie tried to say.

'Yes! We should have written some kind of apology into the script, but Campbell made you look like a nasty, arrogant old queen.'

'Oh well,' Dougie sighed.

'Let me take you to dinner.'

'That's really sweet of you darling, but I'd much rather be alone tonight.'

'Are you sure?'

'Absolutely.'

'Don't be sad.' Carina positioned her head at an angle and rested it against Dougie's shoulder.

Dougie smiled wanly. 'I'll be all right. I will. But right now, what I'd really like to do is jump in my car and drive to the coast. It's not very far, I believe?'

'Ten, twelve miles,' said Newall, helpfully.

Dougie seemed suddenly brighter. There was a glint in his eye.

'I've always found the sound of the sea very soothing.'

'Well, wherever you go, lovey,' warned Carina. 'Make sure you stay away from gents toilets.'

She kissed him on the head and winked at Newall. He followed her out of the room.

'Carina?'

'Yes, treasure?'

She paused outside her dressing room, a half smile playing around her lips. Newall hesitated a moment before continuing.

'Are you hungry?'

'Starving.'

'Would you like to go out for a bite to eat?'

'I thought you'd never ask,' came the reply.

Newall grinned bashfully.

'Really?'

'You are off duty, I take it?' Carina queried.

'Oh, aye!'

'Good.'

She stroked his arm in a brief show of intimacy.

'Give me ten minutes to get my face on and then I'm all yours.'

Number One Star dressing room door slammed shut and Newall was left alone in the dim corridor. He stared over at the sepia portrait of Ken Dodd on the wall.

'Still got it, Doddy,' he said.

At least he hoped he'd still got it. He was a bit rusty when it came to dating women. It had been a while. Small talk wasn't exactly his forte. Come to think of it, big talk wasn't his forte either. He was a man of few words. In his younger days women, at parties and at bus stops had admitted to being attracted by the strong, silent, moody air of mystery he exuded and he'd been quite popular on the old dating front, for a while, years ago. But prior to leaving him, his ex-wife, while accepting she'd fallen for his dark looks, rather cruelly admitted that whilst 'brooding' and 'aloofness' were very exciting attributes in a man - especially to girls in their late teenage years - alas, as youth faded, along with party invitations and the urge to stay out all night clubbing, it became all too clear that 'silent', 'moody' and 'aloofness' were incredibly boring traits in a middle aged man. The ex-Mrs Newall's confession had left Newall with a feeling of inadequacy which rankled. It wasn't at all fair. He'd never considered himself cool and aloof. The 'Man With No Name', Clint Eastwood persona was an image which had been projected onto him, not something he'd cultivated. Still, that was all in the past, all behind him. This was a new start. Aware of his shortcomings in the social skills department, and desperate to prove he was no monosyllabic old duffer, he racked his brain to think of suitable topics of conversation for the night ahead. Lost in thought, he barely noticed when Jez Thompson hurried towards him from the auditorium. His already worried expression took on an even more serious note when he registered the detective's presence.

'What's happened?' he asked urgently.

'Nothing,' replied Newall, putting ice-breaking conversational thoughts of Gilbert and Sullivan and pony-trekking on the back-burner. 'I'm just waiting for Miss Hemsley. I'm er... we're... going to eat something.'

'Oh. Right. Smashing,' said Jez, relieved that no pets or cast members had been mutilated in the past few hours.

'Did you see the show tonight?'

Newall nodded.

'Terrible wasn't it,' said Jez, agitated. 'We'll have to do something about that, I'm afraid.'

He peered up and down the corridor.

'Have you seen Dougie around? Is he still here?'

Newall nodded.

'Right. Right. Well, catch you later, pal.'

He marched down the corridor and rapped loudly on Dougie's dressing room door.

'Dougie?' he called. 'It's me. Jez. We need to talk.'

Newall heard a muffled response from within, saw Jez take a deep breath and enter Dougie's room. A moment later the shrieking and wailing started.

Chapter Seventeen

The Tyne Bridge, brightly lit against the night skyline soared high above as Newall drove down the steep curving bank of Dean Street towards the river. Despite the modern street furniture, the neon signs above bars and the iron foundations of the bridge which dominated this area by the Tyne, the place still exuded a Dickensian feel, with its tall and graceful narrow buildings, separated by alleyways or 'chares' and steep, recessed, crooked staircases of worn stone steps which vanished into the darkness, all nestling under the protective span of the bridge around them. The Quayside. Ever since he could remember, he had loved this part of town. But he'd loved it even more when it was the 'Forgotten Place'. When the river traffic stopped flowing and the area fell into decay. When the finer architectural details and the beauty of the buildings became obscured beneath the black grime of pollution. It felt like his secret. Off the beaten track. Now it was Newcastle's jewel. Proof of the City's rejuvenation. Cleaned and scrubbed up, old architecture co-existing alongside the new, Newall could not deny its beauty. He was as proud of the place as any Geordie could be. Yet, there was something not quite right about it all. The modern Quayside reminded him of the beautiful film actress who'd succumbed to the cosmetic surgeon's knife. The results were startling - sharper lines, wrinkle free, taught skin, enhanced bone structure. Still great to look at. But the natural beauty was gone. She didn't look younger. She didn't look better. She looked different. She looked like a woman who'd had a face lift.

Newall became aware of his guest in the passenger seat. He glanced at her surreptitiously and wondered fleetingly if Carina had been enhanced at all, over the years. It was difficult to tell. If she had, it was fine by him. She looked fantastic.

'Everything all right, cock?'

'Yes. Fine. Short walk that's all. To the restaurant.'

He jumped out of his seat, ran around and opened the passenger door. Carina took the offered hand and climbed out demurely.

'I haven't been round here for years,' said Carina. 'Looks like it's changed a lot. I like it.'

'I preferred it when it was run down and grubby.'

'If you're telling me you've got a thing for crumbling old ruins, I'm off,' she said.

Newall looked at her in alarm but relaxed when he saw her smile. The smile vanished quickly when a wrought iron gate slammed shut in the wind, somewhere behind them. The sound reverberated around the narrow alleyway like a gun shot. Carina almost leapt off the pavement. She clutched her chest, wrestling with her nerves. Newall put an arm around her protectively. He noted that she did not shy away.

'It's okay, it was only a gate slamming in the wind.'

'I'm just a bit jittery at the moment,' said the actress.

'It's understandable.'

'Do you think you'll ever catch the person who... who killed my Fluff? The person who wrote the letters?' she asked.

Newall nodded seriously. 'I promise.'

The smile returned to Carina's crimson lips. They walked along the Quayside, heads bent against the bracing North Sea wind. A fog was beginning to settle and although the hour was late, they passed several shadowy crowds of Christmas party-goers, vague in the mist at first, most of them young, all of them the worse for wear. Some of the lesser inebriated recognised Carina, and called after her, 'Cora! Cora! Merry Christmas!' Carina waved back graciously and wished them the same.

'I love Newcastle,' she said. 'It's full of half-dressed piss-heads but they're a happy bunch.'

They reached the restaurant, 'Salvatore's'. Although it was a short walk, Newall was out of breath and red in the face. Carina asked if he was all right.

'Fine, thanks,' he replied. 'Be better when I'm back in the warmth.'

A doorman ushered them in, and they entered the welcoming dining room aglow with the comforting light from large candles in wrought iron sconces around the room. A log fire crackled in an inglenook fireplace at the far end of the bar. Diners nudged each other. Heads turned to look at the celebrity in their midst.

'This looks lovely,' said Carina, seemingly unaware she was the object of some attention. 'Very Gothic. I'm so hungry,' she added breathily. 'I hope you can keep up with me.'

'I've got a very large appetite,' Newall replied.

'So have I,' said the actress and winked at him.

* * *

Nearer the coast the fog was worse. Luckily for Dougie, who was a nervous driver, there was little traffic on the road. It was almost eleven and he was beginning to have second thoughts about his planned Garbo-esque, under-the-stars walk along the beach. For a start there were no stars to be seen. And no moonlight. The sensible side of Dougie realised it would be prudent to cut his losses and turn back. He could visit the sea-side another day. A day when it was possible to actually see the shore line, thus avoiding driving into it. He was cold too - the heating system of his battered old wreck having packed up long ago. The miserable bungalow, his digs, with the old lady wallpaper and old lady smell suddenly seemed quite an attractive proposition to him. At least it had central heating and now that Carina had moved out he had the place to himself. He could do anything he liked. And that was the trouble. He sighed ruefully. He couldn't think of anything to do. What he wanted, what he really wanted, was company. Just to sit with someone and talk. Or not talk. Just sit. Together. Comfortable in each other's presence. How foolish he had been. All those weeks sharing with Carina, wishing he was somewhere else. How ironic it was that he should discover, on the eve of her departure from the house, her true nature. Underneath the unpleasantness and prima-donna-like behaviour lurked a kind, selfless and good heart. He wanted so desperately to talk to her. Although he wasn't sure if this was the sensible thing to do. She'd threatened to quit the show if Jez sacked him and now that he'd actually been fired, he didn't want to cause trouble for her. Or anyone else in the pantomime. He'd been annoyed with Jez at first. He was convinced that the media interest would die down and people, as ever, would forget about his discrepancy and let him carry on. But it was not to be. Jez was only safeguarding his assets, his show. He didn't like the man. But he understood. At least he had a few days until they found a replacement for him.

157

A sign loomed in front of him at the roadside. Slowing down he noted the junction ahead. What should he do? Carry on to the coast? Or turn around and go back home. To bed. There was little time to make a decision. Painful light, from a bright halogen bulb - the sort of light that burned the retina, exploded in his rear view mirror. There was another vehicle behind him, a motorbike or something like it. A moped? He turned right, hoping to throw off the bike but as luck would have it, the rider behind had also opted to turn right. Dougie flicked the deflector switch on his mirror and the light dazzling his eyes died down. It seemed as if fate had taken a hand. He was bound for the coast after all.

Heading away from Whitley Bay, Dougie pulled over at one point to check Lauren's directions. The bike behind, a moped with chubby rider, revved up and overtook him, its shiny red brake light dimming as the fog closed in around the vehicle, snuffing out the glow. Dougie, alone on the road, wound down his window. The smell of freezing sea air surrounded him, clearing his head. He took deep breaths, consulted his directions and set off again, winding up his window as he went. He felt better already. So he would have to face some personal issues, deal with the Press over the next few days. And maybe his rash actions had jeopardized his career. But there was always hope. He could take up some reality TV offers. Advertise sofas. Who knows what might happen? Horrible times always lead to good times, he thought to himself. It wasn't strictly true, but what the hell.

The headlights picked out a lone high gabled building up on the right. Dougie was pleased. At least he wasn't lost. This was the old pub mentioned in Lauren's directions. The road down to the sea must be just past it. As Dougie indicated to turn right and position himself correctly on the road, light poured in from behind him. Another moped, or indeed the same one he'd seen earlier, was approaching, headlamp shining brightly.

Dougie tutted, adjusted his rear view mirror and made his turn. His old jalopy trundled and lurched ominously as it hit pothole after pothole along the winding lane. There were no street lights now but at least the fog was less dense here. Dougie stopped and turned off the headlamps. Was this the right place? He could see nothing but blackness around him. Common sense told him to go back. The reckless side of Dougie urged him onwards. As ever, Dougie's life-long philosophy of throwing caution to the wind won the day. He reached inside his glove box, took out a torch, opened the door and clambered out, wrapping his scarf tightly around his neck and tucking it under his woollen overcoat as he peered into the night. He could hear the sea, lapping against the shore somewhere close-by, somewhere below. After a minute or two, Dougie, his eyes acclimatizing to the darkness, could make out a few shadowy objects in the distance: a fence, a footpath sign. He set off, comforted by the gravel path underfoot which sparkled and glinted in the beam of his torchlight. The path would take him safely along the cliff and down to the beach.

He wasn't sure just how long he'd been walking when he heard what sounded like an eerie, high pitched screaming. He stopped in his tracks, the hairs on the back of his neck standing on end. With his imagination running riot, he shone the torch out over the cliff edge, half expecting to see an army of Sirens, singing their eerie hypnotic songs of death from the rocks below but the torchlight's beam was eaten up by the mist. All around was darkness.

The screaming continued - sometimes sounding distant, sometimes closer, depending on the wind. Dougie thrashed around frantically with the torch, peering into the gloom away from the cliff edge, desperate to locate the source. Eventually he managed to make out several tall masts in a field and shining his torch in their direction, saw they were a forest of radio aerials, connected to each other and tethered to the ground by an intricate web of wires in a skeletal pyramid-like arrangement. The wind, blowing fiercely through the taught wires, caused them to reverberate and hum erratically. Dougie shone his torch along the gravel path, shivered and pushed onwards through the drizzle.

* * *

'I met her at a night club. La Dolce Vita.'

'Ah, that's romantic.'

Newall was talking about his ex-wife, which was strange, considering he was on a sort of date, but it was at Carina's behest. She wanted to know all about him. His background, his life in the police force, his loves. And quite incredibly, he found himself talking. And talking. In fact he was finding it difficult to stop. He'd rabbited on through the starter, and now Carina had finished her main course and he'd barely touched his own. This was a first! To chatter away on a first date AND to be the last to finish dinner. All the time, as he talked he was aware of the other diners staring at them. It had been uncomfortable at first but he'd very quickly acclimatised to being the focus of attention and he quite liked it. Most of the time people barely noticed him. At work it was different, that's because he was a senior officer. Off-duty though, in the canteen, or in the car park and sometimes at the pub, colleagues tended to ignore him. Except Clifton. Pauline Clifton was always there, always attentive. She spoke to him on a social basis. Good old Clifton. Actually, she wasn't that old. She was much younger than him. Funny that, he always saw her as older. It was because she was so serious. She needed to relax more. And stop frowning.

'It wasn't really romantic,' he said. 'The Dolce Vita was a bit of a dive. Rough. Although,' he went on, 'we did have a pleasant smooch along to Labby Siffrey.'

'See?' Carina said. 'That must have been rather romantic. You must have been quite happy then.'

'Yeah,' he agreed. 'But it was downhill all the way, after that.'

'No kids?'

Newall shook his head and changed the subject.

'When were you really happy?'

Carina sighed. 'What a funny question.' She shrugged and thought for a moment. 'Working on *Winkle Bay*. I was top of the tree. Nobody could touch me.'

'What happened?'

Her face clouded for a moment.

'New broom came in and swept me right out.'

'Why? You were the star of the show.'

Carina sighed. 'It was partly my fault,' she said. 'I handled it all wrong.' She sloshed the wine around in her glass before continuing. 'The business changed, you see. When *Winkle Bay* first started it was run by grown ups. People with experience of life - writers, producers, directors. Then the telly companies, they wanted more episodes a week and it was all 'we've got to grab the teenage audience'. Why I don't know.'

'It's the way of the modern world,' Newall said, with feeling.

'Maybe.' Carina emptied her glass. 'Trouble is, the Suits wanted more episodes a week but they weren't prepared to put more money in so they cut corners. Ended up with a bunch of toddlers running the show. Twelve year olds clutching media studies degrees with no

161

experience of life, sitting in their story-lining office coming up with stupid stories a gerbil would find unbelievable.'

She snorted, bitter memories coming back to haunt her.

'They kept making Cora do things she just wouldn't do. I knew that character. I'd lived with her for twenty years. And so did my public. The letters of complaint, ooh, you should have seen them - came in by the sack-load, they did.'

She stopped to thank Newall for re-filling her wine glass.

'One of my fans came up with a story,' she said, taking a long gulp of chardonnay. 'Very sexy, very dramatic. Cora has an affair with her daughter's fiancé. Smashing stuff.'

Newall apologized. 'I didn't see it, I'm afraid.'

'No bugger did. They wouldn't do it. One of those munchkin idiots in the story department... do you know what he said to me? The spotty faced urchin.'

Newall shook his head.

'He said, "We think it's a bad idea because no twenty two year old man would be attracted to an old lady".'

'No!'

'Yes! Well, it all went crazy after that. After I punched him. I fell out with the new producer, Rufus Frenkel. Little creep. For speaking my mind. And to get his revenge, the petty minded freak refused to renew my contract, turned Cora into a nutter and had me carted off to the loony bin. Twenty years service. Down the drain!'

'There'll be other shows for you. Other hits,' Newall said helpfully. 'You're very good.'

Gratified, Carina stroked his arm.

'Bless you, lovey. But I don't know about that. There's only one show I've ever wanted to work on. Cora's never left me, you see. If

162

they asked me, I'd go back like a shot.'

She played with a piece of salmon on her plate with a fork.

'Of course I'd insist on story control.'

A diner, of similar age to Newall, who had been staring at them for a while, plucked up the courage to go over and speak to her. Carina chatted courteously and signed his napkin and he went away happy. So happy and pre-occupied with the autographed napkin that he walked into a table where two women were gossiping and giggling, heads together, and sent their wine glasses flying across the table.

'I saw you in a restaurant once,' Newall declared eventually.

'Did you?'

Newall nodded.

'A few years ago, now. Quayside Lodge. You were there with your husband. The last one.'

'Oh,' she said. 'Let's not talk about him.'

'Sorry,' he muttered.

'I have a theory, Roy, and it's this. Something my mother taught me. If you don't have anything good to say about someone, it's best to say nothing at all. But he bled me dry, the scrounging bastard,' she added. They both laughed. Newall took a swig of his wine and noticed the two women diners were scrabbling frantically in their handbags. Something about the nearest girls profile made Newall stare. She looked familiar. Twisting around in her seat to get the waiter's attention, he saw her face full on and recognized Heidi, Jez Thompson's wife. She was seated with another woman whose features he could not see without standing up. Newall could only note the long dark hair, and slim stocking-ed legs. He nodded to Heidi and received a curt nod in reply. Her companion did not look around. Something about the set up was wrong, Newall thought.

Was it the unmistakable look of alarm he saw register in Heidi's eyes? Or the way she'd all too quickly dismissed his presence? He returned his attention to Carina who was recounting the tale of her audition for *Winkle Bay*.

'It was the most exciting day of my life,' she said. 'My life was never the same again.' The next time Newall looked over, a waiter was wiping down the empty table. Heidi and her friend had gone.

* * *

The mist was clearing and Dougie spotted a bench on the cliff edge, just off the path. He was tired now, and sat down gratefully. In the distance, out to sea he could make out the lights of a passing ship and wondered where it was bound for. Norway probably. One of those Christmas cruises to the fjords. Panto had been his main source of income for the last few years but if the work had indeed dried up for him, he would spend next Christmas abroad. On a cruise, if he could afford it. To a sunny destination. The Bahamas. Or Antigua. He would suggest it to a few friends, see if they were up for it.

He huddled inside his coat and let his scarf cover his mouth to protect him from the cold air, then sat back and listened to the comforting roar of the breakers crashing against the shore below. Out in the blackness beyond the cliff, he could see, very faintly, the white horses of the waves, racing and colliding on their way to the shore and ever so faintly he could hear, if he concentrated, the wailing wires of the radio aerials, screaming their strange song to the wind. He relaxed and allowed the noises of Nature and Science to wash over him. In that moment, events of the past few hours overtook him, flashed through his mind like a sped up film and raced off back into subconscious recesses leaving emotional traces of humiliation, indignation, hurt and pain in his heart, in their wake. Suddenly he felt drained, both physically and mentally. Funny how the sea air made one feel so exhilarated and then so damned exhausted. His eyelids felt heavy. Mustn't drop off, he thought and stomped his feet to rally his energy levels for the return walk to the car. He'd gone off the idea of a walk along the beach. Besides the tide was coming in. He was tightening his scarf around his neck when he heard the footsteps on the gravel path. Faint at first, they became louder, more assured, and a figure appeared in the distance. Dougie shone his torch along the path and peered intently along the length of the beam.

'Hello?' he called. No reply was forthcoming. The footsteps stopped.

Alert now, Dougie stood up and was about to retrace his steps when a man stepped out of the darkness. He gasped and stared nervously at the rotund figure before him. The man wore a parka, thick thermal gloves and walking boots. Dougie couldn't tell his age, for his face was partially obscured by a dark baseball cap. Dougie tried to smile but his lips were chapped and frozen and he was aware of a nervous tick in his cheek.

'How do?' said the man in a slurred, high pitched voice, at odds with the large frame. 'Bit dark, isn't it?'

'A bit,' said Dougie warily. The man seemed a simple sort of guy. Not bright. But pleasant enough.

The man smiled and Dougie's nervousness started to evaporate. It was a nice smile. Shame about the lumpy body, he thought.

'I was on my way back to my car...' he started to say.

'Oh,' came the reply.

Dougie felt sorry for the lad. Was he a lad? He tilted his head slightly, hoping to get a better view of the man, only the cloud of vapour issuing from his mouth every time he exhaled and the brim of the cap made it difficult for him.

'No! You stay. I was on my way home anyway.'

Baseball Cap Man sniffed and wiped his nose with a gloved hand as Dougie turned around ready for the hike to his car.

'I come here when I'm miserable,' he said eventually. 'To be by myself.'

Dougie stopped. The man was staring out to sea and seemed to be talking to the wind rather than him.

'Does it help?'

'Sometimes.'

Dougie was intrigued now. The stranger was a pathetic sort, hopeless but he was starting to feel sorry for him. He had a child-like quality, a shyness which he found appealing.

'If you don't mind my asking, why are you so miserable?'

The man, still looking out into the blackness, shrugged.

'Lonely.'

'Don't you have anyone?'

'I suppose.'

When no more was forthcoming, Dougie felt compelled to prompt him.

'So you *do* have someone?'

Baseball Cap Man turned to face him. In the torchlight Dougie caught a glimpse of his face for the first time. Underneath the downy, tufted beard, the plump features were not wholly unattractive, but it was a strange face. It was the eyes. For a sad man they were far from melancholy looking. They weren't *anything*. Just dark pools. And his expression. That was all wrong too. It seemed fixed in a sneer. So Dougie had got the 'simple' bit right. The man definitely wasn't

166

the full shilling. He determined to get away as soon as possible.

'I live with me Mam,' the man replied. 'She's not well. So it's difficult to sort of go out with... people,' he said carefully. For the first time he looked at Dougie directly and held his gaze.

Interesting, thought Dougie. Was he getting the come-on here, from this strange creature?

'Oh, you poor dear,' he said sympathetically.

'Sometimes,' continued Baseball Cap Man, 'I think it would be really nice to have someone to love. Someone who loved you back.'

Dougie felt strangely moved all of a sudden. It was almost like a tape recording, listening to his own words coming out of someone else's mouth.

'You know what I mean?'

Dougie did.

'It must be a nice thing, holding someone's hand.'

'Yes,' Dougie managed to say. He had a lump in his throat. How had this happened? Here he was, in an isolated spot and out of the mist a man had appeared and echoed his own longings, his own plaintive desires.

The stranger bit his lip and looked out over the dark precipice again.

'I'll hold your hand,' Dougie found himself saying. He took off his glove. The man hesitated for a moment, then reached out and took Dougie's hand in his own. It was warm. Safe.

'What's your name?' Dougie asked.

'Gordon.'

'I'm Dougie.'

'I know.'

Used, as he was, to public recognition, the short phrase was innocuous enough but in the split second it took Dougie to analyse its meaning and connect it with the malevolent tone in which the words were uttered, he was doomed. He saw the sly expression forming under the baseball cap all too late. Gordon tightened his grip around his hand, pulled him close, then pushed with all his might. Dougie felt himself flying backwards and soon he was falling, plummeting through the cold air with terrifying speed, too shocked to scream.

Standing on the edge of the cliff, Gordon saw the body disappear into the black void, heard the awful thud of bone slamming into rock. He turned away, smiling to himself. That went very well. Dirty Dougie thought he was stupid, he could tell. He was used to the look people gave him. Pity and revulsion all rolled into one. Well, Dougie, you was wrong, thought Gordon and laughed out loud. He'd played the nasty man like a fiddle. Used all the right words, exactly like he'd been told. Mission accomplished! Result!

He moved off the coarse grass carefully, found the gravel path and followed its snaking course back to the spot where he'd parked his moped.

Along the cliff, the massive aerials with their web of wires, taught and invisible under the night sky, continued their unearthly wailing. Down below on the rocks, where the breakers crashed and roared against the shore, salt water ebbed and flowed amongst the broken pieces of a dead man's head.

Chapter Eighteen

Newall paid for dinner while Carina excused herself to go to the loo. On her return, when she asked the waiter for the bill and was told it had been settled, she frowned at Newall with mock anger.

'I thought we were going to split it two ways?'

Newall shrugged. 'Changed my mind.'

Carina grinned, leaned across the table and kissed him on the lips. Newall couldn't help grinning.

'Thank you,' she said. 'It makes a change. When I go out with a fella, it's usually me who pays the bill.'

'I suppose I'm old fashioned.'

'Next time Roy, I'll pay...'

Newall didn't hear the rest of what she said. His heart was singing at the words, 'Next time.' They spelled hope and a promise of further excitement. A tingling thrill rushed through his body. She wanted to see him again. What a turn on. This incredible woman really was interested in him!

'I'll hold you to that,' he gushed. Carina sat there, demurely, staring at him.

'Can I get you another liqueur?' He did not want the evening to end.

'Better not,' Carina said gently. 'Think I've got a busy day tomorrow. After today's fiasco I suspect Jez might want a few changes to the script. Poor Dougie. It's all my fault.'

'No, no,' Newall tapped the table emphatically. 'Anything that's happened to Mr Hunt, he's brought it on himself.'

'You don't understand. I made him into a laughing stock...'

Newall reached out and took her hand in his.

'Listen to me. Stop punishing yourself. You've got enough on your plate.'

Carina looked down at the floor tearfully.

'I guess you're right,' she said.

'I am. I'm probably speaking out of turn here,' he added, 'But I think you might be right about a busy day ahead of you tomorrow.'

'How so?'

'I think Dougie's about to join the ranks of the unemployed. I saw Jez go into his dressing room while I was waiting for you.'

'What?' Carina was aghast. 'No! I told Jez I'd walk if he sacked Dougie.'

'Well, I could be wrong. I suppose.' Newall sounded dubious now. Perhaps he'd grabbed hold of the wrong end of the stick when Jez had spoken to him. And Dougie's weeping might have been about something else. He wished he'd kept his mouth shut. 'I'm out of line,' he told Carina. 'I shouldn't have said anything.'

'Don't worry, darling. You're probably right. Thompson's a slimy old sod. I wouldn't put anything past him.'

She pushed her seat back, bringing the evening to a close.

'I hope Dougie's all right. I hope he doesn't do anything stupid.'

She reached inside her capacious bag for her phone, rifled around, then stopped abruptly.

'Silly, isn't it. I still keep expecting to see my Fluff poking out.' There were tears in her eyes as she said, 'Rest In Peace, my little love.'

Newall tried to look suitably sympathetic but it was difficult. The trembling, baldy-bog-eyed creature had given him the creeps.

Carina produced her phone, flipped it open and declared the battery dead. Newall offered her the use of his own.

'No point, thanks. I don't know his number. I'll give him a call in the morning. That's if he hasn't been caught dogging down Westgate Road,' she said. 'Will you walk me back to the hotel, Roy?'

'But I can drive you.'

The actress shook her head.

'It's only a five minute stroll up the hill.'

'Okay.'

He stood up, picked her coat up off the back of her chair and held it out for her.

'You're a gent.'

They walked out into the evening air. The mist and fog had turned to a slight drizzle now and they set off along the Quayside and up the hill towards the Valmont, a converted warehouse building under a yawning Victorian viaduct. As they passed by the old Crown Pasada pub, with its etched and stained glass windows, glowing brightly from within, Newall pointed to a motorcycle helmet draped over the handlebars of a moped, parked at the side of the road.

'Someone's trusting,' he exclaimed. Carina laughed, linked her arm through his and lent against his shoulder.

A dark figure emerged from the shadows and watched their progress up the hill. Gordon, his face inscrutable, followed at a safe distance, trying to listen to any conversation. If he was hoping to hear something juicy, he was sadly disappointed. Carina and Newall, comfortable in each other's presence, walked in silence.

In the grand reception, modern and bright the last stragglers of a works' Christmas party were milling around, waiting for their taxis to arrive. They gestured excitedly as Carina marched up to the desk to pick up her key.

'I'll see you to your door,' Newall said. 'If that's okay.'

'I'd like that,' she replied coyly.

In the lift up to her suite Newall could hear his heart pounding excitedly in his head. His hands shook and he stuck them in his pockets. Carina linked her arm through his again. He smelled her hair, it wasn't as soft as it looked but it was clean and sweet.

'Well, here we are,' she said, stopping outside a door at the end of the long corridor. Newall felt like a teenager again. Unsure what to say. How to proceed. She slipped her key card into the slot and opened the door. Newall hesitated. Should he wait to be admitted? Or should he take the initiative and enter? Would she be offended if he did? While he deliberated in the doorway, Carina kissed him. He pulled her closer, enjoying the moment, forgetting his dilemmas. Sometimes a man can think too much, he thought. Just go with the flow.

Eventually Carina shied away from him. She was breathless and bright eyed.

'I would love to take you to my bed, Roy,' she purred.

'You can,' Newall assured her.

'Not tonight. I'll be a wreck in the morning. I need all my strength for rehearsals and two performances.'

'Are you sure?' asked Newall plaintively.

'Fraid so.' She kissed him again, hugged him tightly and felt the pulse in his neck racing away.

'I want to see you again, Carina.'

'Ring me. Tomorrow?'

'I promise.'

She kissed him again, on the cheek this time, and bid him goodnight as she closed the door. Newall winced, adjusted his pants and padded silently over lush, thick carpet back to the lift. He was sweating heavily now. Lust, pain, frustration, joy, all were careering around inside him, shaking his very being. He felt so alive, so energized. He stared at his reflection in the mirror as the lift descended and laughed. A woman wanted him, found him attractive. And not just any woman, a sexy, classy famous soap star. Carina Hemsley, no less. And it felt good.

He floated through reception, past the inebriated party-goers without really seeing them and returned to his car. On the way, it barely registered that the crash helmet was still hanging from the moped's handlebar. His mind was on other things.

If Newall had been paying attention he might have noticed that one of the inebriated party-goers in the Valmont's reception was neither inebriated nor party-going. Gordon had been hanging around with them, unseen by management, waiting for his moment. Careful to avoid detection from Newall when he re-appeared, he threw himself into the midst of the drunken crowd until the policeman had left the building and made for the staircase as soon as the coast was clear.

The policeman disturbed him. Angered him. So he would put up with no further delays. From now on he had to assert himself. Tonight would be the night, he decided. It was time. No more delays. This was the new beginning, the future he had been dreaming about for a long time.

Stopping to use his inhaler on the third floor, Gordon began to calm down. There was no real hurry. He knew where Cora was and she wasn't going anywhere. He should savour the moment. Imagine the delights in store. He cackled and took another puff of the inhaler. One by one he counted the steps up to the fifth floor. He opened the door carefully, making sure he was alone in the corridor. It was late, after midnight in fact, but he couldn't risk being seen. He'd get into trouble and he didn't want that. The coast was clear. He entered the corridor, liking the feeling of the deep pile beneath his feet. He would have to get used to this kind of thing. Extravagance. Luxury. This was the world into which he was about to join. No more cheap nylon carpets for him!

A door in front of him opened and he stopped, holding his breath. A tray containing dirty crockery and glasses was pushed into the corridor and the door slammed shut. The occupant hadn't bothered to look out. Good. Gordon carried on, marking off the room numbers in his head as he passed by them. 503, 502, 501, 500, The Bridge Suite. He was outside *Her* room. Sorry, *Her* suite. Suite by name, sweet by nature. At last. He placed an ear to the door, hoping to hear something from within. Never mind.

Gordon pressed the handle down and the door clicked. It was already open. Smashing! It made him feel welcome. Wanted. He pushed the door open wider and entered.

Carina stood with her lovely back to him. She was drinking something from a crystal tumbler, looking at the TV. It was one of those big modern flat ones. Expensive. Gordon took his eyes off her, fleetingly to take in his surroundings. There were sofas and ornaments and pictures. And doors through to other rooms. The place was bigger than his house. More posh carpets. He could smell them, they were almost new. He loved the smell of new carpet.

Even cheap carpet when it was new smelt nice.

Carina took a swig of brandy from her glass, saw Gordon's outline reflected in the cut crystal pattern a hundred times over, like a fly's eye and spun around.

'All right, Kidda?' she said cheerfully.

'Good, thanks,' Gordon replied, as curtly as possible but already he felt his anger dissipating. It was difficult to be annoyed with Cora, especially as she seemed so pleased to see him.

'Come 'ere, you must be freezing cold.'

She bounded over to him, hugged him and set about rubbing his arms to stimulate circulation. He wanted to say, "What was the copper doing here?" only it didn't seem so important to him anymore. Gordon's eyes rolled back in his head and his lips quivered, such was his pleasure. Every caress, even the slightest touch, sent him into paroxysms of pleasure. When Carina stopped, he felt warm all over.

'I must admit, I didn't expect to see you tonight, gorgeous,' she crooned. 'But I'm glad you popped over. Couldn't have picked a better time. I've just got rid of the Law. Miserable plod wants to know all about my life.'

'What for?'

'Erm... just to find out if there's anyone in my past who might want to kill me.' She laughed and stared into his dead eyes. It was difficult to ascertain from them whether he believed her little white lie, or not. After a moment, Gordon giggled and thumped the back of the sofa.

'I thought you - you know!' he said coyly, 'Fancied him or summink.'

'As if!' Carina protested. 'There's only one man in my life.'

Gordon's shoulder shook with joy.

'Now, then,' she said sweetly, 'how did it go?'

Gordon hissed through his teeth and dribbled spittle at the side of his mouth. His was not a pleasant laugh.

'I pushed him over the cliff.'

'So he's dead? Dougie's dead?'

Gordon, excited, nodded. 'I heard his body fall to bits.'

'You are so clever darling.'

Gordon agreed. 'It was dead easy. I said everything you said to say and over he went.'

'Good riddance, I say,' said Carina, winking at him.

'So can we get married now, Cora?'

Carina guided him over to the nearest sofa, pushed him down and sat on one of his big knee's.

'Not yet, Gordy. There's still one or two little things to sort out.'

Gordon, dejected, hung his head.

Carina tucked him playfully under the chin. 'Won't be long though.'

She jumped off him, pulled him up by his arms and ripped off his parka.

'Why don't I make you comfortable for an hour or so, sweetheart?' she whispered, pushing him back onto the sofa. 'And then you can go back to your Mam's.'

'I love you Cora,' drooled Gordon.

He tugged eagerly at her dress and pawed her leg.

'In a minute tiger,' Carina trilled, backing away and collecting her glass. 'I need a drink first... Or six,' she added under her breath, pouring herself a stiff brandy. She looked over at the large mass on her sofa. 'Here's to Dougie,' she cried, raising her glass in a toast. 'To Dougie Hunt who hogged the lime-light and stole my thunder.

No more column inches for you!'

Gordon wasn't listening. He was unbuckling his belt and pulling down his trousers.

'Come on, Cora,' he coaxed. 'Let's do stuff.'

He held out his arms and made mock squeezing gestures with his hands like a podgy demanding baby. Cora knocked back her drink in one and grimaced. The things one had to do for one's career. It didn't bear thinking about. Still, it was a means to an end, Gordon had his uses and things were progressing just fine. In fact, better than fine. Everything was perfect!

She yanked at her dress, pulled it carefully over her head and lowered herself onto the sofa.

Chapter Nineteen

It was cold in the auditorium. Jez, waiting for the cast to arrive, stomped his feet to get his circulation flowing. He knew the heating didn't come on until lunchtime, an hour before the matinée, and even then it wasn't exactly as warm as toast. The cost of heating a space this size was astronomical, it was money down the drain, so if a few punters complained about their kiddies succumbing to hypothermia during the performance, tough! They should have wrapped up warm beforehand. Jez shifted in his seat and dangled his legs over the seat in front. He was not looking forward to the cast meeting. If the atmosphere was cold now, it was guaranteed to plummet to minus figures within the next few minutes. He'd already spoken to Carina on the phone, made her aware of his decision to sack Dougie. She'd shrieked and abused him - boy, was she a pro when it came to dishing out insults and expletives - but she had not threatened to quit, which consoled him, slightly. 'Contrary' was her middle name and she may have been hiding something up her sleeve for later. At least she'd agreed to come in early.

Campbell trotted down the aisle towards him, ancient floorboards creaking and groaning underfoot as he went. He grimaced as Jez looked round.

'Looks like the floor could do with an overhaul,' he declared. It was the last thing Jez wanted to hear.

'Lose some weight,' he said nastily. Campbell glanced down at his skinny body. Was he joking, or serious? He could never work out this man's sense of humour. He wondered if Heidi did either.

'I left loads o'messages for you last night. Why didn't you ring me back?'

'I was out. En... enjoying myself,' Campbell stuttered.

Jez frowned at him. 'Were you with my wife last night?'

'Me? No. Why?'

'Doesn't matter.' Jez dismissed his suspicions from his mind. He had other things to think about.

'We go back to the original script. As of today.' Campbell was about to interrupt but Jez carried on.

'The actors'll remember their lines. It's what I pay them to do. And we have to find another one to play Baron Hard-On. Up, I mean. See? The bloody papers have got me at it, as well.'

Campbell looked appalled. 'We won't find anyone at this late stage.'

'Rubbish,' spat Jez. 'It's Christmas Eve tomorrow. We're closed on Christmas Day, re-open Boxing Day. Plenty of time to find a thesp. I thought ninety-nine-point-nine percent of them were permanently on the dole.'

'It's not just the casting. If, and I say if, we find someone, he'll have to be rehearsed, he'll have to learn his lines...'

'Christ, it's hardly fucking Shakespeare. We're not asking him to memorise 'A Midsummer Night's Murder'.'

Campbell corrected him. '*Dream.*'

'It will be murder if you can't find me a new Baron Hard-Up, pal.'

Campbell slumped into a seat, threw one leg over the other and sulked.

'And don't sit like that,' said Jez, irritated. 'You look like a big Jessie.'

'You snaky bastard!'

Both men turned around to find Carina advancing down the aisle towards them. Cigarette and holder in one hand, flouting several government laws, and with her other hand on her hip she sashayed towards them, ready for war. Jez leapt up.

'Now Carina...' he started to say but Carina wasn't in a listening frame of mind.

'I've been trying to ring Dougie all morning,' she roared. 'Poor love's not answering. He's probably in bed, sobbing his heart out. Or worse - topped himself.'

Jez held up his hands in surrender.

'I know what you think Carina. But it had to be done. I couldn't ignore the complaints. Look.' He held up The Journal, Newcastle's daily morning newspaper. 'Letters page. "*I took my three grandchildren to see Cinderella at 'The Old Tyne Theatre'. I was horrified to watch Dougie Hunt making lewd and rude references to his sexual habits. He was a disgrace...*"'

'Did it say anything about me?'

'No.'

Carina raged inwardly. Dougie was dead and he was still getting more press than she was. Where was the justice?

'And who wrote the letter?' she demanded. 'Fanny the Fascist from Fenham?'

Jez shrugged.

'I can't afford a drop in the box office, Carina. I really can't.'

'We won't find another actor, Jez,' moaned Campbell. 'We really won't.'

Carina made a grand show of looking around. The other members of the cast were starting to arrive in dribs and drabs. Lauren and Ben, Brendan and Justin.

'Where's Dougie?' they all wanted to know.

'I asked him to come in later,' replied Jez. 'So I could talk to you all.'

'Oh please Jez, you can't get rid of him,' begged Lauren from the stage. Ben rolled his eyes and remained silent.

'He made a mistake,' she went on. 'Have you never made a mistake before?' she asked of Jez, with beseeching eyes.

Yes, thought Jez. Getting into bloody show biz, that was my mistake.

'Look,' he said, with a tremulous voice. 'I've made my decision, pet.'

Lauren burst into tears. In the absence of a handy firearm, Carina produced a handkerchief from her bag and offered it in a dramatic show of sympathy and compassion.

'Don't worry, my love,' she simpered, 'we'll get Dougie back somehow.'

She chuckled inwardly. Fat chance!

Sylvie Goggle made a late entrance from the back of the auditorium. She wore a tight knitted black cap with an excessively large matching pashmina over her tweed coat, which swished around her like a cloak. It was a cultivated image: a statement, so Sylvie thought. A statement which said 'respected icon of the stage'. The majority of people she passed in the street mistook her for a different iconic figure: Batman.

'I hope this hysteria isn't about Dougie,' she boomed. 'It's all very tiring.'

'It is,' agreed Jez. 'But we have to sort it out.'

'Well, either sack him and find another Baron Hard-Up or don't sack him and tell him to keep his doo-dah in his pants. It's as simple as that.'

'It might be like that at the RSC, sweetheart - every Ham for himself,' Carina barked, 'but here we're a team. We're all in it together.'

'Could've fooled me, darling,' Sylvie said sweetly.

She sat next to Campbell, leant over and kissed him three times on the cheeks. Carina watched from the stage in disgust. What was it with these classical actresses, she wondered, kissing folk too many times and touching them up like desperate nymphomaniacs at a snogging contest. Just because they'd done a bit of Shakespeare they thought they were better than everyone else. Shakespeare wasn't acting, it was just running around on stage, saying 'doth' and 'verily' in a posh voice. God, how boring. No wonder they spent all their free time sticking their lips on each other. It was to compensate for the daily tedium of having to perform 'Mac-Bloody-Beth' and such like stuff for months on end. Give me soap opera any day, she thought!

She ignored Sylvie's retort, pulled out her mobile phone and speed dialled.

'Jackie? I need you.'

She wasn't in the mood for Jackie's excuses.

'... I don't care. Jump in your car and get over to the theatre, now!'

Carina ended the call and tossed the phone in her bag. Yes, it was going to be a busy day. If only the others knew! She clambered down from the stage, sat by herself in front of Sylvie and let the others put up an argument for Dougie's retention. She'd already made a satisfactory show of solidarity. She sat back and let Jez stumble through his plans for yet another revised show. She looked at her watch and wondered idly how long it would take for Dougie's body to be found. It might possibly have been washed out to sea by now. Would he turn up, bloated and unrecognizable in Holland? Or Hull? Who knew? There were no certainties. The only absolute, shining certainty, was that Dougie would not be turning up for today's performances, or any others, for that matter. Alarm bells would ring and a replacement would have to be found. Jez would see to that. There was too much money at stake. They were sold out for weeks to come. Thanks to her. And, begrudgingly, she admitted, to mad Gordon.

She felt no guilt at Dougie's demise. She saw it as a necessity, part of the scheme of things. The death threat letters were something she'd hatched with Gordon's help to raise her profile in the media. Jez's decision to tell no-one of their existence hadn't helped matters. But the ambivalence of the newspapers. Oh how that hurt. She had been their darling for so long. It was yet another reminder of how far she'd fallen from grace. Her brainwave plan to have Gordon bump off old and smelly Fluff - was a means of salvaging the situation and if it hadn't been for Dougie's outdoor orgy, she would have been front page news on all the tabloids. The producers, the magazines, the TV shows and celebrity bookers, would have fallen over themselves to hire her but it didn't happen! Dougie had ruined it for her. Of that there was no doubt. Getting rid of him was an act of revenge. At first. Later on, when she'd calmed down, the more she thought about it, the more sensible the idea sounded. The media would have a field day! And she intended to milk it for all it was worth.

Jez's pep talk to the cast was interrupted by the arrival of a very serious looking Newall and Clifton. Carina's heart leaped into her mouth. It was starting. They'd found him. She could tell. She glanced at Newall, trying to get his attention but he studiously avoided her. They had! They'd found Dougie. Why else would he ignore her? He was trying to act the professional. Carina took deep breaths to steady her nerves. Three, two, one, action!

'Morning, Roy,' she said brightly.

Clifton looked over at her in surprise, mouth open. She shut it quickly, regaining her composure and watched her boss out of the corner of her eye. He was blushing again. Was she missing something here?

Newall acknowledged her. 'Carina,' he nodded without smiling. For a fleeting moment Carina wondered if she'd been found out.

'Everything all right, Inspector?' Jez asked.

'Well, no,' Newall admitted. 'I'm afraid I have some bad news.' He cleared his throat.

'Early this morning a woman walking her dog along the cliffs near Whitley Bay...'

'Oh My God!' shrieked Lauren.

'... found a body on the rocks. A nearby search of a parked car...'

'Please, no!' wailed Lauren. 'It's Dougie isn't it?'

Newall nodded sadly. 'I'm afraid, yes it is.'

Before Carina had chance to impress them all with an outpouring of grief and regret, Lauren started to scream. She clutched Ben and shook him by the shoulders.

'It's my fault. He went to our spot. I told him to go. It's all my fault!'

'You told him about our place?' Ben looked horrified. 'He's been to *our* secret place?'

He snorted in disgust.

'Well, we can never go back there again.'

Lauren buried her head in his chest and sobbed. Carina fumed inwardly, the little bitch had beaten her in the outpouring of grief stakes. She would have to put Plan B into effect.

Clifton studied the others. They all seemed genuinely shocked. They were pale and, apart from the air-head girl on stage, stunned into silence. Carina, alone in the front row stalls, stood up shakily.

'Are you sure it's him?' she asked in a small voice.

'Yes. It's definitely Mr Hunt,' replied Newall. Clifton frowned. Was there a note of tenderness in his voice she hadn't noticed before? 'From the documents in his car, we managed to trace a sister, in Hartlepool...'

'Hartlepool?!' Sylvie gasped. 'Oh how dreadfully common.'

Newall ignored her.

'She's identified the body. I'm really sorry.'

Carina lurched sideways and collapsed into a seat. Lauren's weeping and wailing reached new heights of hysteria. Newall bounded over and was at Carina's side in a second.

'Carina?'

Her eyes fluttered open.

'Sorry. I'll be okay.'

'Take your time.'

Newall helped her sit upright with a tenderness that surprised Clifton. She noticed their lingering hands, the concern on her boss's face, his arm around her waist and she didn't like it one little bit.

'How did he die?' inquired Sylvie. 'Did he fall? Was he pushed? Or did the snivelling old queen top himself?'

Clifton responded vaguely. 'It's too early to tell.'

'Was there a letter? A sue-icide note?' the actress annunciated.

Clifton shook her head. Justin and Brendan, the Ugly-Sisters,

185

sprang to life.

'That doesn't necessarily mean he didn't kill himself,' said Justin and looked suddenly puzzled. What had he just said?

Brendan nodded eruditely. 'Yes, it's a myth that suicides always leave a note. At least that's what they said on "C.S.I".'

'The Vegas one,' Justin added. 'Not the Miami one. We don't watch that.'

'I quite like "CSI: NY",' quipped Ben, tiring of his girlfriend's histrionics.

Jez, who had been lost in thought for a while, stirred.

'Do you think he did commit suicide, Inspector?'

He went over the last conversation he'd had with Dougie, in his mind. He remembered the tears and Dougie's obvious distress when he'd sacked him. A pang of guilt seared through him.

Newall did not want to speculate.

'It's too early to say. The investigation is on-going.'

'Maybe he fell?' suggested Carina and watched Newall closely for his response.

'Yes,' he said. 'He might have.'

Carina relaxed. There were no guarded clouds of suspicion in his eyes so the police were of the opinion that it had been an accident. Excellent.

'Someone could have pushed him over the cliff. Murdered him,' declared Ben.

She froze, inwardly cursing the big mouthed, empty headed idiot.

Lauren was sobbing again. 'I sent him to his death. It's all because of me he's dead.'

'Could you clarify that please?' asked Clifton, all the time watching her boss who was smiling in a most sympathetic and inappropriate manner at Carina Hemsley.

'He wanted to get away, be by himself. So I told him about a place Ben and I found by the sea,' said the young actress sadly. 'It's windswept and romantic and peaceful.'

'Or it was,' interjected Ben. 'He's spoilt it for us now.'

'There were some handwritten directions found in his car. Was that you?'

Lauren nodded.

'When did you talk to him about this?'

'Last night. Straight after the show. He was feeling down. It was awful for him. All those people booing and jeering. Nobody should have to put up with that.'

Clifton sighed impatiently. 'I thought that's what people did at panto's. Booed and shouted, "It's behind you!"'

'This was different,' Newall answered. 'It was a personal attack.'

'You were there?' Clifton was aware of her voice rising an octave.

'No law against it, is there?' he replied caustically.

Clifton, subdued, tried to carry on.

'What sort of a mood was he in? Did you notice?'

Lauren thought for a moment. 'Quiet. For him. Sad, I suppose.' She burst into tears again. Jez, pale and troubled, stood up.

'I think I was the last person to see him. Here, I mean, at the theatre,' he said, swallowing hard. 'We had a conversation.'

Clifton registered Newall's confirming nod. What was going on with him? What was he doing?

'What did you talk about?' she managed to say, getting a grip of herself. When Jez did not reply, she repeated the question.

'I sacked him,' he replied.

Nobody spoke for a moment.

'How did he take it?' asked Clifton.

Another pause.

'Not very well.'

Carina reached for the handkerchief tucked up her sleeve and blew her nose.

'Excuse me,' she said and hurried out of the nearest side exit. Making sure she hadn't been followed, she looked up and down the passage before pulling out her mobile phone.

'Jackie?' she whispered. 'I need you here.' She paced up and down, angered by the series of excuses Jackie was coming up with.

'... I don't care if it's two shopping days to Christmas, give the brats some cash in an envelope, they won't mind. Kids don't want presents these days, they'd rather have the money... get over here now...'

She brought her up to speed with the news and barked some orders at her. 'Ring the Press straight away. No names, just tell them Dougie's dead, suicide probably and all his co-stars are upset. Best not single me out. Yet. Got that? Good.'

She ended the call abruptly. Newall appeared in the passage-way, seaching for her.

'How are you?'

Carina trembled visibly and put a beautifully contrived, shaking hand up to her mouth.

Newall slipped an arm around her and stroked her back.

'I'm sorry I couldn't let you know sooner. We've had a busy morning, what with finding next of kin and identifying the body.'

'That's all right,' she replied meekly. 'Better get back to the others, eh? We all need each other right now. We're a family.'

They made their way back down the passage way. Newall noticed Carina smiling to herself.

'What is it?'

'I've just remembered something. You know what he said to me once?' Newall shook his head. '"*I don't want to grow old, Carina*," he said. *"I'd rather die young and stay pretty".*'

She chuckled to herself. 'He was about thirty years too late but I guess he did it in the end.'

'He said that?'

'Yes. The other night. Before I left the bungalow.'

Newall considered this thoughtfully. Before entering the auditorium he squeezed her hand.

'Can I see you later? Tonight?'

'Oh, I'd love to Roy but would you mind if we made a date for tomorrow instead? I wouldn't be much company tonight.'

Newall reddened, annoyed at himself for appearing so insensitive.

'Of course.' Mortified, he barely spoke another word when they returned to the others and left most of the talking to Clifton. The two detectives left the theatre soon after.

'So,' said Clifton. 'Did you enjoy the pantomime?'

'I did actually,' Newall declared. 'It was good fun. Entertaining. Value for money. The kids loved it...'

'I wasn't referring to last night, Boss,' she replied severely. 'I meant back there. Just now. All that blubbing and hysteria. They all couldn't stand him the other day.'

'That's just actors.'

They walked back to the car without speaking. Clifton ached to ask him how he suddenly knew so much about the acting profession. She thought it wise to let that one go though.

Inside the theatre, Jez and Campbell sat in the stalls planning an early closure for the pantomine.

'If we close now and open, say the twenty seventh, or twenty eighth, or even the twenty ninth,' Jez was saying, 'with a new Baron Hard-Up...'

'No!' Carina interjected. 'We stay open.'

'But it's disrespectful,' said Campbell, all indignation. 'We can't.'

'Dougie would have wanted us to go on,' Carina said. Lauren, Justin and Brendan nodded in agreement. '"*The show is everything*".' That was his motto.

'Really?' said Sylvie, pithily. 'I thought it was "*Fancy a shag?*"'

Carina ignored her. 'What a homage to him it would be if we carried on with the show that he loved so much.'

'You're forgetting Baron Hard-Up's absence,' Campbell called out.

'No I'm not,' she said and pointed at him.

'What?' Campbell looked bemused.

'You can do it. You know the lines. You wrote them.'

The director's jaw went slack.

'I couldn't.'

'Yes you could. In fact you will. You've acted before.' The command came from Jez.

Carina sat down contented. Things, she thought, could not be going better, and wished straight away she hadn't thought it as Jackie wandered down the aisle towards her with her two children, Evie and Christian in tow. They walked with the dawdling, petulant gait of two kids who wished they were elsewhere. Evie and Christian slumped into seats on the end of the first row.

'What are they doing here?' Carina hissed.

'You said get here straightaway,' Jackie whined. 'My mother can't look after them at such short notice and my mother-in-law doesn't want to at all. I thought I could leave them here for an hour or so while I...' she lowered her voice and whispered in Carina's ear, '... buy their Christmas presents.'

Carina shooed her away. 'I told you what you had to do. Anyway, you won't have time for prezzie buying. You're going to be busy. Did you make those calls?'

'I did,' answered Jackie. 'Everybody was very interested.'

'When they descend,' said Carina regally, 'I want you to fit them all in at five minute intervals. National dailies get priority - am I clear?'

Jackie nodded. 'But if I could nip out to Fenwicks at lunchtime...'

Carina studied the two children. She tried to recall their names. And failed. How old were they? Eight and seven? She went over to them, smiling benignly.

'Hi kids.'

'Hello,' they replied politely, in unison.

'What do you want for Christmas?'

They reeled off a practiced list of things - computer games, dolls, football kit, CD's, clothes. Carina held up her hand.

'You do know that Santa Claus isn't real, don't you?' she said. The children stared at her, wide-eyed and stunned. Especially Evie, the youngest. 'He doesn't exist. It's your father. Although this year, it'll be your Mammy, as Daddy's done a bunk.'

They continued to stare at her in stunned silence as she returned to her seat further down the aisle.

'Sorted,' she said to Jackie. 'No need to go shopping now. Just slip them a few quid in a card.'

An hour later, the Press descended like vultures and Carina was ready for them. This time they wanted to hear her story. She sobbed and laughed and cried and wrung her hands and railed at the heavens as she talked about her dear, dear friend Dougie Hunt and his untimely, tragic passing. What a sad loss. What a personal tragedy. But the show must go on. And go on it did, that night. With a new, slimmer, more neurotic Baron Hard-Up. With an audience on the edge of its seat, with TV cameras and entertainment 'reporters' from all the morning magazine shows in the aisles and with Carina dazzling them all centre stage.

Chapter Twenty

Gordon's mother shifted her position on the make shift bed in the living room and peered at the television. 'Cora', someone was saying. 'Cora Smart from *Winkle Bay*.' It was a blonde woman. A blonde woman, sitting on a bright sofa was talking about Cora. And then suddenly, there she was - the woman herself, live via satellite link, in her living room.

'Beautiful!' she moaned. Cora was beautiful. But why was she crying? What was wrong? And why was she wearing big sunglasses inside, when it wasn't even sunny?'

'Gordon! Cora!'

She heard her son clattering downstairs from the bathroom. He hurried into the room, covered in shaving foam.

'What's wrong Mam?'

She tried to point at the television but only succeeded in falling backwards onto the pillow. Gordon saw his pride and joy on screen and sat down on the bed, crushing his mother's legs. She groaned in pain but Gordon, engrossed in the TV paid little heed to her grunts of distress.

'See? That's my girl,' he said, pointing at the screen proudly. He listened intently. She was talking about Dougie. She was going to miss her dear friend. Such a loss to the entertainment world. He was a sweet, misunderstood soul.

'Don't cry Cora!' he said, puzzled. Was this the horrible Dougie man she'd asked him to get rid of that she was talking about? Or another one? Were there two Dougie's from the pantomime? Perhaps he should find Cora, ask if he'd made a mistake. No. He wasn't allowed to do that. She'd be angry. She always called him and didn't like it when it was the other way round. He'd tried that once before and she'd been furious. Gordon thought back to the previous evening. Cora laughed a lot and made nice noises with him so he *had* pushed the correct Dougie off the cliff. Maybe she was confused.

Gordon's mother groaned loudly under her son's weight. He shifted his buttocks off her lower half and leaned forward earnestly.

'That's my girl,' he repeated, indicating the TV. 'She's mine.'

He groped for his mother's limp hand on the bed and stroked it gently.

'I've got some news Mam.'

It was expressly against Cora's orders but he couldn't help himself. His Mam could keep a secret. He could trust her.

'Me and Cora - we're getting married.'

He listened to the intermittent mumbling that came his way from spit lashed lips and chose to interpret the response as 'congratulations'.

* * *

Carina spent the morning giving interviews via satellite link from the front row of the 'Old Tyne Theatre'. A succession of grinning reporters armed with microphones were quick to pass over Dougie's death and ask her questions of a more meatier nature, like 'Where

194

have you been hiding for the past few years?', 'You look terrific, what's your secret?' and 'When are you going back into *Winkle Bay*?' Carina answered the questions with wit and grace and always brought the subject back to her lovely Dougie.

Afterwards, when the camera's and technicians had gone, Jackie arrived with the newspapers. Carina whipped off her sunglasses and flicked through the tabloids. Every one of them. If she wasn't on the front page, she was on page 2. At last. She scanned the headlines, 'Troubled Dougie, kills himself... heartbroken friend carries on... electric performance... still got what it takes...' The story was the same in every article.

'It's awful to think...' Jackie started to say.

'Then don't think,' muttered Carina.

'No, it's really sad, Carina. If Dougie hadn't died, you wouldn't be in the papers, would you. You're a big brave star and that's great - but it's only because Dougie,' she lowered her voice, '... killed himself that everyone's realised how talented you are.'

'Not *realised*, *remembered*. There's a difference.'

'Yes,' replied Jackie, subdued.

* * *

A few miles away in the foyer of 'A1 North TV', Lauren and Ben sat watching the latest scenes of *Winkle Bay* being recorded, on a large plasma monitor. Ironically the studios, with their glass-walled partitions, high-tech sound stages and stylish office furniture were housed in a former tobacco factory, an ugly, soul-less building further down the Tyne near the former shipbuilding centre of Wallsend. The cigarettes had long since stopped rolling off the production line when executives at 'A1 North' toured the abandoned premises in search of a suitable self-contained new home for their televisual cash cow. It was perfect for their needs, with space to expand and close to all the major roads. Deals were done, contracts drawn up, grants obtained. The TV people moved in. From under the factory's eves, where once, a million cancer sticks a week were manufactured, sorted, wrapped and shipped out to a gasping nation, another type of addictive product - and some would argue, equally as dangerous to public health, was now being churned out for the masses: soap opera.

Ben was engrossed in the story unfolding on screen before him. *Winkle Bay* hadn't reached the Antipodes yet but the girls in the cast looked hot and that was enough to grab his attention. Who cared about plot? Two spunky women in swimming cozzies were arguing with a guy in a suit about the benefits of wind energy over nuclear energy. Or something. Did it really matter?

Lauren had also noted the scantily clad girls and was well aware of the effect they were having on her boyfriend. If she got the part, she thought to herself, well aware that it was a big 'if', she would go out of her way to despise them. She was a serious actor, RADA trained, and girls like those, who wielded their pneumatic boobs around like bouncing melons in a carrier bag, did nothing to further the cause of women on television.

A bespectacled, wizened little thing who looked like she'd fallen asleep overnight on a sun-bed and woken up the next day a darker shade of shrivelled prune, clattered down a flight of stairs and marched up to them.

'Lauren?' she asked abruptly.

'Yes.'

The Prune offered a gnarled hand.

'Suzy Lovell, casting.'

'Pleased to meet you.'

'Come with me.'

She turned away quickly without waiting for Lauren to get up.

'Break a leg,' Ben called out as Lauren hurried up the stairs after Suzy.

'It's an interesting building,' she said, trying to make conversation.

'Used to be a ciggie factory years ago. Full of pigeon shit when we moved in,' came the earthy reply. 'You learnt that scene we sent you?'

'Oh yes,' Lauren gushed. 'It's really well written.'

'Is it?'

They were now crossing the upstairs office, open plan and vast, with rows of desks set out in groups along the length of the floor space. An army of staff, mainly directors and their teams, at various stages of pre and post-production were beavering away, keeping the Good Ship *Winkle Bay* afloat. One or two looked up from their work stations, curious to see the latest auditionee and exchanged words of approval in hushed tones. The others, immune to the plethora of youth and beauty that the soap conveyor belt paraded past them on a regular basis kept their heads down.

Suzy ushered her into a seat outside a glass walled office and went off to chat to two women at the water-cooler. Lauren fidgeted uncomfortably in her chair, aware she was the subject of their conversation. Suzy was talking animatedly to them and they kept leaning back to get a good look at her. She moved her chair slightly and glanced through the glass wall at the good looking man sitting behind the large desk. He had tousled hair, cut in the 'just-climbed-out-of-bed' style which really took hours of teasing and pampering with product to give it that nonchalant appearance. The thick rimmed glasses, the sharp, light brown suit, lilac shirt, green tie and shiny tan shoes were the uniform of a man who lived his life by an un-swaying adherence to the strict rules of The Bible. The Fashion Bible that was 'GQ'.

Lauren had read about Rufus Frenkel, the Boy Wonder Producer in the newspapers. He'd been brought in to revamp *Winkle Bay* a few years ago, to give it an injection of youth and energy although he would be forever known as the man who axed Carina Hemsley. She made a mental note not to mention Carina. She didn't want to jeopardize her chances. The guy looked grim enough already. Rufus's boyish looks weren't so boyish this close up. There were dark shadows under his eyes, deep lines to the side of them. His whole demeanour said 'serious stress levels.' The Golden Boy was starting to look a bit grey.

Indeed, right at that moment, on the other side of the glass, Rufus Frenkel was not feeling particularly Boy Wonder-ish at all - not that he ever acknowledged or used that particular turn of phrase, it was patronizing in the extreme. He'd earned his promotion to producer at the age of twenty four through sheer hard work and dedication. Of course, there'd been some serious brown-nosing along the way but, hey, wasn't that the way of the world?

Usually at Christmas time, Rufus would be jetting off for a well deserved break in the sun with his girlfriend. But not this year. He'd been ordered by his boss to stay at his desk 'til Christmas Eve and to be available, with mobile phone at his side, over the holiday period for possible 'discussions'. About what, his Executive Producer superior, would not say. For the first time in five years, Rufus was apprehensive about his future. He was beginning to suspect that the axe might be about to fall on him. Year on year, the ratings kept tumbling. He'd used every nail-biting plot imaginable - murder, mental illness, disability, incest, explosions, kidnapping, lesbianism - all the usual sensational soap stories, to halt the decline. Nothing had worked. This year's Christmas Day episodes were make or break time for him and he'd pulled out every trick in his bag to make *Winkle Bay* 'must see' television. The Great British viewing public was about to be mesmerized by the increasingly unhinged antics of Angie Makepeace, supermarket shelf stacker and former lesbian nun as she takes her father/lover hostage and threatens to explode the handbag bomb attached to her mobility scooter. All the ingredients for a rip-roaring festive special were in place. But Rufus knew he had placed all his eggs in one basket and the knowledge of this was keeping him awake at night. Like the ticking device in Angie's shoulder bag, the countdown had started.

Rufus picked up the post his secretary had placed on his desk earlier that morning and sifted through the jumbled mix of Christmas cards and fan mail, first with a weary eye and then with mounting anger. Amongst the Seasons Greetings were a number of letters from *Winkle Bay* fans begging for the return of 'Cora Smart'. They were always letters from older fans - the wobbly, spidery scrawl, the damp smell emanating from the envelopes. Carina had put them up to it. It was so obvious. The same post marks, the same wording! Every cluster of fans on coach party outings to her sorry pantomime must have been accosted and primed on a nightly basis, judging from the quantity of mail coming in. The woman was appalling and so lacking in dignity. When would she take the hint? He'd already spoken to that ridiculous fan club woman about it - 'Tell Carina she's never coming back,' he'd said. How blunt did he have to be about it? The actress and the character had had their day. *Winkle Bay* was a different organism now. Didn't she see that? Okay, she was riding high in the media. Today. And for the first time ever she was being presented in a positive light, which astounded him somewhat. He'd watched her earlier that morning on TV, going through her sickening emotional routine. Megalomania will always out, he thought. She didn't fool him. Not one little bit.

He reached across the desk, grabbed his address book and rifled through the pages angrily until he found the number he was looking for. Time to spell things out for her. He picked up his phone and dialled.

'Carina Hemsley.'

The voice was almost gravelly now, though still with the same deep tones he remembered. She'd puffed her way through a few thousand cigarettes since he'd last spoken to her.

'Carina?' he said flatly. 'Rufus.'

'My darling!' she cried, insincerely, 'How are you? It's been ages.'

She was in the foyer of the Valmont, waiting for her driver to turn up. She beckoned impatiently to Jackie who was struggling to get out of the lift, burdened as she was under the weight of Carina's dry-cleaning, her make-up bag and business case. Carina cupped the phone.

'It's Rufus fucking Frenkel!' she hissed. Jackie's eyebrows lifted in a lesser impression of her icon and she teetered over to her.

'I didn't expect to hear from you ever again,' she said into the phone, winking at Jackie. 'Did you see me in the papers?'

'I'd like to set something straight...' Rufus started to say but was interrupted by the gathering ego on the other end of the phone.

'Poor Dougie, it was awful but everybody's been so good to me, so caring, I'm so, so moved by all the lovely people out there. They have taken me to their hearts. They've missed me, you see...'

She crossed her fingers and held them up. The moment she'd been waiting for was about to arrive. She could feel it. Jackie mirrored her actions, held up her fingers and dropped the dry cleaning.

The producer cut in, unable to contain himself. 'Actually Carina, that's why I'm calling.'

'Oh?' Carina found herself short of breath. She felt a tightening in her chest.

'I've had a further flurry of 'Bring Back Cora' letters and cards.'

'Oh, bless them,' she said. "My People'. I've left a gaping hole in their lives, Rufus. They keep asking, "when is Cora coming back to *Winkle Bay*?" All the time. I keep telling them it's not going to happen - I've moved on, but they just won't listen. I don't know what to say to them anymore.'

'Then I'll tell you. Shall I?'

Carina hesitated. She didn't like the tone that was creeping in to his voice.

'Go on,' she said.

'The next time someone asks the question, you say to them, "My character will never be returning to the shores of *Winkle Bay*. The producer saw fit to get rid of me because I am an unpleasant megalomaniac whose delusions of power and popularity sapped what little talent I had and turned me into a self-obsessed, overbearing monster".'

Carina's grip on the phone tightened. She felt the blood draining from her face.

'Did you get that?' he asked, when the silence down the line made him wonder if the connection had been broken.

'Yes.' The response was flat and deadly. Hate, passionate vengeful hate began to well up inside her. She could hear its terrible screaming in her head.

'So there is absolutely no point in getting your feeble minded acolytes to write in, begging me to give you your job back. No point whatsoever. Your return to Winkle Bay,' he raged, 'will be over my dead body.'

Carina was only half listening. This wasn't happening. It couldn't be. Everything she'd planned, the gamble she'd taken, her hopes, her dreams, they all pivoted around Rufus's realisation that he'd made a fundamental and terrible mistake five years ago. In her dreams he'd called her up, invited her out to lunch, charmed her, seduced her, apologized, begged her to go back. It never entered her head that his personal dislike of her might get in the way and scupper her schemes. Business was business. Rufus needed her. That's the way it worked in television. Didn't he know that?! He was an intelligent lad. Lad! That was it. He was a young man. Carina had failed to take into account the arrogance of youth. And the vanity. For a fleeting moment she hated herself more than she hated him. She'd put herself in the position of having to listen to his insults, his derision, his total assassination of her character. And as she considered this, her hatred for the man swelled, mutated, and surged. It ripped through her heart, her head and throbbed through her veins. Every corpuscle cried out 'revenge'.

She ended the call, without replying.

'Well?' asked Jackie eagerly, her fingers still crossed. 'What did he say?'

'I won't be a minute,' Carina replied levelly. 'I've forgotten something.'

She managed a tight smile, strode over to the lift last occupied by Jackie, and pressed the button for the top floor. The smile played about her lips, with only the slightest of facial tics a clue as to her inner rage, until the lift doors closed and she saw herself reflected into infinity around four mirrored walls. The sight of an army of

Carina's stretching into the distance under a harsh and unforgiving light caused something to snap. She started the frenzied attack with her fists, then using her heels, her bag, her elbows, anything she could lay her hands on, she ripped the place apart. When the fury left her and the lift stopped on the twelfth floor she was surrounded by shards of broken mirror and glass. Thick droplets of blood, oozing from a cut on her palm, trickled down her mobile phone as she held it to her ear.

'Gordon, darling,' she said, her throat and tongue dry from the physical exertion, 'There's a little job I'd like you to do...'

She paused, pressed the ground floor button then sucked the bloody wound on her hand before continuing her discussion with Gordon. It took only a few seconds to convey her instructions. When the computer voice announced she'd reached ground floor level, everything was arranged. Rufus's unpleasant words had been most prophetic. They'd given her an idea. She stepped out of the lift, feeling much better.

'Is my car here?' she said to Jackie.

'I don't know.'

Jackie was trying to read Carina, trying to work out from her demeanour how the conversation with Rufus had played out but Carina's expression was inscrutable behind her sunglasses. She was a closed book. Jackie decided to take the plunge.

'What did he say to you?'

'Who, dear?' replied Carina.

'Rufus.'

'Oh. Him. Not much.' She smiled a wide empty smile. Jackie, feeling that something was not quite right, saw fit to refrain from asking any further questions.

Rufus leaned back in his comfortable, ergonomic leather desk

chair after making the call and breathed a sigh of relief. He'd
wanted to say all those things to that awful woman when she left
five years ago but at the time he considered dignity to be the best
policy. Carina had tried to destroy him in the Press by painting
him as the inexperienced 'Yes Man', puppet of his Masters. At
every opportunity, every public forum, she'd criticised and insulted
him. Her comments had hurt. He was only human - not that
he'd let anyone other than his girlfriend in on that particular secret.
Gradually as her star waned and the newspapers lost interest in her
repetitive bile, he put Carina to the back of his mind. However, he
did not forgive and he did not forget. Revenge was indeed a dish
best served cold.

A knock on the door made him sit upright. Suzy entered.

'Hiya, got Lauren Wentworth outside.'

She handed over Lauren's C.V. and head shot. Rufus took in
the photograph and the profile of the girl sitting beyond the glass
wall. He wasn't sure about her. Suzy had persuaded him to call
her for the audition. She was pretty, there was no argument about
that. But the character she would be playing, Daisy Smart, was a
manipulative, gold digging maneater. This girl looked too pure and
innocent.

He speed read the details on her resume and his eyes locked on
to one particular job. Her latest. There was something familiar
about the venue. The pantomime. 'Cinderella'?

'The Old Tyne Theatre?' he queried. 'Why is that ringing
bells?'

'Ah, right.'

Suzy was prepared. She knew Rufus had a complete downer on
anything and anyone connected with Carina Hemsley. It would be
a great pity if this actress fell by the way side because of it.

'She's a good little actress, Rufus. Just remember that.'

'But why is 'The Old Tyne Theatre' in my mind?'

He thought for a moment. Suzy said nothing, merely stood there watching his brow furrow, his eyes crease behind the poseur-ish spectacles and waited for puzzlement to turn to realisation.

'She's in panto with Carina Hemsley?!'

'I know. But I saw her and she's good. She's really good.'

'Being 'good' and working with Carina Hemsley just don't equate, I'm afraid,' he said, unfairly. Suzy picked him up on that.

'She's a young girl, starting out on her career. She has to take the first job that comes along.'

She saw Rufus studying the photo again and decided to press on.

'The other thing. Any chance she can get, Carina tries to upstage her.'

'Of course she does. The girl's beautiful. Carina will hate that. The jealousy must be eating her up.'

'Yes.'

Suzy scrutinized his face. A small smile had broken out across his countenance. Rufus was cottoning on. How Carina would hate it if the young actress she despised (and despise her she must - Rufus knew how the woman operated), was cast in the show she so ached to be back in, as Cora's *grand-daughter*!

'Show her in,' he said.

An hour later, as Ben drove along the coast road back into Newcastle city centre, Lauren's phone rang. She listened for a moment, stunned, then ended the call and stared out of the window. Objects and buildings passed by in a blur - the Alexandra Bridge, Jesmond Dene, the high stone walls of Sandyford Cemetery, they all were as nothing. Lauren was in a far away place. It was several

205

minutes before Ben noticed. He was lost in deep thoughts of his own. His chest was itchy, which probably meant it was due for another waxing. He wondered if he should have his underarms done while he was there. And there was some fuzz forming on his butt which wasn't nice. That's what this bloody cold climate did to blokes. Turned them into gorillas. He never had this problem in Sydney.

'Who was on the phone, babe?' he asked eventually.

'My agent.'

'Yeh? What did she want?'

'I got the part,' Lauren said quietly, at first. 'I got the part!'

She laughed and screamed and cried all the way to the theatre.

Rufus's last day at work before the Christmas break did not end on the high he'd anticipated. He was packing his brief case with the latest batch of *Winkle Bay* scripts when his secretary, Janine, entered in something of a tizz.

'Reception's just called,' she said, her usually calm demeanour showing signs of unease. 'Carl Rogers is on his way up.'

'He's here? Now?'

Rufus's feathers were ruffled. This did not bode well. The Executive Producer, the man who called the shots ultimately, was based in the company's offices in the city centre. He stayed away from the *Winkle Bay* Production Centre and only ever turned up when there was trouble brewing.

'He didn't call before to say he was coming?'

Janine shook her head.

'There's more,' she said. 'He's got someone with him.'

'Who?'

The secretary swallowed. She'd only heard of the other 'guest' by way of reputation, seen him on television, in interviews.

'Mick Flynt.'

Janine watched Rufus's adam's apple bob up and down.

'What?'

There was no time for further interrogation. Rufus could see the two men heading towards them across the production office. Carl, the older, more conventional of the two with his world weary demeanour, contrasted with the younger media mogul, a pretentious Byronic figure with velvet jacket and wild, flowing hair. Flynt exuded the laid-back confidence of the self made man. Janine, a plain speaking, down to earth Newcastle lass, couldn't help but notice that the media mogul's face with its craggy lines and baggy eyes was not the face of a man who smiled very often. She preferred Carl's more elastic, lived in look. Now there was a man who liked a laugh and knew how to have a good time. Just goes to show, she thought, having loads of money doesn't make you happy. And what was with the hair? Mick Flynt was in his late forties at least, too old to be prancing around with a Seventies Bee Gees flick.

'Doesn't he think he's great!' she said out loud. But Rufus wasn't listening.

'Just give me a shout if you want coffee,' she added quickly, before scurrying out.

'Rufus? Sorry to barge in on you like this,' boomed Carl in his avuncular fashion. 'But events have overtaken us rather and we need to act. Have you met Mick Flynt?'

Rufus, unsure if he could trust his voice, shook his head.

Mick nodded courteously and flicked hair out of his eyes. Carl turned to him.

'Rufus's been running the show for five years, done some great stuff. We've got a cracking couple o'Christmas Day eps coming up.'

'Good,' Flynt said, without enthusiasm.

Carl carried on. 'We've got a problem though,' he said, nonchalantly, as if trying to convince himself that by sounding laid back about the whole thing, the problem might go away.

'The *Powers That Be* want to axe us.'

'What?' Rufus managed to find his voice. 'They can't! We've had a bit of a low patch but we're doing great stuff at the moment. The stories are working, the viewing figures...'

'... Are disappearing down the toilet.' Flynt's flat Mancunian tone made the sentence sound even more damning.

Rufus was about to stand his corner but Carl held up a warning hand. 'To cut a long story short, Rufus, we've been given six months to turn the programme round, or we're scuppered.'

'Wait til they see tomorrow's episodes...'

'Can't risk it. We need a new energy, a new approach. I've brought in Mick. You know his track record. He's created two soaps, sexed up the genre, made them more appealing to kids. We want him to work his magic on *Winkle Bay*.'

'So you're firing me?' Rufus said, trying to sound cool and calm.

'No!' bellowed Carl, 'Not at all. You're still the man. We love what you're doing.'

'But,' he added, 'Mick is coming in as "programme consultant". He's got a great idea, a what-dya-call-it, an 'event' to get the punters watching in their millions. Mick?'

'Trouble is,' Flynt said pompously, 'Fish isn't sexy. Harbours aren't sexy. Nuclear power stations aren't sexy. You've got too many middle class characters. Too many older characters.'

'Not any more, we've a lot of good looking...'

Flynt talked over him arrogantly.

'What we have to do is get rid of all the dead wood and start again. When the re-vamped show goes out, we're going to call it 'The Bay'. What's happened before, the last twenty years - all gone. All forgotten. All that matters is *now*.'

Flynt ran a hand through his long tresses and started pacing around the floor, outlining, acting out the great 'event' he'd come up with, the amazing, edge of seat, story that was going to save the drowning soap.

As the plot unfolded, Rufus found himself hardly able to believe his ears. This man had come in and was putting a bomb under all his good work, his good, hard work, and rubbishing everything he stood for. The story was ludicrous, insane! Didn't Carl realise? This act of fictional lunacy wasn't going to resurrect *Winkle Bay*. Quite the opposite. It would destroy it! He must talk to Carl, alone. He had to make him see. Allowing an outsider, a competitor, to take over the reigns was like giving The Big Bad Wolf the key to the Three Little Pigs front door.

He was jolted out of his inner raging by a crucial development in the story and the mention of a name.

'What?' Rufus was almost yelling. 'What did you say?'

Flynt backtracked, repeated his words and smiled nastily.

'You can't let him do this,' Rufus railed at his boss. 'You can't!'

'I've made my decision.' said Carl quietly. 'It's happening.'

Rufus tried to say 'I quit,' but the words wouldn't come. He was thinking about his mortgage. And the loans. The credit cards. The loss of his girlfriend's respect. Instead he sat back in his chair, listened to the twists and turns of Flynt's saga and felt his professional world, everything he stood for, crashing down around him.

Chapter Twenty One

'Glazed Towers', a former Nineteenth Century vicarage at the end of a gravel driveway twinkling with fairy lights in the dull morning gloom, existed as a show case for Jez Thompson's wealth and commercial interests. It featured in all his company brochures and flyers, with its lead effect lower windows, stained glass conservatory and upper floor mix of clear and frosted glass bay windows, all framed in shiny white, wipe-clean plastic. To thousands of potential customers the message was 'your house too could look as stunning as this.' The mansion, his pride and joy was something of a talking point amongst the locals of leafy and sedate Ponteland, who were unimpressed by its 'stunning' façade. Most of them had complained to the local town planning department, claiming the dwelling resembled a fairground House of Fun in the midst of an otherwise sedate conservation area, a paean of sash-windowed Victoriana. A court case was pending. Jez, if he lost, faced the heinous task - for a double glazing magnate, of having to replace his plastic windows with the wooden framed sash variety. It was almost too unbearable to contemplate.

Strolling around the house on Christmas morning in faux-velvet slippers, overseeing the small team of caterers employed to provide Heidi with a stress-free festive dinner, making sure his guests - the panto actors who had elected to remain in Newcastle for Jesus' Birthday - thoughts of upvc versus traditional wood frame windows were far from his mind. He had other issues to contemplate. Top of the list, and most important of all was the question: was his wife having an affair with that idiot director turned actor, Campbell Garibaldi?

He trusted his wife. He really did but there was no escaping the niggling feeling that she was growing away from him. He sensed it quite strongly. When she'd petitioned him to employ the man in the first place he'd considered her request a strange one. Why was she such a fan? A few minor fringe plays to his name, Garibaldi was no great shakes on the entertainment platform. Jez had the means to engage a big named director for the Old Tyne Panto, but no, Heidi wanted Nervous Nellie. During their time together she'd never shown much interest in the day to day running of the theatre. Now she was never away from the place. And he'd seen them in the building, out of the corner of his eye, huddled together, laughing and joking, thick as thieves. Then there were the phone calls and texts. Why did she feel she had to leave the room whenever Campbell rang? If there was nothing going on between them, there was no need to exclude her husband from conversations so what did it matter if he overheard? No, there was clearly something going on.

It was true that the light of love, the passion was missing from their marriage. When was the last time they had sex? Last week. Only last week. That wasn't so bad, was it? Then he remembered Heidi had wanted to make love almost every day when they first tied the knot. The bonds that tied them together seemed to be loosening. They used to do everything, go everywhere together. Now there were last minute excuses of 'dinner with a friend in need' - a 'girlfriend', granted but he only had Heidi's word for it. He'd never heard of 'Camille' until recently and now they were best friends? He sighed and waved to Ben and Lauren who were sipping mulled wine by the real pine Christmas tree in the expansive lounge.

'Oy! Ginger!'

Jez spun round. Carina, cigarette holder in mouth, one hand on hip, was holding up her champagne glass.

'Happy Christmas.'

Jez smiled politely.

'Have you seen my missus?' he asked.

'She was here a minute ago. Went off with the Scottish Biscuit... Upstairs,' added Carina in a loaded manner. She tapped her nose conspiratorially. 'I'd watch him if I were you. The little quiet ones are the worst.'

Jez tried to laugh a raucous, confident laugh but only managed to sound as if he'd got something stuck in his throat. It was not what he wanted to hear. The awful witch must be a mind reader. He wagged a finger at her weakly and moved on. Aware that she was still watching him from the doorway, he dropped into the dining room, pretending to be interested in the catering staff's movements, then doubled back and bounded up the stairs two at a time.

They were in the bedroom. The master bedroom. He could hear them giggling and whispering as he pounded along the mezzanine floor towards them. Surely she wouldn't be doing anything in the marital bed they shared? Whatever she was, Heidi was not a heartless woman. He paused in the doorway, half afraid to peer in. He took a deep breath, then entered the room. At first there was no sign of anyone but the sliding mirrored door to the walk-in wardrobe was open and there she was, his Heidi, standing before him, holding up the dress he'd bought her for Christmas. Campbell, for whatever reason, had opted to wear Baron Hard-Up's frock coat for the occasion. He'd thought it odd when he'd arrived an hour earlier but Heidi had squealed and told him he looked fantastic. Campbell was running his fingers along the dress as Heidi held it against herself.

'What's going on?' Jez said, trying to sound reasonable.

'Hiya, darling,' exclaimed Heidi brightly, as if it was the most ordinary thing in the world to entertain another man in her bedroom, 'I'm just showing Campbell my lovely dress.'

She pulled her husband towards her and kissed him.

Campbell let go of the sleeve and looked at them both uncomfortably.

'I'll erm... I'll go down and... mix a drink,' he said lamely.

'You do that,' glowered Jez.

Campbell closed the door quietly behind him. Jez gazed down at his wife's perfect form. All he had to do was ask the question. 'Are you having an affair?' Simple as that. Five words. And then he'd know. Well, unless she lied. But the more he looked at her, the more beautiful she seemed, the more innocent. And his anger evaporated. He didn't have the heart to do it. Instead he said, 'Why's he wearing that stupid coat? It looks like a dress.'

Heidi laughed. 'He just likes it.'

'Idiot.'

Heidi laid the dress on the bed, still smiling.

'I love my dress,' she said. 'I like *all* my presents.'

'I'm glad.'

She nuzzled Jez's neck and stroked his beard.

'Well, I'd better get back to our guests...'

'Not yet, eh?'

Clinging on to him, Heidi allowed herself to fall back onto the bed, dragging her husband with her. Jez put his hands out to steady himself and found Heidi shifting around under him. Tugging fingers groped for his belt, before moving nimbly and expertly upwards and unbuttoned his Rudolph the Red Nosed Reindeer Christmas waist coat. He knew what this was all about. Diversion tactics. He felt her guiding pressure, pushing him sideways and down and then she was on top of him, pulling off his tie. He yanked at her top, causing her to let go of him, briefly. Then, pushing back the hair from her eyes, Heidi took charge again and the disrobing continued, frantic and more desperate now. With his wife firmly in the driving seat, Jez followed the diversion and rather enjoyed where the bumpy journey was taking him.

Downstairs, Carina was stabbing at her mobile phone with a scarlet talon.

'This is the second message I've left,' she fumed. 'What the hell are you doing, Jackie? Ring me!'

Ben's voice cut in from behind her.

'Can't the slave have Christmas off?'

Carina, tempted to throw her phone at his thick head, aimed it at the interior of her handbag instead.

'Why don't you go away and do some sit-ups, love,' she said. 'Your love-handles are showing.' Ben sneered at her but checked his waist nevertheless.

'And just for the record, her husband abandoned her,' Carina bridled. 'I'm keeping her occupied.'

The door opened and Lauren entered. She went over to Carina, silently and laid her head, rather pathetically on The Star's chest. Now what? thought Carina.

'Something wonderful's happened,' Lauren said in a little voice. 'I've got the part in *Winkle Bay*!'

Carina's body stiffened.

'What part?'

'Daisy Smart!' gushed Lauren. 'I only auditioned yesterday. Isn't that amazing! I can't believe it.'

Carina wrapped her arms tightly around Lauren. Was their no justice in this world? She'd been fighting to get back onto the show, risking everything, giving her all. And this little non-entity with no discernible talent just walks into a role. She hated the girl. Always had done. She despised her youth, her natural beauty, everything!

'I can't breathe!' gasped Lauren.

Carina realised she was crushing her like a python crushes a rat, in a tight embrace. She relaxed.

'I'm so pleased for you,' she said, smiling. 'So, so pleased. How long's your contract?'

'Six months!'

Carina's smile began to disintegrate, but she rallied.

'Six months? Fantastic. You're going to love it.'

'Isn't Rufus Frenkel a lovely man?'

Carina determined to extricate herself from the Christmas festivities as soon as she could.

* * *

Pauline Clifton stood on the edge of the precipice, looking down on the crashing waves below. Further to her right, through the driving rain she could make out the dark, rocky outline of St. Mary's island. A short causeway, exposed to the elements now that the tide was out led to the tall monolith of St. Mary's lighthouse, her whitewashed form made all the brighter by grey, heavy skies. Clifton thought of Dougie Hunt and how he must have stood in this very spot a few nights earlier, looking out into the pitch blackness, depressed and alone. She wondered if a friendly light atop the lighthouse's glassy crown, a fleeting beam of warmth across the ocean, might have made him pause, change his mind and turn away from the edge. Sometimes, all it took was a glimpse of something bright, a shiny object to remind us that the world was not all bleak and dark. Clifton pushed her hands further into her pockets to protect her gloveless fingers from the cold and put away sensitive thoughts. The lighthouse's lamp had long since dimmed. Obsolete, remote, the redundant tower stood in isolation, a reminder to all of the perfidy of progress. Of one thing, when Dougie died, Clifton was sure: there were no beams of light across the sea to warm his heart and dispel his demons. Only darkness and the singing wires. Dougie would not even have known that the lighthouse monolith existed. Suicide. It seemed the most likely scenario. The man had been on anti-depressants for years. Recent events probably tipped him over the edge. Quite literally. The report had shown no scuffle, no suspicious disturbance around the cliff top. Was it really as simple as that? Sadly, yes. Experience had made her aware that suicide rarely lived up to the melodramatic representations she'd witnessed on TV in soaps and dramas - people arranging their deaths so earnestly, with letters and messages, eloquence and tears. Most people just did it. Hurled themselves into oblivion. Matter of fact. Over and out. And that's what Dougie must have done. And yet...

Why were they here? On Christmas Day of all days. The Boss must be suspicious of something. She looked over at Newall, talking into his mobile, pacing backwards and forwards, smiling. Smiling! Such a rare event! Who was he talking to? Carina? No. He was too professional to allow personal feelings to get in the way of an investigation. Clifton tried to eavesdrop but the eerie singing of the

216

nearby aerial wires drowned out his words. She saw him finish the call and pocket his mobile. Instead of returning to her, he stood, unmoving, looking along the cliff top, away from the lighthouse.

'Everything all right?' she asked.

Newall nodded.

'Family?'

'Friends.'

He did not elaborate. Clifton was curious. She wasn't aware Newall had any friends. He never talked about them. He was a loner. Always at home with a takeaway and the football on TV. She realised he was still staring into the distance.

'What is it?'

Newall pointed.

'There's a caravan site.'

'Yeah?' Clifton wasn't sure where this was going. Newall sniffed and folded his arms.

'The last time we were there, it was foggy,' he said.

Realisation dawned.

'That's the place where Carina's ex lives?

'It's within walking distance. Shall we?'

They headed off along the cliff top path, a fifteen minute walk, most of it in silence.

'You think Miller might have something to do with Dougie's death?' Clifton asked as the caravan site loomed ahead of them.

'Could be a coincidence,' he replied. 'I don't like coincidence's.'

Clifton thought about it. 'Lauren told Dougie about this place. Gave him directions. Was she in on it too?'

Newall was candid. 'I don't know. Possibly. No. Unlikely. *In* on what?'

Clifton couldn't say. A moment ago she was convinced Dougie

had topped himself. Now she couldn't be sure.

They followed the path along the caravan park's perimeter fence, away from the cliff and back onto the main road. The high metal gates weren't locked. Newall and Clifton strolled past the empty reception cabin and disappeared into the maze of white trailers.

Clifton knocked officiously on Paul Miller's door. And rapped again. Newall stood on tiptoe and peered through one of the dirty windows.

'No signs of life.'

'Can I help you?'

An old man, in an ill-fitting great coat, his neck buried in a thick scarf was walking towards them, with a small Jack Russell on a lead. Newall offered his I.D. The man took it, scrutinized it. Newall was about to explain but the old boy held up a warning hand and indicated for Clifton to show her I.D. too.

'Can't be too careful,' he said, returning the wallets.

'Five hundred abodes, all empty. It's asking for trouble.'

'We're looking for Paul Miller.'

The man bent down and addressed his dog.

'They've just missed him, haven't they!'

Newall and Clifton shared a look. 'Have we?'

'They have,' replied the pensioner, still talking to the dog. 'Think he's got a new girlfriend. She picked him up, took him away for Christmas dinner.'

He straightened up with difficulty and indicated the dog. 'Pod thought she was a bit of a hound.'

Clifton surveyed the dog and thought that Pod had a nerve. He was no oil painting himself.

'He always asks me to look after the place when he goes away,' continued the old man. 'Back tomorrow.'

218

Newall felt sorry for him. 'Bit lonely for you, isn't it? Wouldn't you prefer to be with your family on Christmas Day.'

'To tell you the truth, I would. But the fact is, they don't want me there. Happy Christmas.'

Before the detectives could interject with sympathetic protestations of denial, the old man and his dog were wandering off through the avenue of trailers.

In the car on the way back to Newcastle, Clifton said, 'I've got an awful feeling that I'll end up like that fella when I grow old. On my own. With a dog.'

'Nah,' replied Newall, sparking up a cigarette. 'You'll be enfolded in the bosom of your family. Worshipped and adored.'

Fat chance! What family, thought Clifton?! Here she was, working the Christmas shift, with no boyfriend, no possibility of one right now. The one man she really liked was at least twenty five years older than she was, and didn't even see her as a woman.

'You fancy going for a drink?' she asked, grabbing the bull by the horns. Newall's eyes remained focused on the road ahead.

'When?'

'Well... Now?' she was beginning to lose her bravado.

'Can't,' came the reply. 'Meeting friends.'

Clifton made a quick dismissive gesture as if it didn't matter. She could feel the tears pricking. What had she expected? An offer of undying love and affection? A proposal of marriage? Yes. It was *Christmas* after all. They drove in silence for the rest of the journey.

* * *

Newall parked his car outside The Valmont and hurried into the hotel. He'd showered and changed in a rush since finishing work but had forgotten to comb his hair. He caught his reflection in the foyer mirror and did a quick tidy job. He hadn't been able to stop himself thinking about Carina all day.

He went straight up to her room without stopping to announce his arrival at reception. Sometimes anonymity was the best policy.

Carina was at the door within a few seconds of his knock. She planted a chaste kiss on his cheek, her lips lightly brushing his stubble. Newall felt his skin tingling against their sensitive embrace, tried to kiss her full on the mouth but she was backing away, guiding him into the room. Later. He had high hopes.

'I always feel sorry for anyone having to work on Christmas Day,' Carina said, offering him a seat on the sofa.

'You get used to it.'

'Well, at least I'm here to look after you now.'

She kissed him tenderly slowly at first, then with more passion. Newall cupped her face in his hands. Her smell, her taste, her feel, he wanted to drag her into bed, drown himself in her. Carina, stroking his right arm as she kissed him, moved her hand around to touch his waist and as she did so, brushed lightly against his groin. It was the slightest of touches but she knew the effect it would have. Before long Newall was on top of her on the sofa. Carina knew exactly what she was doing and she played her part well. She licked his ear, sucked his lobes, used her tongue to good effect, teased him but hung back from full sex. No, she would have to be careful about this one. Didn't want to risk anything, scare him off.

It was only when Newall started pulling at her tights that she remembered her vow of chastity. Sex at this early stage was a bad idea. Carina had to lead him on a bit more, if this one was going to fall in love with her. She just knew instinctively he was the 'married-for-life' sort, a shag so soon after their first date was a no-no. A police officer on her side was a good thing. A police officer on her side who also happened to be mad about her, was even better. One just never knew what was around the corner. He could come in very handy. String him along, girl, she said to herself. Keep him keen!

'I know you want to make love to me, Roy...' she said and felt Roy's ecstatic trouser truncheon thwack against her thigh.

'I do, Carina,' he gasped. Newall's face had turned an unhealthy livid red. He felt as if he was about to burst.

'... But I can't yet...' Carina hesitated. She actually wouldn't have minded indulging in a good old session right this minute. He was overweight but he seemed to know what he was doing. Or was it because she was so used to Gordon's wham-bam three second tremblers? Decent foreplay made a nice change. What possible excuse could she give?

'It's Dougie. And Fluff,' she said lamely.

'Sorry?'

'And we've only just met. It's too soon.' Christ, Carina thought, I haven't said that since I was fourteen.

'Is it?'

'I really like you a lot.'

Ever the gentleman, Newall, took her hand and sat her upright on the leather sofa.

'I really like you too,' he said. 'But it's okay. Plenty of time.'

They sat there, holding hands, side by side. Newall ached to make love to her. Her nervousness, her thoughts for others turned him on even more. She was amazing. Gentle, warm. Underneath all the war paint, she was a delicate thing. Like porcelain. Only nobody knew it. Only him. If she wanted to grieve a bit longer

221

for lost pets and colleagues, that was fine by him. He felt guilty for being so insensitive. It also struck him that caution may have been at play here. She'd had her fingers burnt by the morons she'd married over the years. She must be wary when it came to choosing a new partner and who could blame her?

'Did your ex-husband Paul Miller know Dougie?' he asked.

He kissed her neck, ran his tongue down the muscle at the side, then blew on it, and nibbled gently as she replied.

'I don't know. I don't think so...' she paused, finding words difficult. She was enjoying Newall's attentions. 'Not really sure though,' she managed to add. 'Why?'

'Just curious. Miller's caravan park is a few feet away from the cliff where Dougie jumped.'

His mouth wondered back to her neck. Carina was *really* enjoying herself now. Physical pleasure combined with the thoughts of revenge whirled around in her head.

'You think... Paul... might have pushed Dougie over the cliff?' she gasped.

'Can't say that,' said Newall, pausing to wipe his lips. 'But if they knew each other...'

'I always thought Paul might be a bit of a bi-guy,' she said mischievously. 'The fake tan, the poodle, dyed hair. He saw Mamma Mia eight times when we were together...'

'He's got a new girlfriend apparently.'

Carina wasn't listening to him anymore. Whatever Newall was doing to her, she liked it. An exquisite glow of pleasure began to spread through her body. Two things had happened to her, almost simultaneously and both of them had taken her by surprise. First, the over-riding desire for sex. The hunger was driving her wild. And secondly... she had stumbled across a possible means of reducing alimony payments to a money-grabbing ex-husband. What perfect Christmas presents! Carina decided then and there that she'd had enough of playing the blushing virgin.

'Roy, love, have you got a condom?' she asked.

Chapter Twenty Two

In the hectic period between Christmas and New Year, when much of the UK's population indulged in its favourite past-times of picking up bargains in the sales and partying hard, it was business as usual for Carina at 'The Old Tyne Theatre'. The doors re-opened on Boxing Day and the pantomime whirlwind re-commenced. Thanks to healthy box office receipts and a bombardment of requests for more tickets, Jez had taken up Carina's suggestion and the decision to extend the run by three more weeks. The final curtain would not descend until the end of February, making it the longest running panto season Newcastle had seen for many years.

Carina's efforts to re-invigorate her career seemed to be paying off at last, if not quite in the way she'd anticipated. Three extra weeks work were not to be sniffed at, as she desperately needed the money. She'd started off the year, as she had the previous five years since her ignominious axing, with a paucity of professional bookings. Take last year, the occasional charity event here, the odd Agatha Christie theatre who-dunn-it there, interspersed with appearances at '*Winkle Bay* Appreciation Society' get-togethers up and down the country. Twelve months down the line, the future looked decidedly rosier. The day after Boxing Day, her mobile started ringing with offers of work. TV work, at that! A trickle at first - she'd caught executives on the hop, thanks to the holiday hiatus - the requests for her services had turned into a great tidal wave of interest. She was in-demand again. Just like the old days.

Almost. But not quite. The TV work was of the reality show variety. 'Celebrity' this, 'Celebrity' that. Did she really want to spend a month with a bunch of whingeing no-hopers in a house full of cameras, or have a sweary chef teach her how to make potato gnocci for snooty non-entities in a steamy kitchen? No. The coverage might do her some good in the short term but in the long term, could only damage her reputation. She was an actress and as such had to maintain an allure of mystery. She must hold out for a better offer. Jackie, if she bothered to show her face again (the woman had been incommunicado for the past three days), could fend off the reality show people, keep them at arms length, leaving her agent, Abigail, to deal with the genuine acting offers if and when they came. And they would. She was sure of that. It was only a matter of time. She'd invested too much, gone too far for her renaissance not to happen. As for the one role which she was holding out for above all others, the one she'd already possessed and lost, that too, would be hers for the taking before long. The only obstacle in her path was about to meet with a fatal accident, if Gordon would only pull his finger out and get on with the deed. In the mean time Carina continued to turn up at the theatre, kept the crowds entertained, the journalists happy with witty, bitchy quotes. And in private, after the show in the sumptuous setting of her hotel suite, she played another great role with aplomb: that of adoring paramour to a love-sick copper.

* * *

Across town Rufus Frenkel sat in his office staring despondently at the overnight viewing figures for the *Winkle Bay* Christmas episodes he'd put so much faith in. They were dismal. He'd been hoping for a marked improvement on the previous weeks viewing statistics. If they'd shown an improvement, then they signaled hope for him. He could have used them as a bargaining tool to prevent Mick Flynt from getting his own way, to curb the most ridiculous plot excesses the man was planning for the show. He could have turned to his boss, Carl and said 'See, I *do* know what I'm talking about. Trust me.' But it was not to be. The evidence contradicted him.

In a tiny, private corner of his mind, he conceded that Flynt might be right. Maybe the show did need a new start. Fresh blood. All the stories he'd tried of late had failed to catch the imagination of the public. And the critics. The country had finally tired of *Winkle Bay*. Hell, even The Mid-Afternoon News Bulletin managed to pull in a bigger audience! Rufus sighed. Everything in life had a shelf-life, he supposed. And a TV show was no different. Why had the sell by date expired during *his* tenure at the helm, he thought petulantly? He didn't deserve this. It wasn't fair. Rufus, a stranger to self-doubt, quickly exchanged introspection for blame. Blame was good. Less painful than having to deal with failure, so he deluded himself, massaged his ego, with the well known mantra chanted by despotic soap executives everywhere whose arrogant programme-tinkering skills sent a good show down the toilet: 'across the board, viewing trends for terrestrial TV were shifting. Figures were going down, whereas satellite viewing figures were going up.' Simple! Fact! As soon as he thought it, he felt better. None of this was his fault. The calamity befalling *Winkle Bay* was symptomatic of a trend.

At this point he made his mind up to look for another job.

Diminishing audiences - that was the future for television. There was no stopping it now. Mick Flynt might be capable of hitting the viewers of *Winkle Bay* with a staggering and explosive story (and there was no getting away from it, the story was dynamite - the biggest, most contentious subject ever tackled by a soap) over a few weeks, bumping up the viewing figures in the process, but could his experience and his story-telling skills maintain those figures? No, they couldn't. Television was in an irreversible, downward spiral. Rufus would stay until the story hit the screen and then he would walk away. He was in a win-win situation. If the story worked, then he could admit to playing his part in it, even though Flynt was calling the shots. And if it was a complete turkey, everyone would know it was Flynt's idea anyway. As far as he could see, the only person taking a gamble, (other than A1 TV who were investing an extra £1.5 million on top of the existing budget for the ten episode 'special event') was Mick Flynt himself. The pressure on him to pull it off must be overwhelming. Not that the man himself looked nervous. Quite the opposite. His confidence seemed unshakeable. Only yesterday, after Rufus had cancelled all leave and called in the story-lining and production teams for an emergency meeting, Flynt, turning up late, and facing a hostile audience, impressed the staff with his mammoth vision for the show. He charmed them, convinced them that *Winkle Bay's* loyal, core audience would accept the new direction in which the series was heading and managed to get the team behind it - even though the ditching of existing scripts, re-writing of storylines and sheer logistical upheaval involved meant long days and sleepless nights for most of them. Rufus, no slouch himself when it came to the keen art of persuasion, marvelled at Flynt's skills, the effortlessness in which he wrapped them all around his little finger, steamrollering the opposition. And that's what had impressed Rufus particularly - the way he defeated argument - by talking over it, grinding it down. The story was clear in his mind from the start. All the details, the twists and turns, the nuances, they were all worked out.

Sometimes, during his more excessive creative moods at story conference, Rufus would think twice about progressing with a story when writers and storyliners voiced their concern. Not Flynt. Any criticism - and Rufus had not balked at telling Flynt what he thought of the plan in the beginning - he shrugged off, as if it didn't matter. How could he be so sure the story would work? He was experienced at the game, that was without question - his company, apart from its publishing interests ran two successful soaps, '*Lust!*', an afternoon daily soap aimed at teens and '*Late Nite Lust!*', a post- watershed version of '*Lust!*', with a more adult content. Both aired on a minority satellite station and garnered respectable viewing figures. From the few episodes he'd seen, Rufus, considered the stories and the style of story-telling, naïve and predictable. But Flynt had earned respect in the business, through a combination of two things: longevity - he'd worked in television for a number of years, and self-publicity- keep telling everyone you're great and eventually they'll start believing it. Once again, Rufus's thoughts came back to why Mick Flynt was prepared to take on such a gamble with *Winkle Bay's* regeneration. Why risk your reputation when you didn't have to? The man was a multi-millionaire and respected enough by most of his peers. It didn't make sense. To risk one's career when the outcome - a brief boost to the viewing figures followed by an inevitable decline, was an act of sheer lunacy.

Rufus sat upright, the germ of a suspicion forming in his mind. Mick Flynt *wanted* the episodes to fail. Of course! Flynt was the man in the 'win-win' situation. It was simple. And brilliant. Accept the offer from a rival TV company, sweep in as the saviour of their ailing soap opera, concoct a sensational, if rather tasteless storyline and when it fails, claim that the show's slide towards oblivion was inescapable but hey, he'd given it his best shot. "Oh, and by the way, here's a soap I developed earlier, to fill the slot."

Rufus felt better already. He would bide his time, carry out his commitments as best he could and abandon the sinking ship when the time was right. He swept the viewing figures off his desk, tossed them in the bin and checked his watch. He had a job to do today, the first 'request' Flynt had made of him. He had refused at first, feeling it went against everything he stood for and made him look spineless and impotent, certainly in one particular person's eyes, but after outlining the long-term game plan, Flynt had managed to get Frenkel on side. Rufus, shocked at first by the devious, if not illegal nature of the scheme, saw a chance for revenge. In the short term he realised he would have to swallow his pride and tolerate a large dose of humiliation but it would be worth it. The next few hours would test his mettle to the limit and required a great deal of skill. Right now, the success of Flynt's plans depended on him. Rufus knew he was up to the challenge.

Gordon, sitting on his moped outside the main entrance to the *Winkle Bay* Production Centre, flapped his arms to keep warm. *His* challenge - to rid the world of Rufus Whatsit, was proving extremely difficult to achieve. For a start, he had no information about the man. He didn't know where he lived, what his interests were. Cora hadn't said anything at all about him. He'd followed him from the television studios once or twice and lost him pretty quickly. The speed the spikey-haired fella travelled at in his bright red sports car was disgraceful. As soon as he turned out of the studios and joined the dual carriageway, he would put his foot down and roar off, leaving Gordon's Vespa lagging far behind.

For the third day on the trot, Gordon sat outside the studios, cursing Rufus out loud, to himself. He was really starting to hate him. Really, really hate him. He'd already hated him slightly - for sending Cora off to the mental hospital but now, with frustration setting in, Gordon was not a happy man. Cora wasn't very happy either - she kept ringing him to find out whether he'd done the deed or not. She'd actually shouted at him the last time, called him a 'bloody cretin', whatever that was. Nothing good, he knew that much. He didn't like it when Cora shouted at him. It made him go all cold inside. His heart hurt and he wanted to cry. He produced a handkerchief from his pocket, blew his nose, looked at the snot before folding it away again, then sighed loudly. He would wait out here all day if he had to, to get Specky-Spikey Man. For Cora. Then Cora would be happy again. And so would he. Maybe she would come to his house like she'd promised, months ago. Her presents were still under the tree, waiting to be opened. His mother was dying to meet his fiancée too. He'd even kept some Christmas cake for her.

His mobile phone vibrated in his pocket.

'Hello?'

'Have you done it?'

'Hello, Cora, my lovely darlin'.'

'Is he dead?'

'Not yet...'

'Why the hell not? What's the matter with you?'

'I'm going to do it today, I promise Cora. I'll do it today. I will.'

'You'd better, Gordon. Don't let me down.'

Gordon, said nothing. He heard the anger in her voice and the tears started to flow again. It wasn't nice when people you loved, shouted at you. He sniffed and cleared his throat.

'Co-ra?' he asked, in a pathetic, simpering voice.

'What?!'

'When he's gone will you come round to mine for some Christmas cake and sex?... Cora?'

But 'Cora' had ended the call. Gordon's mouth turned downwards and his bottom lip began to tremble with emotion. She *was* really angry with him. And it was all Specky man's fault. Well, he was for it, now. Gordon dried his eyes, gripped the handles of his moped and wheeled it into the middle of the road by the entrance. The high security gates were closed, preventing unauthorized admission, but that wasn't going to deter Gordon. He would sit here, blocking the entrance until Spikey came out and as soon as he did, he would kill him and Cora would come over to his house and everything would be fine again. Except... how was he going to kill him? Strangle him? Bash him with his crash helmet? That might work. Yeah. A good crack over the head always did the trick. Gordon saw the CCTV cameras around the building. He might have to wait until Specky-Spikey-man's car was around the corner, out of sight of the main gateway, before killing him. Risky. The red sports car always zoomed off as soon as its driver passed through the gates. Dejected, he wheeled his moped back onto the pavement and paced around, muttering to himself. His head hurt. He wanted to cry again.

Gordon was still talking to himself, five minutes later when the electric gates began to swing open. The sound of a revving engine, made him turn. It was him! Rufus Thing. In his sports car, with the roof down - about to rocket off somewhere. He was going to escape again. Without thinking, he ran into the road and threw himself in front of the car, before Rufus could put his foot down.

'Could you get out of the way please?' Rufus asked politely. Mad fan, he thought to himself.

Gordon worked his way around to the driver's side.

'Are you Mr. Rufus?' he asked.

Rufus shivered at the high, slightly lispy, reedy voice. The man sounded like a Geordie Truman Capote. Which might have been amusing if the odd, podgy creature wasn't giving him the creeps.

'Yes.'

'Could I have your autograph, please?' Gordon leered over the driver's window.

'I'm afraid I'm in a hurry, mate,' replied Rufus. 'But if you ring the production office, I'm sure they can send some autographed photos of the cast.'

'No.'

'No?'

Rufus's hand paused on the gear stick. He looked up at the stranger, bewildered. The weirdo had taken off his crash helmet and was opening the driver's side door!

'What do you think you're doing?'

Gordon smiled nastily.

'I'm getting married.'

'That's nice,' said Rufus, humouring him.

'Yes. Me and Cora.'

'Cora...?'

'Smart'.

'Right.' Rufus edged back in his seat and kept his eye on the nutter's right hand, the one wielding the crash helmet. Gordon, preparing to bludgeon Rufus to death, swung the helmet back in an arc and was about to deliver the blow, when a strange thing happened. Out of nowhere, it seemed, a pack of journalists and photographers were tearing towards them. In an instant, they had surrounded Rufus's car and were braying and shouting like wounded animals. They pushed Gordon aside rudely, clicking cameras and wielding microphones like weapons.

'Is it true you're killing off half the cast in a shipping disaster?'

'Mick Flynt - is he running the show now?'

'Is *Winkle Bay* going to be axed?'

Gordon's jaw went slack. 'Axed?!'

Rufus tried to keep his cool. So the news was out. Someone had leaked the story to the Press. Mr Self-Publicist himself, Mick Flynt, no doubt. Ah well, it was bound to happen sooner or later. Only trouble was, the actors hadn't been told yet. Slightly embarrassing. He'd have to ring them all later today.

The staccato questioning continued.

'Are you answerable to Mick Flynt now?'

'Are you about to be sacked?'

'Which actors are going?'

'If you'd care to contact the A1 TV press office, you'll get all the details you need...' he yelled, above the hubbub. Keeping his composure he said, 'Any suggestions that *Winkle Bay*, or any of our characters are about to be axed, are spurious. Thank you.'

Rufus pumped the accelerator and the car nosed its way through the crowd. Gordon fumbled for his crash helmet, pulled it on in a hurry, jumped on his Vespa and set off after the departing producer. Luckily, Rufus was heading into busy traffic and therefore unable to break the sound barrier.

Gordon's heart was racing. *Winkle Bay* axed? Characters sacked? It couldn't be true. And what did 'spurious' mean? Is that why Cora wanted her old boss dead? Because he was going to end the show? No wonder she was angry with him for not finishing him off sooner. He could see the red car, up-ahead, stuck in the stream of traffic heading into the city centre. Shoppers, he supposed. Off to spend their Christmas money in the sales. Must be nice, getting lots of money. Money and presents. He couldn't remember the last time he'd been given a present. Years ago. When Mother could get out and about. He thought Cora might have given him a present this year. Now that they were engaged. There was time yet. She might buy something in the sales for him. As long as she didn't steal anything. That was wrong. Cora had started shoplifting before she was carted off in a van to the psychiatric hospital. He hoped she wouldn't start again. She might get into trouble. His thoughts, forever jumbling fact with fiction, turned to *Winkle Bay's* possible demise again. What would they all do without their favourite programme? He didn't have any answers.

Further ahead, the red sports car ducked and dived through busy lanes of traffic. Gordon kept his distance and didn't lose his quarry this time around. Rufus, pre-occupied with the difficult task that lay ahead, barely glanced in his rear view mirror. Porsche and Vespa, as if connected by an invisible cord, weaved their way through central Newcastle and out towards the west of the city.

Eventually, Rufus's car pulled into a metered space. Gordon, from his vantage point, saw the hood rise up from the back and secure itself to the windscreen frame. Rufus jumped out, shoved some coins into the nearby machine, slapped the ticket onto the driver's window and hurried off. Gordon sighed and set off on foot after him. With any luck he might be able to overtake Spikey, drag him into an alleyway and strangle him. Or bash him with a brick. The area was familiar to Gordon. He knew of an alleyway nearby. Down the side of the theatre! Cora's theatre! There, across the road! Gordon stopped. Rufus had dodged past stationary traffic, crossed over and was standing on the pavement in front of 'The Old Tyne Theatre', staring up at the giant picture of Cora above the entrance. What was he doing there? What did he want? Gordon felt frightened. Something weird was going on and he didn't like it. He watched Rufus walk confidently up to the main doors and disappear inside the building.

Chapter Twenty Three

Cast and crew were preparing for the first show of the day. There was an easiness to the behind-the-scenes regime now. Hysteria and panic were things of the past. The production had settled into a routine at last - there were no more last minute re-writes and the re-cast Baron Hard-Up, Campbell Garibaldi, was settling into his role nicely. Dougie's funeral had taken place down south somewhere, in private - family only, a memorial service was planned for later in the year - during the summer - when the weather would be warmer, more cheerful. It was days, rather than weeks since his demise, yet already it was if he'd never been there.

Campbell, occupying Dougie's old dressing room, sat in his underpants, slowly and meticulously applying stage make-up to his face. Unlike Dougie who played the Baron as a hirsute and bumptious dolt, (except for the one and only unfortunate occasion when he'd played him like a drag queen from La Cage Aux Folles), Campbell brought out the Baron's more sophisticated, feline-side. In looks, with his powdered wig, heavy white foundation, painted eye-brows, rouged cheeks and cherry cherubic lips, he resembled a foppish figure from the Restoration Period. He was almost unrecognizable as the timid, reticent director. And Campbell liked it that way.

He leaned back to appreciate his mask and noticed Heidi watching him from the open doorway. Campbell thought she looked astonishing in her red silk dress and matching Jimmy Choos.

'You look amazing,' he said.

'So do you.'

She came into the room and peered intently into the mirror, scrutinising his make-up closely in the glare of the bright bulbs which framed it.

She picked up the scarlet lipstick. 'Can I?'

Campbell nodded and Heidi went to work on his unfinished mouth like an artist.

'Heidi?!'

Campbell and Heidi continued staring ahead at the reflection of an indignant looking Jez in the mirror. Campbell could see the grey starting to appear in the beard and hair. It looked a mess. How dare he even show his face in public with a beautiful woman like Heidi on his arm. It was an insult.

'Hello, darlin',' she said, matter of factly. 'I was just on my way up to see you.'

There was anger in his voice when Jez replied. 'What are you doing?'

'Helping Cambie with his make-up.'

'He's in his underpants.'

'Is he?' Heidi looked down and laughed. 'Oh, Jez. Actors are always hanging around in their underwear. Don't be such a prude.'

Jez turned around and stormed off.

Heidi called after him. 'Jez!' She shook her head in amusement.

'Better go. See you later.' She blew a kiss and hurried out after her husband. Campbell frowned and picked up the lipstick. The smell of cigarette smoke alerted him to Carina's presence. She was leaning against the door jamb watching him, a smile on her lips.

'You're a dark horse, aren't you,' she said eventually.

Campbell shifted uncomfortably in his chair. 'I don't know what you mean.'

Carina tutted teasingly. 'Shame on you, my pretty! Leave the boss's wife alone.'

She moved off, amused by his startled face and didn't hear his reply because she was laughing so much. The laughter left her when she glanced through the open door of Lauren and Sylvie's dressing room. The place was overflowing with flowers - on the dressing table, windowsill, sofa. There was no sign of Lauren but Sylvie was there, in costume, about to swig from a water bottle.

'What's all this?' she snapped.

'They're Lauren's,' breathed Sylvie. 'Aren't they just divine?'

'Is it her birthday? Or has somebody died? Again?'

Sylvie rolled her eyes melodramatically. 'They're from friends and loved ones - wishing her all good fortune when she joins the cast of *Winkle Bay*.'

Carina tried to keep the sarcasm from her voice but it proved difficult.

'How sweet.'

'Yes. Isn't it,' slurred Sylvie, suddenly misty-eyed. 'It's all so fleeting, though, don't you find?' she inquired. 'Don't you find, darling? One minute you're at the start of your career, presented with flowers and gifts and lauded as the Next Best Thing, the next you're on your own with just a few memories and some...'

She paused, struggling to find the right word.

'... Gin?' suggested Carina.

Sylvie contemplated a deliciously arch retort, something stinging, but the possibility of a volley of bitchy words lost its attraction when it dawned on her suddenly that Carina's quip wasn't catty at all. It was absolutely on the nose. She nodded sadly.

'... and flat tonic,' she said, with feeling.

'Where is she?'

'Gone for a walk with Prince Charming.' Sylvie picked up a lily and sniffed its sculptured funnel. She scrutinized it wistfully before continuing. 'Somebody should tell her - prince's don't stay charming for very long. Once you've provided them with off-spring, and set up a home, put your career on hold, given them your *best years*, Prince Charming turns into Prince Bastard! He ups and deserts you. Abandons you! In the cold, empty pit of...'

'Oh, get a bloody grip, woman!'

Carina, in no mood to put up with Sylvie's self-piteous ramblings, backed out of the room. Whingeing, whining thesps like Sylvie who moaned about their lot in life gave middle aged women a bad name. It was about time she realised, if you wanted anything in this world, you had to go out and take it, plot your own destiny, take charge of it and rely on nobody except yourself. That's what she'd learned over the years, and that's what she was doing right now - shaping her own future.

She returned to her own dressing room in such an intense, self-congratulatory, backslapping frame of mind that she scarcely noticed the timid figure sitting on the sofa, facing her dressing table.

'So, you've turned up at last.'

Carina's low key, subdued tone, intimating deep hurt and disappointment had the desired effect. Jackie only just managed to stop herself from bursting into tears.

'I'm sorry, Carina, I'm so sorry. Christmas was just so hectic, I don't know where the time went.'

'So hectic you couldn't answer your phone?'

'My battery…' Jackie started to say, then realised the excuse was such a flimsy one, it should be discarded immediately. She reached for her handkerchief and the rest of the sentence vanished in a snort of mucus.

'I was having such a lovely time,' she said, when her nasal passages were clear. 'With the children and…'

Again she paused, unsure this time how to phrase the next few words. There was so much she wanted to say. Important things and it was crucial she said them properly, diplomatically. She'd stayed away from Carina for the past couple of days because she was afraid of what Carina might do or say when she became acquainted with certain recent events in her life. Jackie couldn't see her and not tell her, that wouldn't be fair. Or right. Looking at the dark caterpillar eyebrows, raised in their usual angry, questioning way, she could feel her cheeks burning. Where should she start? *How* could she start? It was all so embarrassing. But at the same time, rather unexpected and lovely. She found herself actually wanting to let Carina in on the good news.

'Hang on!' Carina was saying, 'Stand over there so I can see you properly.'

Jackie dragged her heels meekly to the centre of the room and stood under the fluorescent light strip.

'Did you bugger off to The Maldives over Christmas?'

Jackie tried and failed to stifle a hysterical giggle.

'Of course not,' she coughed and cleared her throat.

'It's just make-up,' she added, hurriedly. 'Foundation. Thought I'd try something different.'

Jackie decided against revealing all to Carina. Rightly or wrongly, now wasn't a good time. Tomorrow would be better. Or the day after. Or better still, sometime next month.

Carina scrutinized her sharply. 'New look, taking care of your appearance, has something happened?'

'Like what?' asked Jackie, deeply conscious of the beads of perspiration forming on her top lip.

'That husband of yours turned up at last, has he?' she inquired, unable to hide her sarcasm.

Jackie shook her head calmly. 'No.'

For the first time in goodness knows how long, she didn't twitch or dissolve into hysterical tears at the mention of Alan. She was over him at last. She wasn't waiting for him any more. The sense of relief she felt was wonderful. It was as if a heavy, painful load had been lifted off her chest. Jackie wanted to laugh but she kept herself in check. She hoped Carina hadn't noticed anything unusual in her response. Carina, as ever, more concerned by her own thoughts and needs, was flicking through a note book.

'You've no idea what it's been like for me over the past few days,' she moaned. 'You really let me down.' Carina pointed her cigarette holder at her and effected a mock look of hurt and pain. 'I've been hounded by the Press, TV companies. Reporters. Nightmare time. Been offered all sorts of shit reality shows, which I'm not interested in. But now you're back,' she paused and sucked deeply through her cigarette holder. 'Now you're back, I want you to get onto these people - I've made a list, journo's mostly, looking for tit-bits. See what sort of money they're offering and what sort of stories they're after. Set up some interviews.'

She tossed the notebook at Jackie.

'I'll see what I can do,' Jackie said, without much enthusiasm.

There was a knock at the door.

'Come in,' said Carina in her grandest grand-dame voice.

'Hello Carina.'

Carina and Jackie stared in stupefied disbelief at the sight of Rufus in the door way.

'Bloody hell.'

Rufus slid his hands into his trouser pockets and moved casually into the room. He nodded courteously in Jackie's direction.

'How are you?' he asked pleasantly, as if greeting an old friend. Carina recovered quickly from her surprise and glared balefully at her former boss. Why was he here? What could he want? She hardly dared hope. She sucked hard on her cigarette holder, forgetting that the cigarette had long since died.

'What do you want?'

Rufus cleared his throat. Instinct told him to get out, to run and not stop until he was miles away but he wrestled with his nerves and conquered the desire to flee. Much depended on the outcome of this meeting - primarily, the future of *Winkle Bay* and his own career. The suspicious, dark eyes burning with hatred across the room would not be easily fooled. Yet he had to leave the building with this abominable woman's good will and support.

'Could we talk?' he asked.

'About what?'

Rufus glanced at Jackie.

'I'd rather we discussed this alone, if you don't mind.'

Carina's eyebrows shot up in surprise.

'If you don't *mind*?' she repeated, astonished by his obsequiousness. She turned to Jackie. 'Bugger off and make those calls.'

Jackie scurried out.

Carina rooted around her dressing table for a bottle of vodka amongst the many phials and jars of stage make-up. She unscrewed the cap and tossed it on the sofa.

'Vodka?'

Rufus nodded.

'Why not?' Alcohol was probably a bad idea but what the hell, he needed a drink.

Carina poured generous measures into two glasses.

'So?' she said, handing over a drink and clinking his glass. 'I'll ask again. What do you want?'

Rufus gulped down his vodka and set down the glass.

'No point in beating about the bush. I made a mistake.'

'Only one?'

'I'd like you to come back to *Winkle Bay*.'

It was Carina's turn to gulp down the vodka. Was she dreaming? Could this be really happening? Instinct told her to scream 'Yes!' and leap on the man. Her head told her not to be so stupid.

'What happened to "*over my dead body*"?'

Rufus lowered his head humbly. 'I was having a bad day. Year. I can only apologise for that. I'm so very sorry, Carina.'

He hoped he hadn't gone too far over the top - Carina, wily as she was, could spot insincerity a mile off. He peered up at her fleetingly but she was replenishing her glass and didn't seem to be listening. She approached him, bottle in hand. Rufus held out his tumbler for a refill. One more wouldn't make much difference.

'Why now? What's changed after all this time? Christmas episodes bombed again, did they?'

'No, not at all...' he started to say, then remembering his mission, bit back the retort. Changing tack, he said, 'They could have been better. And that's why I'm here. The network has insisted we make some changes.'

'Really?'

Rufus ignored Carina's unpleasant smirk.

'Yes. So we're clearing the decks, pulling stories and scripts. We've brought in Mick Flynt as a consultant and he's come up with a great story to get rid of all the old deadwood and re-launch the show in the spring. It's a big one. Everybody will be talking about it.'

'Mick Flynt, eh?' Carina studied the young producer closely. If he was upset at someone coming in and usurping his authority - and she knew that had to be the case if Mick Flynt was involved, he seemed pretty calm about it. 'He calling the shots now, is he? Are you his little puppet?' she inquired in a mock childish voice.

'Not at all, Carina. I'm very much in charge. As ever.' He took another glug of vodka and wished he hadn't. He could see his hand shaking as he lifted the glass to his lips. Carina matched him, swig for swig and reached for the bottle again.

Clinging onto as much of his dignity as he could, Rufus said, 'No thanks, I shouldn't.'

Carina ignored him.

'Well, well, well!' she scoffed. 'Rufus Frenkel wants me back.'

'Yes. I do definitely. You're central - *crucial*, to the whole story.'

'And what's that?'

'You uncover a terrorist plot being hatched at the Farne Island Psychiatric Hospital, to bomb *Winkle Bay* harbour.'

'I'm listening.'

Rufus smiled inwardly. He'd hooked her!

'Cora escapes from the Institution and manages to alert the authorities, although nobody believes her at first...'

'Because she's a loony!'

'Exactly! But when the first bomb goes off, they realise Cora's telling the truth. It's a great challenge for an actor. Lots of dramatic potential to explore.'

A whole raft of possible soap and TV awards swam before Carina's eyes - 'Best Performance During An Explosion', 'Best Emotional Scene'.

'What sort of contract are we looking at?'

'Well,' began Rufus. This was the delicate part. He had to handle her very carefully.

'... six episodes to begin with.'

Carina paused, mid-way through a slurp of vodka.

'Only six?!'

'To begin with - for the special eps. But the idea is we bring you back a few weeks later for a longer stint. Say a year?'

Carina mulled over the offer.

'Why bring my character back? What made you change your mind so suddenly?'

Rufus sighed and knocked back the last of his vodka. Unable to meet her eye, he looked down at her feet and concentrated on the leopard-skin print of her stiletto's.

'Look,' he said. 'I'm not very good at putting up my hands and saying *I'm sorry. I got it wrong.* But I guess I did get it wrong. And I *am* sorry. Cora Smart is the most popular character we've ever had. I was stupid to get rid of you. And those things I said to you the other day? Well, I truly regret them.'

Carina, suddenly experiencing the urge to cry – something that rarely, if ever, happened, sank down slowly onto the sofa.

'We've got a big budget for these episodes, Carina,' he continued. 'Millions will tune in to see them. But we also know that millions more will tune in to see their favourite Northumbrian fish-wife back on the screen.'

He swallowed back the bile as memories of her wooden

performance and the dreadful Birmingham sounding 'Geordie' accent she used for the part, swam into his mind.

'Will you at least think about it?' he begged.

She wanted to say, 'Fuck thinking about it, I'll do it.' - It was everything she'd ever wanted. Everything she'd dreamt about for five years. But experience had taught her never to act too rashly or to look too desperate so she replied. 'I don't know.'

Rufus played his trump card.

'You should know, it's only fair,' he said slowly, 'but Mick has suggested we re-cast.'

A cold chill ran down Carina's spine.

'Re-cast Cora?' she spat. 'The audience would have your balls.'

'It's not my idea, Carina. I must admit I'm not keen. Only one actress I know can play Cora Smart.'

'The money will have to be good.'

'I'll talk to your agent. Is that okay?'

'Do that.'

'But I have to ask, Carina. Off the record. Are you interested?'

Carina swung one leg other the other, idly, as she lit a cigarette. It comforted Rufus to see that her hands were also shaking.

'Oh, yes,' she said, blowing a cloud of smoke in his direction. 'Most definitely, cock.'

Relief and the effects of several large vodkas, made him stagger slightly as he stood up to leave. He corrected his posture and held out a hand.

'I hope we can let bygones be bygones.'

Carina wrapped her taloned fingers around his slim hand and shook it with a grip of steel. She held onto his hand for an uncomfortable moment as she looked into his eyes. Rufus felt his heart starting to race. Had she detected anything? He hoped not.

He tried to extricate himself from the handshake but still Carina held on. Then she smiled and released him.

'Let's hope so,' she said. 'See you soon.'

Rufus, anxious to leave, though careful not to let it show, returned the smile, mouthed a polite farewell and left, closing the dressing room door behind him. He walked along the dreary corridor, slowly at first but as the stage door drew nearer he picked up his pace and almost ran out into the grey January twilight. Mission accomplished. He'd done it. Managed to get the dreaded Carina Hemsley on board. Okay, it was at the expense of his dignity: he'd eaten humble pie and hated it but no matter. The end justified the means. When he reported back, Mick Flynt would have to admit it was a job well done.

On the return walk to his car he was forced to lean against a parked van while he took deep breaths and waited for the sick feeling to pass. He knew it was the vodka. Neat, and on an empty stomach, it had taken hold of him quickly. Realising he was in no fit state to drive, Rufus pulled himself to his full height, swayed for a moment on the pavement as he looked around, checking his bearings. He would walk to the nearby Metro station, catch a train, go home and have an early night.

Rufus swallowed, took another deep breath, flicked up the key pad of his mobile phone and speed-dialled.

'Mick? Hi. Rufus. Good news...'

Navigating his way through busy streets to the underground Metro station, phone against his ear, deep in conversation, he became blind to the people, the buildings, the traffic around him. Had he been paying attention, he might have heard the 'put-put-put' of the ancient moped keeping its distance close-by. Had he looked around he may even have recognised the overweight, parka clad figure of its rider, frowning at him from under the protective helmet and visor. But he didn't. He was slightly drunk and too busy telling Mick Flynt how clever he'd been, to notice he was being followed.

Carina put the finishing touches to her Fairy Godmother make-up and sat back, satisfied. She couldn't stop grinning. For the first time in God knows how long, she was actually excited. The future, which for so long had looked murky and depressing, now seemed filled with hope and sunshine. She was on her way again after a five year hiatus. Who'd have thought it a few days ago? One minute Frenkel was telling her she'd never work on *Winkle Bay* again, the next he was groveling in her dressing room, the spineless ant. That was one of the wonderful, if sometimes frustrating, things about life. You just never knew what was around the corner.

Carina reached for the vodka bottle and froze. She was remembering the last phone conversation she'd had with Rufus. And the conversation she'd had with someone else after it...

'Christ!' she muttered, reaching for her mobile.

Chapter Twenty Four

The spikey blonde fella in the fancy clothes, Rufus Thingy, had no idea he was being followed, of that Gordon was sure. At first he thought the man was onto him. All the way to the Metro stop at Central Station, he'd stopped to look in shop windows, hoping for a glimpse, Gordon assumed at first, of possible pursuers following close behind but it didn't take him long to realise the man was only interested in checking his own reflection. He would tidy his hair, straighten his tie, adjust his shirt collar, before lurching on a few more feet to inspect himself again. Which was often. Gordon became convinced the man was drunk, or at least tipsy, which was disgusting. His mother hated drunks. Especially those who drank during the day. No wonder Cora wanted rid of him. Rufus's inebriated condition emboldened Gordon and he'd quickened his pace, to such an extent that at one point he could have reached out and touched him as they descended the steps to the ticket area. His mobile phone had started to ring and he thought Rufus might, at any minute, turn around to look but he didn't seem to have heard. Probably the drink. Numbing his senses. Gordon turned off his phone and stood behind him at the automated ticket machine: stood so close to him that he could smell his aftershave, which was sweet and sickly and made Gordon want to throw up. He'd hung back on the escalator ride to the lower depths, watching, waiting, for the right moment to make his move. As it turned out, the man's drunkenness had worked to Gordon's advantage.

All along the brightly lit platform, shoppers and post Christmas drinkers turned to look down the dark tunnel entrance as the rush of wind and the vibrating tracks warned of the oncoming train. Rufus, lost in thought, had pushed his way to the platform's edge. Gordon took in the narrow gap between the old woman standing in front of him and saw his chance. As the train trundled towards them his hand snaked through the narrow space between commuters, and pushed. He was already backing away when the screams started and the platform echoed with the ear splitting grinding of brakes against iron rails.

Baseball cap visor obscuring his face from unwanted attention, Gordon had ascended the escalator to the surface, pretending to read the gallery of adverts on the walls and escaped into the busy streets. Stopping eventually to catch his breath, he sank down onto a bench in the pedestrianised Northumberland Street, trembling with excitement and nervous energy.

For half an hour he sat there, watching the world go by, dying to tell anyone and everyone what he'd done, how clever he'd been. He glanced over at the two teenage boys sitting further down from him on the bench. Oblivious to his presence, they were tucking into hamburgers, scattering fries and pieces of lettuce all over themselves as they ate. Gordon watched as a piece of tomato fell from the nearest boy's bun, saw him stamp gratuitously on the fallen fruit and kick it into the gutter. He thought of the deaths he'd been involved in - Rufus, Fluff, Dougie. And the others. Murder was as easy as that. As easy as stomping on a tomato. He closed his eyes, thinking of his most recent execution, or trying to. His short term memory was bad - always had been and the details of the afternoon were hazy now. The adrenalin rush was fading, too, and with it his pleasure. The aching emptiness that followed these escapades was like a hunger, gnawing away, unsettling him, making him edgy. He hoped Cora would have some work for him again soon. He would talk to her. Speaking of which...

Gordon fished around in his pocket, turned on his phone and saw five missed calls from Cora's secret phone.

'Oh, crumbs!' said Gordon. The two boys looked across and smirked at each other.

He stabbed frantically at the keypad with fat, shaking fingers.

'I'm just about to go on stage,' Carina fumed. 'Where are you?'

'In town,' replied Gordon in a small voice.

'I want you to stay away from Rufus Frenkel,' barked the voice on the other end. 'Leave well alone!'

'There's a bit of a problem, Cora.'

'What sort of a *problem*?'

'Well...'

'You haven't... Jeez, Gordon, tell me you haven't... You have, haven't you?!'

'Affirmative,' replied Gordon, aware that two pairs of inquistive eyes were fixed on him. 'He's erm... he's shoved off.'

Carina, in her dressing room, screamed down the phone at him.

'You moron. Do you realise what you've done? Why did I trust you? Why did I ever think you could be any use to me, you... you... cretin!?'

Gordon tried to interrupt, to explain. He was puzzled. Cora had asked him to get rid of the blonde man who loved himself. Why was she being so awful to him? Calling him those horrible names?

'Cora? Listen...' he tried to say but Carina was no longer there.

Unsettled by her nastiness, Gordon played nervously with the phone in his hands, his bottom lip trembling. Cora was treating him like one of her employees at the kipper factory. It really wasn't on. He didn't work for her. He loved her. Ever so slowly his distress turned to frustration, then to anger. Cora had no right to talk to him like that. She was his fiancée, the girl he was going to marry. She should respect him. He caught sight of the two boys and their smirking expressions. Quick as lightning he snatched the hamburger from the nearest teenager. The lads looked on in mute astonishment as Gordon hurled it to the ground and stamped it into a pulp.

* * *

Rufus Frenkel was in pretty good shape for a supposed dead man. For what seemed like an age, but was in fact only a minute or so, he lay prostrate, eyes closed, in the narrow trench between the rail track and the concrete buttress of the platform, with the smell of engine oil, hot metal and brake fluid in his nostrils and the sounds of screaming and stampeding footsteps somewhere above, ricocheting around in his ears. Then someone was calling down to him.

'Help!' he managed to shout.

The voice asked if he was hurt. Rufus opened his eyes slowly. In the dim light he could make out the bulky undercarriage of the train, with its dirty metal wheels, inches from his face.

'I don't think so.' He strained to look down his body to make sure all his limbs were in one piece.

'Oh, my God!' he yelped.

'What is it?' asked the voice, urgently.

Rufus's limbs were intact but he'd torn a hole in the left knee of his Paul Smith suit.

'Nothing. I'm fine. I'm okay,' he said. The voice told him to roll into the concrete drain running alongside the base of the platform while the train moved forward. He shuddered as the engine kicked noisily into life again. It inched slowly towards the tunnel, away from him and suddenly he was free. He blinked up at the relieved faces peering down at him. Several sets of arms reached towards him.

'Mind my hair,' he muttered, as his rescuers deposited him unceremoniously on the platform. He swayed on unsteady feet, surveying the crowd of onlookers.

'I've torn my trousers,' he said weakly. A uniformed transport official pushed his way through the crowd, towards him.

'What the hell happened?' he barked angrily.

'I don't know,' replied Rufus truthfully. 'I think I fell.'

He tried to recollect the events of the past few minutes, or was it seconds? And failed. His mind was a complete blank. He remembered paying for his ticket and walking down to the platform. As for what happened next, he couldn't be sure. Perhaps he had died. Was this death? Did Heaven look and feel exactly like life?

'Ah, bless 'im!' said a sympathetic voice from somewhere in the crowd. Rufus looked vaguely at the sea of faces around him. An old woman was pointing at him. 'He's wet himself.'

Rufus became aware of the damp sensation in his pants and noticed the dark revealing stain stretching down his right trouser leg. This is definitely *not* Heaven, he decided.

'You're a lucky lad,' she continued. 'You could have ended up dead. Chopped in half. Imagine the mess! Blood everywhere. Your intestines unraveled all over the tracks and your head rolling around like a football.'

The awful image seared through Rufus's consciousness fleetingly, in the blink of an eye. In that brief moment he saw what might have been. Saw it in all it's graphic and horrific unpleasantness. He felt his extremities go cold. His knees buckled and he pitched forward onto the hard floor in a dead faint.

* * *

'Nice jacket.'

'Thanks.'

'Been shopping in the sales?'

Newall didn't answer Clifton's question. And that concerned his subordinate. In the space of a few days, her boss had turned from a sad old git into a presentable middle aged catalogue model. Almost. Gone were the worn out suits with the curry stained lapels. He'd treated himself to a fashionable hair cut, invested in some new shirts and tailored suits. He was still overweight but there was an energy about him now. The clothes and the contemporary hair style made him look younger, taller. Slimmer. Gorgeous.

'Are you going to tell me what's up?' she asked breathlessly, hurrying to keep up with him, as they walked briskly through the caravan park.

'My personal life is my own business,' her boss muttered irritably.

Newall sighed inwardly, knowing he wasn't being honest with himself. If he'd started seeing someone other than Carina, he would have loved to talk about his new girlfriend with Pauline Clifton.

Truth was, he felt uncomfortable about the way his professional role and private life were coming together, blending. He kept telling himself that Carina wasn't a murder suspect, or a criminal in an important investigation. She was an ordinary woman (sort of), who'd received some weird death threat letters - probably from a crank. Who'd butchered her dog. Distressing as this had been for Carina, it seemed highly likely that nothing would come of the threats. The panto season was almost over, Carina would go back to her old life soon and the hate-mail writer would no doubt find some other outlet for his pathetic obsessions. So there was nothing wrong, he kept telling himself rationally, in his seeing Carina. Didn't he deserve a second chance at happiness? He'd met an amazing woman, whom he really liked, whom he was excited by. And the incredible joy of it all was that she liked him back! Where was the wrong in that?

He looked around at Clifton who had stopped a short way behind him, a hurt expression on her face.

'I wasn't talking about your *personal life*,' she said, adding, 'but if that's the way you want it, fine.'

Suppressing the hurt she felt, Clifton caught up with him.

'I meant why are we here? Again. Hounding Paul Miller. I don't get it.'

'Because Dougie Hunt's body was found a few yards away, that's why,' Newall replied gruffly.

'But he committed suicide.'

'So it would seem.' He didn't sound very convinced. 'I've just got a feeling about this. Something isn't right.'

'Did they know each other?'

'Possibly.' Newall shrugged.

'Its been suggested they could have known each other.'

'By whom?' Clifton asked curiously.

Newall didn't reply. They were standing outside Miller's caravan. The curtains were drawn together. Clifton indicated the liveried Ford Transit parked up beside a smaller hatchback.

'Look's like Mr 'Tan In A Van's' home,' she said quietly.

Newall put an ear to the door. He could hear voices, but they were so low, it was impossible to make out which sex they belonged to. Still listening, he rapped twice on the cold metal: a torrent of urgent, hissing sibilants filtered through the door as the occupants discussed opening up. A male voice cackled nervously. The fearful hissing noise stopped as quickly as it started. Newall moved back in the nick of time, for the door flew open, without warning. A dishevelled, out-of-breath Miller, dressed only in his boxer shorts gazed down at the officers angrily.

'You again,' he said.

'Have a good Christmas, Mr Miller?' inquired Newall.

'Great thanks,' replied Miller sarcastically. He folded his arms in a futile effort to keep the cold out. Clifton could see the goosebumps forming on his mahogany torso.

'We've called a few times but you've been out.'

'That's what people tend to do over Christmas. Visit.'

'Go anywhere nice?'

'A friend's.'

'Male or female?'

'Female.' Paul Miller unfolded and folded his arms. Freezing cold, he was rapidly losing his patience. 'Look, what's this about?'

'Could we ask you a few questions inside, Mr. Miller?' asked Clifton reasonably.

'No, you can't. I'm busy,' retorted Paul.

Newall looked at him with contempt. He wanted to punch him

hard in the face, the greedy, money grabbing creep. Carina had described something of her married life with Miller. He'd bled her dry. Financially and emotionally.

He managed to keep his voice calm. 'Mr Miller? How well did you know Dougie Hunt?'

'Who?' Miller was momentarily puzzled. 'Oh. The actor,' he said, remembering. 'Didn't know him at all.'

'Are you sure?'

'Of course I am. Why do you ask?'

'Are you aware Mr. Hunt fell to his death only yards away from here?'

Miller shook his head. 'Nope,' he said belligerently, adding, 'I don't read the papers and I haven't got a telly.'

'How quaint,' Newall scoffed.

'When your private life's been splashed all over the tabloids and your character asassinated by a lying bitch out to make a quick buck, you tend to lose interest in keeping up with the news.'

Newall pressed on.

'So you never met him. Never had a 'relationship' of any sort with him?'

Miller's face contorted unpleasantly. 'A 'relationship'? What are you talking about?'

'Just asking.'

'I'm going in now. My nipples are freezing.'

A nervous, female voice called out, 'Paul? Is everything all right?'

Newall tried to peer in through the open doorway but Miller's body and the inner gloom of the caravan shielded his guest's identity.

'Coming,' Miller replied, coolly. He turned back to the police

257

officers with a hostile glare.

'I get the feeling you're harrassing me. Why's that?'

Newall shrugged. 'Guilty conscience?'

The door slammed shut in his face.

'What was all that about boss?' asked a puzzled Clifton.

'Just a hunch. Thought I'd rile him, see what happened.'

Clifton, unsettled said nothing. The Roy Newall she knew of old did not go around 'riling' people for no reason. He'd enjoyed annoying Miller. It was almost as if he had some weird macho power trip going on. She wanted to confront him but she lacked the courage.

'Seen Carina lately?' she asked, trying to sound innocent.

Newall pretended not to hear.

* * *

Gordon wiped away the tomato sauce and saliva congealing on his mother's chin with a damp cloth and scooped up the napkin stained with more sauce and pieces of ravioli pasta and filling from around her neck.

'Was that nice, Mam? Did you enjoy it. Your tea? You love ravioli, don't you... Yes!' he said, answering for her. He fetched up a scarlet lipstick from his pocket and retouched her lips, restoring the hideously incongruous 'Cora' mask.

'We'll watch a bit of the news. See what's been happening, shall we?'

He switched on the TV, then turned his mother's wheelchair to face the screen. The local evening news had just started. The old lady stared transfixed at the screen as light from its flickering images poured over her in the semi-darkness. The room felt bare, not at all cosy for a few days following the taking down of the Christmas tree and decorations. Gordon tried not to cry. New Year always made him feel miserable. It was bleak and cold and sad. He closed his eyes and sighed. He felt even more bleak than usual. It always unsettled him when Cora shouted at him. She didn't do it very often, usually she talked nicely and touched him lovingly. She'd been so cross. He wondered if she'd stop having 'The Sex Stuff' with him. He knelt on the floor with his head resting against the sofa, biting his nails, waiting for news of Rufus Whats-it's death. So far, nothing. It was all doom and gloom stories about drunken young people, violence on the streets and shoplifting. What was the world coming to? It wasn't safe to go out at night. He shifted from one buttock to the other, trying to make himself comfortable.

Gordon's ears pricked up at the newsreader's mention of several key phrases 'Metro Station' and 'Lucky Escape.' A library picture of an underground Metro train disappearing down a tunnel played over the reporter's voice-over.

'A man had a lucky escape when he fell onto the tracks in front of an approaching train at the Central Station Metro Station this afternoon.'

Gordon held his breath.

'The man, who has not been identified, escaped with a few minor cuts and bruises.'

'He's alive,' cheered Gordon. 'He's alive, mother.' He pulled himself up with difficulty and kissed her on the mouth. 'She'll be happy now. My Cora.'

He hurried out of the room in search of his mobile phone. He wanted to tell her straightaway. He smiled, relieved, as he speed dialled his beloved. Cora would be so pleased. They would be having 'The Sex' tonight, for sure.

'Cora?!' he gushed, 'Guess what?'

'Don't call me when I'm about to go on stage,' Carina said flatly.

Gordon tried to interject. 'But...'

It was futile. Carina was in no mood to talk.

'In fact don't call me at all. I'll call you.'

The line went dead. Gordon hung his head dejectedly. She was still angry with him. She mustn't have heard. She thought Rufus was dead. He had to tell her. He had to make things all right between them. He switched off the TV and finding what he was searching for amongst a pile of nearby CD's, slipped a disc into the portable hi-fi.

'Mother,' Gordon said, as the catchy tune started up, 'It's Copacabana time.'

He burst into song.

'Her name was Lola, she was a show girl, with yellow feathers in her hair and her dress cut down to there...'

Somehow, Barry Manilow always managed to brighten even the darkest of days.

* * *

'That's great news. I'm really happy for you.' Newall held up his full wine glass to Carina's almost drained glass. 'You're back on top!'

'I suppose I am.'

They were dining in the Valmont's sumptuous restaurant, with its panoramic windows overlooking the majestic sweep of Dean Street. Their after-show evenings together had fallen quickly and comfortably into a routine of dinner, bed and sex. Newall was a happy man. Night after night, they would sit in the discreet booth, hidden away from the other diners and chat - about his day at work, his past, his dreams - Carina was a surprisingly good listener. She in turn would tell stories about the famous people she'd worked with, recount amusing tales of life in the entertainment business and talk about her own past, too. It was clear to him that the abrupt, cold, public persona was a defence, a shield to hide the delicate, warm, beauty within. He felt privileged to be privy to this secret fact. Only he knew the real Carina. It made making love to her all the more special.

'You probably won't want to know me soon, now that you're a big star again,' Newall said. He'd meant it as a joke but the faint hint of underlying desperation in his voice was unmissable. He'd tried to sound and look happy for her when she'd revealed her classified news. Now he was beginning to wonder if he could keep up the pretence.

Carina slid a shoeless foot up Newall's leg. 'This won't change anything between us. I know a good thing when I'm onto it.'

Newall's hand, the one holding the wine glass, started to shake uncontrollably. He put down the glass.

'How can you be certain?'

'Instinct,' she said as her foot reached its target. Newall squirmed with pleasure.

'Shall we go upstairs?' he suggested urgently.

'In a moment,' she laughed. 'We haven't talked about *your* day, yet.'

Like Gordon she'd heard about Rufus Frenkel's brush with death - she'd trawled the local radio news all afternoon and tuned into the TV for information and had been mightily relieved to hear of the 'un-named man's' lucky escape. Now she had to be sure that

Gordon had covered his tracks.

'Nothing exciting to report,' Newall mused. He decided not to mention his interview with Carina's ex-husband. Why spoil a beautiful evening?

Carina studied his craggy face. Lust, adoration, desire, excitement, they were all there in plain view. Suspicion and doubt were not. If he'd known about the Metro incident with Frenkel, he would have said something. Her connection with *Winkle Bay* made the topic unavoidable.

'Then maybe it *is* time for bed,' she said.

She reached across the table, grabbed the lapel of Newall's jacket, pulled him roughly towards her and kissed him hard. Newall felt her warm tongue against his. He pulled her up from the table and slid his arms around her waist.

Outside in the darkened street, a chubby figure on a moped watched the intertwined figures with mounting fury.

Chapter Twenty Five

'I'm watchin you'.

The individual letters were the same as before, a mixture of uppercase and lowercase, multi-coloured, from a weekly glossy celebrity magazine, glued onto a sheet of slightly crumpled around the edges, A4 paper.

Newall, on his way out of Carina's suite early the next morning had stumbled across the folded sheet on the floor in front of the door. He'd almost dismissed it, walked over it in his haste to get to work (he was running late after an exhausting night of passion). At the last minute he'd looked at it again. Letters, invoices, anything in need of Carina's attention would be left for her at reception.

Carina, just out of bed and wondering why Roy was hesitating in the open doorway, went over to him, ran an arm around his waist.

'What have you got there?'

Newall handed her the note and felt her body go rigid. Before he could stop her, she screwed the paper into a ball and tossed it angrily into the corridor.

'You can't do that!' protested Newall, retrieving the paper ball. 'It's evidence.'

'It's just some moron's idea of a cheap thrill,' Carina hissed.

'But how did it get here? Who delivered it? He's around somewhere, watching you.'

He turned and moved off down the corridor towards the lifts.

'Roy?' bellowed Carina. 'Where are you going?'

'Reception,' came the reply. 'I need to see the hotel's CCTV tapes.'

Carina's mouth felt suddenly dry. Bloody-buggering-bastard Gordon! If he was identified on CCTV, all her plans would come crashing down around her ears.

'Don't waste your time. Whoever it is, is just trying to scare me, that's all.'

She set off after him, then remembered she was in her dressing gown. Newall waved to her from the lift as the doors slid together. Carina beat a hasty retreat to her room and hunted around desperately for a cigarette.

* * *

Gordon sat on the end of his bed with the old biscuit tin on his lap. He'd lifted it out of the wardrobe and taken the lid off.

Peering down, he said gently, 'Are you hungry? Are you? Would you like something to eat?'

He felt around in his trouser pocket and produced a liquorice allsort. He looked at it glumly.

'It's all I've got at the minute. I could sneak you something in a bit later on, when Mam's not looking.'

Gordon laid the sweet on the newspaper-lined bottom of the tin. He sat for a moment, without speaking, thinking of the betrayal he'd witnessed the previous evening. Cora and the policeman kissing - the image just wouldn't leave his mind. Every time he closed his eyes, he saw them together. Policemen were supposed to investigate crimes, not steal other blokes' fiancées. Fiancées weren't supposed to kiss blokes they weren't engaged to. Sitting astride his moped on the journey home, fury had given way to anger: anger, to the desire for retribution. Unable to sleep, he'd put the letter together quickly and delivered it to the hotel in the dead of night, knowing its discovery would shock Cora. He would forgive her without a doubt, if she apologised. He'd take her back and continue loving her but things would have to change from now on. He wasn't stupid. She'd started to take him for granted, he realised that. '*Do this Gordon*', '*do that*.' Everything was one sided. Cora hadn't been to his house, still hadn't met his mother, or told the newspapers about him. He'd had enough.

He stirred himself and gazed down at the old tin.

'Cora's being a right bitch,' he complained. 'I saw her last night, kissing a copper. No kidding. Snogging his face off, she was. She never does that to me.'

He would have said more, as there was more to get off his chest but his mobile rang.

'It's her,' he said waspishly, to the tin's inhabitant. 'Hello Cora.'

'What the fuck do you think you're playing at?' screamed Cora.

'I saw you kissing him. That policeman fella.'

'You brain-dead, foul...'

Gordon cut her off.

'You have to be nice to me, Cora.'

Gordon winked good naturedly at the tin but there was nothing light hearted in his voice. Cora detected the implicit threat and realised with a shock that there was some kind of intelligent thought going on.

Revising her tone she said, 'I was doing it for you, you big fool.'

'You don't kiss me like that.'

'He was suspicious, asking annoying questions - about you. I had to throw him off the scent.'

She stopped to listen. There was only silence on the other end.

'Are you there? Gordon?'

'Aye.'

Gordon bit his bottom lip, something he always did when he was trying to think and the subject he was trying to think about was a hard one.

'Why don't you ever come round? Why won't you meet Mam? Why don't you ever talk about me to the papers when you give interviews, or the telly people?'

'I can't come round while the police are suspicious but as soon as they're out of the way, I'll be over like a shot.'

'Yeah?'

'Yes, my darling.'

She grimaced and shivered. 'And if I never talk about you, it's because what we have is special. Private. I treasure it so much and don't want it ever to be spoilt. Do you understand?'

A lump had formed in Gordon's throat and he could only grunt a gruff 'yes'.

'I know it hurts to be apart, but brave heart, my love. We'll be together soon enough.' She swallowed back her disgust and added, 'And we can do 'The Sex' forever and ever.'

Gordon responded with a deeper, more primeval grunt.

'In the meantime, no more naughty letters. Wait until you hear from me. Okay?'

Carina thought she heard a muffled 'Okay' in between the grunting, the excited heavy breathing, the sound of metal-type objects crashing to the floor like colliding cymbals and a dull thud. She ended the call with a distasteful shudder and dropped the phone in her bag. Gordon was a liability. Something would have to be done.

Carina returned to the problem of CCTV footage and Gordon's possible exposure. At the moment, there was little, if anything she could do. Identifying him was one thing, finding him another. For her own sake she had to stay calm. Events, for the moment, were out of her hands.

She bathed, massaged and dried herself, moisturised, dressed. Margaret Frott, using all the magical potions, procedures and beautifying skills at her disposal, transformed herself into Carina Hemsley, Star. Then, with mounting trepidation, she rode the lift to the ground floor.

Pauline Clifton entered the Manager's Office to find her boss sitting back on a chair, feet up, glued to a small TV monitor on the small desk.

'You want to fill me in?' she asked.

Newall pushed Gordon's handy-work over to her with the end of a pencil.

'Carina received another note,' he said, without looking away from the screen. 'Delivered to her door.'

Clifton inspected it.

'Doesn't say much.'

'I've talked to the staff. Nobody here dropped it off. Or nobody's admitting to it.'

He moved his feet off the desk and sat up.

'Trouble is, half the cameras around the place don't even work. Manager says they're just a "deterrant". Useless.'

Clifton's fascination lay in Newall's clothes, rather than in anything flashing by on the monitor. She'd almost acclimatised herself to his new style in natty clothing but the suit was a step too far. He looked like he was ready for a day in The City rather than an eight hour shift with Northumbria Police. There was a day's growth of stubble, too. Why dress like up like Bryan Ferry's slightly chubbier brother and not bother to shave. She was horrified. It could only mean one thing. Dirty-stop-out!

'She could have planted it herself, I suppose,' she offered.

'She didn't.'

'How do you know?'

Newall was about to say something, then thought better of it and tapped the forward switch on the playback machine.

'Did she call you?' Clifton pushed. 'What time did you get here?'

Ignoring her questions, Newall said, 'Two cameras in reception. One behind the counter turned on the staff, the other by the lift. No cameras at all on the stairs - at any level.'

They both turned around as the door opened and Carina entered.

'Oh, good morning, Miss Clifton,' she said politely.

'It's *Ms*,' Clifton snapped, unable to help herself.

But Carina's eyes were scanning the monitor with its split screen display.

'Anything?'

Newall shrugged. 'If he used the lift, we've got him. If he used the stairs - no dice. No cameras.'

Carina prayed that Gordon distrusted elevators.

'Well, good luck,' she murmured sweetly. 'My driver's here.'

Clifton noticed her superior's momentary hesitation.

'I'll see you to your car.'

He put a gallant arm to the curve of her back before opening the door for the actress and escorting her out. Definitely shagging, thought Clifton. Got to be. She dismissed further cogitation on the subject from her mind and inserted another disk titled 'Lift' into the machine and pressed play, then fast forward. A series of singles, couples, groups sped by, approaching the lift, entering. Doors shut, doors opened. Clifton paused the disk only when she recognised a familiar face. Two familiar faces. Newall and Carina. They were waiting for the lift to arrive - he in the clothes he was still wearing, Carina in some glitzy over-the-top number. They were kissing and groping each other like love-sick teenagers.

Clifton was unprepared for the emotional maelstrom which exploded in her chest. She felt as if she'd been kicked violently. Pain, hurt, despair engulfed her. She wanted to weep. Suspecting something was going on between them, was one thing. She'd seen the signs, it was as she thought. But to see them like that, to witness their passion in close-up, so... so *pornographically* - it was too much to bear.

'She's not good enough for you!' she cried out, hot tears cascading down her cheeks. She reached for a hankie and hid her face. When Newall returned she had composed herself and was peering intently at the lift footage from a time later.

'Anything to report?' he asked.

'Only a broken heart,' Clifton wanted to say. Instead she just shook her head. She had her no-nonsense, ball-breaking, ice-maiden reputation to think of.

* * *

Jackie waved to Irene in the box office and scurried past, without stopping to engage her in conversation. Irene shouted a 'good morning' as she disappeared into the theatre auditorium but received no reply. Poor lass, thought Irene. The girl was a prime candidate for a nervous breakdown. Who could blame her? Treated like a slave by that dreadful Miss Hemsley woman, made to fetch and carry for her - for no pay, either! That's what she'd heard, anyway. Not that she listened to gossip. Wasn't there something about being abandoned by a philandering husband as well? Disappeared into the night, leaving her to bring up two kids by herself. Little wonder why she twitched and shook all the time. Terrible thing to have to cope with. Desertion. Deceit. Learning how to master an electric hand drill. People did terrible things to each other. How lucky she was to have found her Jack. Fifty years they'd been married, without the faintest whiff of scandal and not a cross word between them. Jack was a diamond. On their honeymoon night she'd warned him in no uncertain terms, that if she ever caught him playing away from home, she'd hunt him down like a sick dog and shoot him dead. Plain speaking - that was the secret of a long and happy marriage.

Irene opened a bag of wine gums and slipped a green one, her favourite, into her mouth as Jez tripped down the stairs towards her. Here we go again, she thought. The man was forever moping around, searching for his wife, with that haunted, injured look on his silly face. Served him right for marrying a daft lass with no brain, thirty years his junior. The woman was a Jezebel, the way she draped herself over that skinny Scotch lad. Ah well, only a few more days to go and it would all be over for another year. Curtains for the panto, curtains for Jez's marriage as well, she mused to herself. Jez peered in at her through the little hatch.

'Have you seen my wife, Irene?'

'Oh, aye, flower. She passed this way not half an hour ago on

270

her way to the dressing rooms.'

'Thank you.'

'You're welcome,' she replied and added, 'Arm in arm with Campbell. Been shopping, I think. They do get on like a house on fire, don't they?'

Jez smiled and nodded. His eyes, Irene noticed - and Irene noticed a lot of things, were not smiling at all. Oh dear. He was about to set off in search of Heidi but Irene hadn't finished with him yet. An inevitable downside to a job which required human beings to be encased in a wooden construction the size of a small garden shed, with only wine gums and boxes of Milk Tray for company for hours on end, was boredom. Many box office workers relied upon Jackie Collins, or Hello Magazine to get them through the day. And night. Irene, who wasn't an avid reader, preferred mischief.

'I'm so glad you've decided to go back to your natural hair colour, Jez, pet.'

Jez nodded stiffly. 'Thank you.'

''Cos if Hitler'd had a beard, you'd've been a dead ringer.'

Jez, lost for words, hurried away. Irene grinned wickedly. If there was an advantage to being on the wrong side of seventy, it was this - old people could utter vile, rude things and get away with it. She chuckled and popped another wine gum in her mouth.

Jackie knocked again on the door of Dressing Room Number One and tried the handle. The door was locked. She could hear Carina on the other side, talking stridently into her phone.

'Carina?'

She put her ear to the door and strained to listen but it was difficult, Heidi and Campbell were giggling and laughing in the corridor.

Sylvie Goggle threw open her dressing room and bellowed at

them.

'Could you keep the noise down please? I'm trying to prepare for my performance.'

The laughter stopped.

'Thank you.'

She narrowed her eyes myopically and looked Campbell up and down disapprovingly.

'Two hours to go and you're already in full costume and make-up? What on earth for?'

Campbell shrugged. 'Why not?'

'It's ridiculous,' she snorted. 'You look like the Prince Regent's Bum Boy.' She retired to her room, slamming the door behind her.

'Just ignore her,' said Heidi soothingly. She was about to embrace Campbell in a theatrical hug but thought better of it when she heard the steady thud of Jez's footsteps echoing along the corridor.

'Hi, darling,' she said brightly, transferring her affections to her husband.

'We've just been going through a few ideas for the end of run party.'

Jez nodded slowly, suspiciously.

'Come on, I'll tell you all about them.'

She linked an arm through Jez's and guided him away from the thespians' quarters. Jackie knocked and called out Carina's name again. Campbell, who had been watching Jez and Heidi's departure, with a long sulky face, turned to her.

'She's definitely in.'

'Thanks.'

'You look different,' he said. 'What have you done?'

Jackie snorted and pushed a lock of hair behind her ear in an embarrassed gesture.

'Nothing,' she squeaked, and laughed nervously.

'You've been on a sun bed. Or is it fake tan?'

Jackie snorted again but was saved from an explanation by the sound of the key turning in Carina's dressing room door. Phone to ear, Carina beckoned her in. Before she could enter, Lauren was racing down the corridor towards them.

'Carina!?'

'Hold on,' Carina said into the phone and fixed Lauren with her brightest, widest smile. 'Just on the phone to my agent, my darling,' she said. 'What can I do for you?'

'I just thought, well, I was wondering...' said Lauren, flustered, 'I start on *Winkle Bay* in a few weeks and I'd really love some advice, some tips. Could we sit down sometime and talk about it?'

Carina gazed down at her wide, puppy like eyes and said, 'Of course, my love, of course. Anything to help. We'll speak later, eh?'

'Thank you!' gushed Lauren, 'Thank you!' and skipped of back to her dressing room.

Carina pulled Jackie by the shoulder in her room, slammed the door and put the phone back to her ear.

'No... I think we should sign it,' Jackie heard her say. 'I know it's only six episodes but the money's damn good. We can't afford to say *no*...'

She paced around the room, pausing to light a cigarette. Jackie sat down slowly. She wanted Carina to finish her call so they could talk. Her stomach was in knots.

'... Listen, my darlin' just sign the fucking contract. Rufus said they would get me back for a longer stint in a few months, so what's the problem?'

She listened for a moment, clearly irritated by the response.

'Well, *I'm* the client, you do as you're told.' She paused, thinking for a moment.

'Tell them I've only got two small demands. One - I want my old dressing room back, and two - Cora Smart doesn't have a grand-daughter, never has, never will. Get rid. Speak soon, bye lovey.'

She ended the call with a castinet-like flourish.

'Sorted.'

She sucked in a lung full of tobacco.

'It's definite!' she declared triumphantly. 'Cora's back in *Winkle Bay*!'

Jackie gasped and clapped her hands, momentarily forgetting the purpose of her visit.

'Oh Carina. I'm so pleased for you. This is wonderful news.'

'You bet.'

Jackie moved forward to hug Carina in celebration, hesitated, then satisfied herself with a gentle pat on the arm.

'There's been a bit of a coup,' Carina explained. 'Shit viewing figures and crap storylines - it's like I said all along. My public don't want to see a bunch of middle class tossers who work at a nuclear power station, shagging each other silly and whingeing about their mortgage repayments - they want the old days back - fishing boats and working class villagers. Real characters.'

'You're so right Carina,' agreed Jackie cheerfully. Now that major fame beckoned again and mega bucks were on the horizon, Carina was bound to take her news well.

'There's going to be a big story. A crash,' said Carina, lowering her voice conspiratorially. 'They're going to kill off half the cast. Mick Flynt's been brought in to do it.'

Jackie, none the wiser, blinked, 'Mick Flynt?'

'You know! The bloke who makes those over the top, cheap,

scandalous sex soaps with ridiculous storylines. He's always on the box, spouting crap.'

'Oh yes,' said Jackie vaguely.

'So it's bound to get the Press interested.'

'He's going to kill off all the characters?'

'Not all of them. Just a few. Then I'm coming back and they're going to make *Winkle Bay* how it used to be. They're starting all over again.'

'Ahhh,' cooed Jackie. 'And lovely Lauren's going to be in the show with you. That's nice.'

Carina sucked on her cigarette again, pretending not to hear.

'I've done it, Jackie. It's all starting to happen again for me.'

'You deserve every minute of your success,' Jackie said, with feeling.

'You're damned right, sweetheart.'

Jackie suddenly found herself saying, 'Actually, Carina. I've got some news too.'

One of Carina's eyebrows raised in slight interest.

'Don't tell me! Hubby's back.'

Jackie shook her head. 'No, it's nothing to do with Alan. Well, not really.'

'Spit it out, then.'

'I'm in love.'

Carina stared at her. For the first time in all the years she'd known Jackie, she'd actually been surprised by something the woman had said.

'I am. It's absolute, all enveloping love. We've only been together for a short time, really, well, since Christmas and it's early days but we're soul mates, we really are. We love each other so deeply.'

It was like a flood gate opening and she couldn't stop.

'And the sex. Oh, Carina, the sex is just amazing. Like nothing I've known before.'

Carina forced herself to interject. There was such a thing as too much information. Even for her.

'That's fantastic. It is, my pet. You're overdue a good long dose of happiness, you really are. I'm so happy for you.'

Jackie grabbed her hand and squeezed it intensely.

'Do you mean it? Do you really?' she asked earnestly.

'Oh, I so do. It's about time you had the love of a good man.'

'That means so much to me.'

Jackie kissed Carina's hand with trembling lips and said quickly, 'It's Paul, your ex-husband.'

Chapter Twenty Six

'She said *what?*'

Paul Miller sat down hard in the cramped seating area of his caravan and stared at Jackie in disbelief.

'Love each other, cherish each other.'

'Was she drunk?'

'No!'

The tears welled up as Jackie described how Carina, instead of flying off the handle in a furious rage, had been nothing but graceful and dignified when told about their romance.

'She didn't throw anything at you?' Paul asked incredulously. 'Try to stab you?'

'Not at all,' replied Jackie. 'She went about her usual business, applying her make-up, putting her mobile phone on charge. She was happy for us, she really was.'

Miller could hardly believe it. The woman was the most jealous creature he'd ever met in his life and even though they were divorced, he'd fully expected his ex-wife to either stick a knife between Jackie's shoulder blades, or turn up on his door step and attempt to punch his lights out. She didn't want him but she didn't want anyone else to have him either - that was her warped philosophy on life. He knew her so well. Or he thought he did. This was all very odd.

'Something's up. It's not right,' he said, worried.

Jackie disagreed. 'I think I picked her on a good day, that's all,' Jackie opined. 'She's going back into *Winkle Bay*.'

'Is she?'

Jackie nodded.

'Well, thank God for that.'

Miller stood up, the tension of the past few days melting away. He was sure Carina would see his involvement with her unofficial PA as some kind of insult. While he wasn't bothered for himself, it concerned him that Carina might cause trouble for Jackie. Obviously the woman had mellowed now that she knew she would be returning to her beloved soap opera. Hallelujah! Talk about perfect timing. He took Jackie in his arms, kissed her, then dragged her over to the bed, bumping into furniture, knocking pans off the hob in his desperation to make love to her. Tugging at each other's clothes, they fell onto the duvet, a conjoined mass of clumsy limbs.

Jackie allowed herself to give in to passion and lust, yet again. She too felt relief and joy now that everything was out in the open at last. She'd thanked Carina for helping her to find love. If it hadn't been for Carina ordering her to call Paul to let him know about Fluff's demise, she wouldn't be here right now, in the throes of ecstasy, with a revitalised attitude to the future, feeling fulfilled and content. One call, was all it took. She'd phoned him, told him the awful news and been moved by his distress. She recognised a fellow tortured soul immediately. One call had led to another. They would talk for hours - about anything and everything. She'd told him things she'd never discussed with anyone before - her despair, the feelings of utter worthlessness she experienced when Alan left her. Paul in return opened up about his low self esteem, the pain he went through after his marriage to Carina collapsed. And then they met up. The immediate physical attraction between them was electric. They both felt it, surrendered to it without compunction, without any thought for the consequences. The sex had been incredible from the beginning. There was no hesitation, or self consciousness. Somehow, they each knew what the other wanted, needed. It felt as if they'd known each other intimately for years. She'd found herself telling Carina all this and not caring what Carina thought about it. She, Jackie, was happy and she wanted to tell it to the world. And wonderful Carina had understood. She could tell. Her friend was delighted for her. Delighted for them both.

The intense rush, that overwhelming sensation of physical satisfaction, so recently re-discovered, exploded within her, sending nerve endings throughout her body into glorious spasms of pleasure. She shuddered and screamed and forgot all about Carina Hemsley.

* * *

Waves of an altogether different type of physical intensity - those of extreme dissatisfaction, were currently reverberating around the walls of the green room in the former tobacco factory studios of *Winkle Bay*. Rufus, the only hint of his recent brush with death, a slightly grazed nose, had taken a willing back seat while the programme's new 'consultant', Mick, explained to the cast that the axe was about to fall on some of them. They were not a happy troupe.

'But we've got contracts,' protested one of them, a senior member of the cast. It was always the older actors who tended to complain: they remembered the good old days of the actors union, when it had teeth and stood up for artistés rights. They hadn't quite realised those days were gone. Actors in soap opera now, were factory fodder, sucked in, put to work, then spat out. The younger stars, dazzled by the allure of celebrity, accepted this as the norm. It was a small price to pay for selling your soul to the Devil.

'What's the big story you're planning on doing, then?' asked one of the younger breed.

'I can't say much at the moment,' said Mick in his slow, arrogant north-western drawl. 'But it's to do with Icelandic terrorists blowing up the Harbour.'

'*Icelandic* terrorists!?' screeched another aged figure, gawping in disbelief at the self-made media mogul.

'Yeah,' said Mick flatly, his eyes narrowing at the indignant actor. 'It's to do with fishing quotas, and such like.'

'This really is a load of old crap,' opined the actor, Jeffrey Carter.

'How many people are you killing off?' asked a younger, more eager member of the cast.

'Eight,' Flynt revealed, then with his eyes fixed firmly on Jeffrey Carter, added, 'Or maybe nine.'

A murmur of horror went around the room. Mick raised his hands at the crowd, trying to calm the tension.

'It's got to be memorable. No point in killing off just one or two.'

Jeffrey Carter had had enough.

'You're forgetting the audience. They're not idiots. They'll see this as just another cynical attempt by smart arse executives to manipulate the viewing figures. "Oh, I've got a great idea, let's have another murder." I mean is that the best you can come up with? All the soaps do it. People are bored. It's passé. After a week nobody will remember.'

Flynt glared at him. 'They won't forget these episodes in a hurry.'

Rufus joined in. 'It's true. They're going to be pretty spectacular.'

'Oh really?' said Jeffrey sarcastically. 'We haven't heard that one before.'

'Something else for you to digest,' offered Flynt pleasantly, 'Carina Hemsley's coming back.'

A horrified hush descended. The actors who'd worked with her remembered her overbearing ways, the years of behind the scenes unpleasantness. The younger, more recent additions to the series, had heard the awful stories of an ego, out of control.

'This is the end,' said Jeffrey Carter melodramatically.

Mick smiled at him. 'Well, it is for some.'

One of the good looking himbo's put up his hand politely.

'Yes?' inquired Mick, pointing at him.

'Rufus is still our boss, yeah?'

Flynt nodded.

'So what do we call you, then?'

The media mogul smiled thinly.

'You can call me "God",' he said simply.

When the actors left the building half an hour later, grumbling and moaning in outrage amongst themselves, the journalist swarm was waiting for them. One by one, the actors gave their stock 'no comment' quote. The older thespians sped off angrily, the younger ones hung around, teasing the reporters, revelling in the attention. Rufus, standing in the studio entrance, turned to Flynt who was watching the exodus with keen intensity and said, 'I wonder who leaked the story to the Press?'

Flynt blinked at him, mock innocently.

'Who knows?' he replied, with a wide grin. 'Does it matter? Any publicity is good publicity.'

Frenkel nodded. The statement only confirmed what he suspected already. God might work in mysterious ways, he thought, but this particular self-styled deity was as transparent as glass.

* * *

Carina rarely enjoyed a matinée performance. She couldn't quite put her finger on the reason. It was something to do with the attitude of the audience, certainly. Punters fidgeted in their seats more, she'd noticed. They weren't as focussed. Getting them to suspend belief took longer. Theatre was an evening event as far as most people were concerned. Maybe watching a show during the afternoon made them feel guilty. The mundane chores and tasks required of them were put on hold, delayed until the show was over. As an actor, she felt the tension, the distraction. She looked upon it as a challenge, though, usually. That's what made taking part in a long running show like a pantomime bearable. Day in day out, the script was the same. But the audience wasn't. So the performance varied slightly as you tried to bring them into the fold. And for that an actor had to keep his or her wits about them. Coasting through a show on automatic pilot lead to boredom and dissatisfaction. Carina, with all her faults and foibles always gave of her best.

This particular matinée was different. It was she who could not settle, not the audience. She was aware of merely going through the motions on stage, hitting her mark, meeting her cues, singing enchantedly when required. She couldn't wait for the final curtain. No matter how much she tried to rally herself, Carina's mind was elsewhere. Gordon's actions, the surprise letter, had affected her deeply. If he continued to act independently, God knows where it would all end.

From a very early stage, she'd been careful to distance herself from him. The letters he'd written to her all those years ago, proclaiming his undying love for 'Cora', were no longer in existence, burnt in a garden bonfire over a year ago: the occasional meetings - massages for her bruised ego, she'd agreed to in the early days of her 'retirement' from *Winkle Bay* had been held in out of the way, obscure backwaters. She'd known what he was capable of from those illiterate letters. Their violent promises of loyalty to the death, his inability to distinguish between fact and fiction, they were all useful to her as she plotted her return to the fame game. There had been a trial run, a test of Gordon's dedication, his pliability, as soon as she'd signed up for the Cinderella gig last spring and he'd come up trumps, proved to her she could ask anything of him, *anything*, and he would do it. 'The Sex' was a small price to pay for his complete and unstinting trust.

She'd been so sure she could control him. That was the joy of finding someone like Gordon. If the worst came to the worst, and exposure loomed, Carina knew the police would dismiss his confessions as the act of a psychopathic, desperate fantasist. The mobile phone she'd given him, the mobile phone she used solely for his calls, were pay as you go and untraceable - nothing connected him to her. Even if her friendly policeman found video evidence of Gordon entering the hotel lift, he was witness to the fact that she never met with him. But Gordon was a loose cannon. She could no longer trust him completely. She had to act soon.

Then there was Jackie. Jackie and Paul. How she'd wanted to strangle the woman on the spot as she imparted her news of the 'beautiful romance' and the identity of the 'great love' she'd just found. Bitch! Inveigling her way into her affections, her life, pretending to be this neurotic amoeba, then stealing off with her ex-fella. They were probably laughing about Carina right this very minute, cackling at what a mug she'd been. The woman was insane. One of those stupid fans, not content with adoring someone from a distance, she wanted to *be* her. And what better place to start than with the real star's real life cast-offs. Well, she would put a stop to that.

'Yes, Cinderella! You *shall* go to the ball,' she snapped, realising Lauren had just given her her cue.

The next hour dragged. Three more performances, Carina kept telling herself, and then it would be all over. She could wave bye-bye to pantomime. Next Christmas she'd go to Barbados. She'd be able to afford it, earning a steady and more than comfortable living in TV. No more theatrical theatre crap for her.

She took her bow with the rest of the cast at the end of the show and was first off the stage, making a dash for her dressing room before the safety curtain had fully descended. Reaching for the mobile phone charging on her dressing room table, she realised she was not alone in the room. Newall was sitting on the battered old leather sofa, watching her closely.

'Roy, sweetheart!' she exclaimed. 'You gave me a shock!'

'Sorry, I needed to talk to you, I didn't think you'd mind me making myself at home,' Newall said apologetically.

'Of course not. Is everything all right?' asked Carina warily, as he pulled a folded brown envelope from his inside coat pocket.

'I've brought some stills,' he explained, 'All the people who entered the lift between the hours of midnight last night and seven thirty this morning. Would you mind looking at them? See if there's anyone you recognise?'

'No problem,' Carina said brightly. She lit a cigarette and sat down on the sofa beside the police officer. Newall handed over an A4 sized grainy photo of the first lift user. She shook her head. And repeated the exercise with the next photo, and the one after that...

After studying twenty photographs copied from The Valmont's CCTV footage, Carina was pleased to note that none of the photographs included a head-shot of Gordon. He had taken the back stairs after all. The status quo was restored. She could relax.

'Oh, well,' Newall said, 'back to the drawing board.'

'I really do think it's just a stunt. Some kid trying to scare me,' she mused. 'I mean it's the last night tomorrow and nothing's happened to me.'

'There was Fluff,' Newall said, reminding her.

'Yes, Fluff. Bless her,' she replied swiftly, mustering a tragic expression. Fucking dog, she thought, she'd forgotten about the creature. She lunged at Roy across the sofa, pulled him by the hair towards her and kissed him violently on the mouth.

'I'm not worried about anything anymore,' she breathed, 'Now I've got you to look after me.'

Newall broke off the kiss.

'I won't let anything happen to you. I swear,' he promised.

'Thank you.'

She pulled herself up, a shimmering vision in her Fairy Godmother's ballgown costume.

'Give me five minutes to get dressed?'

Newall nodded. 'I'll wait for you outside. I've got calls to make.'

'Have you time for a coffee somewhere in town? I've got an hour or so before the evening show.'

'I'd like that,' Newall smiled at her. 'Don't be long.' He kissed her again and walked out into the corridor.

Carina picked up the phone from the dressing table, turned it on and fingered it nervously, trying to master the unfamiliar keypad. Satisfied at last that she knew what she was doing, she wrote a short text message and sent it. Then she switched off the small handset and placed it in a zipped compartment in her trusty bag. She had been wise not to throw away this particular mobile. Carina possessed a fastidious streak - a useful trait for an actress but even more useful for her present tasks. She closed her eyes and wished she could have been a fly-on-the-wall when the recipient opened up the message.

Minutes later, and wearing an outfit more suited to the northeast winter, Carina stepped out into the corridor and into Newall's waiting arms. Before they could go far, a piercing shriek made them turn. Lauren's dressing room door had flown open and she was running towards Carina, sobbing and wailing, hotly pursued by Campbell Garibaldi.

'Carina! Carina!' she cried, hysterically and fell into the surprised actor's arms.

'What is it, flower?' she asked urgently.

Overcome by emotion, Lauren could only mutter incomprehensibly between sobs and snivels.

Campbell said in a low voice, 'She's had a call from her agent.' He threw her a sympathetic look before continuing. 'The *Winkle Bay* people don't want her. They've decided to cut the character.'

'That's a bit harsh,' said Newall, feeling sorry for the girl.

'I know,' tutted Carina. 'Soap opera - it's a dirty damned business.' She tucked Lauren under the chin in an affectionate gesture. 'Something else will turn up. You'll see,' she said sweetly.

'Carina's right,' Campbell chimed in. 'You're meant for better things. *Winkle Bay's* such rubbish.'

Carina stiffened, let go of Lauren. Campbell took over, wrapping his arms around the young girl and resting his head on her shoulder.

'But I wanted to be in it. I told everyone...' she sobbed.

'I know.'

Ben Tingle appeared at the top of the corridor from the back stage area and stopped in his tracks at the sight of his girlfriend being pawed by a Dandy.

'What's going on?' he demanded, running towards the group. 'What have you done to her?' He shoved Campbell hard in the ribs. 'What is it with you?' he asked nastily. 'Why can't you leave other blokes birds alone?'

Campbell, winded, couldn't reply.

Newall said calmly, 'She's had some bad news, that's all.'

Ben looked at Lauren for an explanation but her lips had turned to a wobbly mush and she was beyond words.

'*Winkle Bay's* axed her before she's started,' said Carina plainly.

'No!' Ben was shocked. 'Bummer!' he said, with feeling. He was looking forward to a few months of being a kept man. Lauren opened her arms wide, like an injured child hoping for comfort from Mummy. Ben hesitated, then patted her on the back clumsily, as if trying to burp her. Her sobbing turned into a sheep-like baa-ing.

Irene hobbled towards them grimacing from the pain in her arthritic hip.

'Yoo-hoo! Miss Hemsley?' she cooed. 'I thought I'd better warn you. There's a crowd of Press people outside. The pack of wolves want to talk to you about your return to *Winkle Bay*.'

Lauren's crying stopped abruptly.

'Thank you Irene,' said Carina grandly. 'I knew it was coming.'

'You're going to be in *Winkle Bay*?' stammered Lauren. Carina nodded.

'Why didn't you tell me?'

Baron Hard-Up and Prince Charming glared at Carina suspiciously.

'Because I didn't want to upset you.'

She smiled at them all with her best Fairy Godmother smile, linked her arm through Newall's and marched him to the stage door.

Lauren, Ben and Campbell stared after her in silence. She turned back to them, reaching for her sunglasses, as Newall pushed open the metal door. Cameras were starting to click amid the din of several eager voices fighting to ask questions at the same time.

'Funny old game this, isn't it?' she said to the trio in the corridor. 'You just never know what's around the corner.'

Lauren began to sob again.

Newall produced an umbrella. Acting as her bodyguard, he used it like a shield, beating a path through the mannerless crowd towards his car, parked at the end of the alleyway.

Carina had to shout to make herself heard. 'I can't answer any of your questions,' she yelled. 'Everything's top secret.'

'But you're definitely going back?', 'Who's being killed off?', 'How many?', 'Is it true there's going to be a big explosion.'

The questions were fielded with a few curt, 'No comment's'. Carina lapped up the attention, paused for photographs, blew kisses, played to the cameras. Newall reached the car and retrieved his key, with some difficulty, thanks to the jostling reporters. Carina grabbed his hand.

'Let's walk. They'll get tired of following,' she whispered in his ear.

He put a protective arm around her shoulders and hurried her around the corner. The press pack followed, the reporters talking over each other, pushing one another around as they jockeyed to get nearer to Carina. Very soon, there was only one solitary man left in the alley.

Gordon didn't seem to notice that he was soaking wet. His trusty baseball cap had been knocked off in the press scrummage. Ordinarily he would have been delighted to hear the news that Cora was going back to *Winkle Bay*. But not today. He stood stock still in the middle of the alley, playing back the events of the last few seconds in his mind, in painful detail. The policeman's arm going around Cora's waist, around her shoulder. The whispering, heads together. The smiles.

Cora had been lying to him. Stringing him along. He could see that now, so clearly.

Carina and Newall shook off the last of the hardiest reporters in the labyrinth known as Fenwick's Department Store. They made their way to the nearest cafe.

'That was mad,' said Newall.

'Is it a problem for you?' asked Carina.

'No!' Newall laughed. 'It was fun.'

Carina kissed him on the cheek.

'Where's your little friend?' she inquired. 'Pity she wasn't here. She would have terrified a few journalists, no problem.'

Newall laughed. Carina was probably right.

'She's gone to see your new boss. Or is it, 'old' boss?'

The actress looked at him blankly.

'Rufus Frenkel,' said Newall. 'Pauline was talking to one of her mates in British Transport Police this morning. Apparently it was

289

Frenkel who fell off the platform at a Metro Station yesterday.'

'Fell?' Carina forced herself to stay calm.

'So he says. We'd just like to make sure.'

Carina suddenly felt a little bit dizzy.

Chapter Twenty Seven

Jackie woke from a deep sleep, yawned and gazed up at the damp patches on the caravan roof. Pushing back the duvet, she checked the time by her watch. Five o'clock! Early evening. She had been in bed with Paul for over five hours of utter bliss. She leant across the pillow and kissed the slumbering tanned figure next to her.

'I have to go,' she whispered. Paul stirred, moaned vaguely and went back to sleep. Much as Jackie wanted to stay in bed for another five hours, she had the kids to think about. They would be home from After School Club in an hour or so and she wanted to be back for them. She wondered if they would get on with Paul and for the first time, began to worry herself about the possible family problems which might arise as a consequence of a new boyfriend coming into their lives. Her 'boyfriend'! She liked that. 'My boyfriend.' The children would like him, she was certain of that. Paul was the sporty type - he would take Christian to football practice, play with Evie in the garden, be their friend. Alan, thanks to his work commitments, had been an absent kind of father to the children. Totally absent, in fact, since his disappearance. She smiled to herself. She'd almost forgotten about her husband. Now she could think about him in a detached, clinical way. Her counsellor would be pleased at the progress she'd made! An unwelcome image of her mother-in-law swam into view. Now, that was someone who *wouldn't* be pleased by Paul's arrival on the scene. Tough! For once in her life, Jackie was putting herself first, and the people around her would have to lump it.

She dressed in silence, checked her appearance in the mirror and perched on the end of the bed to slip on her shoes. Grabbing her bag, she fumbled around in it for her car keys, found them, picked up her phone as an afterthought and stretched across the duvet to plant a tender kiss on Paul's forehead.

'I love you very much,' she said.

'Mmmm,' said the sleeping form distantly.

Jackie glanced at her phone. There was a text message waiting. She'd turned it to silent mode earlier on arriving at the caravan. With shaky fingers she unlocked the phone and retrieved the message. She hoped it wasn't an emergency at home, or Carina. If the children were in trouble, she'd never forgive herself. No, the message was from... Impossible!!!

Paul shot out of bed at the sound of the first scream. Disorientated and bleary eyed, he bumped his head against an overhead cupboard and staggered over to Jackie.

'What's wrong?'

Jackie was staring in horror at her phone, screaming all the while. He tried to enfold her in his arms but she pushed him away aggressively and backed against the door.

'Don't touch me!' she yelled. 'Don't come near me.'

'Jackie?'

Jackie was trembling uncontrollably and her teeth were chattering.

'I can't see you anymore,' she stuttered. 'It's over.'

'Why? What are you talking about?'

Again he tried to approach her but she turned her face away from him.

'Jackie? What have I done?'

'Nothing! Nothing!' Tears were coursing down her cheeks, blurring her vision.

'It's my fault. My mistake.'

Jackie grabbed at the door handle, pushed it open and staggered down the short steps to her car. Paul snatched up the duvet, swathed himself in it and followed her out.

'Tell me what's happened?' he pleaded.

Jackie ignored him. She was in the driving seat, turning over the ignition. Miller banged on the window.

'Please don't call me again,' she begged. 'I can't see you anymore.'

Jackie started howling again. Paul stood back, still in shock, as her car sped off.

'Nutter!' he yelled angrily. Why did he keep falling for mentally unstable women?

* * *

Clifton was finding it difficult to concentrate. She'd never worked in a glass walled office and hoped she'd never have to. How Rufus Frenkel ever managed to do any work was beyond her. There were too many distractions in the large room beyond. What were all those people doing? What were they talking about? She'd go mad with curiosity. If she hadn't already gone doollally from the self-conscious realisation that if she could see what everybody out there was up to, the people out there could just as easily scrutinise her! At any time! It was like being inside a goldfish bowl. What if

Frenkel picked his nose unconsciously, or scratched his arse without thinking? Everybody would see! The shame. The embarrassment. Then again, sitting across from Rufus at his desk, she took in the manicured fingers, the crisp shirt and suit and doubted that Frenkel ever picked or scratched *anything*.

'... To be quite honest with you, Sergeant,' Frenkel was saying, 'I don't remember much about it. It's all a bit of a blank.'

'So you can't be sure that you fell?'

'Well, no, but I must have.'

'No recollection of being pushed?'

Frenkel laughed, as if the question was totally ridiculous. But he sat back and thought about it. Frowning with concentration he tried to recollect, go through his movements in the station that afternoon. Steps down. Ticket machine. Escalator. Platform. Then nothing. He wished he'd turned down Carina's offer of a vodka. Or three.

'The platform was packed with shoppers and commuters,' he said slowly, adding, 'I was jostled - I remember that much, but so was everybody. As soon as we heard the train in the tunnel, we all started moving forward.'

'And that's all you remember?'

'Yes.'

Pauline opened her briefcase and brought out her copies of The Valmont Hotel lift users.

'Would you look through these and see if you recognise anyone. Maybe someone you noticed at the station?'

Rufus, hesitated, wanted to ask *why?* He'd already explained to the Transport Police it had been an accident. End of story. He bit his lip instead, holding back. Time was pressing. He just wanted the woman to leave. He took the photos and inspected them one by one, shaking his head again and again.

'Okay,' Clifton said, disappointed. 'Well, thank you for your time.'

Rufus got up and walked to the door, held it open gallantly for the detective, who was shutting her briefcase.

'Were you in town shopping?' she asked idly.

'No. Meeting. With an actress.'

Clifton paused on the threshold.

'Anyone really famous? Anyone I know?' she asked, trying to sound light and jovial.

'Carina Hemsley,' replied Frenkel.

Clifton couldn't help herself. 'You had a meeting with Carina Hemsley and five minutes later you ended up under a train?'

'Well, I don't think it was her fault,' said Rufus with a laugh. 'Five years ago I think she would have liked to see me dead, but not now.'

Clifton smiled back. 'No?'

'No. We're new best friends.'

'Oh. Right! You're giving her a job again. Of course.'

They shook hands. A secretary sprang up from nowhere and escorted her through the building to the exit. She remained unaware of the art deco architecture, the ultra-modern furniture and was oblivious to the secretary's polite though empty chatter. She had something on her mind. Clifton was thinking that awful things seemed to happen to the people (and pets) around Carina Hemsley. Was she jinxed? Or was there something more to this than met the eye?

'Boss?' She spoke urgently into her phone. 'Rufus Frenkel went to see Carina Hemsley just before he fell off the platform at the Metro Station.'

In the department store café, Newall excused himself, moved away from Carina. Immediately, a couple of old dears, who had been staring at them for the last half hour, found the courage to approach the soap star and took his place at the table.

'I know,' he said quietly. 'She told me.'

Clifton paused. When did she tell him? And why hadn't he let her know? She would ask him in person later, this wasn't a subject for a phone conversation. Instead she explained about Frenkel's inability to remember the events surrounding his accident.

'Call me stupid but I'm thinking, what if those letters *are* genuine, and there's a weirdo after Carina? What if he's getting to some of the people around her first? Am I reading too much into this?'

Newall shrugged. 'I don't know,' he said into the phone. 'It's a possibility.'

He turned to watch Carina chatting with her fans. They were enjoying every moment of being in her presence.

'Look, I'll call you later,' he said into the phone. 'I'm a bit tied up.'

He did not hear the sarcastic reply as he ended the call.

Roy and Carina strolled back to the theatre arm-in-arm. Carina wanted desperately to ask him about his phone call with Clifton. What had he said to her? Newall had been quiet after the conversation, distracted. Why? As they neared the stage door alley, Newall disentangled himself, motioned her to remain where she was standing and peered around the corner. The alley was empty.

'Not a paparazzi in sight,' he said, taking her by the hand. Carina flung her other arm around him.

'Carina?'

'Yes, my darling?'

Newall stroked her cheek, thoughtfully.

'Nothing. You take care. And don't leave the theatre on your own tonight. Wait for me.'

Carina nodded. 'What did Rufus say to your Sergeant?'

'He doesn't remember anything.'

'Something's wrong though. I can tell.'

Newall nodded and said slowly, 'I think it would be best if you kept your fans at arms length for a while.'

'But 'My People' expect to me to make an appearance. You've seen them at the stage door after a show. You know what they're like.'

'We don't know what they're *all* like,' he said sharply. 'Just for a while Carina, keep them at arms length? Eh?'

'But they'll think I'm shunning them.'

'Why is it so important to you?'

'What?'

'The need to be adored?'

Carina looked away and stared at the rain water pouring out of a broken guttering pipe on the wall over Newall's shoulder.

'Because it's a wonderful feeling. Knowing that you're loved.'

'By people you don't know?'

Carina smiled thinly. 'You ever been to those dog rescue places, the RSPCA that kind of thing, where they've got poor abandoned dogs in cages, and folk looking for a new pet parade up and down and pick the cutest one to take home?'

Newall nodded.

'The old dogs, the ugly ones, the difficult ones, they never get chosen.'

'Yeah, I always feel sorry for the ones that get left behind.'

Carina hung her head sadly.

'I was in a children's home 'til I was fifteen, Roy. I was one of those dogs left behind. Nobody wanted me. Not cute enough. You can't even begin to know what that was like. You just ache for someone to come along and say "we'll take you, we'll love you" but they never did. And that stays with you. It never, ever goes away.'

Newall wiped rain from his eyes and ran a hand through his wet hair. Carina knew he'd fallen for her story. It wasn't the truth but it was as near as dammit. Anyway, the truth was boring: unloved by her mother, raised by bossy Grandma, unpopular at school, she wished she had been raised in an orphanage. Hell, she'd told her fantasy so many times, she almost believed it herself.

'You're right,' he said, 'I can't know what that's like, but I'm only thinking of your safety. Stay away from the fans for a day or so, until the panto's finished, that's all I'm asking. And if it's love you're after, well, maybe I can help with that.'

Carina, secretly alarmed by the 'stay away from the fans' part of his speech, nodded submissively. Were Roy and Clifton onto Gordon's scent? Had Gordon slipped up somewhere and given himself away?

'All right. If you say so.'

Newall's face brightened. He kissed the top of her head.

'Why don't we go back to my place tonight?' he suggested.

'I'd like that,' she said and yelped as a droplet of rain, caught the back of her neck.

'Go on - inside,' Newall chided. Ignoring her fake leopard fur coat and matching gloves, the various layers of clothing and high boots, he added, 'It's cold out here.'

Carina teetered over to the stage door, pressed the buzzer and blew him a kiss as the door clicked open. Newall waved, waited until she'd gone inside, then made his way back to his car at the end of the alley. He jumped in, gunned the motor, flicked on the windscreen wipers and drove off into the busy stream of tea time traffic.

A square patch of lighter coloured tarmac was the only clue that a car had been parked in the alley for a few hours. A square, dry patch, and some small, green-brown puddles of brake fluid.

Carina paused outside her dressing room and listened to the hysterical sobbing coming from within. God, the woman was so predictable. She took a deep breath and closed her eyes. One. Two. Three! Caring, concerned Carina, she said to herself, flung open the door and sashayed in, arms outstretched in welcome.

Jackie was prostrate on the sofa, crying into a cushion. Her face, reddened and blotchy from stress and emotion was not a pretty sight. Neither was her nose, with the stream of mucus that drizzled out of it like a leaking tap.

'Jackie, Jackie, love! What on earth's happened?'

Jackie shook her head and wept even more.

'Come on, flower, nothing could be that bad. And even if it is, Aunty Carina's here to take care of you.'

She sat on the edge of the sofa and put a tentative hand on Jackie's knee.

'I've had a text,' bawled Jackie. 'A text from Alan! He's alive. He's coming back! What am I going to do?'

'But that's wonderful news,' Carina said effusively. 'It's what you've wanted for so long, it's a dream come true...' she paused, pretending to remember. 'Oh, shit-sugar-bollocks!' she exclaimed. 'You've been screwing Paul! Shit, Alan'll have something to say about that.'

Jackie uttered a tormented howl and a rivulet of snot poured out of her nose and over her top lip.

Carina grimaced and pointed to the lavatory door. 'Tidy yourself up, sweetheart and we'll talk about it.'

Jackie jumped up as commanded, slamming the door behind her. Carina dived over the sofa and grabbed Jackie's bag. Rooting around, she found the girly pink phone, retrieved the last message, deleted it quickly and buried the mobile deep down in the bag.

Jackie returned, sans snot, and took the vodka Carina had poured for her.

'So where's he been all this time?' Carina asked innocently.

'I don't know,' Jackie said, in a small quaking voice. 'He didn't say. He just said he was coming home and he loved me very much.'

'Did you text him back?'

The thought hadn't entered Jackie's mind. 'No.'

'Are you're sure it was him?'

'Yes!'

'But how, my love?'

'Because it was his number! It came up as 'Alan'.'

'Oh,' said Carina emphatically. 'What are you going to do about Paul?'

Jackie sobbed again. Carina tossed her a box of paper hankies.

'I've ended it. I can't see him again,' she wept. 'I'm a married woman.'

'Yes, you are,' said Carina.

Jackie dropped the box of hankies on her lap. 'I should call the police. He's a listed missing person. They need to know he's coming home...'

She fumbled in her bag for her phone.

'Let's see the message, flower?'

Jackie obliged. Or tried to. She flicked frantically through her Inbox.

'He said... it said... he said... it's here somewhere,' she muttered. 'It was... where is it? It was here. It *was*!' She gave a frustrated howl. 'I don't know where it's gone!'

Carina threw her a sympathetic look.

'Are you sure about that? Now *are* you?'

'Of course I am,' Jackie was puzzled, now. Uncertain. Her hands shook badly as she played around with the phone, opening up old messages, closing them in a furious frenzy.

'It was here. I saw it.' She threw the phone down on the sofa. 'What's wrong with me? Am I going mad?'

'No, no,' said Carina, soothingly. She hugged the poor woman in a tight bear hug.

'But I do have an explanation,' she confessed. Jackie peered up at her through her veil of tears.

'I think there's a little bit of guilt at play here.'

'Guilt?'

Carina nodded. 'Think about it. You meet a fella. He flatters you. He talks you into bed - probably quite easily, and you're having a great time, but at the back of your mind, there's a little voice saying "you can't do this! You're married. You're cheating on your poor missing husband and your kids think you're a slut! What about poor Alan?"'

Jackie looked at her aghast.

'But I didn't think that. I didn't Carina.'

'No, not consciously. It's all going on under the surface. And then what happens?' Carina paused for effect. 'You imagine a text from Alan. It's classic guilt complex, love.'

Jackie shook her head. 'But I saw it. I did!'

'Where is it then?'

Jackie had no answer. No explanation. She hung her head, wept and rocked back and forth on the sofa, hugging her stomach.

'Why don't you go home, kiss your kiddies and lie down for a while?' said Carina, eventually, after she could tolerate the snivelling no longer.

'I think I will,' replied Jackie in a tiny voice.

She walked to the door as if in a trance.

'Should I tell the police, or not?'

Carina drummed the arm of the sofa with her long nails. 'Not,' she advised. 'Unless he texts again. Then I think you should go to the cops.'

'But what if he doesn't? What if he never contacts me again?'

Carina sighed. 'Jackie, love, we all have our crosses to bear. Don't forget, ten o'clock tomorrow night. The Bessie Surtees Room at The Valmont. Wear something nice. Remember, nobody likes a frump.'

* * *

Newall waited for Pauline Clifton back at the office and when she hadn't shown up by half past six, he tried her mobile with no luck. He bumped into some old colleagues on the stairs, on his way out and resisted their pleas to join them for a drink in the pub. Roy wanted to see Carina. He was falling in love with her. It was as simple as that. She made him laugh. She moved him. He felt good around her. It had never been like that with his ex-wife. Not even during the good moments - of which there were few. He hated the time he spent away from Carina and counted the hours until he saw her again. This kind of love, for this is what it was - love. This kind of love was the sort that he had thought, until now, only existed in movies. All encompassing, all consuming. The Big One. At last

302

he understood why men bought flowers and jewellery and gifts for women. He'd only ever gone through the motions with his ex. He realised that now. He almost felt sorry for her. She'd ended up shackled to a man who was only ever half there, a man who wasn't that bothered about how she felt, what she liked, or wanted out of life. She'd done the right thing after all to extract herself from the situation. In doing so she had saved him. Freed him to discover true love. From now on, he would hold no grudge against her. He owed her a great debt of thanks.

Driving through the city streets on auto-pilot while he considered his feelings and laid to rest the bitterness he felt towards his ex-wife, Newall was in Moseley Street when he woke up to his surroundings and realised he was heading for the Valmont instead of the theatre. No matter, he could turn a right at the bottom of the hill by the Guildhall and get himself over to The West End in time for curtain up.

The brakes were rather sluggish, he thought as he picked up speed on the steep descent. He pumped the pedal again. Nothing. Shit, he was speeding up at an alarming rate. The car in front was getting nearer and nearer so he went down to fourth gear. It made little difference. Third gear. The engine whined alarmingly but still the vehicle sped on. He pulled over to the right to avoid hitting the Citroen ahead of him. Luckily the oncoming lane was empty. Think! Think! Pull on the handbrake? No, at this speed he might lose control and do untold damage to traffic in either direction. He swerved again as the car mounted the pavement at a sharp bend in the road. Switch off the ignition? He couldn't risk that either. The power steering would go. Modern cars! Stupid bloody modern cars! He swerved once more to avoid another vehicle ahead of him and yelled as the driving wheel spun round, trapping a finger.

Pumping the brake pedal all the time, and wiping at the sweat pouring down from his forehead, he applied a fist to the horn as he approached the small roundabout and hoped the other drivers would see him coming. Newall was only vaguely aware of the screech of brakes and the dull crump of cars to his right, shunting one another. He shot over the roundabout, struggling to keep control of the car. His off-side wing glanced off an oncoming van and everything became a blur. Roy's car mounted the pavement, collided head on with the crash barrier along the Quayside, flipped twice in an awful grinding of concrete and metal and sailed into the air. There was silence for a moment, then an explosive splash as the vehicle hit the murky waters of the Tyne. The crumpled car floated for a moment, then ever so slowly sank to the depths.

Chapter Twenty Eight

The nurse was speaking to her, Clifton knew that. She was talking because she could see her lips moving. Yet she couldn't make out the words. She was in a silent movie: all she could hear was the pounding of her heart in her ears. Rushing, roaring, boo-boom, boo-boom! Time had stopped for her. It was as if she'd fallen out of the known dimensions, into another universe: a slower, heavier, detached universe where everything looked the same but clearly wasn't. For instance, in her real world, the man in the bed attached to breathing apparatus, with tubes and wires jammed into his body, this man, who looked so peaceful and sweet, he could not possibly be her boss. The laughter lines, the beer belly, the downy tufts of hair on his ear lobes, they were all there, but it still wasn't him. Roy Newall never reported in sick. Roy avoided accidents. He was clever. Things like that didn't happen to him.

'Get up', she wanted to say, 'stop taking the piss,', 'you've had your little joke', 'Wake up!' But there he lay. A sleeping, pink, hairy, damaged Buddha. The same as he always was, cuts and bruises aside, yet not the same. Pauline touched his hand, stroked the still, warm fingers that looked so pale against the clean, white bed covers. How she had yearned to intertwine her fingers with his, to kiss them, feel the strength of his grip around her own. She tickled his palm, dragged a nail gently along his long life line (something of an irony) and traced the leaf shaped scar along the plump base of his thumb, a reminder of another accident, long since recovered from. If she could just get a reaction from him, a response, she would feel better. She could begin to hope. But he lay still, impervious to the stimuli. It was stupid of her, she realised that. He had failed to notice her in life, why would he notice her now, as he retreated from it.

She felt the nurse's touch on her arm.

'You're a work colleague, someone said?' she was asking. 'Work colleague' didn't sound adequate. It meant someone with whom you worked, who went home at the end of a working day and forgot about you. Someone whom you worked with but did not know properly.

'He's my friend,' cried Clifton. 'My friend!'

The nurse apologised. Clifton immediately felt bad.

'No, don't worry,' she said wearily. 'I just can't believe it, that's all. How can this *be*?'

She sat on the plastic chair beside the bed, forlornly and rummaged in her bag for a hankie. She hated it when people saw her crying, a rare occurrence admittedly. Somehow, this time around, she was past caring.

'I see people in this kind of state all the time. It's my job.'

'Different when it happens to you, though. I'd be the same,' admitted the nurse. She produced a hankie from her pocket and handed it over to a grateful Clifton.

'Is there really no chance of a recovery?' the detective asked.

'Oh, pet, I'm not one of the consultants. I couldn't say for sure. All I know is he was a long time in the water, starved of oxygen,' stated the nurse.

Clifton nodded. 'I felt it. I could tell. Part of him was missing.

Just by looking at him. I knew it.'

She wanted to scream and rant at the unfairness of it all. Instead, she took a deep breath, pocketed the hankie and thanked the nurse for her kindness. This was no time for hysteria. There were things to do. Questions to ask. Newall was a careful driver. Always had been. He'd passed his advance driving test a few years ago, a fact he'd bragged about more than once. Road awareness and safety were important to him. He did not, would not, drive recklessly.

From what she'd managed to glean from the preliminary investigation into the accident, eyewitness accounts spoke of Newall frantically working the steering wheel, wrestling to keep control of the vehicle as it sped down Dean Street towards the river, which suggested some kind of mechanical fault. Had her boss aimed for the Tyne intentionally, to avoid damage to pedestrians and other drivers? It wouldn't surprise her. That was him all over. Concerned for the innocent, a noble man. Clifton would have to wait until forensics finished with their detailed examination of Newall's car before she could give full reign to her suspicions. Three hours earlier, when one of her colleagues at the station phoned to give her the news, instinct had told her this was not a straightforward road incident.

'The policeman who came up with him from A&E said there was no next of kin,' the nurse said.

Pauline nodded. 'Divorced. He hasn't seen his wife for years. No kids. I think his parents died a while back.'

'Girlfriend? Partner?'

'Girlfriend of sorts.'

The nurse looked at her quizzically.

'He'd just met someone.'

'Ah, that's sad.'

Clifton looked away, anger welling up inside her as it always did when she thought about Carina Hemsley. She'd called her in the interval to let her know about the accident, the terrible prognosis. There had been much melodramatic weeping and wailing on the actress's part with cries of angst and sorrowful utterances Clifton found difficult to decipher through the distortion and heavy breathing.

Another nurse popped her head round the door, beckoned to the other who excused herself and left the room. Clifton watched them through the narrow glass window in the door, talking animatedly. They were huddled together, exchanging excited gestures. Was their news? Some hope? The ICU nurse returned to her post in the room.

Clifton jumped up, sending her chair skidding back against the wall. 'Has something happened?'

The nurse reddened. 'Oh, not really, no,' she said, hesitantly. Then, lowering her voice, she asked, 'Mr Newall's girlfriend? Is she Carina Hemsley?'

'Yes. Why?' Clifton demanded irritably.

'She's on her way up.'

Excited by the imminent arrival of a huge star, she laughed nervously and said, 'There are photographers everywhere downstairs. Security's going mad!'

Pauline's jaw tightened. She could feel her hackles rising. She was not going to allow her boss's plight to be turned into some kind of media stunt. Newall had dignity.

'You stupid sod,' she cried, gazing down at her boss's silent form. 'Why did you have to get involved with her?'

Lights glowed, machinery bleeped, LCD displays flickered and waned but of the body in the bed, there was no response.

A shimmering apparition in silver sequins burst into the room. Carina was still wearing her Fairy Godmother ball gown. Great swathes of chiffon and white netting engulfed the small room as she rustled and bustled over to the bed.

'My poor Roy. Wake up! Wake up, my darling.'

'It'll take more than a magic wand to revive him,' said Clifton sarcastically. The actress had dashed from the theatre with all her theatrical props - diamante tiara, fur muff and glittering, jewel encrusted wand. She glanced down at the shiny stick in her hand, as if seeing it for the first time, and lowered it to her side. She turned to the nurse, tears coursing down her cheeks.

'Why won't he wake up?'

Clifton shook her head angrily.

'I told you before, he's in a coma. He's never going to wake up. His brain's been starved of oxygen for too long. He's a cabbage.'

'Steady on, pet,' warned the nurse. 'That's a bit harsh.'

She put an arm around Carina, who was hiding her face behind a taloned, shaking hand.

'It's the truth, isn't it?' Clifton couldn't help sounding unpleasant. Upset as she'd claimed to be, during that earlier phone call, Carina had managed to control her emotions enough to finish the pantomime. And that annoyed Pauline Clifton. If it were *her* lover lying in a hospital bed, close to death, she would have been round there like a shot. Bugger artistic commitments.

The nurse glared at the police officer. 'Cora's had a bit of a shock,' she whispered. 'We can talk about the details later.'

She produced another hankie, unfolded it and put it in Carina's hand.

'Have a good blow, dear,' she urged.

Carina blew.

'How did it happen?' she cried. 'I don't understand.'

'Neither do we,' replied Clifton. 'But we will soon. Sounds to me like his brakes failed.'

Carina stopped crying and looked up.

'*Failed?*'

Clifton nodded slowly. 'We'll know for sure by the morning.'

'But it was a new car, wasn't it?'

Carina was panicking inwardly. As soon as Detective Plain Jane called her, she'd suspected Gordon's involvement. It was too much of a coincidence. She could see from Clifton's tone that she had her suspicions too. The woman was in love with Newall. That much had been obvious from the start. Carina would have to be careful. A woman in love spelled trouble - she could be a tenacious foe. If Clifton suspected something, she would not let go lightly. She'd pursue her quarry doggedly, probably to the death. Yes, the girl had it in her, all right.

Carina bent over Newall's prostrate body and kissed him on the cheek. The look of pain in her eyes, the sadness, they were genuinely felt. In that moment. She had liked Roy. Enjoyed his company. The sex. The closeness. In a short term, easy-going kind of way but they would have had no future together. Now that her career was heading for the stratosphere again, any relationship with a 'civilian' was doomed. 'Celeb' and 'Non-Celeb' - they just didn't mix. She would remember his strength of character, his kind, almost naïve manner and think of him with fondness, sometime, somewhere. In a quiet moment. But not now. She had a problem to deal with: a solution to find. No, not to 'find': to enforce. Gordon's time was up.

As if reading her mind, Clifton said, 'Why do accidents keep happening around you?'

'What do you mean?' snapped the actress.

'Rufus Frenkel, Dougie Hunt, The Boss...'

'You think this is all my fault?'

'It's weird, don't you think?' suggested the detective, ignoring the glistening tears which were threatening to ruin Carina's stage make-up.

'Listen to me,' Carina urged. 'You're upset. I know how much Roy means to you. I really do.'

Clifton rounded on her. 'You know nothing.'

Carina aimed for the heart and fired.

'I know that you love him.'

Clifton tried to voice a protest but it stuck in her throat. A throbbing pain pounded in her head and it took all her self-control not to punch Carina hard in the mouth.

'I'm not responsible for this,' Carina said reasonably.

Her tone had the desired effect. Clifton tipped over the edge.

'What I want to know,' she snapped angrily, 'is, if there really is somebody out there determined to bump you off, why don't they just get on with it and put us all out of our misery?'

The nurse placed herself between them.

'I think you should leave.'

Pauline stared at her disbelievingly.

'Me?' she gasped.

'Yes. Now.'

Clifton threw her bag around her shoulder and fled.

'I'm sorry about that,' said the nurse.

Carina shook her head. 'That's quite all right, flower. She's overwrought. They were very close.'

'You're so understanding.'

Carina shrugged modestly. The nurse went on.

'I'm a big fan,' she admitted. 'I'm so pleased you're going back to *Winkle Bay*. We'll be watching.'

'Bless you.'

'Would you like a cup of tea?'

'Ooh, I'd kill for one.'

The nurse hurried out, desperate to oblige the famous actress. Carina watched her hurry along the corridor like a giddy penguin, waited until she had turned the corner, then produced her mobile phone. Ignoring the warnings on the wall, she speed-dialled Gordon.

'Hello, my gorgeous man. How are you?'

There was a silence while he hesitated to answer.

'Hello Cora,' he muttered nervously. 'Everything all right?'

'Couldn't be better. Listen up, handsome, I've got some great news.'

'Oh?'

'You know it's the last night of the panto tomorrow night?'

'Yeah.'

'What would you say to me coming over to yours when I've finished?'

Gordon gasped.

'Really? Tomorrow?'

'Sooner the better,' said Carina, with a sly grin. 'I can't wait to get my hands on you.'

'Hey! You can meet me Mam, as well!'

'You bet.'

'Oh Cora, I can't wait.'

'Me neither.'

She listened to his promises of undying love, tolerated his heavy breathing and tedious, juvenile descriptions of their future life

312

together, waiting for a suitable lull in the conversation.

'Just one little favour, my darling,' she cooed. 'Could you leave your moped for me outside the hotel tomorrow. That way I can get to you sooner.'

'Can't you get a taxi?'

'No,' she said abruptly. She smiled slyly to herself. 'I get all horny riding a scooter.'

'Okay.'

'Leave the key on the tyre under the mudguard and I'll be round a.s.a.p.'

She ended the call moments before the nurse returned with a cup of tea on a saucer with a ginger biscuit.

Carina stayed long enough to give a good impression of the caring, distraught girlfriend - she wept a few times against another nurse's breast, uttered a few token phrases like 'heart-broken', 'never love another man again', and 'my life is over', then composing herself, became a stoic woman, showing her brave face to the world... until she reached the hospital entrance. Unable to hold on to her grief and despair any longer, Carina completely broke down... in the full glare of the waiting British tabloid Press.

Chapter Twenty Nine

The news that Newall's car had been tampered with came as no surprise to Clifton. She sifted through the details of the forensics report at her desk early the next morning. A severed brake line. Simple and ruthlessly effective. Deliberate. Cars, especially unmarked police cars were often the subject of wanton criminal damage - smashed windscreens, slashed tyres, scratched body work. This was not the work of some bored kid armed with a screwdriver. It was something altogether different. Whoever did it, knew exactly what they were doing: they wanted her boss out of the way. There was no other explanation.

The questions of 'why' and 'whom' flashed in and out of her mind along with an awful vision of Newall at the wheel of his car, fighting to gain control of the steering as the vehicle sped inexorably towards its watery resting place. Prolonging the torture, she closed her eyes, placed herself in the driver's seat and imagined, quite masochistically the fear, the terror, that must have coursed through Newall's being during those final moments. Did he think he was going to die, or suspect that his life as he knew it was about to change forever? Probably not. Adrenalin tended to focus the mind. She knew that from first hand experience.

Clifton stared across at the empty desk opposite her, with the half eaten bag of fruit gums perched on the messy pile of folders in the D.I's in-tray. His Queen Elizabeth Golden Jubilee mug, purchased from a charity shop by Pauline and given to her republican boss as a joke, sat where its owner had left it the previous day, dried coffee drips obscuring Her Majesty's gold-leafed profile, crumbs from a dunked biscuit caked to the rim. She remembered handing him the sweet, hot beverage less than twenty four hours earlier.

'One day you'll learn how to make a decent cup of coffee,' he'd moaned after taking his first swig. One day she might. Newall would never be able to appreciate it though. Clifton blinked away the memory. Focussing on the present, she noticed her colleagues watching from the far end of the office. They'd all heard the news. One or two had called her late in the evening to commiserate. On auto-pilot, she couldn't remember what she'd said in reply. Something clichéd, something hollow, something brief, for she could not trust her voice to keep the grief she felt from spilling out. She ignored their concerned nods, the sympathetic smiles and concentrated on getting through the day. The DCI wanted to see her later that afternoon, no doubt to let her know who would be taking over Newall's case load. And to ask her if she knew of anyone who might have a motive for wanting to harm one of his best officers.

Clifton had already rooted around in her memory for potential suspects. During their two years together, threats from criminals, especially the ones they'd seen banged up were considered par for the course. Nobody took them seriously. They were seen usually for what they were: outpourings of irrational rage echoing around a courtroom. One or two possibilities sprang to mind, vaguely. On the whole though, even if a few hardened thugs harboured a grudge, she doubted that they would act upon them. No, this was something different. She sensed it. Something wasn't right. Her thoughts went back to the previous evening and her encounter with Carina at the hospital. Remembering some of the things she'd said to her made her feel ashamed. She spoke in anger, in haste, with the knowledge that she'd been so bloody envious and resentful of the boss's relationship with the actress. Clifton had behaved unprofessionally. Even so, one thing she'd said to her, she still stood by. Odd things were happening around Carina Hemsley. Odd things kept happening to the people around her.

In the canteen she ordered a bacon roll, exchanged a few meaningless words of commiseration with Audrey the chef, who had a soft spot for her boss, always gave him an extra slice of bacon with his breakfast, always laughed too long and too loud at his crass jokes and headed back to her office. It was only on her way out that she noticed the discarded morning newspaper, folded at a particular page and article, lying amongst abandoned trays on a table. The photograph of a teary-eyed Carina Hemsley leaving the hospital under the headline '*Winkle Bay* Star's Heartache' was not the object of her attention. She was more interested in the smaller article next to it about the '*Winkle Bay* Explosive Storyline' with a small photo insert of a smiling Rufus Frenkel standing next to the unsmiling 'soap guru' Mick Flynt. The physical memento's of Frenkel's recent scrape with death - his bruised cheek and scratched nose had not been airbrushed out by the newspaper. Clifton dropped the paper on the table and returned to her office where she made a brief phone call before grabbing her coat. Odd things kept happening around Carina Hemsley?! The woman in the public eye! Well, thanks to the Big Brother society they lived in, Carina wasn't the only person with a camera trained on her.

Fifteen minutes later she found herself sitting before a bank of monitors at Metro Transport HQ with her old Transport Police colleague and mate, Charlie Smith. Charlie was trying to tell her how sorry he'd been to hear the news about Roy Newall. He was a good bloke, he kept saying. One of the best. Clifton cut across him.

'Did you look at the CCTV footage for that afternoon?' she asked.

Smith shook his head. 'There didn't seem to be any point. Frenkel admitted he'd had a few drinks and was quite adamant he just fell in the rush for the train...'

'He wasn't so sure when I spoke to him,' she replied.

Smith shrugged and let his fingers move around the playback machine. A hoard of commuters swarmed across the nearest monitor like speeded up, determined ants as the police officer sought the time and the camera angle he was looking for. He hit play and Clifton leaned closer to the screen to watch Rufus Frenkel as he strode out onto the platform to wait for the train. Two or three travellers appeared behind him, then another few. It was almost rush hour and the platform filled up quite quickly. The actual moment of his fall onto the tracks was obscured by the tide of passengers surging forward.

'Is there another camera angle? I can't see clearly.'

Smith flicked a switch and another monitor played out an alternative point of view of the brightly lit platform. Again, the volume of commuters and an old man carrying his fishing rod equipment in the vertical position, blotted out the view of the 'incident'.

'Okay,' muttered Clifton. 'Go back to the first camera output and play it back slowly.'

Smith obliged and the scene played out before them again, this time with Frenkel looking like he was wading through treacle.

Pauline concentrated on the people behind him. The images were difficult to see clearly, their graininess enhanced by the slow speed of the playback. She was drawn to the small, tubby man in the baseball cap who walked onto the platform after Rufus. There was something familiar about him. Had she seen him before or was it just her imagination, willing her to believe it?

She asked Charlie to rewind and play back at normal speed again. And again. She was not mistaken. She *had* seen him before. Smith saw her staring.

'You got something?'

'I'm not sure.'

He hit rewind again and they both moved forward to get a better view.

'Is it me? Or is he behaving oddly?' she asked.

'I think that's what you call 'furtive',' said Charlie.

'Can you get camera P.O.V from the station entrance?'

'Yup.'

Clifton held her breath while her friend sifted through a pile of discs. If Rufus Frenkel was being followed, then it was possible he might have been pushed. Why, she couldn't say. Yet. Her hunch was telling her that it had something to do with Carina Hemsley.

'Here we go.'

Clifton put her suspicions to the back of her mind and watched the monitor closely. Footage from the camera trained at the foot of the stairs showed a steady stream of people descending from ground level to the subterranean ticket area. Feet and legs came into view first and Clifton recognised Frenkel's highly polished shoes as they came into view. She noticed he was slightly shaky on his feet - he almost missed his footing on one step as he tripped down the stairs.

Seconds later, a grubby parka on top of dirty trainers announced the arrival of another familiar face. The tubby man in the baseball cap. He paused at the bottom of the stairs, watching something beyond the range of the camera.

'This might help,' offered Charlie.

The third monitor on the wall flickered into life with a wide view of the entire ticket hall. The man in the baseball cap was clearly observing Frenkel.

Clifton slapped her leg. 'He *was* being followed!'

'What's this all about Pauline?'

'I'm not sure,' she lied. Charlie looked at her. She knew he didn't believe her. 'The Boss always said, *If you've got a hunch? Act on it.* That's all I'm doing.'

'Whatever you say,' murmured Smith dubiously. His fingers worked the console keyboard and before long the entire bank of monitors were showing a blown-up, enhanced image of Gordon's face.

'Do you know him?' he asked.

Clifton nodded slowly. 'I'm sure I've come across him. Where though, I just don't know.'

'He looks like a right sad git,' Charlie volunteered. 'Ex-boyfriend maybe?'

Clifton laughed and then burst into tears.

The smiling receptionist at A1 TV studios gave her a hard time. 'He's very busy,' she breathed unctuously, 'and doesn't see people without an appointment.'

'This is a police matter,' said Clifton levelly.

'Even so,' retorted the receptionist, still smiling, 'this is a very busy time for us all. We're about to film some important episodes and we're working flat out...'

What was wrong with these telly people? Did they have no grasp of reality, Clifton wondered incredulously?

'I don't care if you're working flat on your back... Jules,' she said, glancing down at the nameplate on the woman's desk, 'pick up the fucking phone and tell him I'm coming up.'

She stormed past the indignant Jules, whose smile had faded as quickly as the celebrity career of a Big Brother housemate, and mounted the stairs.

Rufus Frenkel was waiting for her as she entered the open plan office.

'Is this going to take long?' he inquired, 'I've got a special effects meeting in five minutes.'

'It'll take a minute tops,' Clifton promised. 'I think you were followed into the Metro station the other day, Mr Frenkel, and onto the platform, by this man.'

She pulled him over to the nearest desk in the room and slapped the blown up still from the CCTV tape down with relish.

'Have you seen him before?'

Rufus stared at the bloated features under the baseball cap.

'Yes,' he said, startled.

He sank into the nearest chair. 'He was here - I mean, outside the gates, that day, the day I went over to see Carina. He spoke to me.'

'What did he say?' Clifton could feel her heart thumping. She was onto something and it felt good.

'He said he was going to marry Cora.'

'*Cora?*'

'I know.' Rufus studied the photo closely. 'A lot of the fans, they find it difficult to separate fact from fiction.'

'Why's that?' wondered Clifton.

'Oh, that's easy,' replied Frenkel. 'It's because they're nuts.'

'He didn't give you a name?'

Rufus thought back to the brief encounter. 'No. But he could be a member of the fan club. Probably is, judging by the look of him. Not all there,' he explained. 'Talk to Jules. She'll give you a number for *The Winklers*.'

She stared at him blankly. 'The Fan Club?'

Frenkel nodded.

Clifton thanked him for his time. 'I'll leave you to your special effects,' she said. On her way out, she stopped at reception to obtain the necessary information. Jules's smile had returned but the eyes were as cold as steel.

'I'm sorry I swore at you,' Pauline mumbled, trying to sound sincere.

'Sweetheart,' purred Jules. 'I work in television. Water off a fucking duck's back.'

At The Valmont, Clifton, in an attempt to assuage her biscuit quota guilt, considered mounting the stairs up to Carina's suite. In the end, common sense won the day and she rode the lift to the top floor instead.

'Oh, you poor girl. Come in. I haven't slept a wink. I am destroyed!'

For a destroyed woman, Carina looked the picture of health and vitality.

'I'm sorry about...' Clifton struggled to find the right words. '... About some of the things I said last night. I was upset.'

'I know.' The actress squeezed her arm. 'I do understand.'

'Have you seen him this morning?' Clifton inquired.

'I haven't had the strength,' replied Carina, with an actor's wobble in her voice. 'It's like everything's coming to an end. First

Roy, and now the panto.'

Clifton didn't follow.

'It's the last night of Cinderella. The final performance,' sighed Carina.

'Oh, how awful,' said Clifton, unable to keep her sarcasm at bay. She considered it highly inappropriate, nay, fatuous, to link the end of a stupid kiddies panto run in the same breath as Newall's crash and subsequent vegetative state. Carina looked at her askance before continuing.

'Roy and I were so looking forward to spending some quality time together. It'll never happen now.' She sighed, before adding, 'It breaks my heart to think of him as a cabbage.'

Clifton felt the blood drain from her cheeks. An icy coldness stabbed through her heart like a knife as the insensitive words hit home. She changed the subject.

'I suppose you'll be checking out. Going back home tomorrow?'

'No, lovey! Staying on. I'm going back to *Winkle Bay* for a few weeks - and then back for a longer stint later in the year.'

Clifton, who had stopped listening, looked out at the view of the Tyne and the bridges and the amazing architecture on both the Newcastle and the Gateshead side.

'That's nice for you,' she said vacantly.

Her eyes fixed on one particular spot along the Quayside.

'You can see where his car went in the water from here.'

Carina frowned. 'Can you?' she tutted. 'I'll have to change rooms.'

Clifton continued to gaze down at the river and said nothing for a moment. The actress looked at her watch.

'Did you want something in particular, flower?'

Clifton smiled. 'Yes,' she said, brightening. 'Carina? I hope you can help me.'

'I hope so too.' The woman was starting to get on Carina's nerves. All that sad-eyed gazing into the distance like some kind of tortured Jane Austen heroine. What the Hell did she want? She tried to maintain her air of interest and good-will while the idiot police woman rifled through her briefcase.

Carina had time to absorb the image as Clifton produced the photograph with a flourish. She realised it was Gordon, a split second before Ms. Clifton placed it in full view on the coffee table in front of her and in that split second, she acted, conquering the numb feeling in her legs which suggested that they were about to buckle under her imminently and effected a suitable look - a combination of faint curiosity and nonchalance.

'Have you ever seen this man before, Miss Hemsley?' The police woman was looking at her intently.

Carina played with her bottom lip, pretending to think.

'I don't think so. Who is he?'

'We don't know yet.'

'Is he a criminal?'

'Maybe. It's quite possible he's a member of 'The *Winkle Bay* Fan Club' as well.'

'A Winkler?' gasped Carina, and wondered almost immediately if she'd gone O.T.T. The gasp was a step too far. However, the detective, if she'd noticed didn't give her a second glance. She seemed more interested in the grainy picture. How had Gordon's photograph found its way into the hands of the police? Where was it taken? Carina's palms were sweating. Were the police onto Gordon? Were they onto her? Please God, no. Was it her imagination or was the police officer staring at her in a peculiar way? Suspiciously. Yes, that was it. She definitely looked suspicious. She was toying with her. She knew. This was all Gordon's fault, the big fat twat. She should have put an end to him ages ago. It was a moment or two before she realised Clifton was talking to her again.

'He was seen hanging around the studio gates of A1 TV on the day Rufus Frenkel left in his car to visit you at the theatre. And he was caught later on CCTV camera, following Mr Frenkel into the Central Station Metro station.'

'No!' Carina sounded suitably aghast and it pleased her when DS Clifton nodded in approval at her outrage. Or was she just leading her into a trap? Stringing her along until she'd boxed herself into a tight corner. She didn't know anymore.

'Are you sure you haven't seen him before? At a function for the soap opera perhaps?'

Carina shook her head quickly. 'To tell you the truth I never look at the fans,' she admitted. '*Look down, sign autograph, look up again, get out of there*, that's my motto.'

Clifton smiled coldly, replaced the photograph inside the folder. If Carina's legions of fans ever heard her talking about them like that, her days of living it up in lavish hotels would be over pretty damn quick. Carina noticed the smile, mistook disapproval for suspicion.

'I tried to call your friend Jackie, who runs the Fan Club,' she revealed.

'Any joy?'

Clifton shook her head. 'Phone kept ringing and ringing. No answer.'

Carina exhaled loudly. 'It'll go on ringing and ringing, poor thing.'

'Has something happened?'

Carina exhaled again, deliberated before answering and when she did she tried to use her words carefully.

'It's been on the cards for a while. She's... emotionally...' she wanted to say the word 'crippled' but resisted temptation, plumping for 'exhausted' instead.

'What happened?'

Carina leaned forward conspiratorially. 'Her husband ran off,' she revealed. 'Just upped and left without a goodbye or anything. She hasn't been right since.' She patted Clifton on the arm. 'I've tried to keep her mind occupied. Bless her. I blame myself. Think I overworked her. She threw a bit of a wobbler - not a pretty sight.'

She paused to study her varnished nails, before continuing. 'She'll be at the end of show party, tonight. Probably.'

Clifton pushed her notebook forward and offered a pen. 'Perhaps you could give me her mobile number?'

The actress took up the pen and scribbled down Jackie's mobile phone number. She found Clifton's unblinking stare nerve-wracking.

'You're going to a party, the day after your boyfriend goes into a coma?' asked Clifton.

'I don't have any choice. I'm the head of The Company. It's expected of me.'

She couldn't resist pushing.

'Don't think too badly of me, sweetheart. Inside...' - and here she inserted her dramatic pause, with a sly peek in Clifton's direction to make sure she was with her on the emotional journey. 'Inside I'm *dying*!'

Shit, she thought again. Was that too over the top? The police-woman, who was nodding sympathetically, appeared not to have noticed anything out of the ordinary. The photograph of Gordon had shaken her badly, despite the bravado of her performance. The longer Clifton stayed, the more tense she felt. She took out her cigarette holder and loaded up with shaking hands. She tried to steady them, then realised that she was *supposed* to be in a highly nervous state. She had good grounds. Her boyfriend was in a vegetative state in hospital. How could she forget?!

'Until we find this man and eliminate him from our enquiries,' Clifton was saying, 'I'd urge you to proceed with caution. Stay with your friends, never go anywhere alone. Too many odd things have been happening around you.'

'All right,' replied Carina meekly.

'I shouldn't be telling you this,' said the detective as she made her way to the door. 'I don't have any proof. Not yet anyway. But it could be that this man is behind the death threats.'

Carina gulped. 'Oh, my bloody God!'

'Miss Hemsley?' Clifton, hand on the doorknob, was turning around now. There was no mistaking the more formal tone. 'I've been watching you for a while.'

'Oh?'

Carina's bottom lip trembled ever so slightly and she took another long suck on her cigarette holder as Clifton came back into the room.

'You keep flouting the 'No Smoking Laws'. You really shouldn't.'

Carina dropped the holder and cigarette into the nearby vase of lilies.

'I'm sorry,' she whispered, 'I'm just a sad old addict.'

'Why don't you try a nicotine patch?'

Carina nodded. 'I will.'

Clifton smiled at her supportively.

Chapter Thirty

Day in, day out, twice a day in fact, Jez didn't know how the actors sustained their energy. They were a waste of space as far as he was concerned but he had to hand it to them, this lot knew how to put on a show. He was sitting in one of the boxes watching the last matinée performance. One more show after this and that was it. Thank God. For a variety of reasons, he would not look back on this panto run with a smiling sense of nostalgia. He couldn't wait for it all to be over. As for the future, there was much to think about. His entrepreneurial skills had taken a pounding over the past few weeks. Was it only a matter of weeks? It seemed like years, sometimes, when he thought about it. Perhaps the time had come for him to move on. When you stopped enjoying something, it was time to stop. He'd always believed that and that philosophy had stood him in good stead over the years. Did the same attitude apply to marriage and relationships? No, absolutely not. Sadly, he could not be absolutely sure that his wife was of the same philosophical persuasion. Jez put aside these more uncomfortable thoughts to watch the on-stage pyrotechnics, as the pumpkin transformed magically into a glittering coach. He looked below at the sea of rapt faces in the audience. Oh, to be a kid again. To believe in magical things. To be certain that good triumphed over evil and that men and women fell in love and lived happily ever after. Much as he hated to admit it, perhaps Campbell Garibaldi had been right all along. It was wrong to give children false hope. He should have allowed him to stage his original script, the premise of which was that the course of love did not run smoothly.

The door behind him opened and Heidi sidled in beside him. He noticed she'd dispensed with her usual affectionate greeting of a hug and a kiss. Heidi was whispering in his ear and rifling through an expensive looking shopping bag, tied at the handles with a black silk bow.

'Wait 'til you see what I've bought,' she whispered. She untied the bow and lifted out a series of small blue jewellery boxes. The first one she opened contained a small diamond brooch.

'Very nice. How many have you bought?' he asked loudly, noticing the bag was full of little blue boxes.

'Five,' said Heidi defensively.

'But you only need one!' Did the woman want to destroy his fortune as well as his marriage?

'Silly! They're not for me. They're for the cast. Thank you presents. Brooches for the girls and...' Heidi delved into the bag and picked out a slightly larger box, '... a silver bracelet for the boys.'

Jez surveyed the bulky linked chain sitting elegantly on a bed of black velvet.

'It's what you do in the theatre. Hand out gifts when the play finishes.'

'Aren't bracelets a bit nancy-boy-ish?'

Heidi laughed. 'Campbell thought they were a nice idea...'

'Ah!' said Jez bitterly. 'Campbell. Figures.'

Heidi snapped the bracelet box shut with a snap.

'I didn't spend much money, darling,' she whispered defensively. 'The diamonds aren't real and the silver chains weren't the most expensive.'

Jez nodded distantly and craned his neck to see what the audience was suddenly laughing at. One of the liveried ponies, pulling Cinderella's coach had lifted its tail and deposited a pile of dung on the stage.

'I told that animal handler woman,' he hissed angrily. 'Don't feed the bloody ponies before they go on. It totally ruins the magic when they shit all over the place.'

Heidi ignored his outburst.

'How's Carina?'

Jez shrugged.

'Poor woman.'

'It's one thing after another with her,' muttered Jez. 'She's jinxed.' He looked at his wife. 'Or I am.'

Heidi sat for a moment, deep in thought. It hadn't struck her until now that Jez wouldn't understand. She was not playing fair. She could see that. He needed to know and she wanted to explain, despite the promise she had made.

'Jez?' she said eventually. 'About Campbell.'

'What about him?!'

The anger was there in his voice. She realised this was not the moment to reveal the truth.

'Nothing.'

Heidi picked up her shopping and crept silently out of the box. Jez picked up the box of chocolates perched on the seat next to him, delved into the packaging noisily and slammed one into his mouth. It was a coffee centre.

'Great!' he sighed. 'Just great!'

Backstage, during the interval Carina found Lauren sobbing against Sylvie's shoulder.

'Well, there's a sight for sore eyes. The Wicked Step-Mother consoling little Cinderella! Who'd've thought it?'

Sylvie, whose maternal instincts measured zero on the 'Loving Mother Scale', grimaced at her. Carina grabbed Lauren's shoulders and pulled her off the frosty actress.

'I'm going to miss you all so much,' she sobbed. 'You're like family to me.'

'Oh, Bless!' said Carina.

Sylvie continued to grimace.

'Has she dribbled mascara down my dress?'

Carina shook her head, then spotted Ben passing by. Her shrill whistle, as piercing and confident as any navvy's echoed down the corridor. Ben looked over.

'Here! Mush! Come and grab your girlfriend.'

Prince Charming looked far from charming as he stomped over to them.

'What's wrong with you?' he asked, unsympathetically. 'We're due back on stage in ten minutes.'

'I just don't want it to end,' whimpered Cinderella.

'Come on,' said Ben coldly, yanking her by the shoulders in the direction of his dressing room. The older two actresses watched as, heels squeaking along the floor and ball gown billowing in all directions, Lauren was dragged unceremoniously into Dressing Room Number Three.

'I'll give that relationship another twenty four hours,' said Sylvie unkindly.

'I'll give it 'til half way through tonight's party,' chortled Carina.

Sylvie sighed. 'I do feel for her, the poor child. I know what it's like.'

She looked up and down the corridor conspiratorially.

'I had a thing with Larry Olivier during a run of Uncle Vanya years ago,' she confided. 'Thought it was the real thing but no, it was just sex, sex, sex. And then he dumped me on the last night.'

'I had a similar thing with Tommy Cooper,' admitted Carina. 'He was like his magic tricks - useless. Big clammy hands like shovels, everywhere. I had to keep telling him - not like that! Like *that*!'

She chuckled but Sylvie wasn't listening. Her eyes had a far away look to them. She was back in Nineteen Sixty, treading the boards at Chichester.

'I was so thrilled he was actually interested in me,' she said dreamily. 'The man who was Max De Winter, Heathcliff, Henry the Fifth.'

She jolted herself out of her reverie. 'But it was a long time after all that when I knew him. He'd long since peaked. When he took his clothes off he looked like Gollum. I was in love with the dream of the man, not the actual man himself. Story of my life, darling.'

'Shame,' offered Carina. She smacked her lips together. 'Ooh, I'm parched.'

'I've got just the thing,' said Sylvie, returning to the present day.

Carina rather hoped she might. She followed the Wicked Step-Mother into her dressing room and shut the door behind them. Sylvie was already filling a glass from a large brandy bottle on her dressing table.

'I don't usually drink in the afternoon,' she said. Carina smiled. The woman's breath reeked of alcohol from first thing in the morning to last thing at night. Had done since day one of rehearsals. She watched as Sylvie downed the contents of the large glass in one long, greedy gulp. She smacked her lips and looked at Carina in a startled fashion, as if to say 'aren't you drinking with me?', then realised she'd only filled the one glass.

'Oh, darling, I'm so sorry. There's another tumbler somewhere.' She rooted around her dressing table, overturning pots of stage make-up. 'I know!' she exclaimed and dashed into the en-suite bathroom.

Uncertain as to how much time she had, Carina acted quickly. She grabbed Sylvie's carelessly abandoned handbag and shook it. The contents rattled alarmingly. Bingo! Carina undid the clasp with deft fingers. The interior resembled a pharmacist's drug counter after a robbery, with dozens of multi-coloured pills and capsules - barbiturates, sleeping pills and over the counter remedies lying in piles amongst her toiletries and age-defying potions. Carina sifted through the various bottles of pills, found a brown bottle filled with sleeping tablets and, deciding the contents were perfect for her needs, pocketed it swiftly.

Sylvie returned, waving another glass in the air.

'Found it at last!' she crowed, then proceeded to fill both tumblers to the brim with brandy. 'Chin-chin,' she said gaily.

'Cheers.'

Carina sipped her drink delicately. Sylvie, on the other hand, drained her glass in seconds.

'Awfully bad luck about that policeman boyfriend of yours, darling. Soz and all that.'

'Thank you.'

Carina's eyelids fluttered shut in a show of tragedy.

'Still,' continued Sylvie cheerfully, 'Ordinary Joe's just don't understand our business. When I was in rep at Wolverhampton I fell for a carpenter. Nineteen years old, I was. Slip of a thing. Legs up to here. I thought he was the most divine thing. Looked like Jesus. Both carpenters as well... '

Carina took another delicate sip of her drink and prepared herself for ten minutes of boredom.

* * *

Clifton laid out the photograph of Gordon on the coffee table in front of Jackie. The woman looked as though she was on the edge of a nervous breakdown. Her facial muscles twitched alarmingly and her speech came in gabbled bursts. Her eyes darted about and did their best to avoid contact with Clifton's.

'Take your time,' she said casually. 'I'm in no hurry.'

Jackie's head jerked spasmodically as she studied the image.

'I don't know. I... I... might have seen him,' she said hesitantly. 'I'm... I... Oh my God! It's him. It's the face at Carina's window! Take it away. Take it away!'

She pushed the photo across the table towards Clifton.

'What window?' asked the police officer urgently.

'I don't want to talk about it. I was just sitting in the kitchen, thinking about Alan. Wondering how he was. Where he was. I couldn't remember his face - what he looked like.'

The facial ticks were consuming her entire body now. She sat in the leather Parker Knoll in her cold and functional living room, twitching and thrashing about like a Thunderbird puppet with its strings cut.

'He must have lost his memory, you see. Might even have been kidnapped. He's very good looking, a lot of women fancy him, that was half the trouble. He could be locked in a room somewhere but he managed to text me.'

Clifton frowned. 'Are you talking about the man in the photograph?'

'No. Alan. My husband. Him!' She pointed to a framed photo of Jackie with her arms entwined around a dark haired, sallow looking individual, on the mantelpiece. Jackie must have always looked the manic type, observed Clifton to herself. She seemed to have her husband in a neck lock rather than an affectionate embrace. Alan, although he was grinning and showing off two shiny gold front teeth, had a haunted 'get me out of here' look in his eyes.

'What about *this* man!' she stabbed a finger at the picture of Gordon forcing Jackie to look. 'Is this him? The man at the window the night she gave the dinner party?'

Jackie nodded.

'No-one believed me. I did see a face at the window. And it was him!'

She put a shaking hand to her mouth to quell the rising hysteria as the terrifying ordeal played back in her mind.

'I was right. I didn't imagine him.'

Jackie's head jerked back dangerously. 'Who is he?' she asked, in a moment of lucidity.

'Good question,' replied Pauline Clifton.

* * *

Gordon stirred the pot of chilli con carne cooking on the hob and tasted it with a spoon. Very nice!

'Yum!' he said loudly. 'Mam? Do you want to taste?'

He took the strangulated grunt from the living room as a 'yes'.

Blowing on a gnarled mound of mince on the spoon, Gordon went through to the lounge and stood before his mother.

'You look the bees knees.'

She sat there, in the corner amongst the shifting shadows thrown from the nearby lava lamp, in her best outfit, make-up and wig.

'She is going to be so amazed at you! You look beautiful Mam!'

He moved forward with the tasty morsel on the spoon.

'Better not,' he said, lifting the spoon away. 'Don't want to smudge your lipstick.' Too late. Gordon's mother was dribbling like Pavlov's dog. He sighed and shovelled the chilli into her mouth.

Gazing around the room, he nodded approvingly. Bag of nuts on the table. Bottle of Lambrusco. Crisps. Cheesy puffs. Everything was there.

He went upstairs to his bedroom, took his best suit out of the wardrobe and hung it up on the door. Catching sight of his treasured biscuit tin resting on the sock shelf, he removed it and placed it on the bed next to him.

Gordon smiled down fondly at the tin. 'I told you everything would work out, didn't I?'

* * *

'Five minutes 'til curtain up, Miss Hemsley.'

Carina stubbed out her cigarette aggressively.

'Thank you, Matty my love!' she called out to the old stage door hand.

She lit another cigarette straight away. Her nerves were starting to get the better of her. Timing was of the essence tonight. Every single element of her plan had to run like clockwork. One set back and everything would be ruined.

Another knock at the door.

'Yes, Matty, I know! Five minutes.'

The door opened and Jackie, entered. She had changed into a long evening dress for the party later that evening.

Carina could not disguise her irritation. 'What are you doing here?!'

'I had to come,' said Jackie, hitching up her dress and making herself at home on the chaise longue. 'I didn't imagine it at all. I did see him, Carina! I did!'

Carina sighed. The mad bitch had finally lost the plot.

'I told you. Alan's gone. Move on.'

'Not Alan. The horrible man at your window.'

Carina's eyebrows started to move skywards. 'What?'

'The night at your Christmas dinner party. The face at the kitchen window. The police have his photo. I saw it. I recognised him.' She shivered uncontrollably.

Carina felt her heart begin to race.

She tried to keep her voice calm. 'The police? Did you tell them?'

'Yes. The detective woman. She came round to my house. Oh, Carina! I'm not going mad. He's real.'

Carina thought quickly. So Jackie recognised Gordon. So what? Nobody knows who he is.

As if reading her thoughts, Jackie said, 'They're going to show his picture on the late news tonight. The ten thirty local bulletin.'

The cigarette holder in Carina's mouth drooped as her jaw went slack.

'Fucking Hell!' she exclaimed without thinking.

'I know!' agreed Jackie. 'Isn't it exciting!?'

She lay back on the chaise, collapsing against the pillows.

336

'What are you doing?'

Jackie pulled herself up on one elbow.

'I thought I'd stay here and keep you company,' she said.

'You'll do no such thing,' Carina barked. 'You'll sit out there with the other punters. Go on, out! Out! Now!'

Jackie fled. Carina leant against the dressing table, breathing heavily. She had a bad feeling about this. A very bad feeling.

Chapter Thirty One

Carina kept her head throughout the first half of the pantomime. She spent most of it in her dressing room anyway. Apart from a brief appearance early on in the first act where she duped Cinderella into thinking she was a raggedy old lady in need of some assistance with her load of kindling, and a bigger scene towards the interval where she revealed herself as The Fairy Godmother and turned a pumpkin into a coach, she had time to sit in her dressing room and firm up the plan she had concocted, in her mind. While on stage, she missed a line here, and a cue there which angered her professional nature but this was the last night and other actors were making similar mistakes, or corpsing or worse - improvising. Nobody noticed. There was a part of her that didn't care. She wasn't out to impress anyone - she'd achieved her goal - the return of Cora Smart to *Winkle Bay*. Tonight, it was bye-bye human dross, bye-bye pantomime. No more tat in third rate theatres, no more humiliation in day-time game shows for her. That chapter of her life was about to shut forever. Carina Hemsley was going back to prime-time. Fame. Money. Adoration. And more money. At least, she would be, as soon as she'd removed one last, irritating obstacle. Her tiresome irritation.

Once Cinderella went off to the ball in the pumpkin coach

and the curtain came down for the interval, Carina knew she had a fifteen minute wait while the rest of the cast sat around waiting to go on again. After that, there was exactly an hour - as long as nobody raced through their lines, before she was due on stage again for the finale. One hour to secure the rest of her life.

She faked a coughing fit on her way back to the dressing room and set the scene by announcing she was going to lie down for a while.

'Aren't you coming in for a drink?' asked Sylvie as she pushed open her dressing room door.

Carina declined. 'No thanks,' she said. 'Forty winks and I'll be fine.' But Sylvie, with a thirst from Hell in her throat had bolted and was holed up in her dressing room with a bottle of brandy and a tumbler before Carina had finished uttering 'forty winks'. Carina heard the familiar clink of spirit bottle against tumbler on the other side of the door.

Brendan and Justin had also gone down the alcohol path. Brendan, sweating under his Ugly Sister wig, waved a bottle of champagne at Carina.

'Bubbly, Miss H?' he offered.

Carina declined with a regretful shrug. 'Have to pace myself sweetheart.'

She retired to her dressing room, where she raced around, removing her costume, exchanging white gauze and sequins for black trousers and sweater. She sprawled on the chaise longue acquainting herself with a particular page of the Newcastle A-Z.

The back stage bell sounded for the start of the second act. Carina leaned against the door listening to the retreating footsteps as the rest of the cast made their way to the stage for the Ball scene. When the corridor fell silent, she set the alarm on her phone. Sixty minutes. Carina had one hour to put her plan into effect and return to the theatre.

She set off towards the stage door at a steady pace, not too quickly, in case Matty, geriatric guardian of the door might be at his post. He wasn't - Carina knew he wouldn't be, unless he'd changed his habits of the last two months. He always accompanied the actors to the stage at the start of the second act and hung around in the wings, for he enjoyed watching the delight and expectation on the childrens' faces as the curtain went up.

The cold chilled air of the winter's night hit her as she ran to the scooter at the back of the alley. Carina pulled on the crash helmet, fumbled for the keys under the mudguard, found them. Moments later she set off, unsteadily at first. It had been a while, Rome, Nineteen Seventy Two, to be precise, since she'd last commandeered a scooter. She soon discovered it was like riding a bike. Only noisier. And less exhausting.

Luckily the roads were quiet at that time of night and Carina found herself in the West End of the city within ten minutes. Within thirteen she'd located Gordon's house in the street of dilapidated red bricked houses and was free-wheeling around the back, in order to park up out of sight. Not that it mattered. In the dark, and helmeted, nobody would have recognised her. She knocked quietly at the back door. Gordon, be-suited and reeking of cheap aftershave, answered the door within seconds.

'You're here! You're here!' he shrieked, bouncing up and down on the spot in his excitement. He called back into the house: 'Mam! Mam! Cora's here.'

'Shush!' Carina hissed, worried that the neighbours might hear. She shooed him back inside and followed him in. Gordon attempted to push her up against the sink and kiss her.

'Let me get the helmet off.'

'Sorry.'

She removed the helmet, but kept her jacket and gloves on.

'Can I kiss you now, Cora?'

Carina nodded, closed her eyes, tilted her head back and thought of the future, her career, *Winkle Bay* - anything to take her mind off the fat tongue which was trying to force itself into her mouth. She tolerated it for a few seconds. Carina was aware of time ticking relentlessly onwards. Forty minutes or so, until she had to be back at the theatre. Tick-tock, tick-tock. Move on, move on.

She put an end to Gordon's slobbering by biting the end of his tongue.

'I'm so sorry, darling,' she said, as he yelled in pain. 'Are you all right?'

'Yeth,' replied Gordon. 'Come and meet Mam.'

Carina was about to move into the lounge when Gordon grabbed her hand.

'I don't think we should have 'The Sex', not with me Mam around.'

'Fair enough,' said Carina.

'It won't be for long though, Cora,' he whispered. 'I'm putting her in a Home next week.'

He ushered her into the small, overheated lounge reeking of warm urine and stale sweat. Carina concentrated on the collection of Spanish flamenco dolls dotted around the room and breathed through her mouth to avoid the stench. It was only partially successful. She could taste the cloying stench and thanked God that she would only have to endure it for a short time. Her flesh crawled when she thought about the things she'd allowed him to do over the past few months. All in the name of her 'career'.

Carina's prepared smile for her almost-mother-in-law, faltered at the sight of the grotesquely made-up creature sitting in the wheelchair in the corner. She thought fleetingly of Norman Bates and his mummified mother in Psycho. The same sense of horror and repulsion coursed through her veins. Only this wasn't any film. This was real. And the woman wasn't dead, at least physically speaking. She stared at the bloated, over made-up face, paralysed down one side, and struggled for something complimentary to say. She gave up trying.

'Here's Cora, Mam. She's come to see you.'

Gordon's mother continued to stare ahead at the TV with distant, watery eyes.

'Cora,' she repeated dully.

Gordon laughed. 'Cora from *Winkle Bay*. Yes! My fiancée.'

He pushed Carina forward.

'She's your number one fan, after me.'

Carina fumbled for something to say. 'Pleased to meet you,' she said. 'That's nice lipstick.'

The old woman seemed not to have heard. Gordon reached for the remote device in his mother's lap and switched off the TV. Mrs Crabtree continued to watch the blank screen with the same watery stare.

'I've made a love album for us, Cora.'

'That's so thoughtful, honey.'

Gordon flicked on the hi-fi. Barry White singing 'My First, My Last, My Everything', blared out from tiny speakers. He smirked at Carina suggestively and started jerking his hips in her direction provocatively.

Carina wanted to stab him there and then. Resisting the urge, she said brightly, 'I propose a toast,' instead.

'I've got gin and some lemonade,' offered Gordon, proudly. He was about to return to the kitchen.

Carina blocked his path. 'Let me. You've done so much already.' She gestured to the buffet of crisps and cheesy puffs. 'You keep your mother company.'

At the door she winked at him lasciviously.

'She's a very pretty lady. Now I know where her son gets his good looks from.'

Gordon giggled and squeezed his mother's knee. Carina kept her back to him, took two glasses from the shelf above her and unscrewed the cap on the gin bottle.

Gordon called through. 'Need a hand?'

'No thank you darling, I'm fine.'

Carina felt around in her jacket pocket for the small plastic bag she'd brought with her. The powdery contents were the ground down remains of the thirty sleeping tablets she'd stolen from Sylvie. She tipped a large amount into one of the drinks and hoped it would be enough to send Gordon to sleep forever. She shrugged and emptied the rest of the powder in. Better to be safe than sorry. Adding a large amount of lemonade to the ingredients, she stirred the frothing mixture with a finger.

'Here you are Mr Crabtree.' She thrust the glass into Gordon's hand.

'Thanks - Mrs Crabtree-to-be.'

Carina raised her glass and watched him down the contents of the drink, in one long gulp. She knew he'd do that. He always did.

'Dance?' she suggested.

Gordon lunged at her without replying and enveloped her in a tight clinch. Barry White soon gave way to Stevie Wonder. Gordon rested his head against Carina and hummed along to 'I Just Called To Say I Love You' but by the first chorus, his grip seemed to be loosening and his head felt heavier on her shoulder. The humming became sporadic, then a tuneless slur.

'Let's sit down, shall we?' suggested Carina. She guided him over to the settee. Gordon sat down heavily.

'I love you... Cor...' He never finished the sentence. He was comatose as his head slumped against the cushions. Carina checked her watch. Twenty minutes to get back to the theatre. She was cutting it fine, but it could be done, if she hurried. She studied Gordon's mother who continued to stare with a fixed intensity at the dead TV set. No need to drug her. She was in no position to tell anyone anything.

Carina whipped out her mobile and speed dialled. A muffled and appalling electronic version of the *Winkle Bay* theme tune tinkled away from somewhere around the settee. She felt Gordon's pocket, recognised the small lump of his mobile, ended the call and zipped both phones safely away in her bag. Hurrying through to the kitchen, she opened the oven door, pulled out the shelves, turned the gas on full, blew out the flame as the automatic ignition kicked in and repeated the process with the hob. It took all her strength to grab Gordon by the scruff of his neck and haul him to the kitchen where she pulled him up onto his knees. Taking a deep breath, she shoved him as forcefully as she could. He lay there, on his knees, head in the oven, shoulders wedged firmly in the door, unconscious.

Back in the living room, Carina lit the wick of the novelty candle in the shape of a flamenco dancer, sitting on the sideboard, picked up her glass, took it through to the kitchen, rinsed it under the tap, set it on the draining board, then pulled on her crash helmet. She looked back at the still forms of Gordon and his mother and waved to them.

'Ciao darlings,' she said, brightly.

Carina slipped out of the house, walking with the moped until she felt the noisy engine was out of the range of the neighbours' hearing, then, turning over the ignition, she sped off into the night, hoping and praying that all the loose ends connecting her with Gordon had been tied up. It was out of her hands now. Que sera sera, she muttered under her breath. Concentrating on the stream of traffic heading into Newcastle for Saturday night jollity, Carina made it back to the theatre with six minutes to spare.

She locked up the bike, tossed the crash helmet into a handy industrial skip at the back of the alley and searched her pockets for the new packet of cigarettes she'd bought earlier. At the stage door, she knocked loudly, hoping that Matty was at his post. The old man peered out suspiciously through a narrow crack in the door.

'Miss Hemsley!' he gasped.

'Popped out for some fags, Matty my love,' she said casually, holding up the unopened pack.

Matty opened the door wide, beckoning her inside.

Carina made a show of opening the cigarettes.

'When a girl wants a cigarette, she's got to have one.'

Matty tutted. 'Why didn't you say? You could have had one of mine.'

'Ah, bless you.' She kissed him on the head and hurried back to her dressing room to change.

Carina strode on stage three minutes later for the finale, bowed graciously and was given a tumultuous standing ovation. She accepted the giant bouquet of flowers presented to her by Campbell Garibaldi and made a heart felt speech thanking the other members of a wonderful cast for contributing to one of the most enjoyable times of her life. With tears streaming down her cheeks she asked the audience to remember her loving companion Fluff, her dear, dear friend Dougie Hunt and bid the entire auditorium to join her in a prayer for her darling man Roy Newall, the light of her life who had been rendered a vegetable through no fault of his own. There wasn't a dry eye in the theatre.

A few miles away in one of the poorer suburbs of Newcastle, a massive gas explosion ripped out one side of a small Edwardian red brick council house, scattering charred Spanish flamenco dolls over a wide area. By the time the emergency services arrived, fire had destroyed much of the ground floor accommodation and the occupants were dead.

During the clean-up operation, firefighters, searching upstairs as a matter of procedure, discovered something unexpected in an old biscuit tin lying open amongst the remains of a shattered wardrobe in one of the bedrooms...

Chapter Thirty Two

Clifton parked her car alongside one of the two fire appliances blocking the road and took in the blast damage. The entire downstairs exterior of the small terraced house was gone. Only the upper section brickwork of the house remained. The windows had blown out and charred remnants of curtains billowed out in the chill night. A TV news crew was already there. The reporter setting up her position behind the cordoned off area in front of the house, glanced curiously in her direction as she applied lipstick using a small vanity mirror. A small crowd of onlookers - neighbours and curious ghouls, some of them in dressing gowns and pyjamas had collected and were gawping excitedly at the decimated house. A giant demolition ball couldn't have done a more thorough job. Items of furniture, sections of carpet, a demolished flat screen TV lay in the road where the blast had deposited them. Clifton skirted around acridly smoking pieces of melted plastic as she made her way over to P.C. Thompson. He met her at the gate, or at the space where the gate used to be - it was embedded in the windscreen of a neighbour's car.

'What happened?' asked Clifton, raising a handkerchief to her mouth to protect her from the noxious fumes.

'Gas explosion, we think,' replied Thompson. 'Can't be sure yet.

It's safe enough to come in, though. Forensic's are here.'

Clifton stepped over another smouldering blob of plastic. She pointed at the gooey mess.

'What's all this?'

'Plastic doll collection, apparently. The old woman collected them.'

She tipped her head to one side to study the mess by her feet. Sure enough, she could make out a face, and a hand holding a charred fan amongst the smoke and puddle of plastic.

'Two people, you said? They're both inside?'

P.C Thompson shook his head.

'The mother, if that's who she is - and there's no reason to suspect otherwise, she was found up there.'

He pointed up at the chimney atop the high gabled roof of the house opposite. 'Still in her chair,' he added.

Clifton whistled. 'That was some explosion. And the son?'

Thompson jerked a thumb vaguely. 'He was blown out of the kitchen. Gordon Crabtree's the name. Found him in the back alleyway. Body's not in a good state, looks like he took the full brunt of the explosion.'

'So what have you got for me?'

The police constable took a deep breath and exhaled loudly. 'You're not going to believe it.'

He took her hand to steady her as she climbed up the remains of the staircase. Clifton saw neither the wardrobe with its door hanging off its hinges or the shattered windows as she entered the small bedroom. All she could see were the photographs glued to the walls. Hundreds of them, big and small, with the same grinning face she recognised instantly. Gordon Crabtree had a serious and unhealthy obsession with Carina Hemsley. Clifton felt the hairs on

348

the back of her neck standing up as she took in the photo-collage around her. She knew instinctively she had found her man. The back issues of glossy celebrity magazines, spread around the room by the blast, with pages open revealing cut out sections and missing headlines only confirmed her gut feeling.

'Have you spoken to the neighbours about him?'

'Yeah. "Loner", "Weirdo", "Smelly",' replied Thompson, reeling off quickly some of the character descriptions he'd been offered. 'But you haven't seen the best bit yet.'

He approached the wardrobe gingerly and taking out a pen, pushed the lid off the large biscuit tin sitting amongst paired up socks.

Clifton looked in and gasped. The mummified head, staring sightlessly up at her, mouth agape in a parody of Munch's 'The Scream' was startling enough but it was the two shiny gold teeth which really made her blood run cold. She recognised them from the photograph she'd seen recently on a suburban mantelpiece. The skin had dried and shrivelled and the facial features were shrunken and gnarled like an old prune, but it was definitely him. It was Jackie Humbert's missing husband, Alan.

'What the Hell went on here?' she asked incredulously.

* * *

Carina sighed heavily as Jackie burst into tears at the bar of the Bessie Surtees Room at The Valmont.

'Why not?' she wept. 'Is it something I did?'

'Not really,' said Carina, disinterested. She looked over at Sylvie, who was downing a large whiskey at the other end of the bar, and rolled her eyes at her, fed up.

'But Carina, I've done your publicity for the past five years.' Jackie choked back tears and added, 'For free.'

'That's as maybe,' came the hard reply, 'But from now on, I'll be handled by the Press Office at A1 TV. They're professionals. They know what they're doing. You see, I don't think you're equipped to cope with the increased coverage I'm starting to get. I'm back with the big boys and girls now.'

Carina slammed a cigarette into her holder and lit up. Immediately, the barman hurried towards her, indignation burning at every foot fall. The actress saw him out of the corner of her eye. 'Fuck off!' she said before he had the chance to point out the 'No Smoking' signs. The barman, his bubble of indignation pricked, turned on his heels and scurried back to the other end of the bar.

'But I thought we were friends?' sobbed Jackie.

'Oh! Oh, lovey!' wheezed Carina sympathetically, 'Bless! Whatever gave you that idea?'

Jackie, almost tripping over the folds of her evening gown, dashed from the room.

Carina smiled to herself and allowed her foot to tap away to the music blasting from the disco floor. Lauren, hand-in-hand with Ben stopped to kiss her on the cheek.

'Isn't this great?' gushed Lauren. 'Our hotel room's gorgeous. There was a bottle of champagne waiting for us when we checked in - wasn't there!' She turned to Ben for confirmation but Ben had his eye on the disco where a group of the panto dancers were parading around provocatively. 'Er, yeah,' he said.

'It's so kind of Jez to put us all up. I'm going to give him a big kiss when I see him,' Lauren promised. She tugged playfully at Ben's arm and dragged him off for a dance. Carina checked her watch. The news bulletin must have gone out half an hour ago at least. She hoped the exit she'd arranged for Gordon had worked before the item was broadcast.

'Waiting for someone?' Sylvie had wandered over to her.

'No!' declared Carina. 'Just watching the hours roll by.'

'I know how you feel! I'm not a party person either,' admitted Sylvie. 'All this false jollity and drunkenness. It's shameful.'

Carina raised an eyebrow at her. The way Sylvie was weaving around on the spot in front of her like a hypnotised cobra suggested she was well on the way to being shameful herself. Both women turned to the dance floor as a loud wail went up from Lauren. She was screaming hysterically and attempting to put her arms around Ben, who clearly didn't want anything to do with her.

'You don't mean it. You don't, Ben!' Lauren was saying. 'You can't mean it.'

Ben pushed his way through the dancing throng, hotly pursued by Lauren.

Sylvie opened her clutch bag and slapped a tenner on the bar top. Carina snatched it up and stuffed it down her cleavage.

'I thought he'd wait until at least tomorrow when we were all going home.'

Carina shook her head. 'I know a bastard when I see one.'

'Then that's the difference between us,' sighed Sylvie, 'I never do.'

She shook her empty glass at the barman. 'You know, Larry O sent me a postcard. "Darling it's over", that's all it said. The shit. And Husband. I had him down as a genuine, all round good egg. But no. He turned out to be a bad egg. A stinking, feckless, narcissistic...' she paused to take a large gulp of whiskey from her replenished glass. 'Still, I'm not bitter. Dignity. That's what it's about.'

She nudged Carina with the all the finesse of an un-coordinated lush. 'Here we go,' she said loudly, tipping her head in Jez's direction as he made his way around the room in search of his wife.

'Hi!' said Jez, trying to sound friendly and casual. 'Are you enjoying yourselves?'

'Yes, sweetheart,' said Carina, without much enthusiasm. Sylvie grinned at him glassy-eyed and said nothing.

'Have you erm, have you seen my wife?' he asked, leaning in to them so he could be heard above the loud music.

Carina shook her head. Sylvie beckoned to him conspiratorially, tried to say 'sshhh!' and put an unsteady finger to her mouth but it missed and she poked herself in the eye.

'I've seen them,' she said, with one eye shut.

Jez reared back from her. 'Them?'

'Yesh,' slurred Sylvie. 'Hodi and Camp Ball.' She flung an arm in the direction of the lifts. 'Went that away, twenny minutes.'

Jez, puce with anger, made a dash for the lifts. Sylvie jiggled her glass at the barman again.

'So!' she said, trying to focus on Carina again, 'You're going back to *Tinkle Bay*'

'*Winkle*!' said Carina, irritated.

'Tinkle. Winkle. What does it matter, darling? It's all tosh.'

'Oh, you Shakespeare luvvies,' hissed the soap star, 'you get on my tits.'

Jez alighted from the lift on the third floor and padded along the corridor to face his destiny with a heavy heart. Instinct told him Heidi would be with Campbell in his room. He'd organised the block booking for the members of his cast as something of a test for his wife, to see what would happen when Campbell and she were flung together in an intimate social gathering. Would they be able to resist temptation? Their behaviour so far suggested to him that they would not. Yet even he was surprised at the speed at which they'd fled the party in order to satisfy their lust.

Torturous images of Heidi and the spineless theatre director giving reign to their passion in a hotel room paid for by his own hard earned cash, caused him to slow down as he approached room 323. He'd called The Valmont only that morning to find out where Garibaldi was to be ensconced. The number was etched indelibly on his brain. 323. He knew it would come to this. And here it was. The moment. But how to react? What was he going to say to them? Violence was not in his nature, even though violent thoughts coursed through him. He had a reputation in the double glazing trade as a hard-nosed businessman - a tough negotiator, a fearsome competitor. But right now, as anger and fear drove him onwards to an awful confrontation, he also felt like crying. From his teenage years, through to middle age he had been lucky in love, been in the driving seat, careering through life, an emotionally unassailable vessel, breaking hearts, ending relationships without a moment's hesitation. Until now. He knew at last, what it was to love and to lose that love. Jez thought of his first wife Pat, and how he'd ended their marriage of thirty years with a brief phone call and suddenly the tears he felt like shedding for his own predicament, he wanted to shed for Pat, too. And for the girlfriends he'd treated so appallingly in the past whom he'd tossed aside without a moment's hesitation and never thought about since. He wanted to find them all and tell them how sorry he was. Pat, who gave him two beautiful children and unerring loyalty and support for three decades. Her face at the window, the last time he saw her, pain and betrayal etched on its contours as he moved out of the family home, came back to haunt him. He'd betrayed thirty years of love and commitment without a moment's hesitation after falling for Heidi. Pat's feelings, her hurt, the rejection she must have felt, never once pricked his heart. And now, as he thought about it, he felt a physical pain in his chest and a terrifying, indescribable hollowness that made him feel sick. Had some kind of revenge from a Higher Authority been meted out? "What goes around comes around" his mother used to say. He'd scorned her, never believed in such clap trap - certainly in the business world there was no room for such a ridiculous concept. But could there be something in it afterall? You hurt other people, you get hurt back. It made sense.

He knocked loudly on the door.

'Who is it?' asked a hesitant voice, Heidi's voice, after a moment.

'It's me, Heidi,' said Jez calmly.

Jez heard frantic stumbling and whispering on the other side of the door. Several moments went by before the handle turned and Heidi opened the door but only slightly. She peered through the crack with worried eyes.

'Aren't you going to invite me in?'

His serenity startled him.

'It's not what you think, Jez,' Heidi said.

'Is Campbell there?' he asked, trying to see past her.

'Of course, silly. It's his room.'

Heidi opened the door wide to admit him. Jez, still feeling nauseous, and also very cold, strode past her.

The tall, attractive dark-haired woman standing in the middle of the room was something unexpected. Vaguely familiar to Jez, the woman avoided eye contact with him so he moved around to scrutinize her more closely. With mounting incredulity he stammered, 'B... Bloody Hell Campbell. What's going on?!'

Campbell, resplendent in his black cocktail dress, high heeled shoes and lustrous wig sat down on the bed shakily.

'Don't call him *Campbell*, darling,' said Heidi. 'From tonight, we've got to call her *Camille*.'

Jez, a little out of his depth now, sank into the arm chair next to the trouser press.

'I don't follow,' he said in a small voice. He couldn't take his eyes off Campbell/Camille. There was something unsettling about all this. For a start he was better looking as a woman - Jez couldn't help but notice the long shapely legs, a fact which made him feel very queasy.

'I thought you two were... you know!'

Heidi took his hand.

'I know and I'm sorry Jez, but Camille swore me to secrecy and I couldn't betray her confidence. This hasn't been an easy time for her.'

'Her?' repeated Jez, like a moronic parrot. '*Her?* I'm sorry I don't get it.'

'I have to live life as a woman, for a while,' said Campbell/Camille quietly.

'Why?' asked Jez bluntly.

'She's a pre-op trans-sexual,' explained Heidi.

Jez studied the feminine picture of beauty in front of him, took in the tight velvet dress, then looked at his wife. Something was puzzling him.

'So he's still a man?'

Heidi nodded. 'Until the operation goes ahead.'

'What've you done with your tackle?' Unsavoury as the thought was, he couldn't help but notice that Camille's figure curved and bulged only in the right womanly places

Heidi tutted. 'Jez!' she remonstrated. 'What sort of question is that to ask a lady?'

Jez was still in shock. 'But what about all the whispering in corners, the shopping trips? The secret meetings?'

'Don't blame Heidi,' begged Camille. 'It's all my fault. I just love her style. She's been helping me sort out an identity for myself. It's not easy you know.'

'I'm sure.' He shook his head, trying to make sense of it all.

'I thought you were a bit of a Nancy when I met you,' he admitted. 'But then, when you started sniffing round Heidi... Well, I bloody never!'

Despite the strange-ness of the moment, Jez felt a sense of elation. Heidi wasn't having an affair. She wasn't in love with someone else. She hadn't forsaken her wedding vows.

'I thought I'd lost you, Heidi.'

'Never.'

Heidi sat on his lap, put her arms around his neck and kissed him on the nose. 'Never, never, never.' Jez smiled up at her.

'Tonight's a big deal for Camille,' observed Heidi. 'So we're going to help her and support her as much as we can.'

'Of course we are!' promised Jez enthusiastically. 'Why 'Camille' though?' He noticed Heidi's disapproving expression. 'Sorry. I have to ask.'

'That's okay,' said Camille. 'It's from "Now, Voyager".'

Jez looked at him blankly.

'"*Oh, Jerry, don't let's ask for the moon. We have the stars*"?'

The entrepreneur was none the wiser.

'It's a film, apparently,' Heidi elucidated. 'About a lumpy old lass who turned into a bit of a looker. Black and white. Haven't seen it.'

'Me neither,' said Jez, wishing he hadn't asked. The world was a strange place to him, and getting stranger by the day. Modern Men went on clothes shopping trips with their mates, footballers plucked their eyebrows, used moisturiser and wore pink shirts and other fellas wanted to be women. That was all fine with him. He had Heidi. Nothing else mattered.

Carina saw the detective weaving her way through the room towards her and ordered another drink from the bar. She'd half drunk it by the time Clifton reached her.

'Nice party,' said Clifton, shouting above the din from the dance-floor.

'I didn't know you were invited,' replied Carina coolly.

'Sadly, I'm here on business.' Clifton leaned closer. 'Can we talk somewhere?'

Carina, trying to stay calm, nodded and escorted Clifton over to a small seating area on the other side of the bar. A set of Oriental screens blocked out much of the noise from the wilder party-goers.

'How can I help you?'

Clifton deliberated, choosing her words carefully.

'A few hours ago, I was called out to a house explosion.'

'Oh, no,' said Carina sympathetically.

'Mmm!' agreed Clifton, staring intently at the actress.

'Gas, we think. The two occupants of the house were pronounced dead at the scene.'

Carina cheered inwardly. Thank God, Thank God, Thank God.

Out loud, she said to Clifton, 'How tragic.'

'One of the tenants of the house,' continued Clifton officiously, 'was a Mr. Gordon Crabtree. Does that name ring any bells?'

'Crabtree. Crabtree.' Carina shook her head. 'Nope! Should it, lovey? Who is he?'

'The photograph I showed you earlier...'

'That was him?'

'He was obsessed with you, Miss Hemsley. Or rather, obsessed with your character. Cora Smart. It seems he was also behind the death threats.'

'But why?' asked Carina, pulling off a mean demonstration of incredulity.

'Good question,' replied Clifton. 'On the one hand he was going around telling people he was going to marry you, and on the other, he seemed intent on killing you.'

Damn Gordon and his big mouth! Carina's anger raged inwardly. Why couldn't he do what he was told? Speak to no-one about anything, she'd ordered. His death had come in the nick of time. God knows what he would have gone on to do - or say!

'He sounds like a deranged soul, to me,' she opined sweetly. 'Poor thing. Maybe he was schizophrenic.'

'Possibly.' Clifton didn't sound convinced.

'I just find it strange that he never wrote, or tried to get in touch with you.'

'But he did - if he was behind the poison pen letters.'

Clifton shook her head. 'I meant before all that. Maybe he wrote to you and you didn't reply. He saw red and started sending the death threats.'

Carina sat up indignantly. 'I always reply to fan mail from 'My People'.'

'Do you keep any of it?'

'God, no. My gaff would look like a Philippino land-fill site if I did that. I get letters from fans by the sack load.'

'Even after you left *Winkle Bay*?'

Carina threw Clifton a withering look. 'Especially after I left,' she replied calmly.

'Pity you don't keep anything,' declared the detective. 'It might have been useful.' She paused contemplatively. 'I should tell you,' she said after a moment, 'there's something else. Something we found at the house.'

Carina froze ever so slightly. Her right eyelid twitched involuntarily. She took a swig of wine to steady her nerves.

'I need your help,' continued Clifton, removing a photograph from her pocket. She saw the genuine look of shock from the actress as she looked at the picture.

'You know who it is, don't you?'

Carina nodded slowly. 'It's Alan. Jackie's Alan.' She recognised the gold teeth but little of the mummified features. She'd allowed Gordon to 'practice' on Alan. It was a test to see if the little mad fiend was up to scratch. And of course he was. Still, she'd told him to bury the body, not cut the head off and keep it in a biscuit tin. She gazed at the photograph. She'd done Jackie a favour. The bastard was always trying to get into her knickers. And once or twice, in a weak moment she'd succumbed to his persuasions. What a swine. No loyalty.

'We found the head in a biscuit tin in Crabtree's bedroom,' Clifton explained.

Carina's eyes widened. She pushed the photograph back across the table towards Clifton, who picked it up and deposited it carefully in the inside pocket of her jacket.

'You're her friend,' said Clifton. 'It'd be better if there was a familiar face around when I tell her.'

'Of course,' said Carina sweetly. 'I'll text her, tell her to come over.'

Jackie read the text on the dance floor and considered ignoring Carina's request. One of the young male dancers from the panto had asked her to dance and she was actually beginning to enjoy herself. Seconds before receiving the message she'd decided to resign as president of the 'Carina Hemsley Appreciation Society'. She'd had enough. She was tired of playing the unpaid help to an unpleasant old cow. New Year, new start, she told herself. But old habits die hard and the text sounded important, urgent even. She apologised to her nimble-toed partner, blushed at the kiss he planted on her cheek, then fought her way to the edge of the disco area.

She smiled and nodded at Jez who was about to hit the dance floor with two attractive women on his arm: Heidi and... Oh My God! The dancing stopped as colleagues spotted the identity of the mystery woman.

'What's the matter with you's?' yelled Jez with a grin. 'Have you never seen a pre-op transsexual before, or what?'

Jackie, in a state of high excitement, rushed around the screen to tell Carina the news.

'You'll never guess!' she squeaked. 'Never in a million years. Oh, My, God. But he looks amazing, come and look!'

'Jackie, love?' Carina patted the arm of the chair next to her. 'Come and sit beside me.'

Jackie, calming down, saw the miserable police woman's expression and didn't like it.

'What is it?' she asked. 'What's happened?'

'It's about Alan,' said the detective.

Jackie's knees started to knock. 'What?' she demanded. 'What?!'

'Well, sweetheart,' said Carina, wrapping taloned fingers around her sweating hand. 'It's good news and bad news.'

360

Carina tried to control the glee she felt creeping into her voice. There was enough going on her around her to feed the tabloids for months.

'The good news is,' she sighed, 'they've found him. The bad news...'

The scream that erupted from behind the Chinese screens went on and on and on intermittently until the paramedics arrived.

Chapter Thirty Three

Soap guru Mick Flynt fought his way through the throng of fans, kept back from the television crew by crowd barriers and a police presence and sat on one of the collapsible chairs next to Rufus Frenkel. Wrapped in a thick coat and sheltering under an umbrella to protect him from the cold Northumbrian rain, the TV producer was staring intently into one of the portable monitor's set up for the director and his team to watch the camera output. Down below them, in the harbour, Carina, in character as Cora Smart was climbing out of a fishing boat. The crowd cheered as 'Cora' climbed up onto the pier and was immediately barked at by the assistant director. The cheering was interrupting filming, he raged. Miss Hemsley's time was precious and they all had a schedule to stick to. If it wasn't met, then the new episodes of *Winkle Bay* wouldn't make it to the screen. Carina seemed to be enjoying the attention. She waved and blew kisses to the crowd.

'I promise you,' she cried, addressing her fans, 'Cora will never desert you again. After these five special episodes, I'll be back for more later in the year, and more and more!'

The crowd clapped and cheered, drowning out the protestations of the assistant director.

'You see, this is my life. This is what it's all about,' she enunciated grandly, sweeping her arms around in a grand gesture to include her fellow actors, the crew and the herded fans. 'Just us, the cameras and all you wonderful couch potatoes.'

She waved over at the world weary director. 'All right, Barney, I'm ready for my close-ups.'

Barney glanced at his PA. 'What the fuck's she talking about? We haven't even started the scene properly yet.'

Rufus turned to Mick. 'She's been like this since day one.'

Flynt shrugged. 'So put up with her. It'll be worth it in the end.'

Rufus sighed. It was all right for him to say. The 'consultant' breezed in, stipulated what he wanted, and swanned off leaving a trail of hysteria in his wake as everybody tried to accommodate his ludicrous dictates.

'I've been thinking about that,' said Rufus, looking around to make sure they weren't being overheard. 'Are you absolutely sure we're doing the right thing - you know - in story terms?'

A hint of steeliness crept into the soap gurus Mancunian tones as he replied.

'I *know* it's the right thing.'

'But the viewing figures are already up thirty per cent since the news about her return came out. And all the business about the psychopathic stalker and her personal tragedies, she's never out of the papers.'

'Your point being?'

'I just think, maybe, we should… reconsider.'

Flynt smiled unpleasantly. 'Who's calling the shots here? Me or you?'

Rufus turned away huffily. 'You,' he said, looking out to sea.

'Right. Remember that.'

The director looked over at them.

'We're ready for a take.'

Someone called out 'action!' down by the harbour and Carina stepped onto the pier again.

'She's been asking about the last script,' whispered Rufus. 'Wants to know why she hasn't received it.'

Flynt smiled to himself. 'Better give it to her, then. Give them all the last script of our grand quintet.'

Rufus paled. 'Shouldn't we explain first?'

'What have we just talked about?' snapped Flynt. 'Who's in charge here? Give her the script. Give 'em all the script.'

He jumped down off his chair and set off towards the car park. Barney the director, his face a mass of concern, looked back at Rufus. 'I hope he knows what he's doing.'

'Of course he does,' replied Rufus sarcastically. 'God always knows what he's doing.'

He was pretty sure about what the man was up to. He'd tried to pass on his concerns - that Flynt's real aim was to scupper the show - to his boss, Carl the Executive Producer and to colleagues he felt he could trust. Whilst most of them had been willing to listen to his theory and one or two of them had agreed wholeheartedly with it, consensus was that further and louder talk on the subject was tantamount to professional suicide. So Rufus sat back and watched the man slowly undo all his good work. So much for 'Time will tell and the truth will out.' He laughed out-loud at his own naïveté. This was television. The truth never came out. How could it when the industry was run by bullies? It was like Winston Smith working in the 'Ministry of Truth' in Orwell's 1984 - constantly re-writing and distorting history for Big Brother until nobody knew what the truth actually was anymore. Or cared. As Flynt kept telling him when Rufus's professional pride led him to defend sporadically, the programme he considered his baby, "Hey, it's only television"!'

Flynt sat in his car deep in thought. Rufus Frenkel was a worry to him. Little things he'd said, the way he'd looked at him sometimes, he was onto him. Ah well. The man had one more function to serve - namely, to deal with Carina Hemsley and after that, he could get rid of him. Dealing with actors was something he never usually balked at - he disliked most of them and intimidating them was something of a sport for him - in the same way that cats enjoy playing with mice to the death. In Carina's case he was happy to let Rufus do the dirty work. There was something about her, the dead eyes, the lack of fear, that unnerved him.

Yes, Frenkel could deal with her and then he'd tell Greg Dean, A1 TV's Managing Director that he was superfluous to requirements. Greg would do anything he told him. Stupid bastard. Any MD who thought it a good idea to allow a competitor from another channel and show to come in and tinker around with its programming deserved everything he got. Flynt had it all worked out. Explosive storyline, get rid of a few loved regulars, equals rating grabber! He'd be hailed as a saviour. And then, a few months later after the show's re-vamp had been a re-vamp too far and the programme bore no relation to what had gone before, the viewing figures would slump further still. Nothing to do with him because everyone would know he'd tried his best and achieved a modicum of success with the 'special' episodes.

Already, a team back at his Manchester headquarters was hard at work preparing and storylining that possible replacement. Oh, it was like stealing candy from a baby.

Carina sipped a glass of chilled champagne in the comfort of her trailer as she relaxed between takes. The trailer, complete with all mod cons was a perk her agent had negotiated when sorting out her first short return to *Winkle Bay*. The other members of the cast had to make do with the green room in a converted village hall five minutes from the harbour front when they were on location and already they'd made their resentment felt, excluding her from lunchtime gatherings at The Puffin restaurant and post-filming wind-down sessions at Ye Old Shippe Inn. Carina couldn't care less. She was Top Dog again on the show and that was all that mattered to her. The others could say what they liked. The trailer was a status symbol to show the cast the revised pecking order. She'd never had one before in her career - even in the golden days of *Winkle Bay* and was surprised when A1 TV agreed to her terms so readily. She was thankful they had, for right at this minute she felt ready to drop. Ten days of gruelling filming - up at five, on set or location at six thirty (make-up took longer and longer the older one got), then twelve hour recording sessions, were taking their toll. In the 'old days' three days of location filming were followed by three in the studio but now - the schedule was all over the place: location in the morning followed by studio in the afternoon and then back to location for further shooting. Carina barely knew where she was. On top of that the Press was everywhere. Most of the reporters wanted to know about Gordon Crabtree, her obsessive fan. Did she know him? Had she feared for her life during the threatening letters episode? Carina had handled the Press onslaught with aplomb. Of course she had, it was what she'd been working towards for months. A reporter's dream, she'd provided the media with witty quotes, cried on cue, opened up her heart to the British public and milked the attention like the celebrity whore she was. Thanks to astonishing public interest, Justine from the *Winkle Bay* Press office had almost become her personal publicist, another factor which alienated her from the cast. Grumbling and moaning amongst themselves in the studio green room, they'd nicknamed *Winkle Bay*, 'The Carina Hemsley Show'. Carina took it all in her stride. She was on a high, enjoying every minute of her rise from 'Z' list obscurity to 'A' list most talked about woman. But she was tired too and the idea of her five episode stint coming to an end soon appealed to her. With a healthy bank balance courtesy of her episode fees and the numerous media interviews she'd given, she planned a long holiday and further cosmetic work. Then she would be ready to make the agreed permanent return to the series.

Carina picked up the studio scenes she would be filming later that day, took out a green highlighter pen and marked up her lines. She'd read the scripts for the special week of episodes and been quite impressed. Rufus and Mick had given her some meaty stuff to perform – Cora, mentally ill in the psychiatric hospital overhearing a whispered plot by Icelandic fishermen- terrorists to destroy *Winkle Bay* (she loved 'loony' acting - all the ticks and shrieks and dribbling), escaping to be re-united with her family and her attempts to make the authorities believe her story. She was looking forward most of all to the big budget action sequences where Cora saves the villagers, or at least some of them, from the dynamite packed fishing trawler as it slammed into the harbour wall. Move over Bruce Willis. If she didn't receive a BAFTA nomination for Best Actress after this, there was no justice in the world.

A knock at the trailer door broke her day-dream. Her regal-voiced 'who is it?' died in her throat as D.S Clifton entered without waiting to be asked. Carina buried her anger and smiled graciously.

'D.S. Clifton, what a surprise!'

Clifton noticed that the actress seemed dowdier than usual, then remembered she was probably in costume. Her clothes were the only unimpressive things about her. She looked around at the trappings of success. The trailer was bigger than her flat and packed with more swanky gadgets than an Argos Showroom. She eyed the chrome coffee machine with particular envy.

'This is very nice,' she said, with more than a hint of bitterness.

'Yes, isn't it.' Carina couldn't resist crowing. 'It's on loan from Pinewood.'

'Nice to see that out of all the recent tragedies, someone's doing okay.'

The actress shifted uncomfortably. 'Well, I wouldn't put it like that,' she said.

'Wouldn't you?' She left the question hanging in the air.

'What can I do for you?' asked Carina.

'Oh, just a few questions,' replied the detective. 'Tying up loose ends and all that.'

Carina nodded. There was an edge to Clifton's voice and she didn't like it.

'Any idea why Gordon Crabtree did what he did?'

'Not yet.'

Clifton sat down without waiting for an invitation and took out a note book.

'In the light of what happened to Mr Frenkel at the Metro station, our investigation has been widened,' she revealed, 'We're looking at the deaths of Douglas Hunt and...' she was about to say 'Fluff' but the crass name stuck in her throat. '... your dog. We've also been talking to a profiler,' she added.

'Good,' said Carina.

'Miss Hemsley, what we do find rather strange, is Crabtree's total lack of contact with you.'

'Strange?'

'Our profiler says Crabtree would have tried to make contact with you at some point.'

'I assure you he didn't,' Carina said earnestly.

'And the whole business of the letters - sending death threats, then telling Mr Frenkel he was going to marry Cora. It doesn't fit.'

Carina knitted her brows, pretending to think over the detective's words.

'I don't begin to understand, Detective Sergeant,' she admitted. 'But who knows what goes on in the mind of a lunatic?'

'A profiler,' replied Clifton flatly.

'To be honest, I'm just glad it's all over,' Carina declared.

'Oh, for us, Miss Hemsley, it's just beginning.'

She pulled a pen from her jacket pocket and clicked the top officiously, with her thumb.

'At some point between the second act and the finale on the last night of the pantomine, you went out to buy cigarettes,' stated the detective.

So, old Matty's memory was in better shape than his body, thought Carina. 'Yes, that's right,' she said. 'I did.'

'From where?'

'The pub.'

The detective's face remained impassive. All the same, Carina saw the disappointment in her eyes. Did she think she was stupid? She'd been in the late night shop near the theatre on numerous occasions (apart from the night in question) and seen the CCTV camera behind the till. The tatty old pub down the road, on the other hand, had no such equipment.

'Did anyone see you? Did you speak to anyone?'

Carina shook her head. 'There was no need. I had the right

change. I went straight over to the machine, purchased my ciggies and went straight back to the theatre.'

'Mr Swann the stage doorman said you weren't in costume.'

'Well, of course I wasn't!' snorted Carina. 'I wasn't going to waltz into some old gin joint in a sequinned ball gown and a magic wand.'

Clifton tapped the pen against her pad and stared out of the window, her mind a whirl. So far Carina's answers seemed entirely reasonable. But the gnawing feeling in her stomach was at work, telling her something wasn't right. Was it instinct? Or was it just plain old resentment and hatred. She couldn't be sure anymore.

'Why do you want to know all this?' asked Carina.

'Crabtree's scooter turned up in the alleyway behind the theatre,' Clifton confessed. 'Did you see it?'

'No,' replied Carina emphatically. 'At that time of night it's pitch black in that alleyway - you can't see a hand in front of your face, never mind a scooter.' She gasped suddenly. 'Was he at the panto that night? Or at the matinée?'

'It's quite possible.'

Carina frowned again. 'Why would he leave his bike there though?'

'That's what we'd like to know. It just doesn't make sense.'

Clifton shut her notebook and yawned without thinking.

'You look tired, lovey.'

Pauline Clifton ignored her. She knew she was tired. She didn't sleep at night, that's why. Whenever she tried, all she could see in her mind was the Boss, surrounded by machinery, lying in a hospital bed, fading away, diminishing, in front of her. And all because... because? Why? Why? She could find no answers. And it was tearing her apart.

'If you think of anything, or remember anything - certainly about Mr Crabtree, let me know.'

'I certainly will.'

The detective stared at her coldly. 'I suppose all this business is the best thing that's ever happened to you, isn't it!'

Carina pretended to be affronted. 'That's a terrible thing to say, Sergeant.'

'But true.'

She opened the door and paused on the threshold. 'You know?' she said to the actress. 'Not once, in all the time I've been here have you bothered to ask about Roy Newall. And I know you never visit him in hospital because I asked.'

She went out slamming the door. Carina's nerves gave way to relieved laughter. So that's what it was all about. Nothing to do with a dead end investigation or the suspicions of some swotty profiler. It was about the stupid woman's jealousy, her grief and anger. She poured herself another glass of champagne and toasted the air.

Later that afternoon, Carina's driver dropped her off at the studios in the former tobacco factory. She nodded tersely at the security guard's polite banter when he opened the door to admit her. It did not do to talk to the minions employed by the company. Words could be twisted, regurgitated and flogged to the Press in exchange for financial remuneration.

'Afternoon, Vesuvius,' said Jules pleasantly.

She'd nicknamed Carina 'Vesuvius' after witnessing her fiery temper in reception a few years ago as she reduced a young director to tears for daring to suggest Carina, as Cora, in a particularly un-memorable scene, might like to do some housework as she discussed the purchase of a new kipper curing kiln, with her son Rory.

'I don't do walking and talking! Don't you know that by now, you moronic fucker!?' she'd screamed in the poor lad's face.

'Who are they?' she said to Jules, indicating a group of young men sitting in reception.

'They're the terrorists, darling. Come for their costume fitting.'

Carina's caterpillar eyebrows took a dive.

'They don't look very Icelandic,' she observed. 'They look more... Middle Eastern, to me.'

Jules shrugged and pulled on her ear piece to answer the phone.

'Hello, *Winkle Bay*,' she breathed huskily, 'Jules speaking, how may I help you?'

Carina looked back at the 'terrorists' one last time before disappearing through the green room door.

Jules ended the call, pulled off her earring, started to play with her earlobe and waited for Vesuvius to erupt again. She'd been privy to a few interesting phone calls over the past few weeks...

Chapter Thirty Four

Something was wrong. Carina sensed it. For a start, they were all present. Every single member of the cast. A rare occasion indeed, for on a day to day basis they were in and out of the green room at different times. Another peculiar thing she noticed - all eyes turned to her as she walked in. Over the past three days, whenever she'd entered the Green Room, her fellow actors had tried their level best *not* to look at her, or acknowledge her. It didn't matter to her. Friendship and bonhomie were low down on her list of priorities. Strange then, that they should suddenly start paying her some attention.

Something else was apparent. The place was as silent as the grave. Even with the green room half empty, there were actors huddled around in little cliques, laughing and bitching, carrying on - especially amongst the younger fraternity. Today they were all sitting around in a giant circle, reading scripts. Actually reading them, as opposed to flicking through them scene by scene to find their character name and weighing up how many lines they'd been given. Most unusual. She dumped her bag on the nearest free chair - there weren't many, and was about to head for the canteen, when Jeffrey Carter, still in costume as Reverend Johnny Arthington, peered at her above his reading glasses and said, 'The last episode's in, darling, I think you should look at it.'

'Thanks, honey,' she replied, adding, 'How exciting!'

She hurried over to her pigeon hole at the back of the room, rifled through a pile of letters until she found the large manila envelope containing the script and ripped it open in the way a spoilt and over-indulged child unwraps its presents at Christmas. Sitting down, Carina thumbed through the script, skimming the pages rapidly as she searched for her scenes. So far she didn't seem to have much to do. Perhaps there was more for her later in the script. She continued skimming until a loud crash from the middle of the room made her look up. Jeffrey had thrown his script into the centre of the actors circle.

'The fucking bastards,' he roared, causing some of the younger actors to flinch. They weren't used to the sight and sound of a man dressed as a vicar, swearing like a docker. 'Utter, utter shit!' He spat on the script, to highlight his contempt.

Carina ignored him. Jeffrey's character was about to meet his end in the harbour explosion during the final 'special' episode so he was bound to be a little emotional. She remembered receiving her last episode, or what she thought was her last episode, five years ago. Discovering that Cora was about to be carted off to the Farne Island Psychiatric hospital in a strait-jacket, her immediate response had been to throw a coffee mug through the green room window and push the TV set off its shelf. Jeffrey's reaction looked dignified by comparison.

'Who's storylining this show, now?' he yelled. 'Baboons?'

'I'm sure it can't be that bad,' said Carina.

'No, my darling,' Jeffrey replied, removing his spectacles and pinching the bridge of his nose. 'It's worse.'

Old Joyce Maloney, who'd appeared in *Winkle Bay* since it

started, and was also due, like Jeffrey, to bow out imminently, dropped her script on her lap with a contemptuous gesture. 'He's right,' she said, nodding. 'It's terrible shite. And I should know - I was in Crossroads.'

Some of the thespians in the circle were nodding in agreement: others were gasping and exhaling sharply as they read particular sections of the script.

'I'll give you the condensed version shall I?' offered Jeffrey, in a voice that suggested he was going to give it anyway. Carina set down her script. She would check to see how many scenes she had later, back at the hotel.

'Putting it simply,' Jeffrey was saying, 'they're going to do a Chernobyl on us!'

'A *what*?' asked one of the younger actors.

'Oh, ignorant youth,' moaned Joyce.

'The terrorists detonate a bomb at *Winkle Bay* Nuclear Power Station and we're all going to be fried.'

'The Icelandic terrorists?' demanded another actor.

'They're not Icelandic. They're Middle Eastern,' spat Jeffrey. 'They've been spinning us lies for weeks.'

'Who?' asked Joyce, confused. 'The terrorists?'

'Rufus and Mick Flynt, the spineless bastards!'

Carina, despite her simple grasp of science saw a loop-hole in the plot.

'They can't do a Chernobyl on us! Something like that would take out half the northeast sea board.'

'You're forgetting, darling,' muttered Jeffrey waspishly, 'this is soap opera. We don't let the facts get in the way!'

'Are we *all* going to fry?' - this from one of the more self-obsessed artistés.

'*Fried* as in *dead*?' - this from one of the thicker cast members.

Jeffrey shook his head and waved a hand around at a few of the cast around him. 'Only us.' He pointed at Carina. 'And you.'

Carina looked around, to make certain she was the object of his finger's attention.

'I'm sorry?'

Jeffrey nodded. 'We get vaporised.'

Carina licked the tip of a finger and started skimming through her script again. 'No, no, my love,' she said. 'I jump off the fishing boat before the boat full of dynamite hits the jetty.'

Where was it? Where was the scene? She couldn't find it. But she did spot several scene headings labelled, rather ominously, 'Int. Nuclear Power Station. Day.'

Jeffrey stood up, stretched and drew himself to his full height. He'd played Atticus Finch in a Cumbrian tour of 'To Kill A Mockingbird' and knew how to look important.

'Trust me, my dear. Cora is kidnapped by the terrorists because she overheard them plotting in the loony bin. We've already shot those scenes.'

'That's right,' Joyce confirmed.

'She escapes, tries to warn the village but nobody believes her because she's bonkers.'

'We did all that today,' said Carina.

'And tomorrow we shoot the scenes where we, and when I say "we", I mean "we who are about to die", decide that Cora must be telling the truth.' Jeffrey paused for breath, and for effect, before continuing. 'And next week, we shoot the scenes from that muck...!' He stretched out a foot and stomped on the script, leaving a dusty imprint on the front cover, '... wherein Cora is kidnapped by the terrorists, taken to the power station, tied up with the bomb next to the reactor as the countdown ticks away. Meanwhile her friends are in pursuit and try to rescue her...'

'It's like bloody Goldfinger,' interjected Joyce.

'But why me? Why Cora?' spluttered Carina puzzled. The room was beginning to spin.

'Because Cora's got the pass key to the nuclear reactor room. Jacob Junior dropped it in the kitchen before he went to work and she picked it up.' Jeffrey waved at her script. 'It's all in there!'

'Jacob, my... Cora's son? Why has he got a key to a reactor room?' Carina's voice was becoming increasingly shrill.

'Because he's the managing director of the power station,' hissed Joyce impatiently.

'I am!' confirmed Bryan, who played Jacob.

Carina turned to him. 'But you were a kipper packer five years ago,' she said.

Bryan nodded. 'They didn't know what to do with my character so they took him in a new direction.'

'But this is rubbish,' shrieked Carina. 'It's nonsense.'

She had located the penultimate scene. With pulse quickening and the blood pressure pounding in her head, she read with disbelief the last moments in the life of Cora Smart as a loyal (and soon to die) coterie of friends attempted to free her from her bonds and defuse the bomb next to the reactor. 'Kaboom!!' said the final stage direction. The last scene described the village consumed by a 'small' mushroom cloud.

'It can't be!' she yelled. 'I'm supposed to be coming back. "Five episodes, then a few months off" they said, then I'd be back. They promised.'

'Is that in your contract?' There was an element of glee in his voice as Jeffrey asked the question. Carina shook her head. Abigail her agent had wanted to tie the five episodes to a longer contract but she had shouted her down. Ordered her to sign.

'I think you've been had, my darling,' continued Jeffrey. 'They've brought you back to kill you off.'

'No!' Carina felt the lump in her throat and fought back tears. 'They wouldn't do that.'

'Would you have come back if you'd known they wanted to kill Cora?' inquired Bryan.

Carina didn't answer. There was no need. Of course she wouldn't have come back if she'd known. Rufus Frenkel and Mick Flynt had lied to her, duped her, robbed her of her dreams. They'd used her, exploited her desire to return to *Winkle Bay*. She felt the fury rising. Nobody got the better of Carina Hemsley. Certainly not two ball-less, pint sized television producers. Pushing back her chair as she stood up, she made for the door, the spikes of her high heeled boots echoing portentously around the room as she marched purposefully onwards.

In reception, Jules looked up, recognising the determined foot fall. She saw the face, recognised the expression, before it disappeared up the stairs and knew it spelled trouble for someone. Should she ring up to Rufus and Mick and let them know? No. She liked Rufus. But Mick? He was an appalling man. He treated people with contempt. He was overdue a good kicking.

* * *

'Oh my God!'

Rufus, in his glass walled office with Flynt, saw her coming. Flynt tried to act nonchalant. He picked up his jacket.

'Sort it out,' he said, about to make his escape.

'You've got to stay with me,' urged Rufus. 'You have to help me.'

'She's a washed up old ham. Don't be scared of her.'

'You don't know her like I do.' Rufus was sweating now. Production teams at their desks had stopped work and were following Carina's progress across the office with their eyes. Flynt, aware of the audience, knew he had no choice but to stay, so he stuck his hands in his pockets, effected a half smirk and jerked his head in Carina's direction as if to say, 'I'm cool, I'm not scared of you. What's the big deal?'

'You lied to me!'

'Oh, I wouldn't go that far...' Flynt started to say.

'You've killed off my character,' screamed Carina. 'You told me you were going to bring me back! Permanently!'

'And here you are!' Mick smiled at her.

'I'm getting fucking nuked!'

Rufus could not look her in the eye. Mick Flynt found it easier as he wasn't the one she was addressing face to face. Or face to neck. In her high heels, she towered over the two men like a giantess.

'Let me explain something...' stammered Rufus. He could feel the perspiration trickling down his back now. What was he going to explain? There was no explanation other than they *had* lied to her and got her back under false pretences! All he wanted to do was point childishly at the smug bastard standing next to him and say 'It wasn't me it was him!' Luckily for Rufus, Carina wasn't interested in any explanations.

'You can change the scripts,' she was saying. 'Re-write them. Cora nearly dies, but she doesn't.'

'We can't do that,' said Flynt.

'Yes you can!' she screeched. 'It's easy. I've got a pen. I can do it. "Nuclear blast. Cora survives". Doddle.'

Flynt, pushed hair out of his eyes. 'No.'

'Then bring me back as my twin sister,' she said beseechingly. 'You have to. You told me I was coming back for good.'

'I didn't promise you a thing,' said Flynt, with that hint of a sneer never very far away from his smile. 'And I'm the one in charge. I make the decisions around here. Not him.'

Carina looked at him. Saw that he was toying with her.

'You can't do this to me. You can't offer me the world then just drop me.'

The soap guru laughed. 'Hey! It's only television!'

Carina clenched her fist. She wanted to hit the man. Hit him and never stop.

'I'll walk. And you can sing for your other bloody episodes. I'm not staying another minute in this place.'

'There's the door,' Flynt opened it for her. 'Feel free to leave. But do remember, that if you walk away without fulfilling your contractual agreements, we'll see you in court. I hope you can afford a decent legal team.'

Carina deliberated on the threshold, then walked out. Several dozen faces in the production office, turned away as she strode out. Flynt pushed the door shut behind her.

'She'll be back,' he said confidently.

Carina felt like a caged tiger, cornered and desperate to kill. She hurried down the back staircase, pushed through the fire doors and took deep gasps of fresh air. Hands scrambled around in her handbag for cigarettes and she lit up greedily, without the aid of a holder. She picked up her mobile phone and paced around, waiting for her agent to answer as a refuse collection van arrived to collect rubbish from the canteen kitchen. She raised her voice above the reversing alarm.

'Abigail? Emergency. Ring me as soon as you get this message.'

She tossed the phone back in her bag. This wasn't happening to her. It was a nightmare and any minute she'd wake up. What did Mick Flynt have against her? What had she done that was so wrong? It was as if he was torturing her for some reason. He reminded her of the child who enjoyed pulling the legs of beetles or the wings off butterflies, for kicks. As for Rufus, he was the kid who stood by and let his bullying friend torture the insects. He was spineless and insignificant. If she was going to stay, she had to change Flynt's mind. Persuade him. Make him see sense. The thought appalled her. She hated the man. 'It's only television?' How dare he say that to her. It wasn't only television - it was her life.

One of the refuse collectors in his blue boiler suit, called over to her.

'Hey! It's Cora Smart!'

His other mates looked over at her. She suddenly felt self conscious, standing as she was, by the bins, puffing on a fag, on the verge of tears, not looking her best. The man winked at her conspiratorially and turned to his mates.

'Will you look at that!' He folded his arms and winked at Carina again. 'Sitting with the rubbish! Didn't you used to be a big fish in soap opera?'

Carina turned to face them.

'I still am big!' she declared proudly. 'It's the producers that got small.'

The refuse workers laughed. The cheeky one admitted he didn't watch much TV these days and his workmates nodded in agreement.

'There's nothing on worth watching.'

'You know why that is?' asked Carina and gave her answer before they'd had chance to reply. 'Because the executives at the top? They're just no bloody good.'

She threw down the half-burned down cigarette and hurried back into the building, making for the green room, a determined woman. Ignoring questions from the other members of the cast about where she'd been, she stopped at her pigeon hole and bundled up the scores of fan letters awaiting her attention. She dashed out of the room, leaving a trail of mail on the floor in her wake.

'She's coming back,' warned Rufus, squinting to see her clearly through the glass walls of his office. 'What's she carrying?'

Flynt seemed unconcerned and uninterested. 'I haven't got time for all this crap,' he said.

Carina barged in without knocking.

'You can't get rid of Cora,' she said. 'You need me. This lot needs me.'

She opened her arms and let the bundles of letters and cards fall to the floor.

'I'm not even back on screen yet - and look at it. This is only two days worth of mail.'

She smiled at both men as if no more needed to be said. Flynt gazed down at the floor, unimpressed.

'It smells of pissy old grannies to me.'

Carina nodded. 'Some of them do smell. A lot of them.'

Flynt smiled at her nastily.

'You're a dinosaur.'

Carina reeled. 'What?'

'You're a dinosaur. Like that lot,' he said, pointing to the correspondence on the floor. 'I brought you back to kill you off. And when the idiots who write to you and watch you see you die, they'll stop watching. There'll be no more speculation about Cora-bleedin'-Smart. They'll move on to something else.'

'I don't understand. I thought...' stumbled Carina, '... I thought you wanted to increase the viewing figures.'

'We want a new core audience,' drawled the media mogul in his dull, flat voice, 'Advertising friendly younger people who at the moment are put off by the sad old gits who tune in week after week. That's why we're killing off the dead wood. Out with the old,' he grinned, 'in with the new. We're nuking the place. We're re-naming it "The Bay". Moving the location nearer Newcastle, making it less remote, more urban.'

Carina heard his arrogance but as for his words, only some of them were sinking in.

'But what about all the fans? 'My People'?'

'Let's face it, in a few years time your 'People' will all be six feet under. And that's no good to me!'

He turned to Rufus and laughed. Rufus lacked the confidence to laugh back. Flynt was playing a very dangerous game by antagonising, rejecting his core audience. What if the older viewers did desert the show as he wanted, but the fickle younger viewers failed to jump aboard?

Carina knelt on the floor and started to pick up the letters. She fingered them delicately, gently, stacked them one by one in a pile. This could not be the end, she thought. The fans - they deserved better. She had to defend them. Stand up for them.

'Do you want me to beg?' asked Carina quietly. 'Because I will, if you ask me.'

The half-smirk was on Mick Flynt's face again. 'Well, you could give it a go.'

Carina swallowed hard. This was her last chance.

'Please? *Please* let me stay.'

'Is that it? Is that the best you can do?'

'The fans out there, they've been waiting a long time for me to come back. They've missed me. They tell me all the time.'

Flynt folded his arms and stared down at her as she knelt amongst her fan mail.

'It's not about the fans though, is it? It's about you. You've had five years of being nothing and nobody. You hate it and you're terrified that you've got to go back to it when your little comeback's over.'

'I don't want to do panto in some poxy third rate theatre every Christmas until I drop,' admitted Carina, picking up the letters and clutching them to her chest. 'I want a life.'

'So do summer season instead.'

'Do you know what it's like to be famous and poor?' Carina said suddenly. 'To be recognised by everybody, everywhere you go?' She stood up, still clutching the letters. 'In the end you don't go anywhere, because you can't afford the taxi fares and you're too famous to take the bus. You lose your house but you can't move onto the council estate because the Press'll come round to haunt you and the neighbour's laugh at you, so you find a rented little bedsit somewhere, out of the way. And you hide there. In the dark, with the telly on, watching all the shiny faces you used to work with getting shinier and shinier and their teeth getting whiter and whiter.'

Flynt shrugged at her. 'That's the actor's life. Up and down.'

'I can't go back to being nothing. I can't.'

'Think of yourself as one of those dinosaurs from 'Jurassic Park'. You were extinct for a while, then you were brought back from the dead, and then you died again.'

Laughing, he had turned to Rufus in the hope of receiving some sign of appreciation of his wit, so he didn't see Carina's hand clasp around the dagger shaped letter opener she'd picked up off the floor with the fan mail. The sharp blade, thrust with such great force, stabbed him through the chest and lodged there. Flynt looked at it, blinking with surprise, a silly grin on his face. He staggered back, fell against the glass wall, his legs buckling as his heart stopped beating, the shocked smile still registering on his face. He was dead before he hit the floor.

Rufus began to shake and then scream, along with several people on the other side of the blood splattered glass walls of his office. Carina didn't seem to hear. She was bending down to pick up her fanmail. Rufus backed slowly out of the room and it was only after she heard the door click shut that she looked up and saw the sea of faces on the other side of the glass, staring at her. She stood up slowly placing her mail on Rufus's desk, reached in her bag, lit a cigarette and inhaled deeply.

'See, Mick?' said Carina sweetly to the corpse on the floor. 'The thing about dinosaurs is, they didn't become extinct, they evolved. Into beautiful birds. So you see, the only dead thing around here, is you. But hey?!' She paused to chuckle at some private joke. 'Don't worry - "*It's only television*".'

She was still laughing when the police arrived.

Pauline Clifton led her, handcuffed, through reception, towards the main entrance. Carina had not uttered a word since her arrest. She seemed to have shut herself off from the real world. She was in a far off place. Her eyes looked vague and the half smile which haunted her features unsettled the detective. Why hadn't she spotted the signs of madness before? Surely they'd always been there to see?

'I can take you out the back entrance,' Clifton offered, for already, through the glass doors she could see the hoards of press photographers at the security gates, fighting like animals amongst each other to get the best picture.

Carina came to life, standing tall, straining against the cuffs.

'I'll go out the front!' she declared grandly. '"My People" want to see me.'

The Press went mad as she came out of the building. She was escorted to an awaiting police car but before she was bundled inside, she waved to the crowd.

'I love you all,' she cried.

Clifton placed a hand on her head and guided her into the back seat.

'Why Carina?' she asked as the car headed for the scrum of photographers at the gate. 'Why did you do it? All of it?'

'You couldn't begin to understand, sweetheart,' said Carina, as the car was assailed from all sides by representatives of the media.

'You're not a celebrity. It's the most wonderful thing. A joy. But when it's gone...'

She stopped waving and turned to the detective.

'Do you know what it's like to feel as if you're... *nothing*?'

Clifton shrugged.

The actress, ever the pro, started to wave at 'her people' again.

'Then you're a lucky girl.'

The car began to accelerate through the crowd and soon the sea of journalists and photographers receded into the distance. Carina twisted around in her seat to gaze on the scene for one last time.

'Well,' she sniffed, 'I suppose this'll bump up their viewing figures.'

The End